THE
KINGDOM
OF
SWEETS

THE
KINGDOM
OF
SWEETS

ERIKA JOHANSEN

DUTTON

DUTTON

An imprint of Penguin Random House LLC
penguinrandomhouse.com

DUTTON and the D colophon are registered trademarks of Penguin Random House LLC.

LIBRARY OF CONGRESS CATALOGING-IN-PUBLICATION DATA

Names: Johansen, Erika, author.
Title: The kingdom of sweets: a novel of *The Nutcracker* / Erika Johansen.
Description: [New York]: Dutton, 2023.
Identifiers: LCCN 2023019063 (print) | LCCN 2023019064 (ebook) |
ISBN 9781524742751 (hardcover) | ISBN 9781524742768 (ebook)
Subjects: LCGFT: Fantasy fiction. | Novels.
Classification: LCC PS3610.O2546 K56 2023 (print) |
LCC PS3610.O2546 (ebook) | DDC 813/.6—dc23/eng/20230503
LC record available at https://lccn.loc.gov/2023019063
LC ebook record available at https://lccn.loc.gov/2023019064

Printed in the United States of America

1st Printing

BOOK DESIGN BY DANIEL BROUNT

For Maya Ziv, who goes into the quicksand with me every time

THE
KINGDOM
OF
SWEETS

OVERTURE

EVERYONE CALLED HIM GODFATHER. WHEN CLARA AND I were christened, he came to the ceremony, though he was no relation of ours, and stood in the back of the church, leaning on his cane, grinning like a reaper as we were baptized. He wore a swirling blue cloak like that of a sorcerer in an old tale, the silken lining spangled with moon and stars, and everyone feared him. Our cook, Anastasia, who hailed from the countryside, even said he had the evil eye.

Our parents had not invited him to the christening, but because he attended, they had no choice but to invite him to the small reception at their home. They hoped he wouldn't accept the invitation, but he did, handing my father a handsome present of gold coin before he proceeded to the corner where Clara and I lay comfortably in our cradles, staring up at the ceiling. We were the first Christmas babies that year, born shortly after midnight on the holy day, and the midwives had thought us identical. But it would never be that way again. Drosselmeyer stood over our twin cradles for a long moment, staring down at us, despite our father's nervous attempts to lure him away with offers of cigars and brandy. When he placed one hand on each of our foreheads in the old pagan sign of blessing, our mother began to weep.

"Light," Drosselmeyer said, looking down at Clara. And then, turning to me: "Dark."

My mother screamed, then fainted dead away. Father and his friends tried to pull Drosselmeyer from my cradle, but he laughed and raised his cane. Darkness fell upon the room, and in the commotion afterward—people rushing to and from the kitchen seeking matches and extra lamps, Father fetching Mother's medicine and assisting her to a sofa—it was some minutes before they realized that Drosselmeyer had disappeared, vanishing like one of his tricks. But he was not entirely gone, for in the entrance hall of our house they soon found his other gift: a portrait of the man himself, sitting in a high-backed armchair. This portrait could not be removed; Father tried, even hired carpenters to make the attempt. But the frame defeated all comers. Nor could the portrait be hidden, for no matter what Mother chose to wrap it in, cotton or sheeting or linen, the covering would inevitably fall while the house slept, and the maids would find it in the morning, crumpled on the floor. Thus did Drosselmeyer watch over us, even in the dark.

Father and Mother begged the guests to say nothing of what had occurred, but to no avail. The tale spread far and wide throughout the city, such a celebrated piece of legend that soon no one, not even my parents, recalled which friend or relative had actually stood over us at our christening and pledged to care for us if they could not. We had only one godfather, and everyone knew his name.

———————

LIGHT. DARK.

This became the tale of our childhood. Light, they called Clara, and rightly so, for Clara was all that was bright and charming, blue-eyed and pink-cheeked. Her bouncing curls reflected the sunlight in golden spangles. When she spoke, the lilting charm of her voice enticed others to listen, making her sound far more intelligent than she really was. She lived in the moment, not understanding why anyone should wish to look beyond, and because most people honestly did not wish to do so, Clara was both popular and well-liked. Lucky as well, they said, for the blessing of a wizard was no small thing. Drosselmeyer never attended another christening in the city, and though no one knew why he had come to ours, our family was assumed to be under a kind of protection. So Clara was invited everywhere, to birthdays and soirees and parties and lunches. She was a wildly decorative jewel in our society, and her dance card was always full.

I was the dark child, the unlucky child. My hair fell black and straight down my back, and my face turned broad and dull. As we left childhood, dropping our necklines and tightening our stays, Clara developed a pretty figure, with full breasts and long waist, while I remained short and lump-like. I sat in the corner at dances, watching Clara move, living through her life. Being born on Christmas Day was supposed to be a lucky omen, but our friends and neighbors assigned that luck only to Clara, while I was considered fundamentally unlucky; once I overheard Mrs. Ladd, the railroad magnate's wife, telling the baker that she would rather cross paths with a black cat than that cursed Stahlbaum child. The rest of the neighborhood must have felt the same, for I was never bullied or mistreated by the other children, only left alone.

I did not believe myself cursed, but I could not deny that Drosselmeyer had done something to me, opened my eyes wide. Clara never saw the way boys' faces would change when she turned elsewhere, their smiles becoming hungry and wild. She never saw our father curse in his beard at the rich men who snubbed him in the street, or the brittle disappointment that lay behind our mother's fixed smile. Clara could not see the hidden darkness of the world, but I could. I was cursed to see. Grandmother Kalenov, the oldest woman in our neighborhood, said that I had the evil eye, just like Drosselmeyer, that I could look into a man's heart and know his most terrible secrets. I saw the hidden contempt of husband for wife and wife for husband; the fear of the merchant whose business was collapsing; a mother's jealousy of her daughter's youth. They did not trust me, our friends and neighbors, for they knew I knew them, and people don't wish to be known. They need their secrets, just as they need their illusions, and so although I was christened Natasha—having been born first on Christmas Day—they called me the dark sister, and I was as distrusted as Clara was praised.

Still, we were friends, Clara and I. We squabbled often, but we were loyal. We needed each other, for our parents were never the same after the christening. Mother grew increasingly dependent on the unseen world, her days dominated by mediums and spiritualists as she sought some way to undo what Drosselmeyer had done. Father took his own regrets out of the house, and so often it was only Clara and me, supervised first by nursemaids and then, as we grew older, tutors. When we were four, our brother, Fritz, was born, and he was christened without incident. My parents held the ceremony at home, and the priest did not begin to speak until Father had locked all the windows and doors.

———

AFTER OUR CHRISTENING, DROSSELMEYER REAPPEARED IN THE neighborhood wearing an eye patch. The neighbors said that he had offered his right eye to the dark powers in return for help with his sorcery. There had always been such tales, Drosselmeyer dealing with the devil to curse this or that associate who had crossed him, or to delay his own old age. Drosselmeyer had come to the city long before my parents' marriage, and he was not young even then, but he still walked the streets with the easy movements of a man in his prime. The loss of an eye did not appear to discomfit him either, for he went steadily about his business, doing strange favors and piling up debt . . . the most dangerous kind of debt, not only of money but of service. By the time Clara and I came out into society at fourteen, most of our neighborhood seemed to owe Drosselmeyer in one way or another, and even our own father was forced to beg a loan when one of his foundries suffered a collapse.

Thus did we join the legion of families who lived under Drosselmeyer's thumb. No one tried to cheat him, for he always seemed to know things he had no business knowing, and no one quite understood the limits of his strange power. Mrs. Armistead, one of my mother's more foolish friends, said that Drosselmeyer had threatened to turn her nephew into a toad, but people lost interest in the story when she admitted that he had never made good on his threat. Still, no one was quite certain that Drosselmeyer could *not* do such a thing if he wished, and so no one dared test him. He prowled our neighborhood at all hours, so they said, practicing his dark art, and on nights when I was wakeful I would sometimes peek around the edge of my velvet curtains, hoping to see him down there on the snow-covered path, surrounded by the clutch of gilded boys he kept to do odd errands. And I did see him once, wearing only his top hat and cape in spite of the cold, striding up our street with his boys hollering and baying like a pack of wolves bewitched by the full moon. But no one called the constables, for everyone knew that even the constabulary resided comfortably in Drosselmeyer's pocket, that he had bought their blindness to his misdeeds, so he might do as he wanted and go where he would.

Then one night I saw him alone, his gaunt figure beneath a lit lamp that swung and creaked in the November wind. He seemed to be looking up at our windows, but I couldn't see his eyes, shadowed as they were beneath the brim of his top hat. Still I was afraid, for it seemed to me then that he had blessed and cursed Clara and me in equal measure, and done so for no greater reason than caprice. Several more times I saw him there; I thought that he was waiting for someone, but could not imagine who it might be at three in the morning, and soon I learned not to peek around the edge of the curtains, not wanting to know. Drosselmeyer had made me ugly, cursed me with terrible knowledge, just as he had made Clara beautiful and free of thought, and when I saw him there, leaning against the lamppost without a care at the very darkest hour of the night, I felt that he had somehow come to witness the effects of his work, much as a man who sets two dogs to fighting will watch over the scrap with a benevolent smile and a fistful of cash, not particularly caring who wins.

But he never tried to enter our house, and because he never did, I assumed he never would. As an adolescent, I found myself becoming philosophical about Drosselmeyer's curse. Clara might be beautiful, I reasoned, but I was the one who liked to read, who studied history and languages. Would I have enjoyed these things if I'd been invited to all the parties and had a new proposal every week, as Clara did? She cared nothing for learning; she had abandoned our tutor at the age of twelve with my parents' quiet approval. What need had Clara for history, for language, for made-up worlds? She found her happiness in her waking life, and while I envied her at times, I was pleased enough to be myself. So Drosselmeyer's curse was not necessarily the catastrophe my parents imagined. He had laid upon me a depth of strangeness, something that might allow me to be content with the muted life I would lead in Clara's shadow. On long winter afternoons, while Clara attended dance lessons and I sat in the warmth of the bay window, reading, I mused that while no one would ever ask me to perform in the ballet, they would not expect Clara to write a novel or a treatise either. Perhaps Drosselmeyer had even acted the part of God himself all those years before, bestowing gifts upon my twin and me according to our needs. Perhaps he had meant no harm at all.

ACT I

CHRISTMAS EVE

> Only
>
> There is shadow under this red rock,
>
> (Come in under the shadow of this red rock),
>
> And I will show you something different from either
>
> Your shadow in the morning striding behind you
>
> Or your shadow at evening rising to meet you;
>
> I will show you fear in a handful of dust.

—*The Waste Land*

T. S. Eliot

A NASTASIA, CAN I ASK YOU A QUESTION?"
Our cook cursed, levering a tray of buns from the oven.
The kitchen was her unquestioned domain, but still she always
seemed slightly harried, even in her element. She put the tray on
the cooling rack and turned back to me, wiping her hands.

"Ask quickly, girl."

"You know how to mix . . . medicine." She had told me never
to call it what it was; even the floorboards had ears in our house.

"Aye, medicine," Anastasia replied, tipping me a wink. Above
our heads, the wind hooted in the rafters. A storm was on the way
for Christmas, such a fearsome storm that the railroads had been
shut down, the sailors on the river forced to spend Christmas Eve
lashing ships to the dock.

"Do you know how to make other things?"

"Like what?"

"Like—" I swallowed. "Like a love potion?"

She froze in the act of glazing a joint of beef, fixing me with a
cold glare.

"And if I did know such a thing?"

"I don't know. I just thought—"

"Thought what? Would you be like your mother, gazing into a crystal ball for what you can't have? Would you seek by foul means what you cannot get by fair?"

I shook my head, feeling my cheeks burn.

"I know you've lost all sense about that Liebermann boy, but only the foolish meddle with love magic, child. Being adored is for pretty girls; you must be content with what you are."

"Were you a pretty girl, Tasia?"

The moment I asked, I regretted it. Anastasia was old, with whitening hair and a spinster's sticklike body. But she didn't seem to take offense. She dipped the brush into the sauce and made slow, deliberate strokes with it, as though she were painting a masterpiece rather than glazing a side of beef.

"No, not pretty, Nat. Not unloved, but never adored. And I'll tell you something else: a man like your Conrad may like a plain girl, may even come to care for one. But she'll always be the one he settles for in place of the beautiful woman he can't have. And when the opportunity presents, he will not hesitate."

I shrank from her words, the hopelessness in them. Conrad didn't love me, I knew that. But he could. He *could*. If I could only do the right thing, say the right thing, find the lever that made him look at other girls with such admiration, things might change.

"Are men really so terrible, Tasia?"

"Not terrible. Not even bad-hearted, most of them. But fools, girl . . . men are such fools for beauty."

"It seems unfair."

Anastasia snorted, hefting the tray of beef toward the oven.

"You'll find no fairness in my kitchen. Whatever you feel for that boy will only end in grief; leave him behind."

"I've tried to leave him behind. I tried so hard."

"Try harder, then."

Feeling myself dismissed, I left the kitchen. I shouldn't have ventured in there at all on a day when Anastasia was preparing for a party, and I certainly should never have asked her about a love potion. She had left the country years before, traveling to the cities as so many villagers had since the death of the old king, seeking a better life and more food. Her people were superstitious; Anastasia knew the tarot cards, and would even read palms if she was in an expansive mood. But I should not have asked her about a love potion. I had never sought to entrap Conrad, as other girls did their men, with a full belly or the threat of an angry father, but deep down, I knew that I might have tried such a thing if I thought I would get away with it. I was not the sort of girl men married; Drosselmeyer had seen to that. But hope was a devilish thing. One morning Conrad had torn his cuff climbing down the drainpipe, leaving a thin scrap of white cloth, and I had clambered out onto the sill in the frozen dawn, reaching as far as I could across the gap between window and drainpipe, nearly falling from the icy ledge in my determination to grab the piece of cloth, to have this one thing that would not vanish in the light. Once in a while, I would take the scrap out to look at, to touch, but most of the time it was enough to know it was there, proof that I had not imagined all those nights when we rolled on the bed in a facsimile of love. Bishop Theofan would undoubtedly have called me a harlot, but even the threat of hell did not come into the nights when Conrad climbed through my window. He would knock, and I would let him in, always, because having the nights was better than having nothing at all, even if those nights were no more real than the fog that melted away with the dawn. Conrad did not love me, but that didn't mean he never would. Even the storm outside seemed to feel my certainty, for it picked up suddenly, making the candles flicker, wind screaming against the windows as I left the kitchen.

CHAPTER

2

I N THE PARLOR, SERVANTS WERE DECORATING THE TREE. WE had no ballroom, as the city's truly wealthy families did, but our parlor was certainly large enough to host a party. Our Christmas Eve parties had become something of a neighborhood tradition, but the neighbors didn't know of the penny-pinching that went on behind the scenes to make them as lavish as possible, just as they didn't know how much of our current lifestyle was bankrolled by Drosselmeyer. My father had ordered the tallest tree the woodcutter could find: a bright fir that stretched nearly twenty feet to the ceiling, so fresh that the house still smelled of sap, and later on Drosselmeyer would pay the woodcutter for his trouble, hiding our penury like a magician doing a parlor trick. We couldn't afford these parties, but all the same, we would have them. To do anything else would be to admit our diminished circumstances, and Father could not bring himself to do that.

The youngest of the houseboys, teenage Joseph and Arne, were hanging the tree with tapers and holly now, laughing and throwing berries at each other. They could afford to do so; Mother was shut up in the parlor with the medium, Madame Margritta, a pungent woman, swathed in shawls, who came to our house at least four times a week. She and Mother would sit for hours in Mother's private parlor, wailing over lost relatives, dead royals, and someone named Dominic. Mother spent a fortune on the unseen world, and sometimes Father would complain, but not too much. Father had his own diversions, and he was no more anxious than Mother to have them brought into the daylight, to account for where the money went.

I moved on into the entrance hall, where the dark of late afternoon held sway. Here, Drosselmeyer gazed down from his portrait, his eyes gleaming redly in the shadows. Those eyes followed me as I went up the curving staircase, and though I knew it was only a trick of the painter's skill, still I looked away, quickening my steps. The old man in the portrait frightened me as much as ever, and I wasn't alone. Father had once asked our priest, Father Benedict, to come in and break the spell that fixed the portrait to the wall, but not even the priest wanted to tangle with Drosselmeyer. The neighbors said that the old sorcerer had cursed our house, but they came to our parties all the same, just as a child would poke a stick at an effigy of the devil. Our neighbors might be in Drosselmeyer's pocket, just as we were, but none of them had to live under his eye. The portrait was still watching me; by a trick of the light, it seemed to wink as I went up the stairs.

When I got to the top, I heard Clara humming to herself, some new tune from the latest season. Clara was invited to every ball, even those of old wealth, the landowners and nobility, for she was too charming to remain anonymous among Father's class of merchants and entrepreneurs. Father always said that she would marry well, and his eyes would gleam at the idea of it: our Clara, moving among dukes, duchesses, earls. Father stood at war with his own heart in these matters. He hated the aristocracy, and yet his hate was born of envy. He did not care about ancestral names or heredity; what he really wanted was their ancient, unassailable wealth, and particularly the respect that came with it. Father would have given anything to seal his letters with an ancestral ring, to be invited to the Royal Palace for shooting, to have this and that business associate bow to him as he ambled up the street.

Downstairs, Anastasia's voice echoed from the parlor, exhorting the servants to hurry, the first guests would arrive soon. I should have been getting dressed, but still I paused in Clara's doorway for a long moment, staring at my twin as she stood sideways before her mirror in her shift, staring critically at her own reflection. She had turned her foot out, an affectation she had learned from dance class. Mother had warned Clara that training as a ballerina would thicken her legs and reduce the size of her breasts, but as far as I could see, Clara's body had not altered one whit. She had a beautiful figure, and I felt unexpected jealousy prick me with its claws, Anastasia's words echoing in my head. If I looked like Clara, Conrad would surely have fallen in love with me long before.

"If you're going to stand around in nothing but your shift," I said, swallowing my envy as best I could, "then you should at least shut the door."

Clara shrugged. "The servants have better things to do today. As for Arne, he's already seen it all."

I came inside, closing the door behind me. Gleaming eyes stared down at me, the dolls and stuffed toys and porcelain figurines that seemed to decorate every inch of shelving. My twin's room always reminded me of a fright house, the dolls slumping about like dead children. Clara didn't notice my distaste; she was too busy looking critically at her reflection, relaxing her shoulders and pushing her stomach out.

"It doesn't show yet," I remarked.

"I know it doesn't. I just want to see what it will look like in the spring."

I hesitated, wanting to ask her the question I had been holding back for some weeks: how had she been so careless? After the first night Conrad had climbed through my window, I had gone to Anastasia for help, imagining the worst case, always the worst case. Clara had never taken such a step, though Arne was not her first bedpartner, or even her first servant. But I did not want to accuse my sister, who had never once remonstrated with me for a single one of my mistakes. I envied Clara nearly everything she had, but the envy had never turned to hate, as it did in fairy tales. We were too close for that.

"Does Arne know?" I asked, watching Clara poke her stomach forward again.

"No. I thought to tell him, but—"

Clara reddened and shrugged, and I nodded, thinking of a time when we were little, four or five. We had stolen a chocolate cake and two spoons from Anastasia's kitchen, then run off upstairs to hide in a wardrobe while we ate the entire cake. They found us hours later, asleep in each other's arms, and we were not punished, as I surely would have been if I had acted alone. Things would work out well; so Clara had always believed during every crisis of her life, and she had always been proven right. Even a full belly was not enough to merit serious concern.

"You're right not to tell Arne," I said, perching on the edge of Clara's settee. "He might insist on marrying you, and then Father would sack him. Have him flogged, even."

"Father wouldn't do that!"

I looked at her, surprised and a bit amused, as always, by her strange blend of innocence and experience. Father had flogged two servants when we were young, both for the crime of thievery. How had Clara never heard of it? Father would certainly flog Arne as well, for Clara's purity was worth much more than a stolen cigarette case.

"Does Arne love you?"

Clara shrugged again. "If he does, he's a fool. But I think I was only a bit of fun."

I stared at her, wanting to sit in judgment, yet unable. I, too, had spent many nights with a young man who was not my husband, and I hadn't even been smart enough to pick one I didn't care about, as Clara had. Who was to say that her choices were sins? Not I, for certain.

"Do you think my bosom is bigger?" she asked, taking a deep breath and standing straight, so that her breasts strained the top of her shift.

"I don't know. Why?"

"Arlette said when you're in a fix, your bosoms grow."

"Well, Arlette would certainly know." Arlette was Clara's friend, a pug-nosed blonde who would reputedly show her own bosom in exchange for a box of expensive chocolates. Clara was content with such friends, for she had many, but I had only Clara, and I wished that she would take her situation a bit seriously. If Father didn't find Clara a husband soon, her belly would begin to show, and then the game would be up. Several young men of the city had already offered for her, but none of them were up to Father's standards. We needed money to buy our way clear of Drosselmeyer; Father understood that, even if Clara didn't, and our debt was too great to be satisfied by the salary of a clerk or an architect. Father was determined that Clara should have a noble's son, at the least, but noblemen didn't marry girls with rounding bellies. I knew that much from my books.

"You should be careful," I told her.

"Of what?"

Of consequence, I meant to say, and then shook my head in silence, feeling the futility of the words. It was not in Clara's nature to count cost.

"What are you going to wear?" Clara asked, sitting down at the vanity and taking up her hairbrush.

"My green velvet."

Clara's mouth pursed, as it always did when she disagreed with something but did not think it worth argument.

"What?"

"That dress hardly flatters you."

"No dress flatters me. And Conrad likes green."

"Ah, Nat," Clara murmured, looking up at me in the mirror.

"What?" I demanded.

"Well . . . Conrad is a duke's heir, you know. He's a catch for anyone in the city. Don't you think you would have a better chance with someone else?"

"I'm sure I would. What does that change?"

"There's no need to be so defensive. I'm trying to give you good advice."

"What advice?"

"Boys don't like girls to chase them. They find it tiresome."

"I don't chase Conrad!" I snapped, and that was true. In public, we might have been no more than bare acquaintances. I simply lived with him in my thoughts all the time, hurting, like a stone in my slipper. I had done so for years, but I couldn't tell that to Clara, whose most passionate love affairs lasted no more than a month.

"You should get ready for the party," Clara told me. But her eyes remained grave, and I thought that she had meant to say something else, remonstrate with me about Conrad again. I pushed off the bed, but before I could leave, she rose from the vanity table and came to me, wrapping her arms around me. I returned the embrace automatically, being careful of her hairstyle, which looked to have taken hours to prepare.

"I love you, Nat. I have always loved you best."

"I love you too," I replied, puzzled. We had always loved each other; Drosselmeyer had not been able to take that from us. Clara drew back from me, and I saw that her eyes were sparkling, full of unshed tears.

"What is it?" I asked.

"Nothing. I just—I wish you would find someone who loves you as well as I do."

"I have tried to hate Conrad," I said quietly.

Clara shook her head and turned away, back to the mirror. But I saw the pity in her eyes, and I resented it. As though I had chosen Conrad. As though I had not wished every day since childhood that I had lighted on someone else, or no one, that I could be spared. Beyond the windows, the wind gave another wild, screaming whoop, and I shivered as I moved back into the hallway, watching the candle flames flicker inside the lamps.

"And don't wear that green velvet thing!" Clara called, just as the door latched. "Pick a color that's better on you!"

I stuck my tongue out at the closed door, then moved on down the hall.

CHAPTER

3

ANYONE WISHING TO DEFINE THE DIFFERENCE BETWEEN Clara and me need only look at our bedroom shelving. Where Clara's many shelves were stuffed with dolls and figurines, mine were packed with books. Clara knew how to read, but she rarely did so, only penny novelettes and other rubbish passed on by Arlette. What need had Clara for books, when she was welcome everywhere and invited to everything? She had her own stories, but I had spent countless hours in here, reading book after book in my rocking chair, while Clara went to parties and picnics and dances. Madame Margritta had predicted that I would end up blind as well as a spinster, for so much reading would make me cross-eyed. So far, I had been spared that particular misfortune, but it was only a matter of time before Madame Margritta came up with something new.

The maid had laid the green velvet dress out on the bed, but I ignored it for the moment, sitting down in my rocker and massaging my cold toes. My old fur-lined slippers were beginning to wear through, but I knew we didn't have the money for new footwear yet, not until Father found Clara the rich husband he wanted. In his head, Father was already spending this invisible vault's credit, for he had spoken many times at dinner of the luxuries the money would buy: refurbishments for the house; new suits; a new carriage; perhaps investment in another iron foundry. Father did not mention paying off Drosselmeyer's loans, but perhaps that went without saying. Surely getting the old sorcerer out of our lives must be the first order of business.

Outside, the wind wailed like a woman in grief. I rocked, moving on from Clara now, from Drosselmeyer, thinking of Conrad. He was a duke's son, certainly good enough for Father, but his family fortune and titles had never mattered to me. He was a quiet boy, not blustering in the fashion of the other youths of our neighborhood, and I had first noticed him for that, rather than his good looks. My love of books had inculcated in me a distrust of outward surfaces, a certainty that depth—if depth there were—lay beneath.

I liked Conrad because he thought more than the other boys. He considered the wider world. When we were twelve, Miles Cadwallader had found an injured dog in the gutter outside our house, its hind leg broken, and while the other boys were debating whether to bash its head in with a rock or fetch one of the fathers who owned a gun, Conrad had taken the dog to the surgeon and paid for the man to remove its leg. Money meant little to Conrad, it was true, and yet I had never forgotten the sight of him, marching up the street with the dog in his arms.

That was the day I decided there was more to him than fine clothes and a dukedom. The kindness of the act was almost secondary to the fact that he had chosen a solution that none of the other boys had even imagined, and that singularity seemed to me to denote value, almost a kind of greatness. As we grew older, he was one of the few boys who did not pay much attention to Clara, and this, too, convinced me that he was a boy of original mind. He would dance with the homely girls as well as the beautiful, not seeming to prefer either. Because his parents were unpopular, they had continued to interact with our family long after most of the nobility had given us up as a lost cause, and Conrad and I became friends gradually, a conversation at a time, conversations that I engineered almost as carefully as Clara would arrange her hair. He did not care about popularity, Conrad, and so he could sit with me at a party, talking and laughing, unmindful of his parents' disapproval. We finished a bottle of gin together during our last Christmas Eve party, the night before Clara and I turned sixteen, and though I had been almost too drunk to walk, I had not lost all my wits. I knew what I was getting into.

That was the story I told to Anastasia, to Clara. But in truth, I just didn't want either of them to know what a great fool I had been. That first morning, when we woke together, my bedsheet spotted with blood, I had thought that Conrad would take the inevitable next step of going to speak to Father, asking for my hand. It was only as I watched him dart around the room, gathering up his clothes, that I began to understand. By the time he slipped out my window the same way he had come in, shinnying down the drainpipe, I understood everything. But I couldn't claim ignorance for any of the nights that had come after.

I moved to the bed, staring down at my party dress. Clara was right; it did not flatter me, but it was at least nondescript, dark green velvet with a high neckline. If I were to dress as Clara did, in bright colors and bows, I would only look a fool. No dress would make me beautiful, just as Clara would not look ugly, not even if she wrapped herself in a farmer's sack. I knew my place in the world. I was not to be seen. I was only to watch and know.

Wallow in self-pity long enough and you'll drown, Anastasia whispered in my head. It was a favorite phrase of hers, and she would undoubtedly have mocked me now, standing here feeling sorry for myself, when I was young and healthy and had a roof over my head. The city was full of suffering people; we saw them whenever we went out in the open carriage, and Father would shoo us past those who loitered near the doorway of the church. For the past ten years they had been pouring into all the cities of the kingdom, abandoning their farms to seek better-paid work in the factories and foundries. But there was not enough food, not enough housing. Clara did not see the peasants, but I did, and so did Anastasia, who fed the city's unfortunates from the back door. Yet my own good fortune made it no easier for me to stop thinking of Conrad. Books were more helpful, particularly the tragedies, where people were saved by renunciation alone. Could I renounce Conrad? It seemed impossible, and yet I knew it would be for the best. No one ever got something they wanted so much, and if they did, it would be a curse in disguise, a punishment for the wanting.

"This will only end in grief," I told the Natasha in the mirror, waiting a moment to see whether she would answer, whether she was smarter than I. Then I gasped, whirling around. For a moment, I thought I had seen something over my shoulder, a tall and looming shadow. Then the vision faded and I saw only myself, Natasha Stahlbaum, a girl who fancied herself wise yet was too stupid to take the simple action of locking her bedroom window at night.

CHAPTER

4

I STAYED UPSTAIRS AS LONG AS I COULD, AND SO DID CLARA. WE often did the same things for different reasons. Clara liked to curate her appearance until the last minute, but I simply wanted to avoid the party as long as I could.

At five to eight, Clara drifted into my room and paused in front of my looking glass, taking herself in, her dainty feet pointing outward at that ninety-degree angle. I saw that she had done something odd with her décolletage, so that her neckline hung a good inch lower than it should have. She had painted her lips as well, a bright scarlet to match that of the whores down by the docks. And yet she was lovely all the same, her blond curls drawn back in a blue band that matched her silk dress. Clara was not cruel, but carelessness could be its own sort of cruelty. She took her beauty entirely for granted, not seeing it for the gift it was. It would never occur to her that I would not want to see her now, when the party loomed and I looked ridiculous in my green velvet dress. I tied the ribbon on my shoe and stood, watching the velvet fall around my round legs, my thick ankles.

"You look well," Clara said.

The grandfather clock in the entranceway chimed, beginning to strike eight. In four hours I would turn seventeen and so would Clara, but another year would hardly change anything. We would still be the Stahlbaum twins, dark and light, and I suddenly regretted the envy that had sprung up between us. Whatever Drosselmeyer might have done to us, it was not Clara's fault, any more than it was mine. She turned me toward her and gave me an appraising glance, then jerked my dress's bodice down as far as the velvet would allow. Clara always did her best for me at such moments, giving me advice on hair and corsages and necklines and jewelry, items she had picked up from the fashion periodicals I would never read. She pulled a few strands loose from the pins on top of my head, letting them dangle about my face.

"There," she said. "Now you look less like a schoolmistress, and more like a girl who might want to dance."

I poked her in the ribs, and she tugged me toward the stairs.

IN THE ENTRANCE HALL, THE CHANDELIER WAS FULLY LIT, FATHER pacing beneath it like a caged animal.

"Apple," he said to Clara, kissing her on the forehead. "You look beautiful."

He turned to me, his face changing, becoming a mixture of affection and resignation.

"Nat. You look very fine."

"Where's Mother?" Clara asked.

"In her parlor with that stupid medium. I can't get her to come out. Try, will you?"

Clara and I looked at each other.

"Rochambeau?" she asked.

29

I nodded, clenched my fist, and put down paper. Clara had scissors; with a grimace, I went to the door of Mother's parlor. It was a small room, built beneath the stairs, and Mother had taken it over shortly after we were out of swaddling, cramming an armchair, a settee, and a tea table into the tiny space.

"Mother?" I asked, knocking softly.

"Yes?" my mother's teary voice returned. "Is it time?"

The door suddenly slammed wide, and Madame Margritta's red face was stuck in mine.

"Your mother is engaged," she announced triumphantly.

"Engaged in what?"

"Oh, child," Madame Margritta whispered, her demeanor changing in an instant as she took my hands in hers. Her palms were moist, and the smell of brandy seemed to envelop me in a wave. When I was younger, I had often wondered why Father didn't cut off Mother's allowance, at least enough to pare back the medium's visits. But Father likely didn't dare, for it would have opened the door to questions about his own hobbies and pursuits. A vow of mutual silence; no one ever talked about it, but it was there, implicit in the marriage ceremony. One learned to live with the bad as well as the good.

"Child, your aura is darker than it has ever been."

I nodded wearily.

"I have dealt the cards, many times I have dealt them for you, for your dear mother. Always you turn up the same. The Tower, child, the Tower!"

I rolled my eyes, trying to pull my hands free. Madame Margritta had been dealing me the Tower since I was five years old. I had asked Anastasia about it once; she knew her tarot, had even told fortunes herself on the streets of the city before my mother took her in as a cook. With an expressive sniff, Anastasia had explained that there were no bad tarot cards, not truly, only enterprising frauds with doom to sell. The Tower was neither evil nor good, she said, only an indication of sudden, unexpected change.

"Revelation comes!" Madame Margritta continued, still clinging to my hands. "It strikes at midnight! But from whence, child? The past, or the future? My cards will not say."

"Mother, the first guests will be here any minute."

But my mother still lay prostrate on her settee, her red eyes leaking at the corners and the green bottle on the table, the spoon close within reach.

"My Natasha," she whispered. "Cursed, always cursed. Oh, how many times I've begged the spirits—"

"Oh, for God's sake." Yanking my hands free of Madame Margritta's sticky grip, I stormed into the tiny parlor, hauled Mother from the settee, and walked her into the entrance hall.

"Look, Nat!" Mother whispered, pointing to the ceiling.

"What?" I asked irritably.

"It's there! The shadow!"

"There's no shadow," my father snarled. "That stupid medium has addled your head."

Regally, as though she had not heard him, Madame Margritta swept to the foyer, where Klaus, our butler, ushered her past our father and out into the howling storm.

"She could freeze out there," Mother whispered to Father.

"One can only hope."

Mother's eyes filled with tears, and she delved into the pocket of her dress, groping for the green bottle. Dr. Sackler's Mood Tonic might be the panacea of our times, but whenever I found my mother weeping on her settee, or stumbling from room to room, I wondered.

"She chases that first moment," Anastasia had once told me. "But such moments are only a star falling downward. Even if she catches it, it will be worthless to her now, all brilliance gone." And I had known she spoke the truth, because every night with Conrad had been like that: a diminishment, lessening return. Morning taught me a lesson, always, and now, remembering Anastasia's words, I felt a sudden sympathy for my mother, wondering what she sought in the green bottle, what paradise she had lost.

Our cousins Charles and Deirdre sauntered from the parlor into the entrance hall, wearing identical expressions of contempt beneath their bright red hair. They looked far more like twins than Clara and I, and since Deirdre had taken it upon herself to cut her hair short three weeks before, she resembled her brother more than ever.

"Expensive decorations," Deirdre remarked, looking around her. "But tawdry. I bet the holly isn't even real."

"Of course it is," Charles replied. "The best Drosselmeyer's money can buy."

"That's not your business!" Father snapped, turning around. "And if you're displeased, you needn't come to the party!"

"Oh, we'll come," Charles replied lazily, shooting a pointed glance at Mother. "Someone must keep an eye on things."

"Auntie isn't well, Uncle," Deirdre remarked. "Perhaps you should seek the services of a professional."

Father stared at them with wide, outraged eyes, and I had to smile, that Father thought himself found out only now. I had known since I was eleven, when I saw him meet a red-haired woman beneath a streetlamp. When my father followed the woman down the alley, I had continued on my way home, but that night I sat across the table from Mother, thinking of that single word—*whore*—and how there was such an unbridgeable gap between the

32

good women and the bad. It was difficult to reconcile my father, creeping furtively and glancing over his shoulder as he negotiated a price, with the man who presided over our dinner table, and that night was my first understanding that all men have two sides: right and wrong, give and take.

My mother suddenly stirred to life, fixing her eyes on me. "You must do your best tonight," she said, tucking a loose strand of my hair back into place behind my ear. "There will be no shortage of good young men. You must not alienate them by sitting in the corner as you always do."

I glanced at Clara, wanting to roll my eyes at her, and have her roll hers back. But she only kept smiling, her clear blue eyes fixed on the doorway as the bell began to ring.

CHAPTER

5

BY NINE THIRTY, THE PARTY WAS IN FULL SWING: DANCING couples, shrieking children, tipsy women gossiping, and drunk men discussing the economy. Alcohol governed our Christmas parties, made them tolerable and attractive. The sideboard was covered with glass decanters holding an endless assortment of jewel-toned wines and liquors, and beside it on the table spread the picked-over remains of the buffet: pork, beef, lamb, roasted vegetables, leek salad, and four loaves of the seeded coriander bread that only Anastasia could make well. With dinner more or less concluded, most of the table seemed to be taken up by sweets: cakes and mince pies, candied apples, tarts and marzipan, oranges and raspberry meringue, a bowl of cream. Clara couldn't get enough of the sweets, and one might think the same could be said for Anastasia, but I knew this was simply one of her tricks: desserts, unlike dinner, could be prepared ahead of time and stored in the cold pantry, and Anastasia had spent the past week baking the vast confectionary that covered the right side of the table. As I eased sideways to avoid Mrs. Carmichael's massive bustle, my hand brushed the edge of an apple tart and came away covered in caramel syrup. With only a moment's compunction, I wiped it on the back of Mrs. Carmichael's dress.

Dodging a set of men deep in argument about the merits of various racehorses, I sat down in the cushioned seat beneath the bay window. This was my place every year, so much so that it was now left vacant for me by default. With any luck, I could hide here and avoid the notice of Charles and Deirdre, who were leaning together against the far wall, easy to spot by their garish dress, sipping from glasses of champagne. Someone had even given my brother, Fritz, a drink, though he was not yet thirteen; I had a brief glimpse of him ducking into the shadows beneath the staircase with a full martini glass.

Uncle Angelo was already drunk. In the spirit of the season, he had decided to wrap himself with silken tinsel so that he looked like a round Christmas ornament. Aunt Imogen was begging him to shed the tinsel and behave like a father, but her pleas lacked conviction. Last year, Charles and Deirdre had waited until their father was dead-drunk, then dragged him out to the front stoop and locked him outside. Charles and Deirdre told the tale often, as though it were one of their fondest memories, and since Uncle Angelo had no recollection of the incident, he did not seem to mind.

Mr. Cadwallader and six other men were gathered around our piano, listening to Mr. Holloway play Chopin. Atop the closed lid sat a pretty red-haired woman, swaying back and forth more or less in time with the tempo of the music. Her green muslin dress was no different from the party dresses of any of my mother's friends, yet she somehow had the look of a tart, and I was not the only one who sensed it. The circle of matrons in the corner watched her with barely concealed distaste.

"Nat!"

Charles and Deirdre had found me, just as I had known they would. My cousins were drawn to human misery as surely as carrion birds sought dead flesh, and for all my fixed and pleasant expression, I was fairly miserable. Conrad had arrived more than an hour before, but he had not even spoken to me yet, only danced with several other girls and eaten dinner with his friend Hans. I shrank back into the bay window as Deirdre reached out, her expression predatory, and touched the green velvet that covered my knee.

"You clean up very nicely, Nat. But for who?"

I looked out the darkened window, ignoring her. Frost had furred the border of the glass, and beyond the frame of white crystals was only darkness.

"Charles?" Deirdre asked. "Nat's trying to impress someone. Any guesses?"

"I'll give you three," Charles replied. "Conrad, Conrad, and Conrad."

Deirdre tinkled laughter, cold and strangely delicate, like a glass bell that had cracked years before in some country forever bound by winter.

"Poor Nat. Save yourself the effort. You can put a ball gown on a Holstein, but it's still a Holstein."

"Does he even know who you are?" Charles asked.

I looked away, determined not to answer. People knew I was in love with Conrad, but they believed it nothing more than a dog's love, desperate and hopeless, Conrad lifetimes beyond my reach. That might be so, but still I wanted someone, even a single person, to know that my dog's love wasn't all, that there was so much more to tell.

But I would not tell it to Charles and Deirdre. They had neither pride nor the lack of it, only that razor-sharp contempt.

"Your mother's minding the nursery again," I snapped. "Worry about that."

They wheeled around, delighted, and headed for Aunt Imogen, who was flirting with the oldest Cadwallader boy. I often wondered who had fathered Charles and Deirdre; it certainly hadn't been Uncle Angelo, who was incapable of malice. No, my cousins' vast well of spite had come from somewhere else.

Near the tree, Clara was holding court, seven boys clustered around her, jostling each other in their efforts to make her laugh. When she drained the last of her champagne, they were almost ready to duel over the honor of bringing her a new glass. Clara would never see their real faces, but I saw them, and knew them for what they were: wolves, brought to bay at the hand of a new master. When Clara spoke, they laughed too loudly, and when she smiled, they all smiled back, like marionettes. Clara's silly friend Arlette hung around the edges of the group, trying to work her way in among them, but none of the boys was willing to give up his place near Clara. As Arlette's party laugh grew louder, her voice more desperate, it occurred to me that Arlette, for all her silliness, probably understood men better than Clara ever would.

I grabbed a glass of champagne from a passing servant. I hated parties—the press of bodies, the humid haze of perfume and cigar smoke, and most of all the roar of the crowd. They never spoke of anything meaningful, these people, only that which was vapid and pleasant. Even the group of wallflowers in the corner would be murmuring inanities. I could join them if I wished, and they would welcome another to swell the fold, as though the shame of rejection were diluted by numbers. But there was no honesty there either. I could almost hear their whispered conversation, the saccharine falsehoods about their own self-worth. Lies did the bunch of homely girls no good anyway, for whenever I glanced their way, I would find at least half of them staring at Clara, their faces frozen in poorly concealed jealousy. I at least had the courage to admit my own lack of value in this setting, to stay in the shadows of the bay window and hide.

"Fritz!" my mother shouted.

Fritz had climbed the staircase in the entrance hall, and now perched over the head of the Kalenov matriarch, a terrifying old woman we all hated. Fritz had acquired not only a second martini but also a lit cigar, and as I watched, he took aim and tapped ash into the upswept funnel of Grandmother Kalenov's blue-rinsed hair.

"Fritz!" my mother cried again. But he had already disappeared up the stairs, chortling. Fritz embarrassed my parents, but it was difficult not to smile at his antics. Yet my smile faded, for now Conrad had come back into the parlor, holding a plate of treacle tart. He wore a sober grey suit that made him look older than his twenty years, and his hair had been cut that day. He was not the handsomest man in the world . . . nor, if I was being honest, the handsomest in this room, only a tall, thin boy with dark hair and severe, serious features. Yet I could have gazed at him for hours. He skirted the Christmas tree, avoiding his father, who had joined the worshipful group of men gathered around the redhead on the piano. Conrad's mother had disappeared into a corner somewhere, probably with a bottle swiped from the sideboard. They weren't happy, the Liebermanns, any more than our family, the Stahlbaums, or any of the other families of the neighborhood. Sometimes I wondered whether anyone in the world was truly happy, but the question was answered for me a moment later by

Clara's high, careless laugh. Clara had told me many times that I should put on a proud face, ignore Conrad, teach him a lesson. But I couldn't feign indifference to Conrad, and I would be an even bigger fool than Arlette if I didn't know it.

After saying hello to my parents, Conrad sat down and offered me a bit of his treacle tart. I shook my head—I hated treacle tart—and let him eat, watching him when I thought I would not be observed. I liked Conrad's hands, which were pale and somehow aristocratic without being effeminate. They were not the hands of a worker, or even a merchant. Conrad's hands were made for leisure, for shooting and drinking and waving around during political argument. Noble pursuits.

"You'll be seventeen tomorrow," Conrad remarked, through a mouthful of pastry.

I nodded.

"Was it really an entire year ago we got drunk on that bottle?"

I nodded, grinning. That night had been the one good night, the night I had loved him with a wide-open heart, thinking I needed to pretend nothing, and if all that came after had been a diminishment, it still could not touch the clear memory of that one night. Even now, thinking of it, I wanted him to leave the party with me, take me upstairs, and take all my clothes off. Clara's voice echoed in my head, telling me to remain aloof, to have pride, but I ignored her, for Clara had never been in this place. Boys fell like ninepins at Clara's feet, and so she would never understand the dilemma of the half-wanted, the choice to give in because it was better to have something of the boy you loved than nothing at all.

"Happy birthday," Conrad said, and pulled something from his pocket: a wrapped box from a jeweler. For a moment I was stunned, thinking it was a ring, but the box was too big for that.

I took it and unwrapped it carefully, finding a pretty bracelet: three ruby pendants joined by a series of platinum links. I had never received such an expensive present in my life, and I stared at it for a long moment, moved almost to tears.

"Thank you," I said, and put the bracelet on, not minding that the rubies clashed with my dress. "It's beautiful."

Conrad patted me on the shoulder, and my heart fell. This was one of his thoughtless kindnesses, I saw now, impersonal; he'd had the money, and it had occurred to him that my birthday was approaching. The gift did not mean anything more than that. The dog, the crippled dog . . . for the thousandth time I found myself examining Conrad's attraction, working at it with my mind as though it were some unwelcome weed that had taken hold in the garden, sprung from a taproot that I could unearth and throw into the bin, shutting myself of it forever.

"You understand, Nat?" he said, leaning forward and looking at me, a little earnestly. "Everything will have to—"

A thudding blow echoed against the parlor wall. Out in the entrance hall, some sort of commotion had begun, men's voices raised. Mother would be mortified, but a good brawl would liven things up. There was always a fistfight or two at our Christmas parties. Three years before, one of the Carmichaels had even challenged a Swanson cousin to a duel, although by the time dawn came, both would-be combatants were too drunk to hold tumblers, let alone pistols. The Swansons paid the Carmichaels to settle the grudge, and thus did we all learn that money was honor, that mistakes need not be paid for so long as they were remunerated.

But the argument in our entrance hall grew more heated by the minute. Several men were shouting now, and after a handful of seconds there was a crash of breaking glass, something thrown against a wall.

"What the devil—" Conrad began, standing up. Mother, too, was hurrying in that direction, but before she could reach the parlor doors, they slammed open. The crowd seemed to turn as one, and all conversations faded into a collective, horrified gasp.

Drosselmeyer stood in the doorway, leaning on his cane. He was dressed, as always, in a blue velvet suit, top hat, and silk-lined blue cloak. A matching blue silk eye patch covered his left socket, but the working eye seemed to roll across the room, taking us all in at once. His grin made me shudder. He reached into his pockets, brought out clenched fists, and threw them into the air. Gold coins and walnuts rained everywhere, and the smaller children scrambled after them, shrieking with delight. But the rest of the guests remained frozen, half-drunk glasses clutched in white-knuckled fists.

"Godfather Drosselmeyer!" my father cried, pushing his way through the gaping crowd, his rolling eyes and sweating forehead standing in odd counterpoint to the forced jollity in his voice. "What an honor you do our house!"

Drosselmeyer inclined his head, acknowledging my father's politeness even as that monstrous grin mocked the rest of us, undercutting the very idea of celebration. He placed both hands atop his cane, an avuncular gesture that was likewise belied by the merry blackness of his gaze.

"Thank you, Martin. A joyful Christmas to all!"

CHAPTER

6

THE CROWD RESPONDED WEAKLY, ONLY A FEW GLASSES raised. As Drosselmeyer entered the room, they parted for him, and I saw that he was flanked by his usual pack of boys, six of them this evening, carrying two enormous boxes and one smaller box between them. All were handsome and well garbed, as befitted the occasion; nevertheless, they did not fit in. They were too well muscled for gentility, and they had an air of insouciance. God only knew where Drosselmeyer found them, down by the docks or even—as I had heard—in the red door district. But their murky antecedents would not impede them here. There was a feminine shifting as the pack of boys moved into the room, an adjustment of hair and necklines, a fluttering of fans.

Drosselmeyer gave an imperious snap of his fingers, pointing his cane toward the tree, and the boys, maneuvering with a peculiar grace, deposited the two large boxes beside it. The smaller parcel, one of them brought back to Drosselmeyer, who tucked it beneath his arm.

All of this passed in silence, the crowd still so horrified by the apparition in the doorway that they couldn't even muster the courage to whisper behind their hands. Conrad had left my side, but I didn't blame him; I wouldn't have wanted the wizard's notice either. Father offered Drosselmeyer a brandy, which he accepted with a nod. Only then did I notice the seventh boy standing at Drosselmeyer's shoulder.

He did not match the others. This boy was dark-haired and dark-eyed, tall and lean like Drosselmeyer himself. A distant relative, perhaps, nephew or cousin, though it was strange to think of Drosselmeyer having relatives. The boy's mouth was pulled and twisted by scarring, his left cheek crossed with the marks of old wounds stitched. More scars marred his hands, which dangled beneath the worn cuffs of his suit.

"Nat," Clara whispered, making me jump. She had appeared at my elbow as though by magic, and I found myself absurdly flattered that she would leave her group of admirers, even now, to come and talk to me. She took my hand and pulled me into the corner, just as she always did when she had a secret to tell. Conversation had finally resumed around the room, though muted.

"Pull down your neckline, for god's sake," Clara told me, yanking at my dress. "You've a fine bosom, if you would only take advantage of it."

I batted her hand away, for I had no interest in drawing attention to myself. And Conrad . . . well, Conrad already knew what my breasts looked like.

"Who is that?" I asked, inclining my head toward the scarred boy.

"I don't know," she replied. "Never seen him before. But, Nat, listen. There's something I have to—"

She fell silent. Following her gaze, I found Drosselmeyer's black eye upon us, watching with the speculative gaze of a man who considers the purchase of a horse. I shuddered, and felt Clara do so as well; a moment later, she had darted away into the crowd. Trying to hide from the wizard's gaze, I ducked behind one of the draperies that covered the bay window. Snow drifted wildly outside the glass now, and tiny crystals crusted the border of the pane. I could hear the wild howl of the wind.

"I have brought gifts!" Drosselmeyer boomed, silencing both the minimal talk and the three string players in the corner. Peeking from behind the portiere, I saw Drosselmeyer's boys lifting the two massive boxes to stand them on end. They were plainly gifts, wrapped in silken paper and tied with bright red ribbon.

Adults were moving the chairs to line the walls now, and several of them were busy corralling the children onto a single sofa. At twelve, my brother, Fritz, was the oldest among them, and he sat very unwillingly, a sour expression on his face. When he thought no one was looking, he tipped up his martini glass and drained the last of its contents.

Drosselmeyer reached into his cloak and produced a tiny conductor's baton, waving it like a magic wand. Several of the younger children on the couch wriggled in delight, anticipating a magic show, but I felt foreboding drop over me like a stage curtain. The children might well believe him a harmless wizard, but of course I saw him differently: a bird of terrible omen, casting a shadow not only over the party but over the future, the daydreams I held close. I glanced around the room, but Conrad had vanished, and I was suddenly glad. I looked down at the bracelet he had given me, wrapping my fist around it as though to protect it from harm.

"A trick, Godfather!" one of the little girls cried. "Do a trick!"

Drosselmeyer bowed, a courtly gesture.

"I shall!" he announced. "For I have brought gifts for my two goddaughters, seventeen on this night!"

Clara caught my eye, and I saw my own alarm mirrored in her face. Drosselmeyer waved his makeshift wand, tapping the tall box on the left, and its front fell forward to the floor, revealing the thing inside: a toy clown the height of a man, dressed in garish silken pajamas of orange and green. Its cheeks were rouged, its aspect obscured by white greasepaint. It was not real, only a wooden toy, but still I winced at the monstrous sight of it. Father had once given me a harlequin doll, a horrid porcelain creation with dimpled cheeks and a courtesan's knowing smile. After several nights spent trying to sleep with the thing in my room, I had thrown it from my window into the bed of a passing wagon. Father had never tried to give me another doll, but Drosselmeyer's clown was much worse, its smile bright and murderous, the hands at its sides dangling bone-white, long fingers ready to clutch.

"For Natasha!" Drosselmeyer cried. He whirled, his blue-spangled cape flaring behind him, and threw his hands into the air. I shrieked, and I wasn't alone, as the clown sprang from its box, eyes rolling with merriment, and bounded into a backflip, landing with perfectly split legs in front of the sofa full of children, its paint-smile stretched wide. One of the little Berthoff girls began to weep.

"What poor taste," someone whispered to my left. "Even for the dark sister."

"Appalling," another voice replied. Several parents approached the couch to comfort their children as the clown popped to its feet and began to caper around the room. Some of the drunker guests laughed at its antics, but others, including my mother, looked decidedly uneasy. Drosselmeyer had all the gifts of the magician, prestidigitation and legerdemain, but his tricks were sometimes too good. The clown was clearly made of wood; beneath the silken clothing, one could see the joints where limbs connected to the trunk by some sort of cunning invisible screws. But the thing's face had an almost human mobility, its cheeks dimpling when the gruesome smile flashed. It danced and kicked around the room, its movements mechanical enough to maintain the illusion of artifice as it moved past the fireplace, the Christmas tree, the sideboard, moving steadily closer to the bay window where I sat. Drosselmeyer was watching me, his black eyes bright with interest, and I felt anger kindle inside me, an old anger I had almost forgotten. What had I ever done to this terrible old man, that he should bear me such ill will?

The clown spun a final time, came to a full stop before me, and turned its painted face toward mine. Deep within each of its eyes I saw a cold pinprick of shining red light, the light I sometimes fancied I saw buried within the eye of Drosselmeyer's portrait in our entrance hall. As the clown leaned over me, arms outstretched, I caught the scents of sawdust, sweat, and something worse: the scent of the night moss that grew in the churchyard cemetery. There were actual knuckles beneath the clown's gloves; I could see them working as it settled its hands on my shoulders. Drosselmeyer was gone; the party was gone. We stood in a black circle alone, the clown and I, my mind reeling toward a dreadful understanding: Conrad would never ask me to dance in public, not now. This foul, grinning creature was the only partner I would ever have.

That's Drosselmeyer talking.

The voice broke over me like water. Wouldn't the old wizard like that, for me to sit in the corner and grow old in silence, believing it was all I deserved? With a sudden murderous fury, I threw my glass of champagne into the clown's face.

The creature sank back on its heels, closed its eyes, and seemed to shrink, somehow. Without warning, it was only a toy again, its white face dripping with amber liquid, a lifeless mannequin of cleverly carved wood. The room reappeared around me, and I saw that everyone was looking to Drosselmeyer . . . some with horror, some with amusement, but all with an obscene sort of anticipation. Every Christmas Eve they collected themselves and came to the Stahlbaum house; here, finally, was the show they'd come to see.

"Forgive her, Godfather!" my father bleated, wringing his hands. "Such a fine gift! Natasha forgets her manners. She will apologize."

"I will not."

"Natasha!" Father cried, and I heard real desperation in his voice. But he was looking at Clara. Always Clara. If Drosselmeyer wanted to broker a fortunate marriage for Clara, he could, and if he wanted to ruin such a marriage, he could probably do that too. Father knew it; it was in his eyes as he looked at my beautiful sister, and I fought back a vicious wish that her stomach would show, here, now, that she would be forced to marry Arne, condemning our family to penury forever.

The clown was still standing before me, eyes closed and arms outstretched. Revolted, I gave the thing a push, and it fell backward, hitting the floor with a thump and lying there, at rest, in a small puddle of champagne. Fifty pairs of eyes moved from Drosselmeyer to me, then back again, as though watching a competition of lawn tennis.

"I see my clown has failed to impress," the old wizard said softly. But a smile hovered on his lips, and his lone eye retained that gleeful piratical light. With another flourish of his makeshift wand, he tapped the second enormous box, which likewise opened to reveal a ballerina, her tulle tutu the color of pink marzipan. She was life-size, like the clown, but clearly a toy for all that; her head twitched and turned mechanically as she began to whirl around the room, and her eyes held none of the clown's mad, unnatural life. No one paid her much attention.

I sat down again in my window seat, contemplating the clown on the floor, trying to understand what had happened. Champagne could do many wonders, but it did not perform magic. I had wanted the clown dead, and so it was. Or had Drosselmeyer done that? The group of boys had reassembled around him now, all except for the scarred one, who stood off to one side. Beneath his sleeves, the slim fingers were long and clever-looking, like those of a pianist or watchmaker, and I wondered whether he was in trade. He caught me staring at him, and I turned away.

"Friends!" Drosselmeyer cried again, waving the small white box in the air. "Friends! I have one last gift. Clara, come here."

CHAPTER

7

THE PEOPLE AROUND ME BRIGHTENED AS DROSSELMEYER drew Clara forward. Her curls bounced, and her dress swayed charmingly around her calves. The adults watched her with approving smiles, but Clara's own smile seemed forced, and her eyes were wide with panic. Her gaze met mine for a brief moment, and I was certain that we were both thinking the same thing: Drosselmeyer, for some cruel reason of his own, was about to reveal her pregnancy before the entire room.

"A special gift," Drosselmeyer announced, handing Clara the small box, "for a special girl. Open it, child."

Slowly, Clara began to unwrap the box. Something terrible seemed to hang above our heads, and I looked around to see if anyone else felt it, but the people around me were watching Clara with the same mindless voyeur's gaze as that of the men gathered around the piano. Clara was taking her time with Drosselmeyer's gift, unwrapping it as though it might contain some deadly substance. But when she lifted out the item inside, gasps of disbelief peppered the room.

It was a nutcracker, the simplest and most pointless of Christmas decorations. The little carven soldiers had appeared in the city some fifteen years before, part of a short-lived fashion. But every family still had several nutcrackers in their home, to be brought down from the attic before Christmas and then forgotten until Twelfth Night. Drosselmeyer's nutcracker was even smaller than most, and its white hair and fearsome grin scarcely distinguished it from the rest. This, then, was Clara's special present: an ugly doll that wouldn't fetch five pfennigs in the street.

"Cheap bastard," a man muttered, sotto voce, to my left. Clara curtsied, her face an open book of confusion and disappointment.

"Thank you, Godfather Drosselmeyer."

Taking the nutcracker from her, Drosselmeyer placed it gently on the floor, then gave it a tap with his wand. The toy soldier gave a visible shudder, then began to march forward. Guests backed away as it approached, allowing it to march to the far end of the room, where it did an about-face and then started back. Clockwork, one would have said . . . unless one had also seen a clown with a working pair of knuckles beneath its gloves. As the nutcracker passed, I craned my neck over Mr. Barron's shoulder and saw that there was no key in its back.

Halfway across the parlor, the nutcracker crossed paths with the ballerina as she whirled through the crowd. The little soldier paused, executing a strange, courtly bow as the dancer passed, and then resumed his patrol across the room.

"Oh, isn't he dear!" Clara cried, clapping her hands in genuine delight. She always did love her dolls, and I supposed it was a fine thing to have a doll that would march and bow on its own. But the guests still looked uneasy, and I didn't blame them. Drosselmeyer's toys were simply too lifelike. Coming upon an ottoman, the nutcracker stood there for a long moment, as though puzzled, then reached over its shoulder and drew a saber from its back. Perhaps it was only imagination, but I thought I heard a snarl emerge from between the nutcracker's clenched teeth. It drove the saber into the side of the ottoman with a ferocity that seemed more human than mechanical, and I heard the stitching rip.

"I want him!" Fritz cried, hopping up from the sofa. "I want the nutcracker!"

Father tried to grab my brother, but too late. On Fritz's face was the same mulish look he had worn when he was eight years old and set out to skate the thin ice of the river. He darted between several guests and grabbed the nutcracker from the floor. The little soldier struggled, his mechanical arms and legs almost flailing as Fritz dragged him back to the settee.

"Fritz!" Father cried. But there was futility in the cry. No one had been able to control Fritz since he was six or so. I glanced down at the floor, where the clown still lay on its back, arms outstretched like those of the mustachioed villains at the theater. Its eyes, wide open, were staring at me. One of them winked.

I shrieked, cringing backward into the window bay. But no one noticed, for at almost the same moment, Fritz threw the nutcracker in a single, convulsive movement. It sailed across the room, hit the wall with a brittle crack, and fell to the ground.

Charles and Deirdre began to laugh wildly, and Clara looked reproachfully at Fritz, but his wide, terrified eyes were on the nutcracker. His florid cheeks were drained of all color, just as they had been when we finally hauled him from the crack of ice in the river, half frozen. I chanced a look at the clown, found that its eyes were closed again.

"For God's sake, Fritz!" my father snapped, then turned to Drosselmeyer, spreading his arms in supplication. "Godfather, what can I say? My children are so cavalier with your gifts."

Drosselmeyer ignored him, watching Clara pick up the nut-cracker with great gentleness. One of its arms fell to the floor, splintered into two pieces.

"Ahhhh."

The crowd let out a collective sigh, and all heads turned toward Drosselmeyer. He frowned, lowering one eyebrow as if deep in thought, then gestured for his boys to come. The scarred one came last, reappearing from the far side of the Christmas tree. Clara smiled her enchanting smile at all of them, even the scarred boy, but he turned away from her, causing her mouth to pinch in confusion. I felt a mean pleasure in that.

Drosselmeyer took the broken pieces of the nutcracker from Clara, and the boys gathered round it in a huddle. Then Drossel-meyer tied something white, a kerchief or perhaps a napkin, around the nutcracker's broken arm, binding it to the body. He produced his wand again, waving it back and forth over the toy like a ma-gician trying to summon a rabbit from a hat. There was a bright flash of violet light, and when he whipped off the handkerchief, the nutcracker's arm was whole.

The guests clapped, but now there was some uneasy mutter-ing, which I understood. It was all very well to have a magician in your neighborhood, but it was quite something else to be forced to continuously endure his conjuring at a party, and on Christmas Eve of all nights. Our neighbors had not bargained for any of this; they only wanted to get drunk in peace. Clara set the nutcracker on the floor, where it resumed marching its paces, and the guests drew away as the toy approached.

"Friends, I have one final announcement!" Drosselmeyer boomed, as though oblivious to the crowd's rising discontent. "My gift to Clara is not only a Christmas present, but an engage-ment present! Two honorable families have come to an agreement."

An excited murmur moved through the room. I looked to Clara, wondering whether she knew who the boy was, or whether Father had acted summarily, he and Drosselmeyer cooking this up between them. But Clara's blue eyes were dull, her mouth twisted in an expression I could not quite read. She stared at the floor like a prisoner in the dock.

"So join me, friends!" Drosselmeyer continued. "Raise your glasses!"

The assembled crowd raised their drinks, crying toasts that sounded genuine enough. But I had no champagne, and I was watching my godfather, who seemed entirely too pleased. Looking from his gleeful expression to Clara's miserable countenance, I felt a suspicion awaken inside me, suspicion so monstrous that it took only moments to transform into certainty.

She wouldn't, I thought wildly, putting my hands out as though I might ward off disaster. *She wouldn't do it. She would never—*

"To Clara Stahlbaum and Conrad Liebermann!"

CHAPTER

8

I COULD NOT LEAVE THE ROOM, COULD NOT FLEE IN TEARS AS I wished to do. They were waiting for that, all of them, their glittering gazes now turned from Clara to me. The voyeurs wanted me to run, and so I knew that I could not flee, or break down crying there in the alcove. Nothing to give them the scene they craved. For a spiteful moment I thought of opening my mouth, shouting to the world about Conrad, what we had been to each other. It would not stop the marriage, no, but it would taint it forever. When Clara and Conrad entered a room, no one would ever speak of anything else.

But I couldn't, for Conrad would despise me. I looked down at the bracelet on my wrist again, suddenly understanding its significance, the meaning of Conrad's odd words earlier. He met my eyes across the room, smiling, and in the smile I saw both relief and real affection, horribly fraternal.

Good old Natasha, that smile said. *You never made trouble before, and thank God, you can be relied upon not to make any now.*

Clara was staring dumbly at the floor. Her eyes were filled with misery, but that would earn her no clemency with me. My mother, too, looked guilty; had she known about me and Conrad? My father hadn't, I felt certain, for he was beaming drunkenly upon Clara, his apple, whose beauty and pliancy had enabled this match to benefit them all. I realized then that Drosselmeyer must not only have brokered the marriage but funded it as well. Clara, after all, offered nothing to a duchy but good looks and charm, and Conrad's parents were too mercenary to be swayed by such considerations. No, this betrothal would have required gold. I stared at Drosselmeyer, trying to read him as I would a book. The idea that he might have planned this, waited all these years to spring a trap, made me feel hunted, almost despairing. Had he not done enough? Father had already begun to talk of sending me to the convent next year if I had no suitors, but I had not taken the idea seriously; after all, I'd had Conrad, who in the worst instance might act as a trump card if Father tried to make good on his threat. The sisters didn't take spoiled women, not unless they came with a significant dowry for Christ. Now I could see the terrible future, so clearly that it might as well have been visible through the window: Clara and Conrad at every family gathering, the two of them together, having pretty children, smiling at each other, traveling together, accumulating the warmth of married life together as so many couples did, while I sat in the corner, growing older, unmarried, unwanted, forced to see. Clara would have these things, appreciating them not at all, while I would have nothing, not even a full belly to accuse Conrad with, nothing but a scrap of his white shirt and the ruby bracelet, the traditional present in such situations, the beautiful piece of expensive jewelry that all noblemen gave their paramours when the arrangement was over and no harm done.

THE CLOCK STRUCK TEN. THOSE WITH YOUNG CHILDREN WERE busy corralling them and wrapping them in hats and scarves. Drosselmeyer's ballerina continued to whirl around the room, occasionally striking a guest with her perfect arms and legs; she smacked Uncle Angelo in the gut and then knocked over a row of bottles at the sideboard. My mother grabbed at the ballerina, trying to bring her to a halt, but the dancer continued to twirl, and her outflung hand slapped my mother in the face. The group of men around the piano exploded in laughter.

Something brushed against my leg. Looking down, I saw the nutcracker, its hand tugging at the hem of my dress. I recoiled, then stopped. Its face, which had seemed so fixed before in its pained grimace, must have had some malleability after all, for now the doll seemed to stare up at me with great solemnity, its eyes wide and full of knowledge. Even my own mother had never looked at me with such sympathy.

"I'm all right," I whispered. "I just . . . I didn't expect it."

Across the room, Clara had taken Conrad's arm, and Conrad had covered his hand with hers. Even inside its white glove, Clara's hand looked tiny, and Conrad held it very gently, as though it were something delicate. All men had two sides; I had known it for years, though I had somehow never connected the knowledge with Conrad, and now I sensed that Clara would never know the boy I had known, the boy who had not needed to perform or please because his was an easy audience, already besotted. Clara's Conrad would be another creature entirely, brought to sudden and vivid life by Clara's status as an object of value, and he would be a boy I did not know. Pain broke over me like a wave, and the nutcracker seemed to feel it too, for it patted my knee.

"He likes you."

I blinked, but it was only Drosselmeyer's odd boy, the scarred one, leaning against the wall near the end of the buffet. He was watching me with an almost clinical detachment, the impression enhanced by his eyes, which were a deep, fathomless black.

"It's only a doll," I replied.

"You think so?"

"Mikhail!" Drosselmeyer's deep voice boomed in my ear. He must have crossed the room in mere moments, and he seemed agitated, twisting his hands beneath a smile that was wholly false.

"Do you wish to go home, Mikhail? Your work here is done, I think. All of the other boys have been given leave until the party ends."

"I'm not one of your boys, old man. I've done what you asked of me. Now leave me alone."

Drosselmeyer flushed, color working its way up his jaw.

"You forget yourself. Perhaps you weren't ready to come out after all."

Across the room, a woman shrieked and glass shattered on the floor. Peering over Drosselmeyer's shoulder, I saw Mrs. Gulder clutching one bleeding hand while the ballerina twirled smartly in front of her. I looked down to see whether the nutcracker was still beside me, but it had disappeared.

"That creature is entirely out of control," Drosselmeyer said coldly, as though the ballerina's behavior were a personal affront, rather than his own design.

"Just as you ordered, Godfather."

Drosselmeyer turned to stare at him, and the boy pushed himself from the wall and headed across the room, leaving us alone in the alcove. We had never had private speech, Drosselmeyer and I, but here was a privacy that I would not have chosen. Drosselmeyer looked down at me, and I thought I saw honest pity in his black gaze.

"Are you heartbroken, Natasha?"

"No, Godfather." But I added it, in my mind, to Drosselmeyer's crimes and offenses. He had known, of course he had.

"She blooms, your sister," he remarked, settling himself onto the opposing cushion. "Her condition agrees with her."

I blinked, then wondered why I should be surprised that Drosselmeyer knew that too. He had known everything, yet picked Conrad for Clara. Why?

"They'll be happy, you know," Drosselmeyer went on. "Money, good looks, charm . . . they'll make a fine couple. One of the bright lights of the city."

Drosselmeyer's boys were wrestling the ballerina back into her enormous box, though she was putting up quite a fight; when one of the boys lost purchase on her arm, she began to beat the other two about their heads and faces. Finally they pinned her arms and legs and muscled her back into the box, where she immediately subsided, closing her eyes and resting in a plié, beautiful and glittering in repose. At the same moment Drosselmeyer rose, but I forestalled him, grabbing at the hem of his blue velvet coat.

"What do you gain?" I hissed, keeping my voice low. "What do you gain by deviling me?"

Drosselmeyer looked down at me, considering. There was no goodwill in his gaze, but no malice either. Indeed, I felt that I did not matter to him at all, that he felt nothing for me beyond that impersonal pity.

"You needn't worry, child," he murmured. "Soon you will suffer no more."

"*To Father Christmas!*"

The speaker sounded hoarse and belligerent, as though prepared to fight all those who would not stand up for the laughing man with his bag of gifts. But they all took up the shout, and suddenly the room was a glittering, jagged landscape of raised glasses and toasts, voices that sounded somehow vicious beneath their celebratory words, and as they lowered their glasses, Drosselmeyer was abruptly gone. I looked for Clara and Conrad, but they were blocked by the group of wallflowers, who had migrated as one toward the buffet table. I had the odd sense of being on a stage, a space where actors appeared and disappeared at will. My father was huddled with Conrad's father in the corner, both of them sniggering over something in a monthly, and Conrad's mother was dead-drunk on a settee beside the fireplace. The tart had gone from her place atop the piano, and Fritz and my mother were nowhere to be seen.

"Has he gone?" The scarred boy, Mikhail, had returned to stand above me.

"Who, Drosselmeyer?"

"No. My nutcracker."

"Yours?" I looked up at him, bewildered. "I thought it was for Clara."

The boy began to laugh, and it was not pleasant laughter. The scars seemed to pull at the sides of his mouth.

"The old man doesn't own my creations. He doesn't have the power to give them away."

"You're not one of Drosselmeyer's boys," I said. "Who are you? Who are your parents?"

"Who are yours?"

I didn't know what to make of this question, but a moment later I forgot it, for the crowd had parted again to reveal Clara and Conrad laughing together, their heads bent close.

"He's a fool," Mikhail murmured, making me look up sharply.

"Why do you say that? Every man in the city wants Clara. She's a prize."

"Prize indeed. How far along is she?"

"Keep your voice down!"

"Some men are desperate to be deceived," the boy went on, his tone conversational. "He will take the healthy baby after six months' marriage, your foolish beau, and tell himself any story he must."

"He's not my beau."

The boy snapped his fingers, much as Drosselmeyer would. A moment later, he was holding a scrap of cloth: a scrap I knew, the cuff of a man's white shirt.

"Give me that!" I said furiously, snatching for it. But the boy only snapped his fingers again, and the scrap was gone.

I drew away, curling back into the alcove, no longer interested in finding out who the boy was, only in having him gone. One sorcerer in the neighborhood was enough.

"I have not stolen your keepsake," Mikhail said. "It's illusion, no more, and I am not Drosselmeyer, to entertain myself by bullying a young girl."

I looked away, embarrassed that anyone should know how foolish I was, that I had so treasured a scrap of shirt. But there was no help there, only Clara and Conrad across the room, smiling at each other. The ruby bracelet seemed to hang on my wrist with the weight of lead, yet I couldn't take it off. It was all I had left.

"He's a duke's son, no?" Mikhail continued. "Will he marry your sister for her beauty? Or perhaps he actually needs an heir, in which case a breeding woman would be an asset."

"Perhaps he simply loves her."

The words hurt. I didn't know why I felt compelled to defend Conrad to a stranger, even now.

"Surely your sight is not so limited," Mikhail replied. "There's little love in that boy for anyone but himself."

"You don't know him," I said frostily.

"Neither do you, or you would not sit here weaving a tapestry of excuses. Are all humans so foolish?"

I turned away silently. I had always thought it would be a relief to tell someone about Conrad, to have it in the open. Yet this was somehow worse, to have our dealings raked over by this odd creature, a scavenger inspecting dead flesh. I realized then that I had not wanted to tell someone about Conrad, so much as I had wanted to have something to tell, something real. Yes, that most of all: I wanted something real to tell.

Across the room, the group of boys hefted the great box that held the ballerina, balancing it on their shoulders as they trooped out of the parlor. They must have picked up the clown as well, for nothing remained to show where it had lain but a puddle of drying champagne. Drosselmeyer shepherded them out, crooking an imperious finger at the boy beside me.

"Well, I must go," Mikhail said. He looked down at me a long moment, then said, "Should you happen upon my nutcracker again, I would leave it be. The old man meant it only to walk and talk, but I am not his servant. The finished item holds a great danger for one as poorly used as yourself."

"Conrad didn't use me."

He threw me a final pitying glance, then moved off to follow Drosselmeyer. At the bar, people continued to order drinks, undeterred even by the spectacle of Fritz, who had taken over as bartender after a fashion, busily pouring the leftover drinks into pint glasses and then setting the resulting concoctions on fire. On the far side of the room, Conrad's mother had fallen from the sofa and now lay on the floor. I thought of the many times I had tried to speak to her over the years, to subtly court her approval. When she was drunk, she didn't care, and when she was sober, she ignored me, because I would never be good enough for her son. I turned away and didn't look at her again.

"Oh dear God, what are those children doing now?" bawled deaf Grandmother Kalenov.

The men had succeeded in getting Uncle Angelo to collapse into an armchair, but now Charles and Deirdre were busily wrapping tinsel around both their father and the chair. Uncle Angelo slept blissfully during this process, emitting the occasional gasping snore. The armchair was too close to the fireplace; if the fire didn't die fast enough, Uncle Angelo might literally bake there overnight, but no one moved to intervene. The crowd shifted and moved like a great ocean around me, and I heard snatches of dialogue everywhere, phrases meaningless and almost idiotic in their brevity.

"—best I've ever seen, and good God, you know how I hate the ballet—"

"—fifty pfennigs to the ounce! By winter, we'll be coining our own—"

"—says she won't have him, but you know she'll come round—"

I covered my ears, trying to shut them out. The crowd parted, and there were Clara and Conrad again, whispering, so close to each other that they might have been kissing. Telling secrets. Making plans. Charting a life in which I would have no part. Conrad had released Clara's hand, but now he was toying with the lace that bordered her glove, halfway up her arm. Such behavior was frowned upon, of course, but for a newly engaged couple, society could be more forgiving, and of course Clara would never be reprimanded anyway. I closed my eyes and found a sudden hideous vision: Conrad climbing the icy drainpipe on the side of our house, only instead of going left when it branched, he would go right, toward Clara's room. Images flipped through my head like a deck of sickening cards; Clara and Conrad together, not only in a locked room but a locked life, because that was what marriage was, a magic circle drawn to separate two people from the world, and no one able to look or interfere or know. But I would know. The images came faster now, joining seamlessly like one of the new moving pictures they showed on the high street, and all the while something terrible was growing inside me, some rapacious animal. All these years, when Conrad had talked to other women, looked at other women, clearly desired other women, I had stood aside, eyes downcast. I had never made trouble for him, and perhaps that was why, in his mind, we were still merely good friends, friends who had drunk too much wine one night and fallen into bed together. But now he was ready to be away, on to his future. They thought they would be happy, the two of them, thought themselves shut of me so easily. But it wouldn't be that way; I swore it suddenly, clenching my fists tight enough for my fingernails to draw blood.

Had I possessed Drosselmeyer's sorcery, I would have cursed them. Had we been men, I would have challenged Clara to a duel. Instead, I watched the pair from the corner of my eye, my beautiful sister and her handsome fiancé, who had once made me laugh by taking off my stockings an inch at a time, like a dancing girl's. For the next hour I watched them, and all the while I thought of magical things. Terrible things.

CHAPTER

9

Anastasia was washing dishes, her back to me and the set of her shoulders speaking volumes about her mood. I halted just inside the doorway.

"Anastasia, can I help you clean up?"

She gave me an unreadable look over her shoulder, then said, "You can dry."

I took a towel.

"What a fool's parade," Anastasia muttered. I made a noise of agreement, then began to dry the plate she'd handed me.

"And that old sorcerer! Did you see his present for Clara?"

I nodded in silence, but Anastasia seemed to sense my agreement, for she continued, "The only thing worse than a spendthrift is a mean old bastard. Drosselmeyer's rich as the King; there's no call to be so cheap in public that way."

"It wasn't an ordinary nutcracker," I told her, remembering the scarred boy's warning. "It could walk and talk."

"So it could walk and talk," Anastasia scoffed. "Drosselmeyer's magic costs him nothing, does it? His toys could sprout wings and fly, and that old goat would still be as tight as my fist."

"There's something wrong with the nutcracker, Tasia. I felt it."

"Ah," she replied. "Well, when a craftsman makes something, it takes on the heart of what he is. That old man's creation might well send you upstairs with the screaming horrors. Though why he would take time to craft something worth less than ten apples at market, I don't know. If that old vulture had any sense, he'd use his sorcery to make a machine for washing pots and pans!"

Anastasia's voice moved on, high to low and back again like a flute, cursing Charles and Deirdre; Drosselmeyer; Conrad's mother, who had vomited on one of Mother's best carpets; and one of the Reichler cousins, who had put an elbow through a windowpane in the entrance hall. The pane was clearly the worst infraction, for it would need replacement quickly in such weather, and Anastasia bewailed the dealing she would have to do with the glazier, an old foe. When she had run out of curses, there was silence for a few minutes, a comfortable silence of Anastasia washing and me drying, thinking of nothing at all. Then I felt her hand on my back.

"I'm sorry, girl," she said, in a firm, no-nonsense way. "I knew your hopes."

I turned, helpless, and buried my face in her shoulder. She was warm, and she smelled of cinnamon and pastry and sweets, all good things.

"Take comfort," she murmured, rubbing my back. "Any boy fool enough to want Clara is too much fool for you."

I stilled, contemplating the possible truth of that. Yet what did it change?

"Nat?"

Glancing over my shoulder, I saw my mother, standing in the

doorway. Beside me, Anastasia grunted, a sound that could have meant any number of things, and began to wash a tin cooking spoon.

"Nat, I'm sorry."

I turned, ready with a furious retort, and then stopped. Mother's expression was full of honest regret, nothing of the green bottle in it at all. She had known, then, about Conrad. Perhaps she had even known about all those nights when he had slipped through my window. She held out her arms, as though to embrace me, and my mouth began to tremble. The bloom of darkness inside my stomach was too strong for that pretty word, *sorry*, which after all was no more real and substantial than Mother's laudanum visions. Her regret might be true, but what did it buy me? Sorry was no coin I could use for purchase. I turned away, back to the dishes. Mother lingered for another minute, then I heard her shuffling steps leave the kitchen.

"Let me wash for a while," I told Anastasia.

We switched places. The water was scalding, and for some minutes the pain took most of my attention. From the parlor, I could hear random voices. Many of the guests had begun to take their leave, and that crowd-roar was finally beginning to recede.

"Nat?"

Clara's voice, behind me. I stiffened, dropping a pan back into the water.

"What do you want, princess?" Anastasia demanded, picking up a saucepan. "Haven't you done enough?"

"Nat? Can we talk?"

Turning toward the doorway, I saw that Clara's face was uncharacteristically determined; she meant to have this out, one way or another. Anastasia, too, seemed to know it, for she dried her hands on the dish towel and said, "All right. But not too long in here. I've plenty more to do before I can rest."

She went out into the parlor, closing the door behind her. Clara and I were left alone, facing each other like duelists on opposing sides of the kitchen. Her eyes were glassy with unfallen tears, and she lowered them quickly.

"Nat, I'm so sorry."

I did not reply, only watched her, seeing her clearly now, perhaps for the first time. She might not have chosen Conrad, but she had taken him all the same, because it was easy. Clara danced through life like one of those old Greek goddesses, the Graces perhaps, with flowers strewn at her feet, and the whole world was charmed. But not me. Not any longer.

"What will you do when your time comes, Clara? What will you tell him, when you have a baby in May or June?"

"He already knows," Clara said, not meeting my eyes. "He says he will accept the child as his."

The words hit me like a physical blow. Conrad would not so much as touch my hand in public, but he would marry my sister even though she bore another man's child? How could Clara's value be so great, and mine so little?

"You understand, don't you, Nat?" Clara asked, her voice pleading. "I have no choice—I must get married, and quickly, before I start to show. Otherwise everyone will know."

"And what a tragedy that would be."

Her eyes widened.

"You won't tell them, Nat. You can't."

How I longed to tell her that I would! But spreading gossip was too petty a revenge for the thing inside me.

"I won't tell them," I replied.

Clara smiled, tears hanging on the ends of her lashes. She moved forward and I saw that she would embrace me, as though this business were all done and we were sisters again. She would give up nothing, yet expect me to give up everything.

"Don't touch me."

She halted, and the corner of her mouth curved in a Clara-pout.

"Why must you be so difficult? I said I was sorry. I *am* sorry."

"Sorry isn't magic, Clara. It doesn't heal all wounds."

"Well, what else am I supposed to do?" Clara demanded. "Should I marry Arne and live down by the docks like a fishwife? Go into the convent?"

I thought of telling her that the convent had been good enough for me, but before I could, she spoke again.

"He was never going to marry you, Nat. He told me so."

That cut deep as well. I had assumed that Conrad would tell no one, and that had been something, at least, for the shared secret had put us in our own magic circle, a place and a past, a hundred nights in which Clara could have no part. That they had sat and discussed me, decided how to handle me . . . that had broken the circle, allowed Clara to reach in and pull Conrad forward, into the present. Into their future.

"You've made your choice," I said. "I don't think there's more to say."

"You would let a boy come between us?" Clara's shock was genuine. "After all these years?"

"Conrad has not divided us. You've done that."

Clara's cheeks turned pink. She had been stealing things for years—chocolate from the kitchen, silk from Mother's sewing box—but she was not used to anyone speaking to her in this way. I saw the first spark of anger in her eyes.

"We'll be married at the New Year," she told me, her voice chill. "Conrad says we'll take our honeymoon across the continent, stay away until long after the baby is born. Even if you decide to tell, there will be no proof."

"I've already said I won't tell."

"Then what do you want from me?" Clara demanded. "What am I to do? I want you to forgive me."

"Cancel the engagement, then. Go out there, now, before the guests are all gone, and tell them a mistake has been made."

"I—I can't do that."

"Then you've made your choice."

"But I won't live this way!" Clara shouted, stamping her foot. "You're my sister, Nat, my own twin! Tell me what I must do!"

"I've just told you."

"Why are you so intractable? Why not find someone else? That's what I'd do!"

"Yes, you would, Clara. But I can't."

"Doesn't it matter at all that I'm sorry?"

I began to giggle, helpless giggles that were not in the least amused. What must it be like to have a life so easy that every problem should be resolved by simple wishing, by that meaningless word, *sorry*? I couldn't imagine, and yet what a great pleasure it was to stand in her way for once, to see her face consequence, to watch that Clara-pout deepen!

"Go," I told her. "Go back to your fiancé."

"He's left already, with his father. His mother was unwell."

"Ah, yes. Your wonderful new relations. You should enjoy them."

A knock sounded, and Anastasia peered around the door.

"I must have my kitchen back now, girls. Everything sorted? All friends again?"

I shook my head, and Clara ran from the room, sobbing, hands pressed to her face. Anastasia took her place at the sink with a shake of her greying head, muttering, "Wait until the day the little princess finally has something to cry about."

"She says I should forgive her," I said. "Move on."

"And did you?"

"I didn't. I won't."

Anastasia nodded. "People make much of the bond of blood. Blood does matter, but it isn't a saint's pardon for all sins . . . though the blood of twins might be a different matter."

"Why?"

"Why, twins are a powerful thing, girl, as I've told you before. You and your sister share a single soul."

"Country nonsense."

She shrugged, turning back to the dishes. Yet I saw that I had managed to offend even her, my only friend in this house. A wave of despair seemed to break inside my head.

"Get moving, girl. I must finish drying these before the night's gone."

"Anastasia," I began, and bit my lip. Thinking of the long night to come, I wanted to apologize for my rudeness, to beg her to stay.

"Go on, girl," Anastasia said, her voice gentle, but with a note that said she would brook no refusal. "There's work left to do, and I'm for my bed as soon as it's done."

CHAPTER

10

SHE WAS NOT MERCILESS, ANASTASIA, FOR SHE LET ME linger there in the kitchen doorway, weeping a little, until I regained control. In the parlor, Uncle Angelo was still trussed up in the armchair, his enormous gut barely visible beneath the mountain of tinsel. Everyone else was gone, even the servants, who had lowered the chandelier and doused the candles. I couldn't hear Clara anywhere; she must have gone to bed. Behind me, I heard a click as Anastasia retreated to her solitary room beside the pantry, taking the lamp with her. Everything was suddenly dark. Too dark.

I tiptoed out into the parlor. The room was still softly lit by the fire, but someone had banked it, and it was beginning to die down. In the armchair, Uncle Angelo snored in prolonged drags of breath. Dimly, I heard a squeaking sound near the skirting boards; mice, come to take advantage of the crumbs before the servants tidied in the morning. Mother would be appalled if she knew, but she wouldn't hear it from me.

A rustling came from my right. Turning, I saw Clara, asleep

on the blue velvet sofa. Her eye paint was smeared, as though she had been crying, and she held the nutcracker in her arms, like a child with a stuffed toy. I felt a perverse urge to snatch it away, but heeded the scarred boy's warning to steer clear of the thing. Its painted mouth grinned fiercely at me in the firelight, reminding me of Drosselmeyer, and my earlier question recurred: why had he done this to us? So far as I knew, I had committed no sin, nor was Clara particularly good. There was no morality in our godfather's double-edged blessing, so what had it all been for? I should have shaken the truth out of the old man while I'd had his coat in my hands. Now it was too late.

The Christmas tree was still lit, which was poor vigilance by Father and the servants; someone should at least have extinguished the tapers. I took the capper, meaning to do it myself, but as I neared the tree, I saw a gleam of silver wrapping on the far side: the enormous box that had held the clown. Drosselmeyer's boys had boxed the ballerina and taken her away, but they hadn't taken the clown. Where was it?

It could be anywhere, I thought, and a cold finger seemed to run down my spine. Everything in the room appeared suddenly wrong, enlarged and distorted. Mother's sideboard, normally some six feet tall, now towered above my head. Our parlor had a high ceiling, easily twice the height of a normal room, but the Christmas tree appeared even taller than that, as tall as a several-storied building, growing before me until I shut my eyes. It was time to go to bed.

I moved into the entrance hall, feeling as though I had walked a thousand miles. Halfway across the black-and-white floor, I halted and kicked off the silly heeled party shoes I had chosen, in an early evening that seemed like years ago. Who had I been trying to impress? Conrad? Stupid. He never noticed anything I wore.

Something popped in the hall's enormous fireplace. I whipped around, but saw only flickering shadows and Drosselmeyer's portrait. The painter had depicted him as a concentrated academic, deeply immersed in his book, and it gave me an uneasy feeling to be dismissed by his image when the real man had spent the evening watching me so closely. Drawing nearer, I stared at the portrait, the rough, pebbled texture of cheap canvas and old paint.

"What do you want from us?"

No answer. I hadn't really expected one. Drosselmeyer did what he wanted, and shared his reasons with no one. Yet he must have had a plan. He had been watching us for years, controlling our futures with money as surely as a man would control a lapdog with a leash. I was furious with Clara, but there must be some blame left over for our godfather, who after all had made us what we were.

Now the old grandfather clock in the hall began to chime midnight: one bell, then two. Looking down, I found my feet hidden, the space between my knees and the floor clouded in a layer of white vapor as clammy as mist. I tried to kick it away, but it clung to my legs, inching its way up my thighs in grasping tendrils. Three bells, then four. I looked back through the parlor doorway to where Clara still lay on the sofa. Clara, who had taken everything but the one thing I truly wanted, and then taken that too. The clock chimed five bells, then six. A scraping sound knifed the air behind me and I spun around, my nerves ragged. There was nothing there, yet something had changed, something so simple that I couldn't put my finger on it. Seven, then eight. I spun, frantic, and finally saw it: Drosselmeyer's portrait. The armchair in which he usually sat, so assiduously reading his book, was empty.

Nine bells, then ten. A flapping sound behind me. I turned and Drosselmeyer was there, crouched atop the grandfather clock.

From his shoulders sprouted a great pair of leathery black wings, like those of a bat. His lone eye glared red in the dying firelight. He looked down at me and grinned, vulpine, ready to spring. The clock chimed twelve; there was a flash of light, a bang that made me jump, and Drosselmeyer disappeared in a puff of smoke.

I screamed, clapping my hands over my mouth, and at the same moment, my twin cried out from the parlor. Somewhere very close by and yet far away, I heard the squeaking of mice. I turned back to the portrait and found him there again, our godfather, half-spectacles perched on his nose, reading as though his life depended upon it. He had said something to me earlier, something about suffering. What had it been? I could not remember. Even the party seemed many years ago.

A low giggle echoed above my head, where the staircase met the upper hall. I knew that terrible giggle's owner, knew it as well as though I had seen it standing there, white gloves and a red murderer's smile. And it came back to me suddenly, what Drosselmeyer had said.

Soon you will suffer no more.

Now a shadow moved at the top of the stairs. It was as tall as a man, and it slid from wall to wall, easing to the top of the staircase, trailing its fingers on the silhouette of the marble railing. Beneath the crackle of the fire, I could hear the rustle of silken clothing, the hiss of its white gloves as they paused on the wooden balustrade.

Dear God, I thought. *He means to kill me.*

The shadow began to descend the stairs.

I turned and fled.

CHAPTER
11

I N THE PARLOR, THE CHRISTMAS TREE NOW SEEMED TO TOWER
high into the night, like one of the new American buildings that
were reputed to touch the sky. The cabinets of Mother's sideboard
stretched far above my head, their doors as large as those of the
city cathedral. But I paid these wonders no mind, only ran for the
kitchen, Anastasia's kitchen, always so full of light and sympathy
and blessed practicality. Nothing terrible would come there; nothing would dare.

But the door lay shut, and though I hammered away with my
fist, it did not open. Anastasia was in there, in the tiny room off
the kitchen where she lived, but after a few moments I realized
that she would not hear me, not even if I should scream and
scream. Drosselmeyer's magic had taken us now, Clara and I, and
even Anastasia could not interfere.

Something squeaked behind me, the sound enormous in the
firelit room. Whirling, I saw a slumped and hunched silhouette,
ratlike, scuttling against the sideboard cabinets. More squeals

echoed in my ears, and before the rat's shadow, fleeing, I saw another shadow: a lithe girl with the body of a dancer, her mouth wide and hair streaming out behind her. On the sofa, Clara had begun to writhe and sob, holding her head. The nutcracker fell from her arms, hitting the floor with a thump of wood on wood. More of the shambling creatures rose in silhouette against the sideboard, and I heard the click of their claws, the rasp of their loathsome tails dragging behind them. All around me I sensed motion, yet everywhere I turned, there was only still midnight silence and the bright glow of candles. Clara had always been deathly afraid of mice and rats, and now I began to understand that she, too, was suffering . . . not only suffering, but being made to suffer.

Good, I thought. But the satisfaction was short-lived, for now a tall shadow was edging its way around the doorframe into the room. No mouse, this, nor even a rat; as it straightened, it became manlike, dancing along the wall. The tip of its pointed hat bobbed in the shadows thrown by the fire. It paused, turning its head this way and that, and I knew the moment it spotted me, for it gave a happy little hop and turned a cartwheel. Then it came, dark but agile, leaping along the wall, its hands outstretched.

I retreated toward the center of the room, the sofa where Clara lay. A thunderous boom echoed around us, the sound of a cannon, but still I could not take my eyes from the shadow on the wall. It was questing for me, feeling for me, its fingers flickering in the firelight as though they were reading the air. I took another step back, and my foot came down on something hard: the nutcracker, where it had fallen in front of the sofa.

I bent to pick the toy up, then paused. The scarred boy had warned me to leave it alone. He worked for Drosselmeyer, yes, but he was not one of Drosselmeyer's boys. I had sensed that clearly.

Yet it did not follow that he was my ally either. If Drosselmeyer meant to kill me—and it seemed certain now that he must, even if I could not imagine why—then I could not trust any of them, these terrible toys that walked and talked in mockery of us all.

On the far wall, the clown's shadow was bending to the skirting board. It was stuck on the walls, I thought; I would be safe here, in the center of the room . . . but even as the certainty crossed my mind, the shadow seemed to puddle and collapse, bleeding beneath the skirting. A moment later, two dark footprints appeared on the adjacent floorboards. They paused for a long moment, then began to move, shadows of steps, the print behind disappearing as soon as the forward foot had landed. I stared at them, not believing, even as they crossed the room, moving toward me. I smelled the thing coming, that same dank churchyard scent I remembered from earlier. I couldn't see it, but it was there.

I darted behind the sofa where Clara lay, began shaking her shoulders. But she did not wake. From a distance, as though through a thick door, I could still hear the booming of a cannonade, the screams of dying mice. The footsteps were still coming, around the corner of the sofa now, and I fancied that I could even hear the thing that was stalking me, its gloved hands trailing along the velvet of the cushions, its feet shuffling on the floor. In a moment I would see it as well, I knew: bloodred smile, waxpaint face, and murderer's eyes, and when that moment came I would die of terror, long before it could touch me, or bow, or ask me to dance.

Something tapped my knee. I looked down and found the nutcracker staring up at me, reaching for me in clear invitation, like a young child demanding to be picked up. The little toy soldier both repelled and drew me, smiling with that fierce grin that so resembled a grimace of agony. Drosselmeyer had left it here, left it to Clara's casual mercies and fickle nature; perhaps the nutcracker, too, felt cast aside. Warnings echoed in my head, but those warnings had been given hours before, in a cheerful and well-lit parlor that had no understanding of this dark room. The clown's silhouette rose before me, and without another pause for thought, I bent and took the nutcracker beneath the arms, lifting him up.

ACT II

THE SUGAR PLUM FAIRY

A woman drew her long black hair out tight

And fiddled whisper music on those strings

And bats with baby faces in the violet light

Whistled, and beat their wings

And crawled head downward down a blackened wall

And upside down in air were towers

Tolling reminiscent bells, that kept the hours

And voices singing out of empty cisterns and exhausted

    wells.

—*The Waste Land*

T. S. Eliot

CHAPTER

12

I OPENED MY EYES TO SNOW. NOT THE SNOW OF THE CITY, which I knew well, muddy and tracked by the ruts of countless horses and carriages, its bright white gradually fading to a lifeless taupe as it piled up in drifts at corners and around streetlamps. This was country snow, pristine and silent. Night lay over the land, but the snow seemed to glow with its own light, like that of a pearl, bright enough to illuminate not only my green dress but the vast land beyond, over which snow lay as far as the eye could see, covering fields and hills in an unbroken carpet, so fine that it looked like sugar. As I raised myself to sit, I saw that I had landed with an impact, carving out an enormous divot in the snow.

Looking up, I saw Clara, distant and yet very close, like an object viewed through a spyglass. She was sitting in an old-fashioned sleigh, its sides hung with jingling bells. Two horses were hitched to the sleigh, and their harnesses too were hung with bells, their proud manes strung with bright red ribbons and green sprigs of holly. I felt pity for the poor beasts, but Clara exclaimed delightedly at the sight, clapping her hands as though she were six again, finding the new dollhouse our father had left under the Christmas tree. Beautiful that dollhouse had been: a mansion, almost a castle, all sheer pink and frosting white. Clara had been enchanted, but I had played with the thing perhaps twice and then left it alone, preferring by far the grey stone castles of medieval knights in books, men who fought dragons or undertook the terrible voyage to the Holy Land. But Father had never commissioned one of those, and Clara could not understand why I might prefer piracy on the high seas or war on the Turks to the parties and balls she created inside the dollhouse, placing each figure carefully in a process that might take hours. This sleigh, with its ridiculous trappings, would have fit right in, and so would Clara in her blue dress, all frills and lace. With her hair falling in golden curls down her back, she looked like a doll in the sleigh.

But now I saw that Clara was not alone. A young man sat beside her, holding the reins with one hand, his other arm tucked companionably through hers. He was wearing the same uniform as Drosselmeyer's nutcracker, but with gold epaulets at the shoulders. A prince for Clara, then, who had always dreamed of one. He was so handsome that he made Conrad look like a poor cousin, but it was Clara's taste in beauty, not mine. He was too square-jawed, too bland, an assembly of symmetrical parts, with all the charm of a tailor's mannequin, and at the sight of him, I felt my astonishment recede, my mind turning to the question of what this place might be.

A dream, was my first thought, but I dismissed that immediately. The night was clear; the air felt cold. The curtain of night flowed over my head as black as a deep lake; there were simply no stars. And now I realized that the snow beneath my hands was not cold; nevertheless I could feel it, running through my fingers, clear and real. No, this was no dream, I decided. But what was it?

The nutcracker prince shook the reins and the horses leapt forward, bearing him and Clara across the snow. Though I stood no more than twenty feet away, Clara and her prince did not notice me as they passed; they were too busy chattering happily to each other, like friends who have reunited after years apart. I wondered what Conrad would make of this development, but the question was empty, and I knew it. Whatever this place was, it existed far beyond our well-lit world of parties and presents and wounds that did not heal. Conrad was not in this place, nor would he ever be part of it.

This was between Clara and me.

THE HORSES WERE SURE-FOOTED AND QUICK; I LOST SIGHT OF the sleigh within moments, but it was easy enough to track, for the runners left two clear lines in the white carpet of false snow, which was really some sort of fine powder, like confectionary sugar or morphine, scattered far and wide over the land as across a grand baking board. The trees—mostly pines and other impossibly tall conifers—were blanketed with the stuff as well, so perfectly that the snow looked painted on. In fact, the entire scene struck me as one of art. But my perception was no fault of the artist; indeed, the illusion was so great that I was the only thing that broke it as I followed the tracks of the sleigh's runners, stumbling along.

The land was perfectly silent, and this, above all things, told me that I was no longer in the world I knew. Clara and I had been born and raised in the city, but we had gone for many rides and picnics outside the high walls. The country might seem quiet by comparison, but there was no silence there. One could always hear the farm animals, cows lowing and geese honking, and the sound of the peasants at work. Wagons traveled along the paths, horse harnesses jingling, and birds screamed at each other from tree to tree. One couldn't even get lost in the country, for there was always some sort of market taking place in one of the many hamlets that surrounded the city walls. The countryside was really a very busy place, but this land was silent and still.

After perhaps a mile or so, the sweets began to appear. At first I did not note them, registering only dimly the tree in the shape of a lollipop, the high lamppost that swirled in tones of bright peppermint, red and white. But then, as the sleigh tracks began to curve to the right, I noticed three crystal sugar reindeer, cropping idly at marzipan grass beside the tracks. Yet I was not charmed by these wonders, for I could almost picture Clara, clapping her hands again. This land seemed to align too perfectly with her dreams, her fantasies, her shelves full of dolls.

Drosselmeyer, I thought, with a stir of anger. He had been as evenhanded as ever, our godfather; a murderous clown for me, and for Clara this place, which might have come straight from one of her fairy tales. Yet there was something about it that was not quite trustworthy. Fake snow, a mannequin prince . . . these things made me think of a tale from before I was born, about one of the lovers of the old dowager queen, who was so desperate to impress her that he had created the facades of thriving villages along one of the provincial rivers. The old queen had indeed been impressed, but only because she was nearly blind. Whoever had created this place had admired beauty but forgotten to add life, and in the omission I sensed a kind of desperation, something constructed quickly and without grace, under a dreadful deadline. Who was meant to be deceived? For what purpose?

But the sweets provided some clue. When we were younger, Clara used to steal constantly from the kitchens: chocolates, candied almonds, pastilles, whatever Anastasia left in the pantry. If she succeeded, Clara would share the sweets with me, but if she was caught, she only smiled her winning smile and Father and Mother would forgive her, no matter how Anastasia howled. Here were all the sweets Clara could ever want, and no Anastasia to get in her way. As I labored through the knee-high piles of ersatz snow, I saw that small tracks veered away from the sleigh path to the gumdrop trees, that the snow beneath the trees was scattered with gumdrops like fallen fruit. These detours continued as I went farther, Clara's tracks veering toward another grove of trees that hung low with lemon drops and a stand of bushes that appeared to be sprouting enormous clusters of pure caramel. I viewed each of these depredations with increasing injury, seeing her now in my mind's eye: Clara, who had always been able to eat all the chocolates and cakes she wanted without seeing so much as an extra inch on her waistline. Clara, who had never been forced to face consequence.

More crystal reindeer appeared here and there, cropping the sugary grass. They seemed immune to the cold air, but I was beginning to feel very cold indeed. Rounding a stand of taffy trees, I was confronted with two gingerbread men no taller than my waist, having an argument beside a peppermint lamppost. The fact that these creatures could walk and talk had clearly not saved them from Clara's ravening hunger, for a third miniature figure lay on the snow beside them, his head bitten cleanly off. The two remaining gingerbread men did not seem concerned about their fallen comrade; in fact, Clara seemed to be the subject of their heated argument.

"She was not!"

"She was! She was! I know more than you, lummox, and I tell you, that was a girl! A human girl!"

"You're only three days old, just like me. How would you know anything?"

"I know. A living human! Think of it! Such a thing hasn't been seen here since—"

They seemed to become aware of me then, and the argument stopped short.

"Pardon me!" the first gingerbread man called, bowing with a politeness so exaggerated that it bordered on the burlesque. "I mean no offense, but are you human?"

"Yes," I replied cautiously.

"Thank you."

He turned back to his companion, trying to speak in an undertone.

"You see? I told you. There's another one. The hour has come!"

"The hour for what?" the other gingerbread man demanded. "Where do you get all of this mystery?"

"Shhh!" The first shot me a furtive glance. "Come over here, if you want to discuss it."

They disappeared behind the taffy tree, leaving their be-headed companion behind. The crystallized reindeer nearby had ceased cropping the grass and begun to eye me with interest, so I hurried on, following the sleigh's tracks. They took a lazy, rounded route, as though the nutcracker prince were in no hurry and determined to show Clara the sights. I followed them for what seemed like hours, past a thick forest of shortbread trees covered with melted chocolate, the scent of mint in the chocolate so thick that it made me gag; past a field of enormous candied jelly beans that popped from the snow like colorful new-sprouted cabbages; down into a ravine bordered with high walls of fudge. For a brief time, the tracks even ran alongside a tumbling brook of pink jelly, so sludgy and sickly looking that I followed Clara's path at a wide distance, not wanting to take the slightest chance of falling in.

Many times, it struck me as odd that I felt no desire to sample any of the delights I saw there. I was not so mad for sweets as Clara, but I liked sugary things well enough. Perhaps it was only that everywhere I went, I saw evidence of Clara's progress. Small crumbles marred the walls of fudge; several of the giant jelly beans had been seized and pulled from their stalks; one of the shortbread trees had been felled and butchered, its branches stripped and the chocolate gouged away from the crust as though by an animal. At one point, a trail of pink jelly led from the stream back to the sleigh tracks, and I could almost see Clara there, snuffling greedily as she licked each sticky drop from her palm. Perhaps it was the vision of Clara gorging herself that kept me from feeling hungry . . . the realization that whatever I might touch, might covet, had already been sullied by my twin long before.

And yet there was more. This land seemed designed for Clara, beautiful but simple, full of sweets that talked and walked and did not complain even when her hunger demanded their heads. The nutcracker prince too, I decided, would have been built to Clara's taste, a gallant cavalier who gave everything and demanded nothing. I wondered whether she saw Conrad the same way, then dismissed the idea. Clara had never bothered to look further than Conrad's title, Conrad's fortune. Thinking of him sleeping an easy, dreamless sleep worlds away, I began to weep again, silent tears that froze into fine sugar on my cheeks as I stumbled through the snow. The dog, the wounded dog . . . I had thought that he was kind above all things. But in this place my vision had sharpened, and I saw him picking up the animal, hauling it away in silence. He had not comforted the dog, I remembered now, had not said a word to it. He had simply removed it from the group of boys, taken it to the surgeon, because anything else would have left a mess. The pretty bracelet at my wrist jingled with my footsteps, and I realized that Conrad had not been so much trying to silence me as to enclose me. He needed me inside that bracelet and all of its implications, so that he might view me as a finished bit of memory, no loose ends. Clara, too, had wished to seal me off, wrap me in the finality of that idea, *sorry*, so that we would never have to speak of it again. They thought they could discard me, the two of them, but I was no gullible girl, to be cozened by treats. I tasted nothing, not even when the path of the sleigh presented me with an enormous almond torte, my favorite, which had been baked in the shape of a small hut, the roof thatched with sculpted strands of golden marzipan meant to mimic straw.

After a difficult climb through a field of marshmallow rose-bushes, their blooms as white as the snow surrounding, the sleigh tracks topped a rise and began to descend into a valley so lavishly strewn with sweets that a squinted eye might have mistaken the sprawl for a flower garden. Every color of the rainbow was represented down there, and some that I did not recognize from our spectrum at all. But I did not bother trying to sort them out, for my attention was commanded by the valley's centerpiece: an enormous castle of luminous pink candied sugar, its heights iced in white by what seemed an infinite variety of parapets and seraphim and turrets. I could not even say how tall the castle stretched, for the tips of the highest turrets reached beyond the glow of the snow, disappearing into the arching molasses black of the night sky.

Far below, I spotted Clara's sleigh, wending its way toward the valley floor. I could almost see her there, bouncing with excitement at the sight of the castle, yet I felt chilled. The castle resembled our old dollhouse so closely that I didn't believe it could be coincidence. Who could have found that castle in Clara's memory and built it to scale? Even Drosselmeyer had never seen the doll-house, for Father had commissioned it long before the ruinous foundry disaster had put our family in the old magician's pocket. Clara might think this place had been built to delight her, but I saw something different. Another land lay under this one; I felt that I could almost glimpse it, just beneath the layers of pretend snow, the pink walls of the castle, the rainbow field. Clara had done me a wrong, but it did not trouble her one bit, and if I needed evidence, there was the map of her merry passage, flirting with her nutcracker prince and blithely stuffing her face with sweets. If this place was meant to deceive my twin, I decided, then all to the better. I wondered how she might look, caught in one of Drosselmeyer's traps, the rolling lawn of her life pulled out from beneath her feet. The picture made me smile, and I started down the slope into the valley, not feeling the cold any longer, my bare feet shuffling through the false snow.

CHAPTER

13

B Y THE TIME I REACHED THE WALLS OF THE CASTLE, CLARA
had already disappeared inside. The heavy sleigh had been
dumped over, as though a careless child had knocked it flying,
and next to the larger, booted tracks of the nutcracker prince,
Clara's tracks continued down the slope toward the drawbridge.
Seeing those small footprints in the snow, I felt a great leaping inside my chest.

Several soldiers, all of them dressed as nutcrackers, were
working to untether the horses. But the horses were not cooperat-
ing. They kept stamping their feet and tossing their heads, jerking
their bridles out of the soldiers' hands. Beneath the jingling of the
innumerable bells that decorated harnesses and manes, I could
hear the soldiers' complaints.

"Come on, you whore!" one of them snarled, jerking at the
reins. "Sit still!"

I wondered whether I should try to slip by unnoticed; the
soldiers were preoccupied, and Clara had apparently passed
the gauntlet without trouble. But their swords and pikes were real

enough, cold steel that gleamed almost white in the effulgence of the snow. The weapons were the first things here to strike me as genuine, innate to the landscape rather than constructed illusion, and after a moment's dithering, I veered toward the sleigh.

"Bad enough having to wear this nonsense," one of the soldiers growled as he tried to hold a horse by the bit. "But to not even attend the party and all! When was the last time we skipped a party? Ah, be still, you troublesome bitch!"

He cuffed the horse across the jaw.

"Old Maria told me it's a special party," another soldier grunted, working on the tight knots that laced reins to sleigh. "Not like the others. We might not even want to be there."

"Let's just get it done," a third soldier cut them off, speaking with the tired air of the long-suffering captain. "The girl's inside. It's easy duty from here on out."

At that moment they, like the gingerbread men, seemed to become aware of me all at once. Their attention shifted as a unit, and I felt my confusion return. They had been waiting for Clara, expecting her. But no one had been expecting me, and at the realization my mind spoke up, settling my first question.

This is not Drosselmeyer's work. Drosselmeyer wouldn't have forgotten about you.

"Who are you?" the captain demanded, and that was another good question. Who was I, in this land in which only Clara appeared to matter? If I was not the dark to Clara's light, who was I?

But habit was too powerful. I had defined myself against Clara for too long.

"The girl who just went inside. I'm her sister."

"Sister," the captain said, rolling the word around on his tongue as though it were utterly unfamiliar. "We were told of no sister."

"We have no instructions," another of the soldiers muttered. They had abandoned the attempt to wrangle the horses, and now they moved closer, studying me as though I were an exhibit in a museum.

"What's a sister?" one of them asked.

"I don't know, but I think she's human."

"Her Majesty would know. She understands these matters."

"Her Majesty's at feast."

"We'll test it," the captain said decisively. "Hold out your hand, sister."

I extended my arm, and he took my hand in his. It was cold and lifeless, as hard as marble.

"Human she is," he announced after a moment. "I can feel the blood. The warmth."

The soldiers clustered around me, putting hands on me. They touched only impersonal places—my arms, my shoulders—but still I felt slightly violated by their presumption, the nearness of them all. My mind called up an unwelcome memory, Mother's cautionary tale of a poor witless girl who had been caught in the street at night by a gang of men, down by the docks.

"Warm." One of the soldiers ran a hand down my shoulder. "How warm she is."

I jerked away, the circle of soldiers parting easily, and I moved a few feet back, wrapping my arms around myself.

"This is a difficult business," the captain said, rubbing his jaw. His fingers made a rasping sound, as though his chin were made of stone. "We were told nothing about a second human."

"Should we send word? Ask for instructions?"

"I'd rather not. It's more than my life's worth to interrupt her at feast. Any feast, mind, but particularly a special one like this."

"But sir! An unknown human, wandering the land?"

"It's true," another put in. "She'll have our heads if we don't tell her."

This last bit of dire prophecy seemed to sway the captain, for he nodded and snapped his fingers at one of his underlings.

"Fourth, you go. Say that a second human wishes to enter the castle. A *sister*."

"Yes, sir."

The soldier hurried down the aisle of the drawbridge, under the waiting gate, and into a courtyard lined with alternating varieties of apple trees: candied, then caramel, then candied again. Beyond this orchard, I could see little, though the gleaming pink of the walls seemed to light the land outside for miles around.

"Would you like to sit, sister?" the captain asked courteously, and did not wait for my assent before barking at the remaining soldiers.

"You men! Get that sleigh upright! Clear the snow off!"

I accepted his offer gratefully; now that there was no farther to go, I realized that I was truly tired after my long tramp. With almost overdone gallantry—I was unpleasantly reminded of Clara and her ridiculous prince—the captain handed me up into the now-righted sleigh. The soldiers clustered around, but none of them tried to climb into the sleigh with me, a fact for which I was also grateful.

"What is this place?" I asked.

"This is Her Majesty's castle. We keep the gate."

"No, I mean this place," I said, gesturing around me. "This land."

"This is the Kingdom of Sweets," the captain replied, so smoothly that I felt sure that this was a rehearsed answer.

"And who is Her Majesty?"

"The Sugar Plum Fairy," the captain replied, just as promptly. "She rules the Kingdom of Sweets."

What nonsense, I thought. But it was not purposeless nonsense, for I saw how such answers might appeal to Clara, with her shelves full of pretty dolls.

"Where is this land?"

The question seemed to confuse them. They all looked to the captain, who looked blankly back at them, then replied lamely, "This is the Kingdom of Sweets."

"But where—"

"Are you cold, sister?" the captain asked. "We have drink. Warming drink."

"No," I replied, for I remained suspicious of this land and its offerings, even those that seemed kindly meant. I looked up at the castle walls: silvery pink, the color of candied pearls, stretching upward to disappear into shadow.

"Sir!" Fourth called from the drawbridge. "We're to let the human in and bring her to the feast."

The captain nodded, then offered a hand to help me climb down from the sleigh.

"I would escort you myself, sister, but I'm under orders not to leave my post at the gate," the captain told me. "Fourth, however, is the most trustworthy of my men. He will take you inside."

Fourth offered his arm as courteously as the captain had, and I took it without thinking, just as I would have taken Father's arm—or Conrad's, if Conrad had ever been brave enough to take my arm in public. But as Fourth guided me down the slope, I hesitated, shivering slightly. The arched gateway beyond the drawbridge looked like an open mouth, the crystal sugar daggers of the portcullis like gleaming teeth, and the soldier's arm resting beneath my hand was cold. So very cold.

"Sister?" Fourth asked. "Would you like to continue?"

I didn't want to, but Clara was in there. Clara was about to attend a feast.

"Come, sister," Fourth urged, almost kindly. "You don't want to keep her waiting."

"No," I replied steadily, picturing Clara's ribbons of blond hair, her fine-boned face. "You're right. I don't."

We continued down to the chocolate drawbridge, and as we stepped onto its spongy, sticky surface, I realized that I had not thanked the other soldiers. Turning, I called back my gratitude. But they did not answer, and in that moment I felt the first thrill of genuine fear, for they were no longer watching me, or even trying to untether the horses. They stood motionless at the crest of the hill, their uniforms no longer bright and colorful but vague bits of texture, their faces featureless and translucent.

They had turned to fine, crystallized sugar. Candied glass.

CHAPTER

14

ONCE WE HAD PASSED THROUGH THE APPLE ORCHARD AND entered by a postern gate, Fourth led me down several long corridors lined with doors. These corridors were not symmetrical, or even flat; they wound up and down, left and right, as though dug by some tunneling animal. The floor appeared to be made of marzipan, for with every step I took, my foot sank slightly, then made a protesting sound as I pulled it free. The walls of the castle shone with pink light inside as well as out, and the hot glare soon began to make me dizzy. The place smelled too much of sugar, the cloying miasma of a sweetshop that had gone centuries without an airing. It made me think of our old volume of Brothers Grimm, of the witch who lurked in the forest, waiting for plump children to happen along, nursing her hunger like a sickness. Her cottage, too, had been built of sweets; one of the book's several painted illustrations showed it, gingerbread walls that stood beautiful and deadly beneath a bright pink sugar roof. Even the castle's warmth made me uneasy, for it made me think of the round black oven in the illustrations, of the witch waiting beside its squat shape, holding her atrocity only for the moment when the device was good and hot.

There were many rooms opening off these corridors. None had doors, but still I could not see inside, for each doorway was utterly robbed of light, and it was like looking into the mouth of a deep cave. Yet these rooms were not empty, I could have sworn to it. Someone was in there; I felt their eyes on me as I passed. Whenever I paused to investigate, Fourth pulled me along, murmuring, "Please, sister. You don't want to see."

Up and up we went, following staircases that curved first one way and then the next, meeting and then diverging, as though the castle were one of those ancient and fabulous pyramids, creations of the ancient Turks, constructions that were not pyramids at all but labyrinths, obstacles designed to keep ordinary men from reaching the gods. For a fearful moment I wondered if that was our destination, to meet God, and then told myself not to be a ninny. I had not believed in God since the Sunday when I was eight and saw Father Benedict shuffling the notes of his sermon at the altar. If God meant to speak to us, I thought, he would do it himself. He would not choose a medium, and certainly not one as feckless and venal as our priest. I had refused to attend church from that day on, and not all of Father's threats could compel me. At last my parents had put about that I suffered from a morning ailment and took religious instruction in private, an announcement that seemed to confirm the neighborhood's worst suspicions about me.

Clara, of course, continued to go on Sundays like a good girl, though she believed no more than I did. She once confessed to me that she thought it was all a game, and though she did not have the vocabulary to elaborate, I thought I knew what she meant. Church was only a set of rules, and any set of rules could be navigated, manipulated to create the illusion of a saved soul. If God was not reduced to speaking through Father Benedict, then I could hardly believe He would be reduced to creating a land where sweets grew on vines and pink sugar palaces reared up into the molasses night. No, fantastical as this place might be, it was the work not of God but of some other.

At last Fourth led me down a long, straight corridor that ended in a set of massive doors. These doors were actually carved slabs of dark chocolate inlaid with curls of pink icing, and when Fourth rapped smartly on the surface, creating several dull thuds, I noticed muddy smears of chocolate on the knuckles of his white glove. Fourth, too, looked at them with surprised distaste, adding to my certainty that the castle had been altered just for this moment, just for Clara.

The doors opened onto a crescendo of sound that made me wince and clap my hands to my ears. At least once a year we attended the symphony outside the King's palace, the performance for commoners. It hurt Father's heart to do it, but Mother loved the symphony, and of course we were not invited to the closed performances for the nobility. I knew the sound of an orchestra, but this cacophony was like nothing I had ever heard. I pictured a hundred violinists, two hundred cellists, fifty flutes. The sound of the strings seemed to squeal across my ears. But when I looked through the doorway, I could see nothing, only darkness.

"I don't want to go in there," I told Fourth, in a voice that sounded very small to my own ears.

"But you must," Fourth replied, his own voice as inexorable as it was kind. He extended a hand.

"Come, sister. Her Majesty is waiting."

CHAPTER

15

A S WE WENT INSIDE, I CLOSED MY EYES AND COVERED MY
ears, expecting to be deafened. But at the instant we passed
through the great arch of the doorway, the sound of the orchestra
was suddenly muted, as though a damper had been applied. Now
it was a pleasing volume, the tune bright and cheerful, almost lilting, and when I opened my eyes, I saw that the room was not dark
as I had expected, but brightly lit and beautifully appointed.

We stood on the edge of an enormous dancing floor, so large
that it dwarfed even the outsize ballroom that took up the fourth
floor of the Buhlers' mansion. The dance floor was a cherry-colored
wood, polished almost to gleaming, its vast expanse covered with
human snowflakes, lithe and graceful dancers dressed in white
satin. There were no outliers, no weak dancers; they whirled and
arched toward each other, their movements so perfectly choreo-
graphed that I could not distinguish one from the other. I might
have watched them for hours, but after a few moments Fourth
placed a marble hand at my back, propelling me along the wall.

Beyond the dancing floor were countless round tables, each

packed tightly with people. I looked around for the grouping that might contain the mysterious Sugar Plum Fairy, but could see nothing to distinguish any one table. All of the guests were utterly beautiful, and they seemed to have dressed for Clara's pleasure, in pastel outfits decked with tulle and lace. Yet theirs was a frozen beauty, not wholly human but carved from marble, the way angels looked in old paintings. They seemed without urgency, even as they raised glasses or beckoned servants, and their movements were altogether languid, marked by a lithe grace that put even Clara's to shame. As we inched around the edge of the floor, I looked up and saw that the room was lit by five glittering chandeliers, each of them holding hundreds of tapers.

"Where is the Sugar Plum Fairy?" I asked Fourth in an undertone.

"She is here."

Where? I meant to ask, but the question stuck in my throat, for I had spotted Clara now, at one of the tables nearest to the dancing floor. The nutcracker prince was seated next to her, holding her hand, and Clara appeared to be regaling the table while the other guests hung on her every word. Her eyes were overly bright, as though she were drunk, but whether on wine, or sweets, or the handsome man sitting next to her, I didn't know. Instinctively I moved toward her, but Fourth grabbed my hand.

"Sister, this is not the way."

"Is she the guest of honor?"

"That will be as Her Majesty wishes."

For a long moment I thought of simply bolting, tearing free of his marble grip and leaping over tables and blocking chairs to reach her, my pretty twin who had apparently decided the way to atone for her sins was to enchant a new man while gorging herself on treats. Then I saw that Fourth was terrified, that he was actually trembling inside his soldier's garb. In the face of his fear, my anger seemed to subside, and I put a hand on his marble shoulder.

"Do not cross her, sister," he whispered. "I beg you."

"No. I won't," I replied, looking around the dance floor, the hundreds of tables. "But what is this place? Is it even real?"

"I can't say."

"Why not?"

"We watch," Fourth said in an uneven voice. "We watch, but we cannot interfere. Please, sister. Please."

I followed him then, sorry for the fright I had caused. Fourth led me around the dancing floor and into the thicket of tables, and as we wended our way between chairs, I gradually realized that the guests were reaching out to touch me, gentle brushes against my arms and waist, not threatening, only curious. Whispers followed in my passage, a susurration of sound through which I could make out only one word:

Warm.

IT HAD BEEN MY IMPRESSION UPON ENTERING THE ROOM THAT all of the tables were full, but I had been wrong, for Fourth led me to a table in the center of the crowd where a single chair sat empty. In front of the chair lay a clean plate and goblet, bordered by a napkin on which lay several knives and forks.

"Sit, sister."

I sat, and Fourth pushed the chair in behind me, nestling me comfortably against the table. I turned to thank him, but he was already gone, maneuvering between tables, making his way back to the door. As he went, the music changed, becoming bright and sprightly, almost mischievous, and I saw that an enormous papier-mâché dragon was making its way across the dance floor. The legs of some twenty people poked out from beneath the hem of this clever contraption, another entertainment clearly designed for Clara. She was pointing at it excitedly, tugging on the sleeve of her nutcracker prince.

Trickling sounded; the man beside me was filling my goblet with a clear substance that looked like water, though I didn't believe it was. My neighbor was tall and slim and well-muscled, as beautiful as the rest of them. I thanked him, but the only reply I received was a bemused glance. None of them expected thanks; what did that mean? And what did it say about the Sugar Plum Fairy, who presided over it all? I craned my neck, trying to catch a glimpse of her, but none of the painted ladies around me seemed any different, any more or less grand, than the others.

On my other side, a woman only slightly older than I was leaning back in her chair. She was sullen, almost pouting, and she did not eat, only fiddled miserably with the food on her plate. I had the distinct impression that she was annoyed at being forced to sit next to me. She caught me staring, and returned my gaze with such challenge that I found myself forced to turn away. The rest of the table, five men and four ladies, was staring at me avidly, as though waiting for me to talk, but I was caught by the high, sweet sound of Clara's voice, tremulous with excitement, so piercing that it echoed over the company, and even over the music.

"Then my prince led his army into the battle. They fought so bravely, with cannon and sword! The mice were frightened, but their king was not; he challenged my prince to single combat. My prince tried to cut off the Mouse King's head, but there were seven of them, and they grew back as fast as he could cut them off. Oh, we were in a difficult spot—"

Once again I tried to catch a glimpse of Clara, but the crowd had shifted between us, and the most I could see were the blond ringlets at the back of her head. Clara's tablemates were watching her with breathless interest, and when Clara told how the nutcracker prince had fallen to the ground while the Mouse King stood over him, drooling and ravenous, one of the ladies at Clara's table actually gasped.

"What drivel," a voice muttered beside me.

I turned, startled. It was the man who had poured my water. He was leaning back in his chair, watching Clara with undisguised disdain.

"Watch yourself, Dmitri," one of the women across the table muttered.

"Oh, come now. A *Mouse King*?"

A woman tittered nearby. Some hint of their derision must have reached Clara, for now I saw her look around, her brow slightly furrowed, her expression disturbed, as though she had caught the sound of distant thunder on a clear day. The man beside me said nothing else; the dragon continued to move across the dance floor in time to the pretty, mischievous music. After a moment Clara's face cleared, and she went on.

"Then I threw my slipper, and it felled him in a single blow!"

The pouting woman next to me snorted, then took a long pull of her wine.

"Then what happened?" demanded one of the women at Clara's table. Her voice dripped with excitement, but I heard the ring of falsity there, as ersatz as the pile of sugar lying all around us. Clara might have fooled everyone in our city, our entire kingdom, but they knew her here, and I felt a sudden gratitude toward all of them, even the invisible Sugar Plum Fairy, wherever she might be.

"Sisters," the man beside me remarked. "I remember little of humanity, but this word I do know. From the same womb, yes?"

I nodded.

"Yet all is not well. It shows in your eyes and mouth. Why?"

That was a fine question. Only hours before, Clara and I had stood with linked arms, giggling together. Not alike, never alike, but at least friends. How could everything have changed so quickly between us? Conrad, after all, was the one who had been inconstant . . . or had he? He had never made any promise at all, and through all the nights when he climbed through my bedroom window, I had made no demands. No, Conrad was not the villain, though it would have been easier to cast him that way. It was Clara who had committed betrayal, Clara who had known me best. I thought of all the times she had sat on my bed, or I on hers, listening to each other's heartaches; all the times she had tried to help me improve my appearance so that Conrad might love me, or at least notice me. For all our differences, she was the one who had known me well, the one from whom I had hidden nothing. She had gotten me out of trouble more times than I could count, simply by claiming my misdeeds as her own. I had thought that she had done it all out of love, but she hadn't, not if the simple knock of opportunity could obliterate all that had come before.

"My sister did me a wrong," I finally replied. I liked this phrase; it seemed to encompass the magnitude of Clara's betrayal. It must have satisfied my companion as well, for he raised his glass, smiling slightly over the rim. I raised my glass in return, and in my mind I suddenly saw my brother, Fritz, throwing the nutcracker away with a disgusted cry. What had he seen? I couldn't imagine, but the answer hardly seemed important now.

What mattered was Clara, smiling her best flirtatious smile around a forkful of potato. Clara, who thought she could say a simple sorry and escape unscathed.

But you won't, I thought, remembering how she had run sobbing from the kitchen earlier, as though her heart would break. *You won't.*

"Aren't you hungry?" my companion asked.

Looking down, I saw that food had appeared on my own plate, as though by magic: pork and potatoes, confit and pudding. It smelled wonderful, and I picked up my fork, turning it this way and that in my hand. In truth, I was very hungry, and the hunger was so sharp that it seemed to eat away at my caution. What harm could they do me, all of these beautiful people? What harm greater than that which Clara and Conrad—*and Drosselmeyer,* my mind whispered, *mustn't forget him*—had already done?

The music changed again—though I still saw no signs of an orchestra anywhere around the floor—becoming dark and rich and haunting. On the dance floor, two men in flowing robes were moving slowly around an enormous golden set piece that I gradually came to realize was a lamp. It was Aladdin, then; Aladdin, who had been stupid enough to believe that wishes were granted without price. My gaze returned to Clara, who was tossing her head and giggling at something the nutcracker prince had said. I could tear Clara's pretty curls from her scalp, but what would that solve? Come the New Year, she and Conrad would still stand before the priest, hand in hand.

I closed my eyes, opened them again. The food was still before me, almost staring at me now. Deliberately, almost defiantly, I took a forkful of creamed potato and jammed it into my mouth. Then I took another bite, and another. The food was good, so good that I felt myself suddenly relaxing, my limbs losing the soreness of their long hike through the snow and softening, like taffy. An image flashed across my mind—my mother, gripping the green bottle as she wept on her settee—but then it was gone, and after another moment's thought, I took the goblet full of clear liquid, found that it did at least taste like ordinary water, and drained it.

Only when the first edge of my hunger had eased did I lean back in my chair, surveying the table. They had gone back to their own whispered conversations, though the man beside me remained casually attentive, filling my glass whenever it emptied, retrieving a spoon when I dropped it on the floor.

"What is this place?" I asked him.

"This is the Kingdom of Sweets."

"Yes, yes, the Kingdom of Sweets," I repeated. "But what *is* it? How does Drosselmeyer know about it?"

All conversation at our table came to a sudden halt. My tablemates looked horrified, as though I had committed some unpardonable social gaffe, and to my confused eyes, they seemed suddenly predatory as well. Unease rippled through me, making the confit stick in my throat. The tables around us had quieted also; in fact, the whole room had gone quiet.

"Be careful," my companion cautioned in an undertone. "That's a name best not said in the Lady's hearing."

"She can hear us? Where is she?"

"She hears everything."

I accepted this in silence, not wanting to attract any more attention. The music returned, a rousing allegro that seemed made for dancing, but I paid little attention to the melody. They knew Drosselmeyer, these people. At least they knew his name, and that name was not popular here. I felt another rush of sudden warmth toward the unseen Sugar Plum Fairy, a sense of kinship. Whoever she might be, we shared at least this one thing.

After a few minutes, the table appeared to relax again. But I sensed that I was on a kind of grace, and decided it would be prudent to remain silent for a while. I turned my attention back to my food, eating my way steadily through the plate, turning the puzzle over in my mind. But the pieces kept jumbling, losing their clarity. The nutcracker was not supposed to be special, the scarred boy had said; it was only supposed to march and bow. But the nutcracker was not Drosselmeyer's creation. The scarred boy had made it, and he did not take Drosselmeyer's orders. He might have sent us to this place for any reason, or no reason at all. I had finished the last of my pudding now, and after a moment's hesitation I helped myself to more. It was some sort of almond tart, sweet but not too sweet, and utterly delicious.

The music changed yet again, a happy chirping of pipes twittering like birds over the heads of the company. I found that our Christmas party was growing more dim and distant by the minute. Conrad and Clara were still there, sitting in the corner with bent heads, but the memory was hazy, the pain dulled, as though it were a tragedy I had seen at the theater. A plate of peppermint canes went around the table and my companion offered me one, but I refused; I had always hated the taste of peppermint. The sullen girl beside me had finally drawn herself back to the table, and now she was sitting up, sampling her cane with a dainty lethargy, as though she could not be truly bothered. I could no longer see Clara through the crowd, which shifted and moved like the surface of the ocean, but I could hear her high, affected party laugh, almost see the pert toss of her head. I longed to ask about Drosselmeyer again, but didn't dare, afraid that I would again awaken these languid people, like lions at the zoo.

Something cold touched my hand, and I jumped. The man beside me, Dmitri, had intertwined his fingers with mine.

"There is nothing to fear," he said quietly. "We are not cruel, any of us, not even the Queen. We are only patient."

I could make no sense of this statement, but oddly, it did serve to calm my fright, simultaneously convincing me that they were certainly dangerous and that I was not the prey they sought. Yet I extricated my hand from his, for his fingers were so cold, and they did not yield. Perhaps he was meant to partner me, to distract me from the real world, just as the nutcracker prince had clearly been meant to do for Clara. But the idea only made me angry. I was not Clara, to be so easily deterred from what mattered.

"Why am I here?" I asked.

"Only you can say that. What brought you here?"

Given world and time, I might have constructed a complex answer to this question, something comprising Clara's betrayal and Conrad's inconstancy, even Drosselmeyer's terrible magic. I would have explained that I hadn't chosen to come. But my mind had turned sluggish from the food, and after all, they did not seek complex answers, these marble people. They could not interfere, only watch.

"Justice," I finally replied. "I came for justice."

"I have seen enough," a voice announced beside me, making me start. It was the pouty girl, but when I turned to her, she was no longer slouching, and the peppermint candy had vanished from sight. She was not sullen now but tall and proud, her dark eyes pinned on me, and in their black depths I saw both victory and agony, somehow coexisting, feeding each other, a cycle of pain that would never stop. She understood me well, this woman.

I felt as though she had been everywhere I had been, had gone infinitely further into the void of suffering, and I felt both wonder and terror, to be in her very presence.

"You," I breathed.

"Me," the Sugar Plum Fairy replied.

CHAPTER

16

S HE WAS QUITE BEAUTIFUL, AS BEAUTIFUL AS ANY OF THE other painted ladies around us. But always afterward, when I remembered that conversation, I would think that I had known somehow, that just as her land could not entirely conceal itself, neither could she. It was her eyes, twin points of black coal . . . not coal as it sat in an early morning grate, flames out and purpose finished, but coal in a well-banked fire, burning steady and hot.

I thought she would properly introduce herself, but the Fairy was not one for pleasantries. She leaned forward, appraising me, and after a moment she said, "I can smell his stink all over you."

I stared at her, confused, almost hurt.

"Drosselmeyer," she continued, and a slow shuffle of unease went around the table at the name, a subtle shifting of weight and limbs.

"Tell me, Natasha, what did he do to you?"

I stared at her, surprised out of my confusion. The tale of our christening had been told and retold so many times that I could not imagine anyone, even in this strangest of places, who might not know it.

"You need not say," the Fairy went on. "But I will guess, all the same. I know Drosselmeyer, you see. I know his tricks."

She said his name with such loathing that I felt an involuntary welling of camaraderie. I swallowed, trying to clear my head— what had they put in the food?—but I could only feel her will, and it was like a compulsion. Before I knew it, I was telling her all about Drosselmeyer, our christening, about Clara and me, and I did not mind that the entire table was listening. In all our lives, there had been only Clara and Anastasia to listen to my woes, but they had no ability to change things. Perhaps that was the reason I spoke. The Sugar Plum Fairy, for all her painted face and dainty clothing, struck me as a woman who might have the power to act.

"Light and dark," the Fairy said, when I had done. "He said those words?"

"Yes."

"And you and your sister were born at Christmas, the both of you?"

"Yes. What does it mean?"

"Why don't all of you go and dance?" the Sugar Plum Fairy suggested. But it was not really a suggestion, for chairs scraped and the rest of the table rose hastily, dropping their napkins. The man next to me was the only one who hesitated.

"Go on, Dmitri," the Fairy said softly, but there was steel in her tone. "She will still be here later. I promise."

Dmitri smiled ruefully, bending to kiss my hand.

"Thank you, Majesty. I do not mean to be difficult, but she is . . . so warm."

The Fairy smiled indulgently, waving him away, and I felt a

bright stab of fear. I didn't want her full attention, didn't want those burning-coal eyes focused on me.

"I have been watching your sister for some hours," the Fairy remarked. "I needn't have bothered; she is not complicated. But I know little of you, Natasha, beyond your role as Clara's sister. Is there more I should know?"

I shook my head miserably. Whatever had been in the food certainly limited recollection, but it seemed to compensate in sharpened perception. I saw now that my life had been defined by Clara, by the little actions I took to emulate her, the greater actions I took to distance myself. Either way, I did little without thinking about how people would compare me to Clara: how I would look standing next to her; how I would fare by contrast, how I could prove that I did not care when I fared badly. But that tale was too humiliating to admit to a woman like this, ruler of a kingdom who clearly allowed no one to define anything about her.

"I'm no one," I said finally. "Only Clara's sister."

"Twins, yes?"

"Yes."

"Twins born at Christmas," the Fairy murmured, her voice soft, almost musing. "Yes. I see. Drosselmeyer always did fancy himself a master of magic. But he has overreached now, and I will have him."

She looked at me suddenly, seeming to come back to herself.

"Do not worry yourself, child. Dark, he named you, and of course dark sees all, nudges into the cracks and corners that the world wishes most to hide. But look at your sister over there. She wants to know nothing."

Turning, I found Clara on the dance floor now, the nutcracker prince whirling her along, guiding her deftly through a sea of waltzing snowflakes as the pretty melody ebbed and flowed, lilting above our heads. Had she even noticed that I was here? I thought not. Perhaps, in this place, she had forgotten my very existence. But I could not forget hers, and I watched her with narrowed eyes until a new act appeared on the dance floor: a woman swathed in yards of crepe and plaster, so that her skirts resembled an enormous gingerbread house. Men periodically darted in and out from under the gingerbread contraption, each with a foolish grin on his face, and against my will I smiled back. The costume was ludicrous, swaying back and forth like the elaborate hoopskirts of the last half century, and the dress took up so much room on the floor that the snowflakes were forced to decamp and form a glittering, disgruntled huddle on the far wall. Clara left the floor as well, her arm tucked into that of the nutcracker prince. I craned my neck to follow her, then jumped as the Fairy laid a cool hand across my wrist.

"She's not going anywhere. Not unless I allow it."

"Will you allow it?"

"That depends on you, Natasha. We work similar threads, you and I."

"How?"

The Fairy looked away, considering.

"We are not so far removed from your world, child. Not in distance, anyway. We move close to it; we observe it. Sometimes, in the right circumstances, we can even visit it."

I blinked.

"Is Drosselmeyer one of you?"

"No, only a man, albeit an extraordinarily gifted one . . . so gifted that I once gave him freedom of my land. But he took more than was offered, stole a great prize. Many times I have tried to lay hands on him, but he is not an easy quarry."

I nodded, for I seemed to see everything here, my vision wider than it had ever been in our crowded neighborhood. Drosselmeyer the hunted; it made sense, seemed to place him in the scheme of our lives. Neighbor, godfather, sorcerer, usurer, thief . . . Drosselmeyer had always loomed large in our neighborhood, but he had no intimates. There were his boys, of course, those gilded youths just on the cusp of manhood with whom he surrounded himself. But they were not kind, only handsome; Drosselmeyer's favor alone elevated them from their previous professions as enforcers and pimps. All but the scarred boy, and God only knew where Drosselmeyer had found him. Yet this new, hunted version of Drosselmeyer seemed to make his odd existence conceivable. Hunted men did not have companions, only tools. Hunted men might do anything, for they were desperate . . . desperate enough, perhaps, to stand over two newborns in their cradles, blessing one and cursing the other. I saw now that although I had mistaken the Fairy for one of these many beautiful people, she was not like them at all. She stood out, a black rose among daisies. She placed her hand on top of mine, and her fingers were as warm as my own.

"I wish to bargain with you, Natasha."

"Bargain for what?"

"I wish to settle accounts with my old friend. He is not fool enough to come here again, so I must go to him."

"How?"

"Very easily, and yet it can be the most difficult thing in the world, for we cannot reach your world without an invitation. Such invitations are of high value, worth a terrible price, but I think your price will not be so terrible for me to grant. I see your anguish when you look at your sister. The boy, yes? The one she stole?"

"She didn't steal him," I replied stiffly. "He gave me away."

"But you want him still?"

"Yes."

The Fairy seemed amused by this. She picked up her wine-glass and, finding it empty, signaled a servant, who came running.

"Your kind never fails to entertain me, Natasha. Your emotions are so divorced from sense. This man scorned you, but you want him anyway. Would it not be better to seek revenge? Vengeance is greater than want."

I nodded, seeing the sense of this. But Conrad wasn't the vengeance I needed. I looked across the spread of tables, seeking Clara's head. Her blond curls.

"But this will make the bargaining easier," the Fairy continued, her voice jovial now. "I can give you what you want. More, perhaps."

"You can't give me Conrad. He wants Clara now."

"They all want Claras, child, but I have made a long career of punishing fools."

"I don't want Conrad hurt."

"Why not? He has hurt you."

Yes, he had. But there had been more than that, though it was hard to explain. All those nights when Conrad climbed through my window . . . in the long dark of my life, those nights had been the only thing I had ever prized, and the fact that they had been built on illusion, evaporating in the light, seemed to make them mean more, not less. I found that I was unwilling to speak of Conrad. Perhaps I simply didn't want the Fairy to know that I had been such a fool.

"You spoke of a bargain," I said. "What is the bargain?"

"Vengeance for vengeance, the highest of bargains. You will have your sister, and I will have Drosselmeyer."

"How can I have Clara?" I asked bitterly. "I can't even find her in the crowd."

"This is my kingdom, Natasha. Everything in it belongs to me. I could order the moon to rise westerly, if I so desired. The fate of one young girl will trouble nothing."

"Is that meant for Clara, or for me?"

She smiled blandly. "I do not threaten you. Indeed, I had not planned for you at all. I saw your sister very clearly, but you crossed the borders of my land without my knowledge. Do you not think that strange?"

"The nutcracker. It was magic."

She shrugged. "The object does not matter. Drosselmeyer is powerful, but not always precise in his magic, one of many reasons that he fell from my grace."

"But Drosselmeyer didn't make the nutcracker. His boy did."

Her face stilled. The music ceased, dancers freezing on the floor and diners pausing with forks halfway to their mouths.

"What boy?" the Fairy asked, each word a sentence of itself. Beneath the painted mask of her skin, I saw something terrible, shifting and moving. Her eyes were so black that they appeared to absorb the room's light, and while I watched they seemed to grow, turning her face into something desolate and alien. I shrank from her, as frightened as any messenger who ever feared to lose his head for being the unhappy bearer of misfortune. But there was no question of not answering.

"Drosselmeyer called him Mikhail. He was my age, or perhaps a couple of years older."

"And?" she asked, snarling. Between her white teeth, her tongue was black and glistening, like a slug squirming under a rock.

"He said—" I struggled, trying to remember. "He said that he was not Drosselmeyer's boy. He had dark eyes, black eyes."

"What else? What else?"

"He was covered with scars."

The Fairy threw back her head and screamed. I recoiled, covering my ears, for the sound was terrible, not human in the least, echoing across the wide, well-lit ballroom, engulfing all sound, and in its wake the dancers seemed to become almost insubstantial, as though they were gossamer rather than flesh. The room shimmered, and for a moment I almost saw the castle for true, something less beautiful but far more authentic, a crumbling edifice of black soot and ruined stone.

But a moment later the Fairy took a deep breath and the room solidified again. The dancers resumed their graceful movements. And now I spotted Clara again, mincing across the dance floor as though she had noticed nothing, staring adoringly up at the nutcracker prince. He bent to kiss her, and I looked away, anger flooding my veins.

"Drosselmeyer," the Fairy said softly. "He was always clever. So clever, and so spiteful. I thought he sent your sister here to taunt me, to let me know that he still lives beyond my reach. But this is not his doing at all."

I listened closely. Her face had returned to its pretty lines now, but what had been seen could not be erased, and I was more frightened than I had been at any point in this long, strange evening. I could almost see the thing inside the Fairy now, carefully hidden under the bright smile, the pretty clothes, the paint: a dark creature, old and vengeful. Father Benedict had spoken entire sermons on such creatures in our youth, and though I had napped through most of them, I thought that even the priest would have quailed at the look in the Fairy's black eyes, thrown away his crucifix, renounced God, and fled into the dark.

"Since you have been so honest with me," the Fairy continued, "I will give you a bit of free advice, though it works against my

interest: forget your fool. You are very young; you are not breeding, as your sister is; there are no ties to bind. Forget your foolish
boy and find someone else."

I smiled sadly at that, for how many times each day had I
given myself the same advice? How many thousands of times
since I was a child, since I had realized that the game was rigged,
that girls like me didn't get to have the Conrads of the world?

"Ah," the Fairy remarked, a smile dancing at the black edges
of her mouth. "I see that you will not take my advice. Perhaps you
cannot. But keep it in mind. You humans would do well to mistrust your own dearest wishes, for these things never work out
the way you believe they will. The way you hope they would."

I nodded, feeling the truth of her words. Clara's little-girl happiness, free of all darkness—that had never been for me and never
would be. Even if someone should hand me the world in all of its
trappings, I would still know the rotten nature of that gift.

"Why do you hide?" I asked. "I know this isn't the way this
place really looks, or you. Why do you cover yourselves up?"

The Fairy smiled appreciatively. "Well spotted, but to be fair,
this place was not built for you. Had I seen you coming, Natasha,
I would have constructed something entirely different."

"Like what?"

"I'm not sure. But it would certainly have been more difficult
to design."

She surveyed the dance floor. Clara was still there with the
nutcracker prince, her head on his shoulder and a beatific smile
on her lips. The music had changed to a lush waltz, and the floor
had been overtaken by a new set of dancers, all of them dressed
as flowers. Clara moved among them, ruining the effect; her grace,
which had perhaps been noteworthy in the corps of the royal ballet, was far below the standard here. As she moved past, one of

the dancing flowers pantomimed an exaggerated kick toward her backside, and an icy frisson of amusement passed through the room. Clara sensed nothing, but I felt the shift in the air, changing of winds, darkening.

"I have not dealt directly with a human in a long time," the Fairy remarked, still watching Clara. "Your kind used to know the rules of such transactions, but the world has changed. So let me be clear. Bargains such as the one we will make are more powerful than any one life. But the bargain is not sealed until you act. You may go back to your world right now, if you wish, and I will not hinder it. Our dealings will be done. Do you wish to?"

I stared at Clara, Clara and her prince, his gloved hand cupped against her cheek. We were in a land of night here, all pain dulled, but morning would come, and the thought of the future seemed to burn my heart. Clara would not need to undress quickly, huddling beneath the sheets in the hope that her body would remain hidden. Conrad would not cap the candles before they began. They would make a fine couple, just as Drosselmeyer had said, and where would I be? In the convent, wiping tears with the edge of my veil?

"No," I said. "I'm staying."

"Your choice. You may leave at any time; you need only ask. Execution of the bargain is wholly in your hands, blood for blood. But know this: if you enter into such an arrangement with me, you do not forfeit. You do not back out."

"Or what?"

The Fairy grinned, and I saw that beneath her even white teeth, her gums were black. She turned back to me and her eyes were wide ebony pools, so wide that it seemed I could drown in them, and I recoiled at what I saw there, what *she* had seen: vengeance and justice, one and the same.

"Forfeit, my girl, and you belong to me."

The Fairy rose, leaving me frozen in my chair. As she moved away, I saw that she, like many of the women in the room, had a pair of gossamer wings, pastel blue and purple, affixed to her back. But in the light cast by the chandeliers, her wings looked far more solid than those of the other women. They looked, in fact, almost real. As she went, she did not walk but seemed rather to fade, as though into the very room itself, becoming a tall and flowing darkness, almost like a figure in a cloak, a cloak that was constantly shifting and changing, revealing shapes and objects and places, dark oceans. There were faces there as well, anguished faces, eyes tight and mouths yawning in screams, rippling in and out of sight as the thing glided across the room. A pale oval appeared in the dark fabric, something like a mirror, and for a moment I thought I saw my own face at its center, wailing in agony. Then the shadow disappeared, fading to nothing somewhere between the final chandelier and the chocolate doors. For a moment there was a lingering hint of vapor, like a wisp of smoke, then it was gone.

CHAPTER

17

I BEGAN TO SHUDDER THEN, AS THOUGH THE ACCUMULATED cold of the night had seized my body at once. The party was over, the brightly lit room around me empty, all of the chairs sitting vacant, the dancers gone, the floor a polished void. And now I saw that the candied flowers of the table's centerpiece were wilting, their petals decaying as the crystallized sugar melted into a glistening sludge. The food on the plates was beginning to rot as well; on my own plate, I could see something moving within the leftovers. I stumbled toward the chocolate double doors, wending my way around table after table, fighting nausea that had brought sudden beads of sweat to my forehead. That darkness had been no part of Clara's fantasy; I alone had seen it, and suddenly I felt that the room was not empty in truth, that every chair was still filled, all of them watching me, waiting to see what I would do.

"Clara," I called hoarsely, still stumbling along. I thought I saw a flash of blue around the edge of one of the doors, blue like Clara's dress, there and then gone. The doors were melting, the chocolate beginning to run in great drips, puddling on the floor. Clara's fantasy, melting away . . . but to be replaced with what?

At the outer perimeter of the tables, I paused and looked back. The room was buried in shadows, the glow of the chandeliers faded almost to nothing. The centerpiece on the nearest table had tipped over and a puddle of brown liquid was working its way across the tablecloth. The room was almost suffocating with the stench of spoiled sugar and rotting molasses. And now it seemed that I could see something there, between the legs of the tables: a figure on the floor. It moved this way and that, its form almost human as it pulled itself along, one arm after another. Yet it was not human, for as I watched, it lowered itself to lap something from the floor.

I fumbled against the doors. Warm chocolate dripped onto my hands as I scrabbled here and there, looking for a knob, a key, something to turn, as the last of the light left the room. Behind me, I heard the thing pulling itself toward me, the eager, clumsy scuffling of its trunk on the floor. I began to dig at the door, scooping out great handfuls of melting chocolate and flinging them to the side. Light showed at last; first a tiny gleam and then the empty corridor, and I dove through the hole I had made, the chocolate sucking at me, trying to hold me back. Something seemed to grab at my heel as I went through, but I kicked my way free and then I was on the other side of the hallway, on the floor. The hole held for a minute, then the chocolate facing collapsed into a pile of melting sludge. There were real double doors beneath, ornately patterned and set with scrollwork, doors such as any wealthy man might have on his own ballroom. I sat for a long moment, waiting to see whether the doors would rattle, whether one of them would click open. But they lay still.

I pulled myself to my feet. I was alone in the long corridor, the only movement the flicker of tapers in the lamps. Even the rest of the chocolate had melted away, quickly and quietly, as though evaporated, and when I looked down, expecting to find myself covered in brown streaks and smears, I found my green velvet dress as clean as though it had just come from the laundress. The castle was silent around me, though as I hesitated, I thought I heard a distant pounding, almost like the beat of machinery, or the thud of a heart. I listened for Clara, but there was no human sound, only that disturbing heartbeat and the low moan of the wind outside. I could go home at any time, the Fairy had said, and in that moment I almost asked to do so, though God knew there were few comforts waiting for me there. The bargain was in my hands, the Fairy had said that too, but did I really want to bargain on any of this?

Yet just as I was about to say the words, make a wish, something caught my eye at the end of the corridor: two small forms, their heads bent close together. They wore identical nightgowns, and yet they were not identical, these girls. The tapers illuminated the thick braids, dark and light, that fell from the twin nightcaps. Drawing closer, I saw that the two girls were crouched over a dollhouse, one I knew well: a massive pink mansion with a white-shingled roof.

"I'll be the duchess."

Clara's voice, brash and confident even at the age of seven or eight.

"But I want to be the duchess."

She shook her head.

"You're not pretty enough to be the duchess. You can be the maid."

I stilled, the words echoing in my head. But this wasn't real. I had never wanted to play with the pink dollhouse. I had left it alone.

"I don't *want* to be the maid!" my smaller self hissed.

The tiny blond Clara rose suddenly, running off down the hall. I watched her for a moment, then squatted down next to my younger self, wanting a look at the dollhouse. Truthfully, now that I was older and could admire craftsmanship, I saw that it really was a marvel. It must have cost a fortune. Had Father paid for it, or had Drosselmeyer? We had received it on our sixth birthday, right in that strange middle ground of time before Drosselmeyer began to enter our lives again, unseen but always present.

Clara came running back, dragging a tall, pretty woman, but it took me a moment to recognize her as our mother. Never before had I been given an opportunity to see the havoc wreaked by years of the green bottle, and the contrast was stunning. This woman was lovely, pink-cheeked and energetic, her eyes bright and inquiring as she dropped to her haunches beside the two small girls.

"Now, what is the argument?"

"I told her," Clara declared, putting her small hands on her hips. "I told her that duchesses are beautiful. Maids are always little and ugly and dark, like Anastasia or Nat. So Nat should be the maid."

"I'm always the maid," the little Natasha complained. "Why can't I be the duchess for once?"

My mother threw back her head and laughed. Again, I wondered at the sparkle in her eyes, the life in her face. Had I been too young to notice? Or had I just not wanted to remember?

"Oh, Nat, why not just be the maid? What difference does it make, when it makes Clara so happy?"

I stared at this scene in dawning alarm, each word seeming to pull a different string inside my memory. This had happened, and more than once. The vision faded, my mother and the two little girls becoming fainter, until they were only wisps of mist that seemed to evaporate into the corridor. But I didn't need them any longer, for I had suddenly remembered. We had argued endlessly about that stupid dollhouse, Clara and I, and finally I had done something to it. Broken it? No, I had tried to paint it grey, tried to make it match the stone castles of my imagination. Clara had caught me, and Father had given me a spanking. Why had I never remembered it before now?

You should get out of here, my mind whispered. *Just leave. Ask to leave.*

But I could not find my voice. Straightening, I moved down the corridor in the same direction from which Fourth and I had come, seeking the staircase. But the corridor was not the same. Instead of one staircase at the end, I now found two, branching to the right and left. The banisters were green marzipan, sinking into rot. Everywhere I looked, I saw traces of candy, of sweets, but even as I spotted them, they disappeared, seemed to absorb back into the walls. Turning, I saw that the corridor behind me was no longer floored in chocolate, but plain wood. The walls were rough stone piled on rough stone, the joins sealed with mortar. Broad wooden beams supported the ceiling. I recognized this construction, had seen it in my book of medieval castles at home. I half expected to see knights and ladies walking down the corridor, the knights in armor and the ladies in those foolish pointed hats the French had favored until the plague had come, laying them low. No such vision came, but still I found myself charmed, for this was not Clara's pink and sugared castle anymore. This was the dollhouse I had wanted.

Below me, down the right-hand staircase, I heard a scuffling noise. Leaning over the banister, I saw another flash of blue silk, so brief that I might have imagined it. Clara. She was down there somewhere. The sweets were gone, but this great maze of a castle remained, and even now Clara might be running down the corridors, laughing, pursued by her nutcracker prince. Later, they might make love in some dark corner, and Clara could congratulate herself on her cleverness, managing her infidelity in a place Conrad would never see and could not go. But I knew. I always knew, and so I started down the staircase, hardly aware that my lips had lifted in a snarl, seeking my twin.

CHAPTER

18

I STILL DON'T KNOW HOW LONG I TOOK TO EXPLORE THE CASTLE.
It seemed only a few hours, but could have been much longer,
or much shorter. Time had odd dimensions in the Kingdom of
Sweets, though how odd, I would not discover until much later.

At first I saw no one, but I did not think I was alone, there in
those empty corridors. Clara had eluded me somehow, but still I
felt eyes upon me, just as I had in the ballroom. The fathomless
black rectangles that had represented doorways earlier had been
replaced by rough wooden doors to match the rest of the castle,
but they were equally inaccessible. Each door had a keyhole, but
I had no key, and none of them would open, even when pressed.
When I bent and tried to peer through the keyholes, I could see
only darkness.

Coming around a corner, I found a scene I did recognize: Clara
and I, arguing with Mother and Father in the parlor. We were
fourteen, only recently come out into society, and the family had
been invited to a royal ball to celebrate the establishment of
the gold standard throughout the kingdom. But the royal family,

apparently unaware that the Stahlbaums had two daughters, had invited only my parents and Clara.

Normally, I would not have cared—or would at least have dissembled not caring—but I knew that Conrad would be there, and so I had gone to beg my parents to ask the palace for a fourth invitation. Clara had come with me, though I saw now that her pleas to my parents were halfhearted, her eyes on the invitation in her own hand. I watched, still feeling the sting of it, as my younger self ran from the room, crying. These memories seemed to have little purpose beyond causing pain, and so I was surprised when the scene did not fade as the earlier one had, but remained vivid, Clara standing before my parents in the parlor.

"Should I tell her?" Clara asked.

"God, no," Father replied. "What would be the point?"

"No, no," Mother said, and this was the mother I knew, staring dreamily at the ceiling, barely touched by our family squabbles. "If she should ever chance to meet the royals, she might cause a scene."

"It's not fair to her," Clara said.

"No, but life is not fair," Father said, bending a keen eye upon her. "We could always refuse the invitation ourselves, of course, stay home with Natasha, keep her company. Would you like that, apple?"

Clara shook her head.

"Then say nothing. There may be many more events like these, events where the price of your admission will be Nat's exclusion. You had best get used to it, and Nat too."

"Yes, Papa."

Now the scene did fade, their forms melting away into the stone of the castle. Yet I remained standing, staring at the place where they had been. I had not been accidentally excluded, but deliberately, and worse than the pain of that was the pain of not having known. I had always thought that I saw everything, but now I felt as though I had spent a day walking around with my shift stuck, showing my garters, or with lipstick smeared across my teeth. They had known, but they had not told. Even Conrad might have known. Everyone had known, except for me.

"Clara," I whispered, feeling the first hot stab of rage. Clara had known. She had not said anything, and of course she would have told herself that she had kept quiet to protect my feelings. But really it was just Clara, wanting as ever to keep life simple, to avoid the unpleasant. She had known about Conrad, known for weeks, but of course she had not spoken of that either, confident in her smug certainty that everything could be managed and mended, that everything would turn out for the best. How many other secrets had she kept?

Another figure appeared at the end of the hallway, and I tensed, steeling myself for more history I would not wish to witness. But this was no wisp of memory, rather a young man in a doublet embroidered with a purple fleur-de-lis. His hair was parted at the crest. Beneath the doublet he wore some sort of stocking trousers that left nothing to the imagination, belted with a cloth scabbard at one side, the handle of a wooden sword within reach.

A page, I thought. The boy was too young to be anything else. And now more denizens of the new castle began to appear: lords in fine velvet, ladies in beautiful dresses, knights, even servants in homespun and cloth aprons, who ducked and begged my pardon as they went by. Despite my earlier anger, I was charmed, for what was a dollhouse without dolls? They were all beautifully reproduced, almost copies of the illustrations in my childhood books, and I watched them with pleasure, following some of them up and down stairs as they went about their routines. Even the staircases in this castle were correct: built with uneven steps, as the old ones had been, to confuse and stymie invaders. I thought that I could spend days in this place and never get bored. But my pleasure soon began to deepen into unease. The Kingdom of Sweets had been built for Clara, to charm her, tempt her somehow. Whatever this castle was now, it had just as clearly been built for me.

Rounding a corner on the ground floor, I came upon what at first appeared to be a grandfather clock, just like the one that stood in our entrance hall. But this was like no clock I had ever seen before. The number 100 sat where midnight should be, and the circumference was broken by tiny marks. The clock's hand— it only had one—stood where two o'clock would sit on a normal clock; counting the ticks, I found that it was number eighteen.

I stared at this clock for a very long time, so bewildered by its numbers that at first I failed to notice the mirror which stood alongside: a vast sheet of glass, bordered in silver, which would have taken up half the parlor wall in our house. The mirror was the more extraordinary piece, but still I could not stop staring at the clock. Clara and I were seventeen now—or would be, if we ever got back to the world we knew. Did the ticks represent years? Was the clock meant for us? I leaned forward and listened, but I could hear no ticking, and though I watched the clock's lone hand for a long time, it did not appear to move.

A servant passed, bowing and ducking her head. I thought of asking her what the clock meant, but my question was stifled as she passed before the silver-edged mirror. She cast no reflection there, nor so much as a shadow on the ground as she continued on up the corridor, and so I remained silent, nearly paralyzed, lest she should turn around and reveal something I didn't want to see.

Down the hall in the other direction, I saw two small girls, dark and light, squabbling over something, but I closed my eyes, not wanting to know. I didn't need details, for I understood now that all things had been resolved in Clara's favor. I thought again of the times we were caught sneaking sweets from the kitchens, how Clara had always shielded me from punishment. An act of kindness, I had thought, but now I saw it as an odd sort of pre-atonement, as though she had already known how our lives would be.

Leaving the strange clock, I moved to stand in front of the mirror, studying it more closely. The silver border was not plain, as I had first thought, but decorated with small figures, creatures I recognized from old mythology: nymphs and satyrs, little round cherubim. But there was also early Christian imagery here: a tree wrapped round by a serpent; a tall tower in the midst of collapse; winged angels, waving swords and blowing trumpets as they battled hideously ugly creatures, demons or devils. There was even a crucified figure, though he had been hung upside down, in the manner of old traitors. The artistry was magnificent, finer than any silverwork I had ever seen, and I leaned forward, tracing the engraved lines, so engrossed that at first I didn't even notice the figure standing behind me.

I whirled, but there was nothing, only the far wall of the corridor, lined with doors. Looking up and down, I found the corridor empty, not so much as a servant in sight. With a feeling of foreboding—for I knew already that I had not imagined it—I turned back to the mirror.

She was behind me again, her mouth open wide in a scream. For a mercy, I could hear nothing, but the woman was certainly screaming; I could see the cords protruding from her neck. She was naked. Her blond hair hung limp about her shoulders, her body smutched and smeared with black streaks that looked like grease. Her eyes were deep and circled, dark with pain.

Steeling myself, I turned around.

There was nothing there. Only the empty corridor . . . and, directly across from the mirror, one of those blank and faceless doors.

I looked back—God help me, she was still there, still screaming—and then, with a feeling of trespass, I moved away from the mirror and crept toward the wooden door, walking on tiptoe. In the distance I heard that thudding heartbeat, so much a part of everything here that I had ceased to even notice it while I explored the castle. It seemed louder here on the ground floor; I felt that the sound was buried beneath my feet.

I pressed my ear to the door's rough surface, then bent and tried once again to look through the keyhole. But it was just as fruitless as it had been before, darkness and more darkness beyond.

"Empty," I whispered to myself. "It's an empty room."

But it wasn't. I knew that if I turned back to the mirror again—if I could only gather the courage—I would see her there, still screaming. It was a magic mirror, of course—what was an old castle without a magic mirror?—and in my mind I saw the miles of corridors I had already walked, all of them lined with doors; the Fairy, that vast darkness I had seen as she departed; the creature who had crawled on the ballroom floor, licking the remains.

I put my hands to my temples, rubbing gently, as though I could wash the thoughts away. Clara was the one who mattered, Clara who had done me a wrong. I had to find her, find her and get away from this place as quickly as I could. The doors, the rooms, these things were not my business, and whatever this place really was, I didn't want to know.

"You really have no choice, my child."

My eyes popped open, for I knew that voice. I turned and found Drosselmeyer and Clara standing in the corridor, almost beside me. It could not have been long before, for Clara had her hair pinned in the new style, secured by two tortoiseshell combs that Father had bought for her at the King's Fair.

"Is there no one else?" Clara asked.

Drosselmeyer shook his head. "The Liebermann boy, or no one, I'm afraid."

"What about Nat?"

"Your sister will find her own way. The convent, perhaps. Or she would make a fine maiden aunt to your children."

"What of my baby?" Clara asked.

"He will accept the child," Drosselmeyer replied. "So will his parents. I will see to it."

Clara looked away, considering. My anger rose again, seeing how neatly my life had been managed for me, the decisions that had been made all around me, carefully hidden by the scenery.

"Of course, I could arrange the same match for your sister," Drosselmeyer said casually, and I took a surprised breath.

"Nat as a duchess?" Clara laughed, and the laughter echoed cruelly up and down the corridor. "Come now, Godfather."

"Yet she would be happy, I think," Drosselmeyer said quietly. "And it could be arranged. Natasha has not your beauty or charm, of course, but when an engagement is a matter of money, as this will be, a greater quantity can solve almost any problem. Of course, you would then have to find some other young man, and quickly—"

"No," Clara said. "No. I'll take Conrad."

"Very well," Drosselmeyer replied, and there was no mistaking the satisfaction in his gaze. "I will arrange it."

I let out the breath I had been holding, feeling something like numbness in my fingers. Clara turned away from me and I tried to follow, to see her face, but in that moment she and Drosselmeyer both began to fade. Within a few moments, they were gone, leaving me alone in the corridor, staring blankly at a wall.

"Clara," I whispered. But she was gone, only a memory. The real Clara was off somewhere else in this castle, celebrating her betrayal with a handsome man who wasn't her fiancé. She could have given me everything I had ever wanted, but instead she had reached out and taken him, because that was what Clara did. She took and took and took.

"Clara," I said again. "Where are you?"

Something lifted my hair and I turned with a gasp. But it was only the wind, blowing through the great gate of the castle, a broad archway some twenty yards to my left. It hadn't been there before, but that didn't matter. I walked away from the mirror, the clock, and moved down the corridor toward the gate.

Outside, the world was dark and silent. Beyond the rows of apple trees, now twisted and reeking of rotten cider, the portcullis stood open. The drawbridge beyond was covered with sugared snow, granules glistening in the soft pink glow from the walls. There were no guards on the gate any longer; the sleigh in which I had sat hours before was long gone. Even the winding parallel tracks of the runners had disappeared, leaving a vast field of new-fallen snow, and in that snow I saw the tracks of small bare feet. Dancer's feet. The tracks disappeared up the hill into the snow, back the way we had come, in great strides; Clara had been running. At the sight of those small footprints, I felt the same rush of mingled power and joy that I imagined a hunter must experience with his quarry finally, firmly in sight.

A low, practical part of my mind whispered that it would be

cold out there; I should find some better clothing than my now-ragged party dress. But who knew how much time that would take in this place, and meanwhile, Clara might vanish, find her way back to the parlor, to the real world, where she would reward herself for her betrayal with a noble husband and the title of duchess. Conrad himself no longer mattered; I couldn't even remember what he looked like. He was a Christmas present that Clara and I had wrangled over, spitting and kicking. Come Boxing Day, it would lie broken on the floor, utterly forgotten, with no more value than the cheap brown paper that had wrapped it, and by the New Year it would lie in the gutter.

But today, after all, was still Christmas.

"Merry Christmas, Clara," I whispered, and in the distance I heard laughter, as cold and crystalline as the deadly icicles that hung from our house's roof, waiting for unwary passersby. They *were* watching, all of them, somewhere beyond my vision. They were amused by my predicament, perhaps even sympathetic, for they knew pain in this place. But I would gain nothing here unless I was prepared to take it myself. All our lives Clara had been better, luckier, beyond my reach, but now I sensed that I had the chance to close on her, if only I did not soften, did not weaken. If I held on to my hate.

Running lightly, almost skipping, I began to follow her tracks up the hill.

CHAPTER

19

A MOON HAD COME UP WHILE I WAS IN THE CASTLE, BUT NO moon I knew. This moon was a dark, sinking creation, many colors somehow mottling into black. It gave off its own strange light, cold and diseased and frightening, and after an initial disturbed glance, I ignored it, keeping my gaze to the ground.

Clara had fled up the high hill without direction, and come down the far slope the same way. On my initial journey I had been struck by the bounty of color, the variety of sweets. But where Clara's feet crossed, the sweets were now spoiled, their colors leaching into black or brown decay. The marshmallow roses had sunken into a melted-looking sludge. The fudge walls of the ravine were crumbling and the caked chocolate inside looked decades old, desiccated and stale. When I reached the field of swollen, glistening jelly beans, I saw that most of them had split open along the sides, revealing cores honeycombed by squirming black worms.

Thank God, I thought, *I ate none of that*. But this thought raised the equally disturbing question of exactly what I *had* eaten, of how much this land was now a part of me, how difficult it might be to expel. The screaming woman appeared behind my eyes, mouth wide and neck distended, but I shut her away. Once I found Clara, there would be time enough to consider these things.

Something glimmered up ahead, and I came to a stop as I recognized a pair of crystalline reindeer, keeled over now in the snow. They whined and gasped, their breathing shallow, and when I tried to bend and pet one, it snapped at my hand. I felt a terrible pity for them, these creatures that the Fairy had created and then abandoned so easily. But after all, perhaps she had no control of the way her land was melting, fading, changing. In my books of fairy tales, spells never lasted forever, and they often broke of their own accord. Even the sugared snow was melting now, its bright luminescence slowly fading into a pearly gleam, like the light of a crescent moon. I could barely see Clara's tracks anymore, and I had to bend over to follow her pattering steps as they wended through the field of spoiled jelly beans and emerged on the far side.

The river of pink gelatin had dried up now, leaving only a shallow streambed. At some point Clara had almost surely fallen into the stream, for her tracks veered toward the crevasse, disappearing for a few feet before they reappeared in a flurried mess of slime and snow. A nasty-looking residue, pink streaked with black, oozed over the streambed's floor. After a moment I realized that the black patches were some sort of insect; at my running approach, they broke for cover, skittering across the rocks with a hissing, crackling sound that made me feel slightly sick. I didn't look into the streambed again.

Something had been chasing Clara, for certain. Her path was too hurried, too panicky, to be without pursuit. For the first time in many hours I thought of the clown, Drosselmeyer's clown, its shadow chasing me along the walls and skirting boards. But I knew nothing of Clara's nightmares. Were it not for that ridiculous story about the Mouse King, I would have sworn she had none. What had she seen, chasing her across the snow?

What do you care?

That was the right answer, the right sentiment for this time and place. I could almost feel the Fairy's approving nod. I straightened and followed the tracks away from the streambed, wrapping my arms across my breasts. Ice had crystallized on my skin—real ice now, not sugar—but I barely felt the cold. Clara's footsteps were less neat now in their stride, the snow churned between the tracks, as though she had begun to stumble, or to limp.

Ahead, a thin line of black appeared across the snow, growing as I continued forward, looming nearer and nearer until I finally recognized it for the shortbread forest. But it was different now: a wasteland of tortured trees, utterly bereft of leaves. The symmetrical oblong shapes of the upright shortbread had shrunken and twisted, their tops splitting into gnarled black branches that reached for the sickly moon as though begging for relief. Tiny patches of branch-dappled moonlight were visible through the wreckage, but they could not hold against the wide swaths of dark.

In front of the forest, Clara's tracks veered left and right, as though she had briefly run hither and thither, looking for another route. Then they disappeared between the trees. Clara had not wanted to go into the forest any more than I did, and I wondered why, what she had seen there. The trees, perhaps, the trees with their contorted, tormented branches, bent into shapes that nature never intended. In that instant I saw each tree as a man, a man who had sinned and fallen and now tried hopelessly to repent. It came to me that perhaps this was merely the way trees really looked in their deepest hearts, stripped of all summer, all disguise. I felt something terrible waiting inside the forest. That dark heartbeat I had heard in the castle seemed twice as loud here, twice as strong, so that I could even feel it in the earth beneath my feet.

But Clara's in there, my mind whispered. *Clara's in there, and she can't get away with it.* We stood on a set of scales, Clara and I, she at one end and I at the other, but the scales were not even close to balance, for Clara had stolen something much greater than Conrad; she had stolen my future, the future I could have had.

She was not happy, though, that unwelcome part of my mind reminded me. *When Drosselmeyer made his announcement, she looked miserable, remember?*

Well, even a petty thief had the sense to look miserable when they clapped the irons on his legs and stood him in the dock, yet all the while the loot was still stolen, hidden away beyond the reach of any law, any justice. There would be justice here, I decided, and with only slight trepidation, I moved forward, into the shadows beneath the trees.

CHAPTER

20

THE GROUND WAS TREACHEROUS, FOR SOME OF THE TREES had fallen, and their scabrous, twisting trunks were barely visible against the darkened earth. The scent of mint and rotten chocolate was now overpowering, forcing me to cover my nose as I stumbled over the loose branches. Clara's tracks had disappeared, but I continued forward, convinced that I could track her by spite alone, that I would simply know. We were twins, after all, and twins shared a bond, though ours was no bond that either of us would ever have desired or pursued. Drosselmeyer had not intended us to come to the Kingdom of Sweets; it might have been planned by the boy Mikhail, or might only have been an accident. But here we were, and something told me that Clara's light would not help her in this land, as it had done everywhere else.

After an untold length of time I passed between two wrecked trees and found myself in a clearing. It was a small space, perhaps only ten yards in diameter, but that was room enough for the thin light of the black moon to filter down, illuminating the patches of melting snow on the ground. There was no sound, not even the hoot of an owl or the scurrying of a mouse. Nothing could live here; nothing grew, and I suddenly understood that this broad patch of land was somehow the very nexus of this place. The terrible force I had sensed on the outskirts of the forest lived here . . . lived and breathed, and waited.

Before me a figure crawled out of the trees, wriggling its way into the patch of moonlight. I shrank back, but then saw that it was too small to be a man. There was a second moment of horror when I thought it was a young child, and I crept closer, unable to help myself. Only then did I recognize it as one of the gingerbread men, his arms and legs badly mangled, as though he had been attacked by some animal, a dog or a bear or even, perhaps, a clever, hungry fox. Who really knew, after all, how the old fairy tales died, or where the story might end? The gingerbread man dragged himself forward, panting pitifully, crawling almost to my feet before he looked up at me, his face barely lit by a patch of snow.

"Human," he breathed. "I know you now."

I knelt beside him, finding at last a tiny bit of fascination in Clara's fantasy, a sense of child's wonder. The gingerbread man's chocolate buttons were gone now, and so was his red gumdrop nose, but I could still make out the shallow divots that served as his eyes, and I marveled at the craft of the Sugar Plum Fairy, the work that must have gone into bringing a child's dream to life. The gingerbread man tried to crawl another foot, and his mangled arm tore cleanly off. He whined painfully but left the arm behind, a fat pastry grub wriggling helplessly in the snow.

"You could help us," he whispered. "You could—"

A low hiss emerged from the trees ahead of us, and the little man fell silent. The air suddenly reeked of ginger, ginger that had outlived its usefulness and turned rotten. The light from the snow had died entirely now. My eyes were adjusting to the blackness, but not quickly enough, for I could no longer even see the features of the gingerbread man's face. A chill wind had begun to blow; I could hear it soughing through the forest around us, making a sound like sharpened fingernails on stone.

"Natasha."

The sound was neither male nor female. The voice was not human, any more than the poor mutilated creature at my feet. Looking down, I saw that the gingerbread man had melted into liquid, little more than a dark puddle of sugared molasses atop the slick melt of the snow. My insides felt suddenly hollow, and I closed my eyes, but that was no help, for my head was pulled up as though by invisible fingers. Though I did not open my eyes, I realized that I could still see everything, as though my eyelids themselves had melted away, become as insubstantial as everything else in this land. Spun sugar.

In the mottled shadows of the forest, a deeper shadow had come to stand in the space between trees: an upright form, vaguely human, blackly statuesque. The shadow carried something in its right hand, a stick or a beam, perhaps, something that stood as tall as its shoulder. I squinted, trying to see its face, and caught only a gleam of metal, there and then gone.

The figure moved forward, dragging a sack behind it across the ground. It flung its burden forward into the sickly moonlight, and I saw that the sack was Clara, her blond hair tangled and matted against her face, her blue dress shredded almost to rags. Her eyes were closed, and my first thought was that she was dead.

"I am full of gifts," the black figure whispered, and at the sound of its voice Clara began to moan. She opened her eyes, saw me standing above her, and clutched at my leg, as a drowning man might clutch a spar.

"Nat," she whispered. "The Sugar Plum Fairy—she's not—none of them are—"

She fell silent, weeping, and I felt a stirring of pity, unexpected and utterly unwelcome. On that long-ago day when we had stolen the cake and eaten it together, Clara had been taken by terrible stomachache; I had comforted her there in the wardrobe, speaking in a quiet voice until she fell asleep in my arms. Now I was astonished to find myself wanting to bend down and speak to her in the same low, comforting voice. But I was held back by the Fairy, by her black silhouette that towered over us both, making mercy impossible.

"I'm sorry, Nat," Clara whispered through her sobs. "Conrad. I'm sorry. I didn't know what he meant to you."

I stiffened, for that was an outright lie. Clara had known. She simply hadn't cared. But then, Clara was a master of reordering the facts to fit her own self-image as a heroine. Nothing in her charmed life had prepared her to be the villain. Her face seemed to plead with me, asking whether I could truly hold her responsible for anything she had done

"You could have said no," I said. "I know what happened with Drosselmeyer. You could have given me everything I ever wanted."

Clara's face stilled. I saw deception there, an almost animal cunning, and I wondered how much of her innocence had been calculated, designed to get her out of trouble just like this. She had begun to cry again, but I knew her tears for what they were.

"Why are you doing this to us?" Clara demanded of the Fairy, sobbing. "What have I ever done to you?"

The Fairy leaned forward, such a predatory look on her face

that I instinctively tried to pull away from Clara, to get away. But she held fast to my legs.

"I know your kind, child," the Fairy whispered. "I have made meat of them throughout time. You believe others unimportant. You are all that matters."

"That's not true!" Clara howled.

I almost smiled, for this was the Clara I had been looking for, the spoiled child who got everything and fell to pieces when something didn't go to plan. It was a relief to see her again, allowing me to let go of that unhappy moment of pity, so unexpected and unwelcome.

"It is true," the Fairy whispered. "Light, he named you, and so you believe you can do no harm, following your charmed life."

"He blessed *me*," Clara replied brokenly. "Not Nat."

"I see," I replied. There was no light now—even the many-cornered moon had disappeared into whatever hell housed such things—but still I stared at my sister, suddenly seeing her in her entirety, understanding her more clearly in this vast darkness than I had ever done in the sun.

"Light," I said, "and so you thought you had the right to Conrad. To anything you saw."

"I'm sorry, Nat," Clara wept. Her beseeching hands took new hold of the torn fabric of my dress, and she buried her face in my skirts, sobbing. "I'm so sorry."

But I had had quite enough of that word, *sorry*. I could not remember ever thinking it useful, but now it seemed worth less than nothing, devalued entirely by the sight of Clara's streaming eyes, her clear certainty that I would surmount this indignity, let it go as I had let go all the others. Clara's entire life had been paved with forgiveness, with indulgence; she existed in a kind of grace, free from all consequence, and she had courted that grace, smiling prettily through it all. I was supposed to forgive her, her eyes said, that was the way the play was meant to go, and the certainty of that, the entitlement of it, suddenly seemed worse than anything else she or Conrad might have done.

"It's done now," Clara murmured, smiling timidly at me. "You're still my sister. Can't we just—"

I kicked her squarely in the stomach. She coughed and rolled over, whooping hollowly, robbed of breath, and I leapt on top of her and grabbed her head, slamming it into the rocky ground. The forest was forgotten, the clearing gone, even the unseen Fairy merely part of the background, and every time I thought of how Clara expected to be forgiven, what she thought she deserved, I hit her again, long after she had regained her breath and begun to sob, long after the sobs quieted and she fell silent and limp. I felt the struggle go from her limbs, but that only made me angrier; having taken everything, would she deny me even the pleasure of the fight? I called her names, filthy names, all the profanity I had ever heard the dockworkers shout as they loaded the ships on our side of the river. But still Clara did not resist, not even when I grabbed her neck in both hands, pressing my thumbs down on her throat. The breath tore from my lungs, but even the pain of exertion was pleasurable now, for it suited my rage.

"All these years," I panted. "All these years you had every- thing, and still you thought you deserved more, anything you wanted, anything you saw—"

Clara gagged, her breath rattling in her throat. Her body bucked beneath me, jerking wildly, but I bore down, driven by the images in my head: Clara and the dollhouse, where she was always duchess; Clara and my parents, plotting my life behind my back; Clara and our godfather, stealing my future. The pictures seemed to fuel my hatred, galvanizing it, hardening it into the purest emotion I would ever experience, making what I had felt for Conrad seem like nickel plate.

Now I felt the Fairy behind me, so close that I could have reached out and touched her leg, had I dared. But she did not interfere, and in her stillness I sensed silent approval, a quiet feeling of roundness, of rightness, as though we had reached the only logical end. Clara's struggles were weakening, dying, her arms lying flat now, not so much as a twitch. But I could not let go of her throat, not even when I felt the life gone from her, when I knew she was dead. I kept on throttling her, shaking her, until one of those clawed hands descended on my shoulder, making me jump.

"It is done, child. The bargain is sealed."

"Bargain?" I asked stupidly.

"At a time of your choosing, you will find yourself alone with Drosselmeyer, in a place of privacy. And at that time, you will ask me in."

"What does that mean?"

"Difficult to explain. You will take no lasting injury, if that is your concern."

That wasn't my concern. I had not even thought of injury to myself, and certainly I didn't care what might happen to Drosselmeyer. The Fairy had promised not to harm Conrad, and her price seemed small to me, as small as mine apparently did to her. But my hands trembled, as though I stood on the edge of a precipice. I didn't dare look up.

Clara.

"When?" I asked. "When does this happen?"

"You will know."

She tugged at my shoulder, pulling me to my feet. At last I

stood, still unable to take my eyes from Clara where she lay sprawled on the ground, eyes wide, staring at the sky.

"You should make your peace with it now, here," the Fairy said. "Accept what you have done, or in your own world, it will drive you mad."

I nodded, though that was easier said than done. We were far from home, certainly, but sin was sin. I had murdered my twin, murdered the child inside her, and murder could not be undone.

"Be comforted," the Fairy whispered, and her breath came to me, old and sour, like rotten ginger. "Be comforted, for I am full of gifts."

"What gifts?"

"You will see."

Clara's face suddenly seemed to ripple, the eyes deepening, the skin peeling from her bones. I stumbled backward, but the Fairy's hand gripped my shoulder, holding me in place. And now I felt my own face, my own skin, pulling taut, brief pricks of pain as the flesh beneath upheaved and augmented. The sensation spread over my entire body, trunk to limbs and back again. The pain made my eyes water, forcing me to close my eyes.

Clara.

The sensation faded.

"I have fulfilled my part of the bargain," the Fairy murmured, and I fought not to recoil, realizing that the sound I had taken for the wind in the trees was actually her voice, old yet ageless, sharpened claws scraping over anything they could reach.

"Enjoy the novelty you will experience, Natasha. The new life you have reaped. But do not think to cheat me. You will deliver me Drosselmeyer, or you will find yourself in a hell even your priest never imagined."

I closed my eyes, thinking again of the screaming woman, locked forever behind the silent door. The Fairy made no empty threats. There was hell here; I had seen it.

Clara.

"I won't cheat you," I said. "I wouldn't dare."

The Fairy smiled, and the needles of her teeth gleamed brightly, bright as reflected metal in sunlight, though there was no longer even the hint of a moon. She began to turn away, but I spoke suddenly, not knowing I meant to, only needing to know what she was, what this place was. What had been done here.

"You're not the Sugar Plum Fairy. Who are you really?"

The Fairy turned back, her face a blackened horror in the moonlight, and I instantly regretted the question, regretted seeking even the smallest fragment of her attention. But she did not seem angry. She paused, and when she spoke again, her voice was abstracted, as though I had forced her to consider old memories, things buried deep.

"Names are only a lessening, child. They do not describe us. Before my real life began, I was enslaved, but I have left that time behind. In the years since, I have been called many things by many peoples of your kind. But none of them knew me, not really, and for myself I have always enjoyed the quiet names, names bestowed in the heat of the moment, without thought of history or consequence."

The Fairy turned, grinning, and now at last I saw them clearly: black wings spreading from her back, wings of midnight, arching over her, seeming to arch above the forest, blotting out everything, drowning even the darkness of the sky. She raised her arm, and I saw that the implement in her right hand was not a weapon, not even a stick, but a gardener's tool, a long-handled spade. Blood dripped wetly from the iron head, puddling on the ground, and the last thing I smelled in that terrible land was the scent of rusted copper.

Clara.

"This is a land of retribution, Natasha Stahlbaum, and I need no name to rule it. But if you must, you may call me the Queen of Spades."

Clara.

Clara.

Clara.

CHAPTER
21

CLARA."

I woke on the sofa to find Father leaning over me. His eyes were bloodshot with hangover, his face drawn and old in the merciless light of dawn, yet his hand was gentle on my shoulder. The stale odor of drink poured over me in an unwelcome wave.

"Are you all right, apple?"

I stared up at him, momentarily unable to assimilate anything. But my mouth knew the right response before I did.

"I'm all right, Father. I must have fallen asleep here."

He smiled then, his lined face softening. Over his shoulder I saw the Christmas tree, now reduced to normal size, all of its magic gone, candles tawdry without flame, needles coarse and dry in the sickly daylight that bled through the frosted windows. As Father pulled me up to sit, my foot knocked something away: the nutcracker. Its eyes glittered as it spun across the floor, like a last bit of magic from the night past, and then it lay still.

"You've made us all so proud, Clara," Father said, patting my hand.

I looked around, but there was no one in the parlor but Father and me. Even Uncle Angelo had escaped his prison of tinsel at some point in the night past. Father continued to smile at me, that kind smile that he reserved only for her, for his apple, and now, at last, I began to understand.

I am full of gifts.

"Clara? Are you all right?"

And I was. I was all right. I took Father's outstretched hand and sat up, stretching my limbs, Clara's lithe limbs, tipping my head to one side and smiling Clara's guileless smile.

"Merry Christmas, Father," I said.

ACT III

THE DOLLHOUSE

Here is Belladonna, the Lady of the Rocks,
The lady of situations.
Here is the man with three staves, and here the Wheel,
And here is the one-eyed merchant, and this card,
Which is blank, is something he carries on his back,
Which I am forbidden to see.

—*The Waste Land*
T. S. Eliot

CHAPTER

22

CONRAD AND I WERE MARRIED EIGHT DAYS LATER, ON THE second of January, in the great city cathedral. The entire neighborhood was in attendance, and the ceremony was performed by Bishop Theofan himself. There, in front of more than four hundred family and friends, in the exact spot where Clara and I were once baptized, I bent my head and made all the right responses, promising to love and honor and obey Conrad, to be the helpmeet of his life.

Drosselmeyer stood up with us, in his place as my godfather, clad in one of his customary velvet suits. I did not look at him during the wedding, but I could sense him there, a foot behind my left shoulder, and my mind never left him for a moment, not even when Conrad leaned forward to place his dry lips against my cheek.

I had worried that Drosselmeyer would be able to sense the change in me, that he would smell the Fairy's work just as she had been able to smell his. But Drosselmeyer treated Clara with the same careless generosity as ever. It turned out that he had given her a vast bolt of white satin nearly a month before to make her wedding dress in secret, and it was he who gave me away during the ceremony, with Mother and Father smiling on. Mother's smile, at least, was a bit anxious, and she spent much of the ceremony sniffling and weeping, certain that disaster would fall upon us. The crowd, too, seemed certain of trouble, hungry for it. But the ceremony concluded without incident, and afterward Drosselmeyer even made a very fine toast at the reception, a veritable ode to Clara's beauty and charm, his speech delivered without the benefit of a single magic trick.

I looked beautiful on my wedding day. During the reception I sensed the men's envy of Conrad, sensed his pleasure in displaying me as an item he had acquired through his own worth, by both paying more and being somehow more deserving than the rest. Beauty made me valuable, and so I increased Conrad's value, and because I was supposed to be Clara, I smiled and kept my eyes downcast, murmuring inanities whenever anyone asked me a question, which almost no one bothered to do.

There was trouble at the reception, of course. Several men challenged each other, but only one actual duel was fought, and that with such poor aim that the lone injury was a broken statue in the Liebermanns' extensive back garden. One of the Lazarev boys was caught in the wine cellar with Clara's old friend Arlette, both of them stark naked and defiant upon discovery, declaring their intent to marry the next day. The incident almost provoked another duel before Drosselmeyer stepped in, hushing up the business with coin.

My brother, Fritz, who had been acting oddly ever since Christmas Eve, set a fire in a wardrobe, a fire that might have burned the house down if Mr. Cadwallader hadn't smelled the smoke. Anastasia was forced to injure an old friend of Conrad's father who cornered her in the hallway, laboring under such a cloud of drunken blindness that he apparently believed her to be his estranged wife. Aunt Imogen scandalized the neighborhood by taking home not one but two of Drosselmeyer's boys, neither of them a day over twenty, and the only person who didn't notice was Uncle Angelo, who slept the party off in a rubbish bin next to the service entrance.

Later, we discovered that Charles and Deirdre had augmented the bowl of sickly-sweet brandied punch with a bottle of grain alcohol, and in the end nine or ten guests, including Fritz, went to the hospital. But even so, all agreed that it had been an unforgettable party, one of the wildest in the history of the neighborhood, and in the years to come I would sometimes hear people reminiscing about the Liebermann reception with a sort of fond disgust, as though the party itself was to blame and they could not be held accountable for their own misdeeds, for whatever had happened, for what the night had become.

Of course, there was one notable absence from all of these events: Natasha, the dark sister, who had vanished on Christmas Eve and was certainly dead by now, though her body was never found. Popular rumor said that she had thrown herself into the river, for it was well-known that she was in love with Conrad Liebermann herself, and his engagement to Clara had been announced on the very night of her disappearance. Natasha's fate cast no pall over the nuptials; rather, it seemed to enliven them. The unlucky history of the Stahlbaum twins was dragged forth yet again, and it seemed the opinion of the neighborhood that Natasha had been destined for such a tragic end. No corpse ever washed up on the shores of the river, and within two weeks of Natasha's disappearance a funeral was held without coffin: a small affair, private, for family only, and Drosselmeyer did not attend.

———————

MY PARENTS GENUINELY SEEMED TO BELIEVE THAT I WAS DEAD. When the constabulary failed to find any information, Father asked Drosselmeyer to offer a reward, and Drosselmeyer agreed, perhaps because he was certain no reward would ever be claimed. But even my mother seemed to know that the reward was a matter of form, for after my wedding, she climbed further than ever into the green bottle. Whenever I visited the house, I would find her on her sofa in the parlor, barely conscious, her eyes streaming and an old daguerreotype of a six-year-old Natasha clutched in her hand. If I felt any guilt as I watched her mourn, the daguerreotype removed it handily, for it was the only picture of me she had. Clara had been photographed many times, her portrait painted by the most fashionable artist in the city when she was fourteen, but my mother had only this coarse-grained reproduction to remember me by. I wondered whether her grief was genuine, or whether it was simple guilt, as false as Clara's mourning would have been, had I not found her nutcracker and stolen her life. Father's version of grief was more efficient; when I asked him whether I might have Natasha's collection of books to remember her by, he informed me that they had already been sold.

IN THAT WEEK BEFORE NEW YEAR'S, THE LAST WEEK WHERE I might have changed my mind and taken a different path, I considered the idea of marriage to Conrad often, how it would be and what it would mean. Fool though he might be, I still loved him, and so I assumed that marriage would be the easy part, the part that would naturally arrange itself. All Conrad had wanted was a girl who looked like Clara, and all I had wanted was for him to adore me as though I were a girl who looked like Clara. Now that we both had what we wanted, I felt sure that all would be well, and so I raised no demur to the wedding plans, not even when they told me that Drosselmeyer would be giving me away.

Conrad did not touch me before the ceremony, not so much as a kiss. He explained that his mother had made clear that a gentleman did not expect favors for engagement, did not molest his fiancée as though she were a piece of merchandise that he had already paid for. At first I believed Conrad was simply indulging in a sham of virtue, but as I watched his solemn face, I came to understand that he was not wholly hypocritical, that he thought he was both being honest and impressing me deeply with his honesty. I had known that Clara would see a different Conrad than mine, but I had always assumed that would be a matter of playacting on his part, to convince Clara of something untrue. It was a strange feeling, to realize that men would not only say different things to different women but actually become different people, and that was my first hint that our marriage might not be the easy matter I'd hoped.

Conrad had promised Clara that they would spend the first six months of their marriage touring the Continent, but I quickly quashed that idea. I wanted to see the European capitals, particularly London, but not like this, not the trip they had planned to hide Clara's pregnancy. Four days into our marriage, I told Conrad that I had miscarried, and Conrad, knowing little of women's workings and not wishing to know more, accepted this turn of events with simple relief. He did not even call for a doctor, for that would have raised questions with his parents, whom he had never informed of Clara's misfortune. I made a full and speedy recovery, and when Conrad asked if I still wished to go on our honeymoon trip, I told him yes, but another time, perhaps next year or the year after that.

CONRAD'S PARENTS WERE A TRIAL. HIS FATHER DID NOT TOUCH but liked to leer, and his mother was determined to show me off, as though I were a new carriage. All of the wealthy ladies of the neighborhood were the same; they would have made me an ornament, would have had me in all of their clubs and cotillions, but I had no interest in them. As I refused all invitations and rebuffed all attempts at friendship, Conrad's mother and her friends settled into a stiff, hurt silence.

I enjoyed their hurt.

But my own parents were scarcely any better. My father visited the Liebermanns' house as often as he could, particularly during parties, when he would try to meet as many titled people as possible and pass himself off as nobility. He did not bring my mother along on such occasions; in fact, I heard from the servants that he took the precautionary step of buying her a new bottle of laudanum before leaving the house. My father enjoyed himself enormously on these occasions, dropping names left and right, oblivious to the distaste of Conrad's parents, who clearly felt that my father, like me, was failing to act his place. I had all of Clara's beauty now, but none of her charm, that charm which had, after all, been part of the contract they made with Drosselmeyer. One night I passed the door of their bedroom and heard Mrs. Liebermann telling her husband that they should have waited for one of the King's daughters to come of age.

"What rot!" Conrad's father snapped back. "The oldest can't

be more than . . . what? Six? Seven? We would have waited years!"

"Still," his mother returned, "it might have been worth it."

WE HAD NO CHILDREN. I NEVER PUT ANY EFFORT INTO PREVENT-ing them, as the old Natasha had done, using Anastasia's skill with herbs and simples; it just didn't happen. But I couldn't deceive myself as to fault. I sometimes thought that I could feel it inside Clara's stolen body: that other life I had taken, no longer a baby now, but something dark and malign. Conrad was relieved when I supposedly miscarried, yet as the years passed and no further children materialized, I sensed his puzzlement over the matter, his unspoken questions. Sometimes I was tempted to feel sorry for him, but I comforted myself with the knowledge that he had not been without options, that if he had only asked a young and foolish—and fertile—Natasha, she would have leapt at the opportunity. He had had the chance, and thrown it away.

But I must be fair in my recollection. To his credit, Conrad never reproached me for my childlessness, as many other husbands would have done. He was kind to Clara, taking her shopping and bringing her presents, but in truth that only deepened my suspicions, my discontent. Would Natasha have enjoyed such kindness, such understanding? Natasha was the one who loved Conrad, but all she had ever had from him was a torn scrap of shirt and that damnable bracelet, now lost somewhere in the Kingdom of Sweets. As a woman of leisure, a future duchess, I had many hours to ponder this state of affairs, these terrible misalignments of obsession and interest and value, but I could conclude nothing from my study, save that the world was a merciless place.

Despite these challenges, I tried to take the Fairy's advice and enjoy my new life. It was nice to wear pretty clothes and have them enhance my beauty, not to be relegated to the drab fabrics and dark shades that would call the least attention. It was good to have this and that shopkeeper greet me with pleasure, to have a full dance card at every ball, to have men bow as I approached and turn their heads appreciatively when I walked down the street. The servants, too, would bow when I walked through the door, though I soon stopped that practice. Always, on the inside, Natasha reigned, the memory of those inferior days drowning the fleeting pleasure I might have felt at their misplaced courtesy. I tried to be kind to the servants, always; indeed, I was much kinder to servants than I was to my own class. Yet this introduced a new problem in our marriage; in the end, the most damning of all.

While we were only bedpartners, I had not known how Conrad saw the world, had never even given it a moment's thought. Ever since that day of the wounded dog, I had assumed that he was good-hearted, and because he was good-hearted, I had assumed that he would believe what I believed. But from the moment I moved into his parents' mansion, I began to discover many new things about the boy I loved, and none of them were good. I discovered that Conrad not only condoned the flogging of servants but had done so himself on several occasions, with his father's enthusiastic approval. I discovered that Conrad did not believe in charity, not even when small children without shoes ran begging after our carriage as we rode through the park. On one such day I gave the children what pocket money I had, tossing it out the back, and Conrad tried to stop me, grabbing my wrist hard enough to leave a bruise, though I missed the injury until later, so happy had the sight of the children made me as they straightened with coin in their hands and smiles on their dirty faces. I pictured them that night, their families sitting down to the first good meal in months, and suddenly it all seemed worthwhile: my in-laws, their gloomy mansion, even the awkward way I moved in Clara's dancer's body, never feeling quite right there. But Conrad glowered at me all the way home, not handing me down from the carriage as he would usually do, and as I went up the steps, I heard him ordering the driver not to tell his parents what I had done. *You humans would do well to mistrust your own dearest wishes,* the Fairy had said, but I could not admit that she had been right, not then, not yet. Still, as we dined that night I found myself staring at my husband, wondering at how well I thought I had known him, how fine a tapestry I had been able to weave from those nights in my bedroom and the long-ago rescue of a dog.

That night I asked Conrad casually, as Clara would have done, what he thought had happened to Natasha. I was curious to hear his answer, for he had neither attended my funeral nor shown any undue concern at my disappearance. On the rare occasion when my name came up, he gave no sign that we had ever been anything more than bare acquaintances.

"She probably fell in the river and drowned," Conrad replied briskly, and then turned the conversation elsewhere. If he was covering a deep angst over the matter, I could detect no sign of it; I sensed that the topic was neither interesting nor painful to him. That did not wound me, not now, but it was instructive. He did not think of me, my Conrad, any more than I thought of Clara. We had both made our own accommodations with the past, and on the rare occasion when I considered that strange Christmas Eve so long ago, it was only to think that Clara had reaped her own reward, that if she had been only a bit less selfish, a bit less two-faced, she might have been alive and well. I had put the past in a high cupboard, just as Conrad had done, and there I meant it to stay. As the strangeness of that distant Christmas Eve faded further and further into memory, I sometimes even tried to convince myself that I had imagined much of it, whipped into a fever of hysteria by my own anguish over Clara's engagement. But that was a lie, and if I needed proof, there was my brother, Fritz, who might begin screaming with no provocation at all and would occasionally run mad throughout the house with one of the fireplace pokers, trying to break anything within reach.

FOR A MERCY, CONRAD'S FAMILY CONNECTIONS DID NOT INCLUDE Drosselmeyer. Early in our marriage, Conrad confessed to me that he had always found the old wizard repellent, for no reason he could ever pinpoint, and his parents felt the same way. Several weeks after my wedding Drosselmeyer's portrait fell from the high wall in our house where it had hung for years, splitting into pieces on the parquet floor of the entrance hall, and so I was generally spared the sight of my godfather, save for the single night each year of my family's Christmas Eve party, where Drosselmeyer remained a fixture for years to come. But he brought no more presents to our house, and his entourage never again included the strange, scarred boy who had made the nutcracker. Indeed, I sometimes forgot that Drosselmeyer was even there, for as Clara I found our Christmas parties far more difficult to negotiate. Even my Clara, surly and unsociable, was expected to circulate, to decorate the room, and if I tried to withdraw, they would find me. Beauty and charm were double-edged blades, and I sometimes wondered whether my own dealings with Clara might have been different had I known that she inhabited her own prison, her own set of expectations that she could not escape. But I dismissed the question, not liking the tenor of my thoughts when they wandered down this road. Done, after all, was done.

Yet I had not escaped Drosselmeyer's eye, not entirely. One night in our fourth month of marriage I was awakened by a noise like a pack of hounds, all of them baying and slavering at the moon. When I went to the window and parted the curtains, I found Drosselmeyer waiting below, surrounded by his crew of pretty blond enforcers, just as though I were young again. The boys were clearly drunk, laughing and shouting at the tops of their voices, but Drosselmeyer merely stood there, clad in his top hat and twirling his cane, leaning against a lamppost, looking up at the Liebermanns' house. His appearance struck me with the same unformed dread I had always felt as a young child, and I drew quickly back from the window, away from his gleaming black eye, certain that to be seen was to be marked somehow, cursed to endure our godfather's meddling forever.

But what could he possibly want with Clara? This was the question I could not answer. Drosselmeyer had not appeared to grieve Natasha, but Natasha was supposed to die; for all he knew, she had. I sometimes asked the new servants in my parents' house whether they had ever seen any sign of the clown, or even any life-size doll, but they returned negatives with a wide-eyed politeness that told me they thought my question privately ridiculous. They had not been there that Christmas Eve, any of them, had not seen the clown come to life, and so they perhaps thought me a bit touched. But I was not mad; far from it. Among the many possessions I removed from my parents' house with my trousseau, the nutcracker held pride of place. It stood just to the right of the fireplace in my bedroom, and the servants soon learned not to move it, even to dust the andirons, for the nutcracker would snarl and draw its sword when touched. The servants feared the little soldier, and feared me as well. Yet I didn't dare get rid of it, for I wasn't sure it was truly mine. I felt that it was standing guard over me, but for what purpose? Was it a spy, keeping an eye on me for Drosselmeyer? The scarred boy had said the nutcracker belonged to him, but who knew what such a boy might intend with his creations, or whether he had even told me the truth at all?

I told myself that I should leave it alone, that once the Fairy got hold of Drosselmeyer, whatever he had intended would not matter. We had a made a bargain, the Fairy and I, and though the time had not yet come for fulfillment, I thought I would know when it did. Yet when I saw Drosselmeyer beneath my window, hat tipped down to shadow his one eye, it suddenly seemed to me that the past was no longer shut in its high cupboard, that the strange Christmas Eve in my memory had been a piece of a story, a much greater story of which Clara and I were only a small part, and that if Drosselmeyer was still watching me, still waiting, then I was not out of the story yet.

ONE DAY THE DUKE'S BURSAR LEFT AN ACCOUNT BOOK ON THE breakfast table, and because no one had told me not to, I picked it up and leafed through it. My understanding of numbers had never been great, but the account book was not complicated; after some initial confusion, I discovered that the farmers on the Liebermanns' vast landholdings in the east were paid less than three pfennigs a day.

Ever since I was young, my father had bemoaned the wave of peasants who poured into the city every year, seeking jobs in the factories. Clara and I barely listened, only nodded along. We saw the peasants every time we went out, huddled against walls or around fires, too poor to afford rent even at the dockside, and sometimes I wondered why they had come to the city, where there was no housing and even less food. But when I saw the column of three pfennigs in the account book, I finally understood. Even work in the killing factories was better paid, and while there was no housing for the peasants here, they still needed to eat. Who could blame them for inundating the city?

But when I raised the subject at table, Conrad's father said that the emancipation of the serfs was the worst action the old king had ever taken, and that he had personally counseled the new king many times to simply call out the army and eject the peasants from the city. They could go back where they came from, Conrad's father said, and Conrad nodded right along. My casual informality with my maids and the kitchen staff had already become a continual source of arguments with Conrad, who told me in all seriousness that I should occasionally reprimand my maid, even if she had done nothing wrong, so that she should not grow too complacent. I still loved him, or thought I did, but at such moments I did not respect him. And so I began to learn another hard lesson about marriage: that even love might begin to warp and buckle under the accumulated weight of daily contempt. For days or even weeks after such arguments I did not want to look at Conrad, did not want him to touch me at all. We shared an enormous suite on the second floor of his parents' mansion, two bedrooms joined by a vast drawing room, and at such times I would be grateful that I had a bedroom and bathroom of my own, a door to lock.

Still, there were days when we were happy, Conrad and I. I would be lying if I said there was no pleasure in being married, in waking beside someone each morning, seeing his eyes light when I entered the room, clad in a pretty dress with ribbons in my hair. At night we liked to sit together reading in his parents' library, a vast room with towering shelves, stuffed full of classics and religious tomes that had never been cracked. Conrad's parents, like so many wealthy nobles, had to display a library as a sign of status, but they were not readers; they kept the enormous collection of books only for show. But Conrad enjoyed works of military history, particularly the Greeks, while I loved to comb through the shelves, seeking interesting titles, looking at the pretty engraving on the covers. Two ladders provided access to the higher shelves, and some part of me must still have been a child, for I enjoyed climbing up and pushing off with one foot, sending the ladder sailing down the long length of the room. Conrad would laugh, and make a joke about being able to see up my skirt to my pretty ankles, sometimes more, and sometimes we would even end up making love right there in the library, where any servant might walk in. These were good days, and when I thought of my own parents, who had perhaps once been in love, but whose marriage was now a series of compartments designed to keep their lives separate, I thought that Conrad and I were doing tolerably well, and if our marriage was not perfect, it was at least a success. *Enjoy the new life you have reaped*, the Sugar Plum Fairy had said, and most of the time, in truth, I did.

Four years passed in this manner, and I was content.

CHAPTER

23

THEN CAME A WET MORNING IN EARLY DECEMBER. THE
snow was melting, water running down the drainpipes and
icicles dripping outside each window. It would be a long and teasing winter, one in which the snow melted and fell, melted again
and fell again, and each time we hoped it would be the last time,
and each time the snow reappeared the city became more disappointed, more despondent.

I had spent most of the morning reading, tucked into the most
comfortable chair, unmoving, utterly absorbed in a new novel
that Conrad's father had just received in his regular shipment of
books from England: a tale of vampires, told entirely in journal
entries and epistles. For better or worse, my literary tastes had
darkened since that night in the Kingdom of Sweets, and I sometimes thought that this fantastical novel by an unknown Irishman
might almost have been written there. When the knocker sounded,
startling me out of the author's deep world, I bared my teeth.

The servants were well trained; the knocking stopped in moments, and I bent my head gratefully. But after a minute I was

forced to stop again, for there was some sort of commotion going on downstairs. The visitor at the door wasn't going away.

With a muttered curse, I pulled the ribbon down to mark my place, untucked my feet from the chair, and got up. Conrad's father was out gambling, his mother on one of her interminable rounds of social calls, and Conrad at his hunting club, a gathering of noblemen who seemed to use their meetings mainly as an excuse to drink and discuss the perfidies of the poor. If there was a real problem at the door, I would have to be the one to deal with it. It was the butler's job, perhaps, but I wasn't Conrad or his parents, to make the servants clean up every mess.

The creature at the door was a woman, filthy and ragged, neither old nor young, her feet bound in two mismatched scraps of old carpeting. She was deep in argument with Kroll, our butler, but as I swept down the curve of the staircase she stopped badgering him and looked up at me, her gap-toothed mouth dropping open in a grin, her dark eyes unnaturally large.

"Clara."

I stopped dead. The broken, rasping voice I did not recognize, but the tone . . . it was a like a low hum, teasing and dancing, undermining everything, denying the name she gave me even as she spoke it, whispering: *You are not Clara. You are not Clara, and you never have been.*

"Leave," I ordered, directing the command to Kroll and the three parlor maids who had gathered to watch the scene from various doorways. "And close the doors behind you."

"They need not leave," the homeless woman croaked, "for my message is brief and to the point. You have taken your ease long enough. You made a bargain. The time has come to honor it."

I nodded, clenching my hands to keep them from trembling. The homeless woman stared at me for a final moment with eyes that had deepened to a fathomless shade of black, then collapsed on the threshold.

After that there was much activity, a commotion of hurrying and fetching. The servants brought the woman into the kitchen and produced blankets, a basin full of warm water to revive her. At my command, they reluctantly washed her hands and feet—the toes, as I suspected, betrayed the distinctive charcoal encroachment of frostbite—and scoured the grime from her face. But when she finally woke, she was merely a poor homeless woman, a bit scattered in the mind, not entirely sure where she was, and when I asked her about the Sugar Plum Fairy, she stared at me in honest bewilderment. On my orders, the cook prepared her an enormous breakfast, but the woman could eat only a tiny portion, and when I offered her a place to sleep for the night, she gave me a suspicious look, gathered up her bundle of rags, and went on her way.

I dismissed the servants, who clearly thought I had taken leave of my senses, and stood in the comfortable kitchen, my skin warmed by the sunlight pouring through the high, rectangular windows. Yet I was cold inside, so cold. I had forgotten what it was like to be near her, this dreadful creature who dealt vengeance, and though her presence had been diluted by the medium of the homeless woman, she had been close enough to freeze my blood. I did not care what might happen to Drosselmeyer, but still I wondered how I would find the ability to do what she commanded, what I had bargained for: to stand before him and invite her in.

You had best find the ability, my mind whispered. *Or she will find you.*

CHAPTER
24

A PPLE!" FATHER CRIED, HOLDING OUT HIS ARMS.

I went forward and dutifully endured his embrace, trying to ignore the hot gush of his rum breath, so powerful that it seemed liquid where it clung to my cheek. Conrad, too, grimaced as my father clasped his hand, and made a great show of bustling off to deposit our cloaks with the maid.

In general, I had done a fine job of putting away the past, but the past was always harder to escape on Christmas Eve. The Stahlbaum house might be far grander these days, with the walls refinished, the marble replaced, and Anastasia's kitchen now opening onto a vast conservatory, but it was still the same cell in which I had once been trapped, and the people did not change either. Here was Mrs. Armistead, regaling a group of obligated listeners with the tale of her late husband's reckless courage in the war. Here was Grandmother Kalenov, sitting in the corner seat of one sofa, barking deafly when she felt she was being ignored. Here was Morgan Wiegand, raving about a new rifle he had imported all the way from America. Here was Mr. Loring, trying to talk anyone who would listen into buying the lint brushes which he claimed were the wave of the future. And here were Charles and Deirdre, doing their best to torment Uncle Angelo by sticking lit matches into the pockets of his trousers.

Strangely, of all these familiar faces, it was my cousins' I now viewed with the most warmth. They found their pleasure in odd places, certainly, but they found it all the same, and stubbornly resisted all attempts to civilize them, to make them into anything other than what they were. Neighborhood gossip said that Aunt Imogen had been trying to arrange an engagement for Deirdre; she was seventeen now, after all, more than old enough for a beau, and she might even have been pretty if one could ignore her sneers. But Deirdre showed no interest in the company of any man except her brother, and she would not cooperate in the slightest with Aunt Imogen's attempts to feminize her. Tonight she wore a black velvet suit, and she appeared to have taken shears to her own hair again, the result being a carrot-colored mop that straggled this way and that. She and Charles had never looked more identical, and I thought that Aunt Imogen's quest could only end in despair, for the wild delight in Deirdre's face told me that nothing would ever please her more than spite, no beau ever approach the incomparable joys of trying to set her father on fire.

For a long time Drosselmeyer did not appear, so long that I felt certain that he wasn't coming, that his sorcery had warned him to stay away. But a low part of me was also relieved. *You will ask me in*, the Fairy had said, and while I didn't know exactly what that meant, I could not imagine that it would be pleasant, or anything that anyone would willingly endure. Of course I could not avoid payment forever, for she had made it plain that she knew where I was, that I could always be found. I would have to fulfill her terms, and soon, but my craven side was quite content that it should not be tonight, and so it was with both relief and regret that I saw Drosselmeyer waltz through the parlor doors, bowing and flourishing, just on the stroke of ten o'clock.

"Ah," Conrad murmured beside me. "He always has to make an entrance, doesn't he?"

"Yes," I replied, watching my godfather's blue cape swirl around him. "Yes, he does."

Drosselmeyer's boys followed behind, a new pack of grinning adolescents, clothed in handsome suits that did nothing to hide their essential status as rough trade. I wondered how Drosselmeyer found them, how he seemed able to select the most beautifully gilded boys from the most squalor-filled areas of the city. Most of all, I wondered why they needed to be so beautiful. As far back as I could remember, there had been rumors about Drosselmeyer and his boys, of course there had, but I had always believed the rumors to be false. Magicians, after all, needed misdirection, and it seemed to me that the boys were a part of Drosselmeyer's great performance, that he surrounded himself with beauty just as his blue cape might flare behind him, distracting the world with a view of the moon and stars. If I could only look behind the cape, *see* behind it, I might understand such disparate factors as our christening and Drosselmeyer's toys, perhaps even the existence of a Kingdom of Sweets. But at this moment I could see nothing beyond the glare, and so I sat nursing the single glass of wine Conrad had procured for me, augmenting it with water when I felt I would not be observed, and waiting for Drosselmeyer to get drunk.

This was not an easy business. Everyone wanted to offer Drosselmeyer a drink, but no one wanted him to drink it; they had come to talk business, loans, repayments, favors, and Drosselmeyer was simply mobbed. Around ten thirty I followed him out of the parlor, but Marko Kashelt's father followed him out as well, begging for a short-term loan.

Finding myself thwarted, I stood in the entrance hall for a moment, examining the changes. Shortly after our engagement, Conrad's family had bankrolled Father's latest venture, investment in a new iron foundry on the far side of the city, and now that the foundry was built and operating, Mother had plenty of money to indulge her tastes, which were, in truth, admirable. The fall of Drosselmeyer's monstrous portrait from the wall had made room for several new paintings, and I squinted upward in the dim light, examining a pretty portrait of a woman sitting before a warm, bright river that looked nothing like the ice-packed canal down by the docks. The portrait made me think of England, and particularly of London, the extraordinary city of the future that I had always longed to see. I moved beneath the canvas, trying to make out the woman's features in the dim light.

"Natasha?"

I spun around, but the hall was empty. The voice had been little more than a hoarse croak, and for a moment I froze, certain that she was there, that she had been unwilling to wait.

"Natasha? Is that you?"

The voice came from beneath the stairs, from the open doorway of Mother's parlor. I moved that way cautiously, then saw that it was only Mother in there, lying on the settee, staring up at the ceiling, her eyes wide and dark.

"It's me, Mother. It's Clara."

Gradually her eyes wandered from the ceiling, and as they fixed on me, a bright smile lit her face.

"Natasha. You've come back."

I halted, a step inside the doorway.

"It's *me*, Mother. Clara."

But she shook her head, smiling, her eyes a streaming mess as she reached for the green bottle. The old daguerreotype lay on the table beside it, my round six-year-old face immortalized forever.

"My Nat," Mother whispered, beckoning me toward her. "Drosselmeyer said you were gone, but I knew you weren't."

I closed the door behind me, then perched on the edge of the armchair. I had seen Mother under the laudanum before, but she was usually content to lie there, staring happily into space. I wondered whether she somehow saw me, Natasha, in truth, or whether she was entirely in the grip of the drug, tormented by visions.

"Did Drosselmeyer say where I went?"

"Into the dark," Mother whispered. A tear leaked from the corner of her eye, running down to her hairline. "But I knew he was wrong. Margritta said she had seen you, happy in heaven."

"I'm sure she did," I replied drily, thinking of Madame Margritta, who claimed she could summon dead relatives from the grave for ten marks and a stiff drink.

"I always meant to tell you one day, my Nat. But it never seemed the right time."

"Tell me what?"

Mother sat up and grabbed my arm, her eyes so wide they were almost those of a child. And it suddenly seemed to me that she *was* a child, imprisoned in her own dollhouse, all of her joys locked away in the green bottle. Of course no one had forced her to marry Father . . . but in another, truer sense, we were all forced to it. What else was there for women, for any of us?

"We didn't know," Mother whispered. "We didn't know. When we went to Drosselmeyer, to beg him—"

"Beg him for what?"

"For children. Twins, as I always wanted. We didn't know the price."

"What price?"

"Drosselmeyer said we must make him godfather. And it seemed a small enough thing. But oh Nat, that day—"

"I see," I replied, wishing now that she would wake up, snap from her delirium, see me only as Clara again, simple Clara who never demanded explanations. It was exhausting to consider our christening now, when so much had occurred to render it meaningless. Yet behind my closed eyes I saw Drosselmeyer beneath the streetlamp, the top hat tipped low on his forehead. Waiting.

"We didn't know what he would do . . . ah, God—"

Mother began to weep, rocking back and forth, almost keening. I stood up quickly, as though her wretched state might be contagious.

"Do you know why he did it?" I asked, backing toward the door. "Light and dark?"

"No! We only asked him to use his magic for us. We never dreamed—"

"Of course you didn't. But you were fools all the same, you know. Fools, to think that anything you wanted so badly would come without price."

"Don't go, Nat!" she wailed, reaching for me. "Stay here! Don't go back into the dark!"

I threw open the door and hurried from the tiny parlor. Mr. and Mrs. Carmichael, taking their cloaks from a maid in preparation for departure, looked at me oddly, but I ignored them, moving to stand beneath the three new paintings, the spot where Drosselmeyer's portrait had once hung. He had begun his scheming long before our christening, even before our conception. What could possibly have been so important? For the first time I found myself wondering whether there was a portrait of our godfather hanging somewhere in Conrad's house, deep in some room I had yet to find.

Two more hours and it won't matter, my mind whispered. *Two more hours and it will be done.*

That seemed good advice, sensible and welcome. Drosselmeyer's plans, the Sugar Plum Fairy's plans . . . two more hours and I would be shut of them both. I could live a normal life, and never mind that I would live it behind Clara's face. Pretending to be Clara was still more pleasant than actually being Natasha had ever been. Two more hours, and we would all be quits.

"Can I help you, my lady?"

It was the maid, several cloaks still piled in her arms. I didn't recognize her, but then my parents had hired many new staff since I'd left the house. This girl looked very young, and I found myself wanting to ask her whether she had ever seen anything strange in our house: a shadow on the walls, or a life-size clown, or perhaps the Christmas tree, growing and stretching and rising, until it might have been an American skyscraper towering above her head.

But the girl was smiling and pink-cheeked, her eyes bright, and in the end I could not prick her kind understanding of the world. Pressing a five-mark coin into her hand, I thanked her and went back to the party.

CHAPTER

25

MIDNIGHT APPROACHED, AND THE GUESTS BEGAN TO DE-
part. Many of the neighborhood fathers had stayed late,
drinking and fuming indignantly about the rumblings of discontent among the industrial workers, but Father, mindful of the
hospital visits after my wedding reception, had kept a careful eye
on both the buffet table and Charles and Deirdre, who had been
forbidden access to the kitchen. So there had been no chance for
guests to progress to that wild state of drunkenness in which the
party might go on in the quiet corners of our house until the next
morning, when the last revelers, still tucking their clothing back
into place, would be poured stumbling out into the street. Our
Christmas Eves were staid affairs now, and I was surprised to find
myself grieving for the old days, for the way the character of the
celebration had somehow diminished, shrunken from a wild night
where anything could happen to an affair no more debauched
than a village social, so many infinite possibilities closed off,
flown forever, never to return.

Fritz had poured an entire carafe of wine over his head, then sat there giggling in his foolish way, his tongue busily lapping rosé from his chin as he pretended to wash his hair. He had never been quite right in the head since that Christmas Eve so long before, but I seemed to be the only one who connected his condition to the nutcracker; the rest of the neighborhood thought his madness sprang from a bout of brain fever, a rumor undoubtedly started by my father. Fritz was as impulsive as ever, but his impulses ran in more dangerous directions now, lighting fires and destroying furniture. He had been removed from all schooling, for he was just as likely to chew his pens to pieces as use them, and though Father Benedict still allowed Mother and Father to bring Fritz to church on Sundays, he insisted that they sit in the back pew, for Fritz had an occasional embarrassing habit of unbuttoning his trousers and attempting to urinate in the font of holy water.

Once, years before, I had asked Fritz what happened when he'd picked up the nutcracker, what he had seen. But he'd clapped his hands over his ears, making a strange cawing noise like that of a crow, and I had not pressed the matter, not wishing to upset him further. My mother defended Fritz as though he were a young child, and that seemed right, for in many ways he remained little more than a child, wanting things and reaching for them without thought, just as he had done on that long-ago Christmas Eve. Now he clapped his hands delightedly as he watched the last few couples dancing, and cheered when Marko Kashelt demonstrated his latest hobby, juggling several balls from the Christmas tree, smashing five of them before Father forbade him to continue.

Since the clock struck eleven, Conrad had been dropping increasingly unsubtle hints that we should leave. But I resisted, and finally my stubbornness paid off. At 11:36, Drosselmeyer left the room with no one to follow him, and I excused myself from Conrad's side.

The downstairs washroom was open for guests, but Drosselmeyer headed straight up the stairs to our family rooms, whistling and humming. I knew exactly where he was going: to the bright, new-built bathroom that serviced my parents' suite. I followed slowly, for although no one would suspect Clara, lovely Clara, I thought it best that Drosselmeyer not see me, not have even the slightest opportunity to feel that something might be off. In the upstairs hallway I peeked around my parents' bedroom doorway just in time to see the bathroom door closing behind him. I could not make myself follow him in there, so I retreated to the hallway and waited, holding the loose folds of my organdy party dress off the floor. She was waiting too; I sensed her there, in the darkest part of me, biding her time. Perhaps she had been there all along.

A few minutes later Drosselmeyer emerged from my parents' bedroom, and I whirled to face him, as though surprised.

"Clara, my child," he said, his voice only slightly slurred with brandy. "Happy birthday, and merry Christmas!"

I laughed, Clara's tinkling laugh, and replied, "It's not Christmas yet, Godfather. Still twenty minutes to go."

He moved forward. I ignored the impulse to back up, holding my ground, sticking one leg out from the other at a ninety-degree angle, pointing my toe daintily, as Clara had always liked to do. Clara had given up the study of ballet when she married, as was expected of a woman of means, but after careful thought I had kept this one mannerism, feeling that it was an easy way to ape my sister, to allay suspicion. Yet Drosselmeyer of all people would not be fooled by such easy signs and symbols. I would have to be careful here.

"And how is your marriage, Clara?" Drosselmeyer asked. "Young Liebermann, he makes you happy?"

"Very happy," I replied, thinking of Conrad, of the way he

would shout at his valet whenever he lost a cufflink. "I have much to thank you for, Godfather Drosselmeyer."

Drosselmeyer smiled indulgently, and I privately congratulated myself, that I had mimicked Clara's inanities so perfectly. Yet behind my answering smile I wondered at the things the world rewarded women for, how easily satisfied they all were, and most of all how beauty covered everything like the tide, enhancing cleverness and expunging sin, erasing all marks, washing the past clean.

"What brings you up here?" Drosselmeyer asked.

"Oh, I was just going up to the roof for some fresh air. I have missed our view of the city."

"I have never seen your view," Drosselmeyer remarked as I opened the door to the rooftop stairway. I was not fool enough to invite him to accompany me, for Drosselmeyer did not like invitations; he wanted to invite himself, to create discomfort, to push in where he wasn't wanted. He belonged to the Sugar Plum Fairy now, and I sensed my time closing, these final moments in which I might ask him questions, demand answers. Thinking of the past five years, I suddenly felt a fool. Why had I not spoken with him before this? No one ever went to Drosselmeyer's house, but I could have invited him to tea, even pretended to meet him by accident in the street. It was not a thing Clara would have done, true, for she did not seek explanations. Yet I felt certain that I could have managed it somehow, if I had only thought to do so.

But it was too late now. Drosselmeyer was following me up the stairs, his footsteps slow and measured, and this was all the time we would have. He was not as drunk as I had first thought, but perhaps that was all to the good. I needed only lure him to the roof; what happened after that was not my concern, and I suspected that the black thing waiting inside me was more than equal to Drosselmeyer, even if he was stone sober. More, I sus-pected that she would *want* him to be sober for this, would not want him to miss a single moment.

And what will happen to me?

The question was an empty one. I knew the Fairy's answer, as well as though she had spoken it in my ear: we had a bargain, and that was all. The aftermath would be my business, my affair. We reached the top of the staircase and there was the city, its houses and shops and mansions all around us. Cold December wind stabbed through my thin dress. This late on Christmas Eve, most of the windows were dark, but it was still a stunning view, the skyline almost dreamlike beneath the clear black sky, the bright moon. In the center of the city, the King's palace welled upward like a monstrous pearl, its white marble walls gleaming in the moonlight.

"Beautiful," Drosselmeyer remarked, his voice unmoved.

"Yes, it is," I said, and for a moment I forgot to be Clara, my voice equally cold, my mind distant. She was with me; I could feel her now, just beneath the surface, straining, almost wild in her impatience, but still I waited because I felt that I was owed this moment, this single moment with Drosselmeyer in which I did not need to fear him, or his tricks.

"You seem different, Clara."

"I am," I replied, with laughter in my voice . . . not Clara's laughter, but my own, deep and full of knowledge. "Do you never wonder how Natasha died, Godfather?"

Drosselmeyer hesitated a moment before replying, and now his voice was guarded, cautious.

"Why do you ask?"

"I wonder sometimes. I wonder whether Natasha was meant to die in one way, and died in another."

I waited for a long minute, but Drosselmeyer did not speak.

"Why did you do it?" I asked, unable to help myself. "Light and dark. What value to you, in dividing us?"

"I had my reasons."

"And what were they?"

"What are all these questions, Clara?" he asked, clasping his hand over mine. His face was open and friendly, just as a godfather's should be, and that was somehow the worst of all.

"You killed my twin."

The goodwill in Drosselmeyer's face vanished suddenly, and he was the godfather I knew, the godfather Natasha had always seen, malicious and secretive.

"An outrageous accusation, child. Why would I do such a thing?"

"I ask myself that every day." I placed a hand on the edge of the wall and drew it back quickly, stung by the cold. Yet the pain was useful, for it helped me to force her back, to gain another minute of myself. "Why would you midwife us and watch over us and even bankroll us, only to kill one of us at the end? And why at Christmas?"

"You've been drinking," Drosselmeyer said flatly. "Go back to your husband, Clara. I will try to forget that we had this—"

"What were you trying to do? It wasn't for us, and I know for damn sure it wasn't for Mother or Father. So what did we do for you? What did you gain?"

Drosselmeyer grabbed my arms, giving me a good shake. He was stronger than I was, but it would not matter, for I could feel her coming now, rising up inside me on black wings. I jerked free of him, slumping my shoulders, relaxing my smile, dropping Clara's mannerisms one by one.

"They never found the clown, Godfather. I have the nutcracker, but where is the clown? Is it still waiting downstairs, hiding in the walls, just in case I might come home?"

"Natasha," he whispered, stumbling backward. His face was a mask of horror, far too much horror for the simple revelation of my presence. He stared at me as though I were something monstrous.

"The clown was going to kill me," I said. "You needed me to die. Why?"

"Clara," he muttered urgently, grabbing my shoulders again. "Where is she?"

"Dead, old man. Dead as your schemes. And someone wants a word with you."

Drosselmeyer's eyes widened, his horror blooming into sudden, blazing terror, and that was a good thing, good enough to replace the answers I would not have. There could be no more delay, for she was here; I felt her inside me, could almost hear the hissing of her breath. She would not wait any longer, and I was not brave enough to ask her to.

"Come," I said, meaning it with all my heart.

Something turned over inside me, like tumblers falling in a lock. I heard a dry rasping, the sound of a snake that had turned inward on itself, rubbing its own rough scales . . . or perhaps the sound of a pair of monstrous black wings, unfurling to the light.

"Natasha," a voice hissed, and it was *her* voice, not diluted as in the case of the rag-picking woman, but full and sibilant, just as I remembered it in the forest.

I bent my head, for what could one do against that voice? The light changed, becoming neither day nor night but some sort of dusky amalgamation of the two, and though I recognized our rooftop, I also knew that we were no longer there, that it was not the house I had grown up in, the rooftop where I had gone to cry on summer days when people praised Clara too much and me too little. We were in the Fairy's world now, not ours, and Drosselmeyer knew it too; I saw terror in his eyes, utter terror, such that I could not even imagine what he saw, what the Fairy looked like beneath all of her disguises, for I somehow understood now that even the draggled horror I had seen in the forest was only a poor representation, that she had a deeper self, one kept cleverly hidden, waiting for moments like this. She had plans for Drosselmeyer, plans long nursed and long perfected, and I turned, not wanting to see, fleeing down the stairs and out the front doors. But no matter how fast I ran, I could still hear Drosselmeyer's screams behind me, muted now but unflagging, following me up the road.

CHAPTER

26

THE BOULEVARD OUTSIDE WAS MEANT TO SEEM REAL, covered as it was with vendors and fishwives and urchins and ragmen, all the accoutrements of our daytime street. Yet it was not quite a success. I saw no faces I recognized, no one to say hello. Our house was there, but I knew none of the buildings around it, identical marble fronts that seemed all built from the same mold. The boulevard had a familiar feeling of quick construction, illusion built on scaffolding, just like that long-ago land covered with false snow. But illusion or not, I was stuck there, for I had no idea how to go home.

Not knowing what to do, I wandered the boulevard, taking in the sights, even accepting a tidbit from time to time, for all of the vendors seemed determined to ply me with free food and drink. When I selected a painting from a stall, a compelling yet disturbing picture whose matter I could never remember later, the vendor did not charge me for this either, saying only, "I am full of gifts." When I tried to insist, he executed a courtly bow, such as one would expect from a dancing master, and then withdrew into his stall, as silent and still as the ballerina in her box.

I am full of gifts.

This phrase remained in my mind, troubling me as I wandered, for I could no longer take it at face value. The Fairy had given me my new life, certainly, but how well had she foreseen its outlines? I had all the outward trappings of happiness: money, a fine husband, a pretty face. But the money I spent so freely was earned by the misery of others, the husband I had thought worth all the world was not what I had believed him to be, and although my pretty face had bought me everything I had, it was not mine.

Looked at in this light, I was not so sure that the Sugar Plum Fairy was truly full of gifts. Rather, I saw her as full of tests. *Forget your fool*, she had said, and I had not listened. Now I wondered whether I would not have been happier if I had taken her advice. Clara's transgressions were real, and they had demanded punishment. But after nearly five years of marriage to Conrad, I could not help but regret that he was the fissure that had divided us, for I knew now that he was as duplicitous in his own fashion as Clara herself, showing one face to the world and another to the servants, merciless to those whose lives did not touch his, certain that he had somehow earned his good luck.

At the water's edge I saw a short dock with a small boat moored, little more than a skiff. Beside it stood a ferryman, tall and gaunt and unsmiling, waiting with his oar. As I approached, he pointed across the river. I expected to see the view I recognized: the bridge; the train crossing; the rising turrets of the King's palace. But I saw only a dark line of buildings and a dock, and after a moment I realized that I was looking at a mirror image of our own waterfront, a mirror image without sunlight, the cheerful skyline of our city fallen into shadow.

"I don't want to go there," I told the ferryman. "Can you take me somewhere else?"

He shook his head. Behind me, I could still hear Drosselmeyer screaming, but the sound was reduced to a strange, liquid distance. There was no reason for me to travel across the river seeking answers; I had given Drosselmeyer to the Fairy, and our dealings were done. Yet something about that dark shore pulled at me, compelling me to seat myself in the skiff.

I half expected the ride to be free, as everything in this land had been, but the ferryman held out his hand for payment, his smooth face free of all expression. I had no coin, not in my flimsy party dress, but when I reached into my pocket I was surprised to find several small objects: a silver crucifix, one of a matched pair that my mother had given to Clara and me on our fifth birthday; a small green velvet bag that smelled of lavender, in which Anastasia had once wrapped my first charm to prevent pregnancy; and, last and most surprising, the scrap of Conrad's shirt I had pulled from the drainpipe. When I had removed my belongings to Conrad's mansion after marriage, I had taken my journal as well, and so far as I knew, the piece of cloth lay there still, crushed flat between the pages. Once upon a time, it had been my most treasured possession, but now I selected it easily, for what did I need with mementos of Conrad? I already had the real article, and if my old beloved was not the fairy-tale prince I had always believed him to be, no scrap of fabric would change that.

Yet I felt a flash of pain as I handed the piece of torn linen to the ferryman. It hurt me to realize how innocent that Natasha had been, innocent enough that she could be satisfied with a bit of shirt in lieu of the life she would not have. Miserable days those might have been, but they had been true days all the same, and I felt a sudden urge to ask for the scrap back, to hold on to that single tangible piece of the real girl I had been. But the ferryman's grim expression told me that he would not take kindly to a request for exchange, so I said nothing, grasping the sides of the boat as we left the shore. As he poled us across, drops of spray hit my face, stinging my cheeks.

When I climbed from the boat, I felt the change immediately. The waterfront was a ruin of abandoned buildings and dark warehouses, with unlit streetlamps sticking out of the snow-covered ground like skeletal black arms. There were no vendors or artisans on this side of the river, only trudging men and women who seemed not to notice my presence at all. All of them were hooded, and try as I might, I could not see any of their faces. When I asked them questions, they did not look at me, only hurried away.

Now I began to be afraid. The far shore was still bathed in sunshine, but there was no light here, only that strange diseased dim. Flakes of snow had begun to swirl before my face. Something smelled off, as though I might look left or right and find myself before a butcher's or a fishmonger. I thought about reboarding the ferry, but the ferryman would likely want additional payment, and I felt that I could not give up another piece of my old self, not when I had so few left to lose.

I turned away from the river and began to walk away from the light, moving ever deeper into the shadow of warehouses and outbuildings. I recognized this place, or at least its bright mirror; it was the waterfront near our neighborhood, though it seemed eerily quiet without the crowd of sailors and dockmen who usually mobbed it during the day. I could no longer hear Drosselmeyer's screams, and that was a relief, but the silence was its own sort of punishment. I had no cloak, only my silken party gown, and this was not the Kingdom of Sweets, where I had hardly felt the cold. The tips of my fingers were turning blue.

Far up the street I saw a tiny figure, not even tall enough to be a child, beckoning me through the snow. A gingerbread man, I felt certain, and with some hesitation I followed it, up the darkened boulevard, through the park, past our old church. That smell of butchery was intensifying, becoming actively unpleasant, and I thought suddenly of Clara, wondering whether she had been properly buried in the Kingdom of Sweets, or whether she still lay on the ground in the clearing, her flesh rotted away into corruption. I had resolved to be done with Clara years before, but in this dark land she rested particularly uneasily. As I followed the gingerbread man, I saw a scrap of blue fabric caught on a nail, blowing in the wind, and knew that it was a piece of her party dress. One of the buildings had been burned in a fire; the charred patches on the wall seemed to ape Clara's silhouette, though when I turned to face them they reverted to what they were: simple, idiot patterns of blackened brick.

"You won't devil me, Clara," I whispered, quickening my pace, for the gingerbread man was already disappearing around a distant corner. He ran very quickly despite his short legs, almost as though he were taunting me, and it occurred to me that this might be the Fairy's doing, her trick to get me lost in this place until I froze to death. Clara was dead; Drosselmeyer was dead, or soon would be; perhaps this was the Fairy's way of tidying up. Yet the gingerbread men in the Kingdom of Sweets had been friendly, or at least willing to talk. So I pushed faster, fighting my way through the curtain of snow, taking shallow breaths to minimize the stench that seemed to grow stronger with every step despite the freezing cold.

At last I came around a corner and saw that the gingerbread man had halted before an enormous mansion, turned grey in the shadow. Without its facade of distinctive white stone, the house

was not immediately recognizable, but at last I placed it: Drosselmeyer's home. Familiar, this place was, yet different, as though
our neighborhood had turned itself inside out. And where were
all the people, the faces I knew? I had seen no one except those
trudging, servile figures, their faces all masked in the same dull
shroud. The fear inside me suddenly seemed to bloom.

"Hello?" I shouted.

There was no answer, only the wind blowing hollowly around
corners. Above my head, the sun was a dull bronze coin, barely
visible through the haze of clouds. Yet I felt watched, observed
coldly by something I could not see. And now, as I approached
Drosselmeyer's mansion, I realized that the creature I had taken
for gingerbread was not gingerbread at all, but a tiny man, almost
a puppet. It turned its head up to mine in the darkening light, and
I saw that its face was shrunken and wizened, lined like a dried
grape, crushed down in a vise with no regard for how the compo-
nents might fit together afterward, one eye a dark, unknowable
pit, but the other even worse because I could not see it, as it was
covered with a patch.

"Godfather," I whispered, and stumbled, would have fallen
had there not been a lamppost within reach. I clung to it, staring
in horror at the creature before me. I had thought she meant to kill
Drosselmeyer, and I would not have mourned him. But this . . . in
my mind's eye I saw our godfather as he had moved through our
childhood: the tall wizard with the silken cape, all agility and
grace, throwing his hands into the air and showering the neighborhood with coins, with tricks. For the first time in a long while
I thought of the mirror I had seen in the Fairy's castle. The shrieking woman. The corridors full of doors.

The grotesque puppet turned, pointing to Drosselmeyer's

house. With a tiny hand, it tugged at the skirts of my party dress, urging me forward.

"I'm not going in there," I said, for it seemed the only thing I was sure of. I did not want to enter Drosselmeyer's terrible mansion, the place where he had lived alone, working his dark magic and planning his dark deeds. The puppet pointed again, and I fancied that its one eye was beseeching. I shook my head. The puppet squealed in dismay, and at the same moment I realized that the lamppost I clutched was not steel but bone, worn white with age and driven into the ground. More such posts lined the street, up and down, placed equidistant like fence posts, each one topped by a ragged nub of splintered joint. The air was darkening around me, shadows closing. The flakes of snow swirling around my face now looked more like ash.

The puppet Drosselmeyer had begun to whimper. It backed away from me, its lone eye darting this way and that, down alleys and into doorways, its twisted mouth quivering. The darkness kept falling, as though dusk were too slow, the entire world rushing toward night, and now I saw it: a vast shadow, standing just behind Drosselmeyer. Above its shoulders loomed a black monstrosity of wings. I could not see its face, but I knew it for what it was: a terrible thing, old and twisted, existing without mercy, its hands hooked into claws. The puppet squealed in terror, then turned and fled down one of the narrow alleys that ran between warehouses. The shadow followed him.

More hooded figures scuttled past, each one carrying a heavy bundle thrown over one shoulder, so heavy that their bodies were bent almost double. They reminded me of mice or ants, for in their down-headed concentration I sensed a shared goal, a shared destination. I followed them deeper into the dark city, past the park and concert hall. The concert hall's doors were wide open, and a bright scarlet smear streaked across and down the steps of the marble staircase, as though someone had swiped them with a giant's paintbrush. The wind howled above our heads, and only now did it occur to me that I might not want to follow these huddled figures, might not want to see where they would go, what they were about.

Of course you do, my mind whispered. *You're the dark sister. You always see. You're doomed to see.*

I stopped, but they were behind me now, so many of these hooded mice, their paths filtering them into this one street, and they pushed me from behind, carrying me along with them toward the King's palace, that palace which no longer gleamed in the night but now seemed to loom above our heads, grey and cracking and dead. And now I realized that what I had taken for the howl of the wind was not the wind at all, but screams . . . so many screams that they had joined together, male and female, high and low, in a symphony of anguish. The tide of hooded figures carried me along, and at last I halted on a high rise overlooking the palace, seeing our destination, the future we would reach, the place where all paths would end.

Before the palace, where the great green lawn had once stood, there was now a vast pit full of flesh. I could not begin to count the bodies, for they were legion, stretching away from me in a confused mass of arms and legs and heads and hair and bloodstained clothing, so much blood that there seemed to be more red than pink in the sinkhole before me. Around the pit, ever more cloaked figures poured in from all corners of the city, passing me as though I were a stone in the middle of the river, flowing around me on both sides, and as I watched, each of them reached the pit and unburdened himself of his bundle, pulling it down and dumping it over the edge. Bodies fell in, faster than I could count or even see them, and suddenly, as though I had only now become able to breathe again, the smell overwhelmed me, the stench of decaying flesh, and I saw that the corpses were covered with flies.

Something grasped my shoulder. I turned, expecting to see another of those hooded figures, but there was nothing behind me but darkness, a vast darkness that seemed to rob the world of what little light remained. The darkness bent over me, cloaking me in shadow, the air reeking of rotten ginger.

"Go home, Natasha Stahlbaum," it whispered. "Our bargain is fulfilled, and we are pleased."

"What is this?" I asked. "What happened here?"

"Nothing you need worry about. The future is not your concern. Forget what you have seen here and go home."

She pulled me away, her fingers gentle enough. But though I closed my eyes, I could still see them, that field of corpses, women and men and children all mixed together in the pit like a dreadful piece of embroidery. Dimly, in the distance, I heard Drosselmeyer squealing again, like an animal caught in a snare. The sound cut off all at once, and when I opened my eyes I was lying in my own bed.

CHAPTER

27

CONRAD'S MOOD WAS SOLICITOUS. HE HAD WATER WAITING, and a headache powder, and coffee; all of the magical treatments needed to revive the overindulgent. I had drunk very little at the party, but still I held my head, trying to recapture my memories of that dark world. But even as I grabbed for them, they receded. I sensed that something dreadful had occurred, and for a desperate, cowardly moment I wished that it had been nothing more than a dream, wished that Drosselmeyer was alive and well, that I still held the choice of whether to fulfill the bargain.

Then I told myself not to be such a ninny. I was at last done with the old fiend with the eye patch, shut of him forever. The thought brought me fully awake, sent me almost hopping out of bed and into the bathroom.

"We found you in one of the rooms!" Conrad called, still in bed.

"My old room?"

"No, not yours . . . another's!" Conrad replied impatiently, and I knew that I had wandered back into my own room, Natasha's room. I tried to remember why I had done that, but it was all a fog of dim light and blinding snow. There was something there, behind the snow; I sought it, but only halfheartedly. If there was some black work afoot, surely it was the Fairy's business now, not mine.

When I emerged from the bathroom, Conrad followed me into my dressing room, holding out a china cup filled with coffee. I took it, though I did not need it, tasting the extra bitterness of headache powder beneath the heat.

"Did anything else happen?"

"Your mother and father had a screaming fight on the stairs, but most of the guests were gone by then. And your cousins locked your uncle Angelo in a broom cupboard, but he woke up and started shouting, so we got him out."

Conrad smiled, his expression one of fond resignation.

"All this, and a drunken wife to boot. If pressed, I would say it was a fairly well-behaved romp for the Stahlbaums."

I smiled back, for I knew he thought himself utterly generous in his indulgence, this boy who even at the age of twenty-five remained just that: a boy, arrogant and satisfied in his position of comfort. He would have liked me to climb back into bed with him; I saw it in his eyes, but I felt that I could not bear his hands on me, not even for an instant. For no reason at all, I thought of the bruise he had left on my wrist, and behind my own eyes I seemed to see a flash of something, a great darkness. But I could not remember it, and after two more cups of coffee, I went off to my own suite and began to dress.

IT TURNED OUT THAT MOTHER AND FATHER HAD INDEED HAD an argument, such a vicious scrap that it drove them both out of the house, Father to his whores and Mother to Madame Margritta's crystal-laden parlor. They stayed out all night, and when they arrived home in the late morning they were both exhausted, so exhausted that they fell into bed right beside each other, all acrimony forgotten in the need to sleep off the night's excess, and did not wake until the late afternoon. So it happened that a maidservant was the first one to go up to the roof to feed Mother's pigeons, and thus became the unfortunate soul who discovered the entire length of the rooftop dappled with blood.

The butler did not even bother to wake my parents before sending for the constabulary, and a search was quickly instituted across the entire neighborhood, constables knocking on doors and ducking in and out of alleys and rubbish bins, looking for a body. It didn't take them long to discover that Drosselmeyer was missing, that he had never returned home the previous night.

Mother and Father were appalled, or at least they did a good job of seeming so, good enough for the constables to exonerate them almost immediately. The servants were questioned thoroughly to no avail, and Clara's old lover Arne must have been impertinent somehow, for my maid told me later that he came back from the constable's office with a black eye and a split lip. No one thought to question the rest of the house—not even to question me, though I had been found asleep in the bedroom closest to the rooftop stairway—and from this I gathered that the constables themselves would not much miss Drosselmeyer, that although his wealth and bribery had likely kept their children in fine clothes and their wives in better jewelry than they could afford, they had not loved him and would not mourn him. Business would go on just fine.

IN THE WAKE OF DROSSELMEYER'S DISAPPEARANCE, PEOPLE IN the neighborhood speculated about who would inherit his fortune, which was assumed to be vast and invested so diversely that not even the King's disastrous war in the Orient and the resulting erosion of the economy had been able to diminish it. But in the end, word leaked out that Drosselmeyer had not had so much as a bank account, that all of his money, if there had been any, had been in cash, and it had vanished, presumably taken by the pack of pretty boys, all of whom promptly decamped to parts unknown, leaving Drosselmeyer's mansion picked clean.

Left empty, the mansion began to decay almost immediately, so that even a bare few months after Drosselmeyer's death, one could walk by and see the broken windows, the peeling paint of the front door, and the vines climbing the outer walls, their tips not flowering but black as they worked their way through the mortar, tearing the brick apart. Old women crossed themselves as they passed the house at dusk, and children would dare each other to dart up and touch the front door, then run squealing away. No one could find a deed to the mansion, and in the absence of one the property could be neither sold nor repaired. And so Drosselmeyer was revealed not as the neighborhood wizard with a bottomless magic purse but rather as a cheap fraudster, his holdings so nefarious that he had not even dared to leave a will.

Oddly enough, after Drosselmeyer's death, the theory began to circulate that the Stahlbaum house itself was unlucky, haunted by a sinister being that had taken not only Drosselmeyer but also Natasha, the dark sister, so long before. These rumors were idle, but they lingered nonetheless, fueled by the fact that they never found Drosselmeyer's body, and by the further disclosure that the medium Madame Margritta refused to visit the Stahlbaum house ever again, would not set so much as a foot over the threshold and would not see my mother at all, not even in her own fortune teller's parlor. When pressed, or offered a free drink—as she often was in the ensuing days, giving rise to a morbid joke that Madame Margritta's drinks were going on Drosselmeyer's bill—the old medium would hint at unseen forces, saying that on her last visit to the house she had seen a green mist hanging in the front hallway, a demonic black dog on the stairs.

The loss of her medium may have pained my mother, but she surely took comfort from all of her newfound friends. Few people shared Madame Margritta's scruples, and my mother was besieged with calling cards from curious visitors despite persistent rumors that Drosselmeyer's ghost waited for unwary souls on the roof, and that the suicide Natasha haunted one of the upper bedrooms and would appear to anyone who dared to spend the night. In this way my mother soon found other wounded souls who shared her addiction to the green bottle, and on the rare occasions when I stopped by the house unannounced, I could usually find her at the heart of a circle of overwrought women, all sparkling eyes and wan, tearstained cheeks. My mother never again seemed to know me as Natasha, and that was a relief, but still I did not enjoy her company, waiting always for that moment when she would look up, her hazy eyes sharpening, and see me for what I was. It was exhausting, particularly since I had little fear of discovery from any other quarter. Conrad no doubt saw similarities between Clara and me, but he would put those down to the natural affinity of sisters, particularly twins. And while Clara had always pleased Father by being beautiful and ostensibly pliable, he had never known her well enough to see past my performance. No, only Mother had sensed something off, and so I did not seek her out, particularly not in the parlor where she went to weep, clasping the green bottle between her hands like a woman at prayer.

———————

NEARLY TWO MONTHS AFTER THE NEWS OF DROSSELMEYER'S death was printed in the newspapers, a tidy little man showed up at our door, dropped a card that introduced him as Mr. Armitage, and asked for a private audience with Mrs. Liebermann.

For a mercy, Conrad was at his club, while his parents were out shooting with old friends, a marquis and his wife who had a private game preserve. Our butler, Kroll, tried to argue against admitting the stranger, but then Kroll would argue against admitting the King himself if Conrad or his father were not home. Kroll felt certain that all women needed protection against male callers, or more likely, against themselves. At such moments I took pleasure in being Natasha, rather than Clara; I ordered Kroll out with a sharp word and led Mr. Armitage to the parlor myself, trying to guess what his business might be. He was neatly put together, this fussy creature, and yet not comfortable; he seemed determined to place distance between us, to avoid my gaze. As soon as we were seated alone in the parlor with a tea tray, he pulled out a sheaf of papers and told me that his firm had been engaged some years before to look after the affairs of Irving Drosselmeyer.

"Affairs?" I asked. I didn't know whether to be more surprised that Drosselmeyer had a first name, or an attorney.

"Yes, his affairs," Mr. Armitage replied, smoothing his well-oiled hair down behind his ears. "Mr. Drosselmeyer engaged our firm of solicitors to make sure that his wishes were honored after his death."

"What wishes?" I asked, pouring him a cup of tea.

"His will is very simple, at least in terms," Mr. Armitage said. "But the bequest is so odd that it has taken us these many weeks to secure royal approval of the disposition. We might not have done, but if I may say so, your godfather wielded an enormous amount of influence, even in death."

"Ah," I said, thinking of the old rumors, that Drosselmeyer was owed favors even by the King himself. I passed Mr. Armitage the cup of tea, noting that he took it but did not drink.

"Now, as I say, we have secured the King's approval of the terms," Mr. Armitage said, waving a sheet of paper that appeared, at least at distance, to bear the King's seal; I had seen it often enough on documents in the desk of Conrad's father, where I sometimes liked to snoop when I was wakeful. "All that remains is for you to accept the bequest."

"What bequest?"

"All of his holdings. Mr. Drosselmeyer maintained a number of accounts around the city under various business entities, hundreds of thousands of marks . . . and then, of course, there is the deed to his house. All to go to you, Miss Stahlbaum . . . ah, pardon me, Mrs. Liebermann. We have spent so many months dealing with these old documents, you see, that it becomes hard to update the news in one's head."

He offered me a perfunctory smile; this was his attempt at a joke. But I could only stare down at the pile of scrawled papers he had placed in my hands: Drosselmeyer's last will and testament. I began to read through it, and found all just as Mr. Armitage had said. Drosselmeyer had left it all to her, to Clara. But why?

"Will you accept the bequest, Mrs. Liebermann?" Mr. Armitage asked impatiently.

I smiled, Clara's charming and slightly bewildered smile, then nodded, thinking of my new resolution. Past was past. Whatever Drosselmeyer had purposed, he was dead, and his intentions no longer mattered. It would be a wonderful thing to have my own

assets, to not have to ask Conrad—or worse, his loathsome father—
for pocket money. Drosselmeyer's mansion, too, would fetch a
pretty sum, if it could ever be sold. In Europe and America, so I
had heard, women were not allowed to own or transfer their own
real property, but here such things had been allowed ever since
the freeing of the serfs forty-odd years before. The idea of having
my own wealth seemed suddenly wondrous, even more of a mir-
acle than the Fairy's so-called gifts. Mr. Armitage offered the pen;
I signed, and so took not only Clara's life but her fortune as well.
And I did not regret it, not even in the mornings when I woke
feeling as though I had missed something, forgotten some crucial
event, when the past seemed to nag at me like a throbbing tooth.
But I refused to allow it room. Drosselmeyer was dead; Clara was
dead; I had fulfilled my bargain with the Fairy, and we were quits.
If I was to have any chance at a normal life, any ability to fit into
Clara's skin, it would begin now. And so I resolved firmly: No
more magic. No more nonsense. I was Clara Liebermann, née Stahlbaum, and that was all I would ever be.

CHAPTER
28

THAT SHOULD HAVE BEEN THE END OF IT. BUT IT WAS NOT.

THE TOYMAKER

Who is the third who walks always beside you?

When I count, there are only you and I together

But when I look ahead up the white road

There is always another one walking beside you

Gliding wrapt in a brown mantle, hooded

I do not know whether a man or a woman

—But who is that on the other side of you?

—*The Waste Land*

T. S. Eliot

CHAPTER

29

I T WAS IN THE EIGHTH MONTH AFTER DROSSELMEYER'S DEATH that I began to feel distinctly uneasy whenever I left the house. I had the sense of being followed, watched closely by something I could never quite see. I would be out walking, looking idly through the wares of the many stalls in the flower markets, when I would catch a shadowy figure at the corner of my vision and know that of all the people on the boulevard, I alone was the one it observed. But when I whirled to look, there was nothing, not even something that might have fooled my sight: a hanging dress for sale, or the tip of my own sash blowing in the wind.

The feeling persisted. We would be at the theater, where I might or might not pay attention—plays were often interesting, but unlike Clara, I found myself bored to tears by the ballet—and I would sense someone sitting just behind me in the box, in the seats that Conrad's parents never bothered to use. Sometimes I thought I could even feel the lightest touch on my shoulders, a faint mist of breath on the back of my neck. But when the lights came up, there was no one behind us, not even the hint of an indentation in the chair. We would leave after the curtain, my gloved fingers tucked neatly into the crease of Conrad's elbow, and as I climbed into the carriage I would feel a teasing brush of air on my cheek, like a kiss from an old acquaintance. But it wasn't Conrad, who always handed me up the steps like a gentleman, remaining on the ground to make sure I didn't fall, and when I collapsed with a sigh into my customary corner of the velvet upholstery, it sometimes seemed to me that the seat was already warm.

Conrad knew nothing of this, and in any case he was busy elsewhere. The King's worst fears had been realized: the peasants and industrial workers had combined and found common ground, and had even staged several small riots to demand better housing, better pay, better conditions. All that summer and fall, Conrad's club of noblemen met several nights each week, trying frantically to think of ways to quell the uprising. They considered all sorts of outlandish actions to take, except the simplest and most obvious solution of building better housing, augmenting pay, and improving conditions. Conrad would not hear of such a step, not even when I suggested it in Clara's mincing, feckless voice. They could not give in to such demands, he said, or the peasants would want it all.

My father, who was a foundry owner and thus beset by similar concerns, had tried to join Conrad's political club. But his lack of noble blood had doomed him, and the rejection had wounded him so acutely that he even stopped making his tiresome visits to our house. So I was left on my own several nights each week, a development that pleased me. Among the many difficulties of being Clara, perhaps the greatest was the constant vigilance, the endless performance she demanded. It took a great deal of work to pretend to be such a fool, and only when I was alone could I truly relax. On the nights when Conrad and his parents were out, I would retreat to the library with a glass of wine and a good book and feel almost like my old self.

Yet I was not alone, not anymore. The shadow sat just over my shoulder, watching me even in the library. Sometimes the candles flickered without a draft, dripping wax across the tables or, worse, my open book. I felt myself considered, studied from all angles, and under the pressure of that cold regard I often closed my book and retreated to my bedroom. Perhaps it was my imagination, but I thought the nutcracker, too, seemed more alert, almost as though he were on guard. Several times I found him marching back and forth from wall to wall, his saber in one hand and his other hand held out before him like that of a conductor. As autumn deepened toward winter, I began going to bed earlier than I had at any time since I was a child, and if I heard a noise in the silence of my bedroom, I did not look for the source, only buried my head beneath the covers and waited for sleep to come.

ONE DAY IN EARLY OCTOBER, AFTER YET ANOTHER ARGUMENT about my excessive familiarity with the servants, Conrad brought me home a gift as a peace offering.

"They're all the rage in the city," he said, smiling proudly as I unwrapped the ribbons from the pretty box, which had been painted with a charming scene of children picnicking near a riverbank. "Hard to find too; I had to outbid several others with the shopkeeper."

I drew back the soft cloth and saw a figurine of a reindeer, beautifully carved from glass. The legs were separate pieces, attached by some sort of cunning crystalline hinges I could not see. I reached to examine it, but Conrad grabbed the figurine before I could.

"Watch!" he said. "Watch what it does!"

He strode to the dining room, heedless of the two maids who were trying to lay settings for lunch, and placed the figurine at the head of the table.

For a moment the reindeer only stood there, a prism, its many surfaces reflecting sunlight around the room. Then, with a slight tremor, almost a shiver, it leapt into motion and began to move down the table, prancing just as a real deer might, legs working and tail twitching behind. As it moved in and out of the bands of sunlight that lay on the tablecloth, its crystalline body broke the light into rainbows and sent them dancing along the walls.

"Isn't it clever?" Conrad asked. "You can't even see the clock-work."

I did not reply. Cold had seized me, a cold I had almost forgotten. I couldn't see the clockwork; no one could, because there was none. The reindeer was moving of its own accord, and never mind that it was made of glass. That only made things more clear.

"Who made it?" I asked. My voice seemed to stick in my throat.

"Ah," Conrad said, and went back to dig into the box. "There's a card, I remember. But it's all very mysterious."

He pulled a folded white card from the box. It occurred to me that another man, a different man, the man I might have found and married one day if only I had been a bit less young and foolish, would have simply handed me the card to read for myself. But Conrad had already opened it.

"Here it is," he said. "Designed by Orlov."

I stared at the reindeer, which had ceased prancing and bent to drink water from the bowl of cut flowers in the center of the dining table. In the sunlit silence, I could hear each tiny slurp of its tongue.

"The shopkeeper says these Orlovs will be the toys of the season," Conrad told me, perching on the edge of the sofa. "There aren't many of them, and the toymaker doesn't take special orders. People will be dueling over the things before Christmas."

"No doubt," I replied, though my voice seemed very far away in my own ears. No one had ever seen him again, that seventh boy covered with scars. He had left his nutcracker, which after all was only supposed to march and bow, and vanished into the night.

"Don't you like it?" Conrad asked, his voice turning sullen. His brow had furrowed in a gesture I knew well, Conrad's version of a pout.

"I do," I said, trying to sound enthusiastic. The reindeer had moved to the edge of the table now and was looking down, judging the distance so that it could jump from table to chair and chair to floor. From there it could go anywhere, I thought, and in another moment I was moving, snatching the thing off the table. I felt a pinch; it was trying to bite me, straining in my hand so that its teeth could close on a fold of skin. The branched prongs of its horns stabbed into my palm, sharp as needles.

"I love it," I said to Conrad, smiling brightly; Clara's smile, free of all darkness and doubt. "I want to keep it in my bedroom."

Conrad nodded, cheerful again, and kissed me on the forehead. He forgot the reindeer almost as soon as he had given it, certainly did not notice when the thing disappeared entirely after I threw it into the river the next day. But though Conrad had forgotten, I did not. In the coming weeks I asked around among such acquaintances as I had not wholly alienated, and thus heard more about the mysterious Orlov. No one knew where he could be found, not even the shopkeepers who sold his wondrous creations. He dealt in secrecy, was rumored to be a wizard, a genius in the mold of Tesla or Edison. But this Orlov had no such distinguished colleagues, because the scientific community was already disgusted with him. He refused to attend academic conferences at the universities, to lecture or speak, or publish his methods. He did not deal in the great new technologies of the times, engines or electricity or steel, or even in something shamefully prosaic like plumbing, some baseborn branch of science that would make up for its lack of glamour by immeasurably improving human existence.

No. Orlov made toys.

CHAPTER

30

IN MID-OCTOBER A YOUNG MAN WAS FOUND DEAD DOWN BY the docks. There was no shortage of death among the poor that autumn, but this man's murder seized the imagination of the entire city, for it had been achieved in such an ingenious way as to leave even the constabulary utterly baffled. The victim had been killed inside his shabby furnished room, the door locked from the inside. He had not merely been shot or stabbed, as one would expect from the waterfront and its denizens. No, the newspapers said he had been savaged, nearly torn to pieces, as though by a wild animal.

There were no wolves in the city—though we sometimes heard them howling on distant hills during carriage rides to the estates of friends—yet the early speculation that a rogue wolf might have taken the taste for blood was enough for the King to declare a curfew at dusk. When I asked Conrad how a wolf might open a locked door, he had no answer, but said we should not question the King.

This subservience on Conrad's part was new, but not entirely a surprise. The King had now attended several meetings of Conrad's club, and each time Conrad would regale me with every word the great personage said, as though Christ himself had descended to join them in their grousing. Just before Hallow's Eve, Conrad advised Kroll that, on the King's advice, we would not offer sweets to the poor children of the city on the festival night, as tradition dictated, but would rather shut the back door and keep the kitchen dark, so that they would not knock. In the resulting row—one of our most acrimonious—Conrad told me that the steadily increasing unrest in the city and the surrounding lands had made the King nervous. He had advised all of the city's noblemen to take a firm hand with the peasants, both those who worked their land and those they might meet in the street, and offer them no charity that might incite them to greater presumption.

This was in keeping with the character of the King, but I was surprised that Conrad should take such wisdom to heart. He was not a man of original mind, my Conrad—his choice of Clara showed that, if nothing else—but I had not thought him such a fool. When the ragged children stood outside our house on Hallow's Eve, hoping for treats where they had always been before, Conrad explained to me, with the air of a man who knows all, that the children would take the sweets home to their parents, who then traded them at market for coal or scraps of wood. To me, this seemed an even more pitiable state of affairs than the children eating the sweets themselves, but I saw that Conrad did not think so. Worse, I saw that he was not being mean or even spiteful, as so many of our noble friends liked to be in their dealings with the poor. He truly believed he was being somehow swindled by their desperation; he begrudged even the few pfennigs a starving family might reap from such a scheme. And now, looking at my husband, I began to wonder whether I had ever truly loved him, whether I had even known him, or whether I had simply taken his shape and filled it with the virtues I wanted, inventing myself a prince, just as Clara had done. I wondered that I had ever wept over Conrad, or gasped his name in the night, and when I closed my eyes I seemed to see again that terrible darkness behind them, the darkness that had never left me even though I had settled things, put all to right.

"Clara?" Conrad asked. "What are you looking at?"

"Nothing," I replied. "Nothing at all."

THE DAY AFTER HALLOW'S EVE, I SENT MY FOOTMEN TO BUY OUT every sweetshop on the Prospekt. When they returned, carts loaded with bundles of boxed chocolates and wrapped boiled sweets, I directed Ivan, my driver, toward the slum district on the far side of the river where most of the city's poor lived. I had never been there, but Ivan seemed to know the area well, and there we threw the sweets from the windows, from the coach box, from the foot of the carriage, while more than a hundred children ran after us down the street, their excited screams echoing among the run-down buildings and their parents staring at us from open doorways, confounded. The shadow that had tracked me for months seemed suddenly gone; I found myself laughing out loud, and it was only as I threw the last of the sweets out the window that I realized I was speaking, whispering the words to myself: *I am full of gifts*.

Conrad knew nothing of this. Using Drosselmeyer's money, I had begun to augment the pay of both Ivan and my two footmen in return for their discretion. Like most of the servants, they disliked Conrad and absolutely loathed his parents, so secrecy was no hardship to them. The newspapers carried a small note about the occurrence—Mother Christmas, they called me, riding by in her sleigh—and the King was reputedly angry enough to send a detachment of the army down to investigate the matter. But if any of the riverbank denizens had seen anything to identify me, they kept it to themselves, and at any rate the army's attention was soon needed elsewhere. The protests in the center of the city were growing more heated, peasants and workers marching together under banners and signs, their differences forgotten. The newspapers said that several small skirmishes had taken place, a few workers injured. But even the papers eventually forgot to pay attention to the riots, for as November marched onward and ice began to freeze across the river, five more men were murdered down by the docks.

These victims were as anonymous as the first, being without name or family, their deaths tied together only by the brutality of the killings, the locked doors behind which they had died, and the odd fact that all of them had been extraordinarily handsome men in life. The constabulary proceeded diligently, but they got nowhere, though the King raged daily, threatening to replace them all, lock them in the city jail, or send their families to the farthest icy reaches of the kingdom. Conrad's uncle, who knew the head of the constabulary well, told us that while the constables had made little progress in solving the murders, their efforts down by the docks were not wholly wasted; several petty theft and smuggling operations had been dismantled, and a fair deal of stolen property recovered. When Conrad's father asked whether they had made any progress in discovering the ringleaders of the protests, Conrad's uncle said he thought not, and the duke threw his pipe across the room, shattering it into wooden shards.

I knew who the murdered men were, could not have been more certain if they stood before me, gilded angels now grown out of the last of their boyhood and reduced to working the seedier areas of the city. Drosselmeyer chose beautiful boys, but they did not emerge from his tutelage either good or kind. Without their master, they would have created their own small operations, robbery or confidence games or gambling dens. That most of them had locked their doors, barricaded themselves in—the newspapers even said that one victim had stocked in provisions enough to last a small siege—suggested that they had expected to come to bad ends, as well they might.

This all sounded fine, and yet, and yet—when I pictured the scene, the locked rooms and, behind each door, a handsome man cowering for his life, I saw something else. If one wished to kill a man for business, one would shoot him with a revolver, or knife him in the throat. One would not rip him to pieces with implements unnamed. Such brutality seemed personal, too personal for the denizens of the docks. The Sugar Plum Fairy could do such a thing, might even enjoy it, but I could not see what she might gain. Drosselmeyer was dead; surely his incidental tools would mean nothing to her. My thoughts came back again and again to the mysterious toymaker, Orlov. But I had no evidence to connect him with the murdered men, and because he hid himself so successfully, I had no way to even find out whether he was the same scarred boy I believed him to be. In the end I did not bother to contact the constables, for what information could I really give them? Drosselmeyer's boys were orphans, rough trade. No one knew anything about them, not even their names, for Drosselmeyer kept them interchangeably; they came and went, and so many of them looked the same. So I kept my hidden knowledge to myself, even when the information emerged that two of the sets of murdered men had been brothers . . . not only brothers, but twins.

CHAPTER

31

THE COLD DEEPENED. SNOW COVERED THE CITY IN A PRETTY blanket; the lakes iced over, and well-to-do children took to the glassy surfaces with skates. On the waterfront the lamps were lit up and down the docks, so that sailors and loaders could continue working until suppertime. Open carriages were traded for closed; enormous Christmas trees began to proliferate in the front windows of the mansions that lined the boulevard, and as the wealthy of the city began to hunt down Christmas gifts, Orlov's name seemed to be everywhere. His creations were indeed in great demand that season, with every wealthy father scouring the markets and department stores, determined to procure an Orlov for his children. But the genuine articles—dogs that leapt and barked of their own accord; clocks that announced the hour in rich, deep tones; dolls that moved and even spoke—were increasingly difficult to find, and desperate parents despaired. No one quite seemed to know where this Orlov lived, or how to contact him directly. The shopkeepers who sold the toys were no help, for someone had put a fear upon them, deeper than the power of money, and they would reveal nothing, not even how they received their goods. And so, despite the popularity of his creations, Orlov's name began to take on a sinister tone in the city. People whispered that he was not a scientist or even a wizard, but a sorcerer, much like the Drosselmeyer of old. Yet they did not stop seeking his toys.

I was the only one who was not charmed. I already had a genuine Orlov, a nutcracker that brandished its sword and snarled at the slightest movement, frightening the servants and sometimes waking me in the night. Drosselmeyer had given the nutcracker to Clara, but I had no idea whether it thought it was protecting Clara or me. There were no answers to be had, so I did not buy any of Orlov's creations, not even when I saw a gingerbread man being hawked for an exorbitant sum by a vendor down at the docks, a gingerbread man who ran merrily along the table, tiny arms and legs flailing as he spoke and laughed and even wept.

ONE NIGHT IN EARLY DECEMBER, WE JOURNEYED ACROSS THE city to have dinner with Conrad's grandparents. Conrad's grandmother was horribly boring, her remaining energies expended on orthodox religion and flower arrangement, but even she was not as bad as Conrad's grandfather, whose political ideas aligned beautifully with the ideologies of Deuteronomy, and who would have been quite happy to see a return to the days when servants were flayed over an open fire for delivering lukewarm tea.

Clara's guileless face was a great help at these dinners; she had always been one to stare vapidly, murmuring only such occasional inanities as she thought were expected, that it was no difficult feat to imagine, to wander, to construct an entire secret life behind that beautiful face while the world turned round it. But these occasions had become more difficult since Conrad had joined his damnable club, for he and his grandfather would happily complain about the many encroachments by the peasants until the sun came up, while I was forced to listen to Conrad's grandmother explain the difference between hothouse orchids and wild. At such times I found myself hating my husband, and even more, hating our world, which rewarded women only for dumb endurance. Sitting at that absurdly overdressed dinner table, it occurred to me for the first time that I could have been more, even without Clara's face, Conrad's wealth and family. Perhaps we could all have been more.

When we returned home, I dismissed the maids. I had never gotten used to having people help me dress, and though I needed someone to pull my laces tight, I still preferred to undress on my own. For a time the maids had giggled over this, thinking perhaps I had something to hide, a hideous birthmark or perhaps an extra toe. But eventually they came to accept it as simply one more oddity of the young duchess, like the nutcracker that stood beside the fireplace, snarling if anyone got too close.

Dimly, I heard Conrad moving around in his room on the far side of the suite, discarding his suit and putting on his nightshirt. I could even smell him, for he had not bothered to wash out the foul hair ointment that he affected now, another of the King's recommendations. Once we might have talked the evening over, even laughed about it, and then fallen into bed together, giggling as we tried to pull off each other's nightclothes. But those days were gone, and I certainly didn't want his attentions tonight. In truth, since Hallow's Eve, I had not wanted them at all. On the rare occasions when he visited my bed, I tried to remember the nights when we were young, when he would climb through my window and I would want him with a desperation that closed on madness.

But even if the past still held that sort of power, it could not measure up to the horrible memory of the children outside our house, their bewildered faces as they considered our dark doorstep, their bare feet in the snow. Conrad had never found out about my little excursion; even after the papers described Mother Christmas, he never thought to connect the incident with his wife, with simple Clara, who despite her mystifying sympathies for the servants had never shown any real signs of rebellion. So I was not found out, and yet when Conrad climbed on top of me, his brow furrowed in that supreme concentration that I had once found so bizarrely endearing, I found myself wishing that the footmen might let something slip, that Conrad would discover the whole thing. I wanted to see his face.

Putting out the light, I went quickly to sleep. But I woke only a few hours later, chilled by the sure feeling that something was wrong. I could hear nothing, not even Conrad's drunken snores. For a few minutes I lay there in the darkness, trying to go back to sleep. But that uneasy feeling persisted, and in the darkness I found the shreds of the dream that had preceded it. I was in a city, a strange, doomed city covered in snow, and the air stank of blood and corruption. I had dreamed this dream before, I thought, but I had never been able to remember it. I could barely remember it now, and yet it gnawed at me like a forgotten task, or some mistake I had made.

Now something bumped in the sitting room. Squinting at the small clock that ticked away on the mantelpiece, I saw that it was exactly three o'clock, the very darkest hour of the night, the hour when I used to hear Drosselmeyer and his boys come roaring down the street. But they were gone now, all gone. So what was the thing I could hear now, moving on the far side of the sitting room, come out of the dark?

Whatever it is, my mind whispered, *it doesn't belong to Conrad. You're the one who has earned it. You have brought it here.*

I shook my head at that, almost frantically. We were done, the Fairy and I. Weren't we?

I climbed from my bed, piling the many layers of covers at the foot. The floor was freezing, but I didn't hunt around for my slippers as I would normally do. I heard footsteps, the gentle thump of small items being picked up and replaced. My heart thudded mechanically, like the heartbeats I had once heard in the Kingdom of Sweets, seeming to mock my certainty of closure, that high cupboard I had protected all these years. What did I know of such creatures, how they thought or what governed their decisions? How did I know when the dealing was done?

Opening my bedroom door, I found the sitting room full of moonlight, a series of broken shafts that fell to the carpet and then elongated in a strange perspective, growing larger from left to right. As I crossed the room, I made an unconscious game of it, the same old game that Clara and I had once played with such shadows: tiptoeing along, trying to step only in the light, always avoiding the dark. Clara would have come along on my wild ride through the far side of the city, I thought. She would have thrown sweets out the windows, just as I had, laughing at the delight in the children's faces. She would have enjoyed it, even if she—

A shadow stood in Conrad's doorway.

I halted in the middle of the sitting room. For a long moment I could see only a black silhouette, the outline of long hair visible against the pale walls. Something struck me, some memory I could not quite retrieve. I parted my lips and found my mouth parched.

"What do you want?"

The figure did not respond, only stood still, watching me. I could feel menace there, lying heavy upon me, as though regard had weight. After a long, helpless moment, during which that unseen but murderous gaze seemed to bear upon me like lead, I asked, "What have I done?"

The figure shifted slightly in the darkness. Its lower half moved into a shaft of moonlight, revealing the ruins of a dress of indeterminate color, little more than faded rags that swirled emptily around the thing's legs. Stumpy legs they were, peglike, streaked with mud, and after a moment I saw that one of the legs was bent, the calf turned outward in a dancer's pose.

Outward at a ninety-degree angle.

I scuttled backward, all the way to my vanity table, rocking it against the wall, never taking my eyes from the shadow that was coming for me now, moving silently across the sitting room.

"Natasha," it whispered, and it was not the sibilant hiss of the Fairy but *her* voice, lilting and promising. As the shadow moved through my doorway and stood at the far post of my bed, regarding me steadily, I smelled it as well, a hint of decay that blended easily with the French perfume Clara had worn since our twelfth birthday. Moonlight shone through the tatters of its dress, illuminating hands that had long since gone to rot; the fingers ran with rivulets of some dreadful substance that could have been green but under the moonlight shone no color but black. As she moved in and out of the shadows, I saw that she wore the ruby bracelet; a foul thing now, its links covered with verdigris.

"What do you want, Clara?"

"I have made my own bargain," she whispered. "She said I could kill you."

She was stalking me now, following in my footsteps as I retreated around the bed, breath hissing between her teeth. I could not see her face beneath her dark hair, which hung in strings and clumps that blocked even the gleam of the moon. I was afraid, but beneath the fear I felt a sudden spark of anger as well. Clara was supposed to be dead, but here she was. Somehow she had found a way to break the rules yet again, escape consequence, just as she had done all her life.

Now she came around the bed, backing me against the vanity table. One of those corpse-black fingers, half decayed, reached out to touch my cheek. I flinched but did not pull back. Somewhere, I reminded myself, beneath the withered skin and the dark hair that had once been mine, lived my twin sister, Clara. Beneath the skin, I had not changed, so why should Clara, who would not have harmed anyone, save by carelessness? Yet that carelessness had been so monstrous that it would sometimes trump outright cruelty, and for all my good heart, I had strangled Clara when given the chance. We had spent long years in different places, my twin and I; who knew what we were now, what we had become?

"I thought you were dead, Clara."

Clara giggled, not her old charming giggle, but a sound like the screech of a rusty carriage wheel.

"How could I die, Nat, when you still live?"

I blinked, not understanding.

"Did the Sugar Plum Fairy bring you back to life?"

"She's no Fairy, Nat. She's a devil. She makes use of all things, even me."

I closed my eyes at this, but that was no help, for the woman I had seen in the castle's mirror was right there, eyes wide and mouth stretched in an endless howl. I couldn't move, not even when Clara's hands went to my throat, squeezing mercilessly.

Below us something snarled, and a moment later Clara released me, staggering backward. Looking down, I saw the nutcracker, saber in hand, its tufted eyebrows bent downward in rage. As

Clara straightened, it moved to stand in front of me, growling like a dog, waving its saber back and forth.

"My nutcracker," Clara said. "So you even took that."

"I'm sorry, Clara." And I was. I had had my revenge, just as the Fairy promised, but it was no revenge I would ever have imagined inflicting on my twin. Nearly five years had now passed since that long-ago Christmas Eve, but time ran differently in the Kingdom of Sweets; that night in the castle had seemed to stretch forever between our midnight and dawn. And now, for the first time in a long while, I thought of the clock I had seen just beside the mirror, the hands standing at eighteen. I longed to ask Clara where the hands stood now, but she had turned away from me and begun to examine my things, running her black-grimed hands over the vanity table, the boxes of jewels that rested on top. Her touch spoke of covetousness, and my old anger resurfaced. None of this would have happened if Clara had been able to keep her hands from other people's belongings. Then I wondered why I should still feel possessive over Conrad, or even over the jewelry he had given me, when I had never cared about such things, when I had begun to routinely lock my bedroom door at night. *Your emotions are so divorced from sense,* the Fairy had said, and that was only the truth.

"What do you want, Clara?" I asked. "What will it take, to make you go away?"

"Why, Nat, I want my face back. My life. I want what you stole. If I can't kill you now, I will wait."

"For what?"

"Even magic has its tides, Nat. They ebb now, but soon they will flow. We are all waiting."

"Who is we?" I asked, thinking again of the clock, the hand standing still at eighteen.

But Clara said nothing more, only flickered and vanished.

CHAPTER

32

HERE IS A THING I NEVER KNEW ABOUT MY TWIN SISTER: she could be vengeful. Spiteful. The old Clara, the Clara I knew, had been as incapable of nursing a grudge as she was of suffering a broken heart. But she had clearly acquired some education in her travels. She liked best to wait, in rooms I meant to enter, behind doors I was about to open, on the staircase when I was preparing to come down for breakfast. When I read in the library, she would lean over my shoulder so that her hair dangled above the page, smelling of rotten molasses and blocking the light. When I picked up a pastry from my plate at table, I would like as not find the corner of it nibbled and torn away, the edges surfaced by a black grime that looked like traces of coal, or licorice. Sometimes Clara would even trail me through the city when I went out, riding with me in my carriage and following in my footsteps to the dressmaker or the bookshop. She meant to take even my ordinary pleasures, those small things that made my days passable, and as the days went by, I realized that her tactics were working.

Winter had come, and I began to drop weight, unable to eat or sleep, always watching out for her, standing on my guard.

No one saw Clara but me, and I felt that this was just as it should be. This was between the two of us, as it had ever been, and I would have been almost disappointed if Conrad had spotted her, or one of the maids. Despite the horror of her initial appearance, she was, after all, only Clara, and I was determined to prove that I was still more than a match for her, ghost or no.

But I also gradually became sure that Clara had not returned only to devil me. Her presence was too inconsistent. Sometimes days would go by without a glimpse of her. The Sugar Plum Fairy had said she was pleased, but if she bore me no ill will, then clearly there was no goodwill either. Clara had made her own bargain, and the Fairy had offered me up, but in exchange for what? I had given her Drosselmeyer; what was Clara meant to do?

Sometimes I found myself regretting the death of Drosselmeyer—he, I thought, might have had some idea—but not often, for I knew how self-serving such regret was, and I was not Clara, to take up and discard others as they met my purposes. I had helped to kill Drosselmeyer, or at least remove him from our world, and so I had no right to wish for his assistance now. Yet had he been alive, I thought I might have been brave enough to ask for it. I had begun to feel a strange kinship with our godfather, who had spent his life hunted by these dark shadows. He had been clever enough to keep himself from the Fairy's clutches for a long time, and for that I respected him. She had found me with no difficulty at all when she wanted me, showed up on my very doorstep, but she had not been able to do the same to Drosselmeyer, and I found myself wondering why. He had thwarted her, protected himself somehow, but there was no one I could go to for answers. Everything of Drosselmeyer was gone . . . everything, I realized one morning, but his abandoned house.

WHEN I WAS A CHILD, DROSSELMEYER'S HOUSE HAD LOOMED over the neighborhood like a castle in a fairy story, an impregnable fortress where the wicked enchanter worked his malevolent deeds. Shortly after receiving the will from the tidy Mr. Armitage, I had contacted the city's best property agents and contracted them to put the white stone mansion on the market. There it had sat for the past nine months, and the accelerated disrepair into which it had fallen only seemed to enhance its fabulous credentials. The high walls were cracking, the darkened windows covered with grime. Ivy had climbed the house, splitting the fine stonework, and the paint was peeling from the iron sculptures that lined the front walk. I touched one of these sculptures, a pretty representation of a leaping deer, then withdrew my hand as a nest of dark spiders boiled from its marble base, swarming over the toe of my heeled boot.

Several gentlemen had been in to look at the house, the property agents assured me, but none had approached a serious offer, and most left the viewing looking decidedly ill. Neighborhood gossip said that one prospective buyer, a steel manufacturer, had begun to scream as he beheld the enormous looking glass in Drosselmeyer's front hall, and he would not be comforted, not even after they bundled him into his carriage and sent him home. As I hesitated at the foot of the front steps, I found myself thinking not of such tales but of the man himself, our godfather as he had been in my youth: the sinister figure in cloak and top hat, standing beneath the lamppost at the very darkest hour of night. The Fairy had dealt with Drosselmeyer, dealt with him severely, and yet that was not the comfort it might have been. If Clara had returned, bent on revenge, was it not conceivable that the old sorcerer might return too? And who would he wish to close his dealings with, if not me?

Taking a deep breath, I started up the steps.

DROSSELMEYER'S HOUSE WAS NEITHER SO BIG NOR SO IMPOSING as it had once seemed from the outside. Indeed, the entryway was even smaller than that of my parents' house. The walls, denuded of whatever decoration they might once have boasted, were only white-painted brick, now yellowing with age. Pale rectangles denoted where rugs had lain on the cracking floorboards, and the air smelled of mildew and must. I kept my cloak and gloves on, for the rooms were cold, bone-cold, and my own icy breath preceded me everywhere I turned.

The house had been picked clean, the only valuable piece that remained the enormous looking glass, which stood just to the left of the front door. I wondered how it had survived pillage by Drosselmeyer's boys, for it was a fine piece, edged in silver. But of course it was exceptionally large, more than ten feet tall; perhaps they had simply been unable to shift it. Perhaps Drosselmeyer had used the same trick as he had with his portrait, so that even the most determined effort could not dislodge it. Thinking of the manufacturer who had been reduced to sobs, and again of the other mirror in the Kingdom of Sweets, I ignored my reflection, walking past without so much as a glance.

The property agents had done their jobs, more or less; the interior of the house had been restored to its best state. But there were still odd elements here and there, things they had missed, disquieting glimpses of what the house had been. In the flooring of one of the upstairs bedrooms lay an old bloodstain, scoured and scrubbed to a light red, but still visible. In another room I found a crescent moon on the wall, a black moon, the shape burned into the brick. The upstairs windows were covered with a smeary grime that did not wipe away, not even when I tried to scrape through it with one fingernail. In the dining room, several pieces of furniture lay strewn across the floor: chair legs, half a table, a broken strand of crystal from a dead chandelier.

All of this seemed indescribably sordid in the light of my lamp. Opening the rich plum-colored curtains did not help, for when I drew them back, grey moths fluttered out, dozens of them, and the room's details were revealed as even uglier in the full light of day. As I looked around, I could not escape a rogue feeling of pity for Drosselmeyer, who was after all only a sad old man full of tricks, unloved in life and deserted in death. I could not imagine that he had been happy in this house, which had clearly been constructed as a fortress, or even in the wider world outside, where he must have always been watching, on guard, his entire life defined by wariness and graft, all friends bought and paid for. Even the massive library at the back of the house was empty, full of sham covers behind which no books lay. Drosselmeyer was not the only rich man in our neighborhood to pull that trick, but still I wondered at the effort: who had he been trying to impress?

The mirror still stood in the entrance hall. I tried not to look at it, but I could not ignore it either, and so I sat down on the staircase, considering the glass from an oblique angle. No prints or smears obscured the surface, which looked freshly polished, as though the property agents had been in just this morning. Yet the rest of the house was covered in dust.

For long minutes I considered this discrepancy. Drosselmeyer had taken extraordinary measures to keep the Fairy from him; at any rate, she could not simply enter his house in one of her many human guises, as she had walked into mine. She had been forced to bargain with me, a bargain I now recognized as far beneath her, yet it was the only way she could get to him. Drosselmeyer's whole house might well be ringed with spells and enchantments to keep her at bay, but I didn't think so. The mirror was special. Nowhere else in his decaying manse, not even the library, had I sensed anything comparable to the force exerted by this one piece. Also, of course, there was the fact that the glass had remained here at all, when it would have fetched a good sum anywhere in the city, when even the candles had been stolen from the chandeliers. Drosselmeyer's boys had not dared to touch the mirror, I decided, let alone try to move it. They would have been warned not to.

After another long moment's thought, I moved to stand in front of the glass.

The girl who stared back at me was Natasha, and that was a strange relief, to see no hint of Clara there. But she was not the Natasha I had always known. I had not aged, not precisely, but there was something austere in this version of myself, a hardness to the planes and contours of my face that I had never seen. Yet I sensed authenticity in the image before me; it seemed a clearer picture of me, my true self, than even that long-ago daguerreotype. My eyes were twin spots of darkness, lacking even a gleam, only absorbing the daylight. As the minutes passed, I came to notice a shadow over my left shoulder, a vague shape that moved when I moved, so that I could not get a good look at it no matter which way I turned.

"Is it you?" I asked, leaning so close that my breath misted the frozen glass. The bargain was done, but I knew her now; she might decide to do anything, might even decide that our dealings were not done, after all.

But the shadow did not answer, only lingered behind my shoulder, barely visible in the glass. At the same moment I felt something move behind me, heard a scrape in the hall. Clara had not accompanied me on this little trip, which seemed a mercy, but now I wondered if there were not worse things in this house. From the kitchen I heard Drosselmeyer's voice, hoarse and drunk.

"Light! Dark! I've done it! Let's have another, boys! I'll be free yet!"

The voice was true, no echo but alive. In the next moment I smelled ale, and heard the sounds of some mad revel taking place in another part of the house. The dead, dust-covered chandeliers seemed to suddenly glow with life. And now here came Drosselmeyer himself . . . a younger Drosselmeyer, his hair not yet threaded with grey, dancing down the staircase with those lithe movements I remembered so well. As he reached the entrance hall, his shadow followed on the wall, and I suddenly saw the silhouette of a giant rat, its tail slinking behind. The silhouette began to stretch, elongating and drawing upright, its humped back resolving into two grasping hands and a head . . . the head of a clown, wearing a pointed hat.

I turned and fled, back down the hallway, cursing myself for a fool, a fool who had been tricked by Drosselmeyer one last time. I had told no one about this errand, not even the property agents, and now I saw that I would disappear, just as the neighborhood had always thought I had done. They would find my body here in the spring. Or perhaps I would simply vanish, sinking into whatever dreadful world such creatures inhabited.

But the very instant I crossed the library threshold, all sounds of pursuit vanished. The chandeliers in the hallway went dark, and the party noises cut off as though someone had lifted the needle from a phonograph. The house was once again still and silent, a cold fortress above my head. Still, I did not take my eyes from the library door, only stood there for a long moment, waiting to see something: a shadow, perhaps, or the outline of a footstep on the deep-pile carpet. But nothing showed itself, and after a few minutes I relaxed, for my nerve endings told me there was nothing there. Whatever strange visitation had brought Drosselmeyer back had gone . . . or perhaps it did not mean me any harm.

This last thought should have seemed ridiculous—when had the old wizard not been waiting to ruin everything for me?—but as I glanced around the gloom of the library, it seemed to carry an odd credibility. Drosselmeyer was a trickster, a gambler, a creature of risk. He would have understood the deal I had made with the Fairy. Perhaps, long before, he had even made such a deal himself, not wholly understanding what it might mean, because of course we couldn't; we were human, unable to see the entirety of consequence. I had sold myself cheap, purchased a dull and hopeless future, but there had been no way for Natasha to know that, not on that long-ago night when she was still only sixteen, blinded by pain and rage. Drosselmeyer, too, had visited the Kingdom of Sweets; the Fairy had said so. Had he been as blind as I was?

Now a breath of air moved my skirts, making them sway in the gloom. Turning to look for the source of the draft, I noticed something curious: a single book on the bottom shelf of false fronts, its tortured spine identifying it as real. Drawing closer, I even recognized the spine, that peculiar choice of yellow. I saw it every morning when I opened my eyes, sitting on the small bookshelf in my bedroom where I kept my own particular favorites, little worse than new, for I had ordered a copy from London with my own money after I had read the duke's cheap volume to pieces. Drosselmeyer's copy looked equally well read, and yet as I pulled it from the shelf, the worn red lettering seemed to gleam against the yellow cover, even in the thin winter light that diffused through the windows.

DRACULA

I touched the cover, feeling the strangest sense of kinship. Drosselmeyer had a fake library, yet he had read this novel—and more than once, for as I thumbed through it I could see the wear on the yellowed pages, the thin pink lines where the crimson bookmark's dyes had bled into the vellum. As I finished flipping through the pages, a bundle of papers fell from the book to the floor: handwritten pages bound with black ribbon, cleverly tucked between the cover and the frontispiece.

Untying the ribbon, I sank down on the carpet, making a wide spread of my skirts. Then I began to sort through the pages. The first two were a letter, presumably written to Drosselmeyer, although it was impossible to tell because the salutation was only "My old friend." The letter was undated, and the writing was a thin, wild scrawl . . . the scrawl, I thought, of a madman. Yet I had spent years deciphering Clara's poor attempts at letters, helping her to avoid the sharp raps on the knuckles which our tutor, Miss Gude, had favored as a teaching tool. Bringing the paper to the window, I stared at it for a long minute until words began to resolve themselves.

My old friend,

Your letter has amused me greatly, and I have few amusements these days. I am pleased that your plan has borne fruit, so pleased that I enclose a few more pieces of information that I have found in my travels. I hope they will be of use, and yet I feel compelled to caution you.

You have lived a long life, my friend . . . a charmed life, considering that from which you fly. I myself once dared to meddle with such magic as you consider, and paid a steep price. Why not let well enough alone? I well remember your fascination with twins, but these two have served their purpose. None of us knows what might happen after the soul is divided, and guesswork in such matters is ill-advised. A single twin could be a very dangerous thing. Were I you, I would kill both of your creations and simply wait. After all, you have the acorn, and the acorn will outlive the oak. You lose nothing, save time, and meanwhile you would remain safe, much safer than you will find yourself on your present course.

Ah, well. You will do as you choose, as we all do. But for myself, I do not like our chances in this world of science and machinery. Soon there will be no room for our kind at all, no matter what magic we may master. I hope that we will meet someday as toothless old men, men with nothing to do but tell stories. But my heart says it will not be so. We have meddled with terrible things, you and I, and I think we will pay for it in the end.

Whatever your decision, let me know how it all falls out. I hope we will see each other again before the century turns.

Grigori

There were two more sheets, written in the same wild hand, but they were truly indecipherable; after a long moment, I realized that they were in the English alphabet, but the language wasn't English. I thought I recognized it as Latin, but I didn't know enough to translate; Clara and I had learned Greek. There was no date.

Muttering a curse, I rose from the carpet, glaring at the words as though I might force them to translate themselves. When they did not, I folded the sheaf of papers and tucked them into the pocket of my skirts, then sat looking around the dim, musty room, with its rows and rows of sham books. If I was reading the letter rightly, Drosselmeyer had divided us in order to somehow protect himself from the Sugar Plum Fairy. Perhaps it had worked for a while, might even have worked forever if the scarred boy hadn't intervened with his nutcracker, the little toy that was only supposed to walk and talk but had instead opened a dreadful gate. That business about souls being divided reminded me of Anastasia, who had told me more than once that twins shared a single soul. She had said other things about twins too, but I had barely listened, dismissing her words as superstition. I had never thought to connect Anastasia's simple country wisdom with Drosselmeyer's doings, and more fool me. I picked up the letter again, reading down its barely decipherable scrawl until I found the line I was looking for.

A single twin could be a very dangerous thing.

Drosselmeyer had known that. In getting rid of me, he had been trying to turn Clara into something extraordinary, something more than the charming creature of light she had always been. But what? The letter didn't say. I looked at the two attached sheets written in Latin, the language of alchemists and sorcerers, wondering who I knew who might translate.

My skirts were covered with dirt from sitting on the filthy carpet. I dragged myself to my feet, tucking Drosselmeyer's correspondence into my visiting bag, and then, because I couldn't bear to leave his library bereft of all honesty, placed the pretty yellow book with its bloodred lettering carefully back on the shelf.

CHAPTER

33

I N THE FRONT HALLWAY I STOPPED AGAIN BEFORE THE ENOR-
mous mirror, alarmed. That dark shape behind my shoulder was
still there. Not a person, but something else. I twisted, trying to
get a good look at it, and that was when I noticed the half-size
door built into the wall behind me.

I turned, but there was no door. The wall behind me was unbroken. Yet I saw it clearly in the glass: a door that stood no higher
than a small child.

I had seen this trick before, but still it took me a moment to
understand it. Leaving the glass, I moved to the wall and began
to feel for the edges of the door. I felt nothing, and after a moment's thought I returned to the mirror, staring at that tiny door,
thinking of the vast glass in the Kingdom of Sweets. The servants
had been invisible in the mirror, and of course that made sense,
because there were no servants. Whether it was Clara's house of
treats or my fantasy of knights and ladies, neither was real, only
a clever bit of make-believe. But the screaming woman, now, she

had been there, whether I could see her or not. The mirror only showed what was real, I thought, still looking uneasily at the broad shadow just behind my shoulder. Or perhaps these things were only real in the mirror.

Don't you touch that glass! my mind shouted, the voice a clever imitation of Drosselmeyer's. *Don't you dare do it!*

Yet I was compelled. Reaching out, I touched a finger to the glass, not wholly surprised when it met not a flat pane but a liquid surface through which my finger pushed after meeting only brief resistance. Beneath the surface of the glass I felt bitter cold, as when I was a child and used to slide my hand through our letter slot in the dead of winter, enjoying the tangible magic of that disparity: warm and cozy inside, freezing without.

Behind me, in the mirror, I saw the twin of my own finger, grown almost monstrous against the far wall. I traced the outline of the door in the mirror, and as I did so, the wall began to crack and shudder behind me. Dark lines appeared in the reflected stone, and as I turned around, the door swung open into darkness.

I NEARLY FLED THE HOUSE. THE FRONT DOOR WAS RIGHT BESIDE me, after all, and though I felt some triumph at figuring out how to open the miniature door, I had also reached a kind of exhaustion in the revelations of Drosselmeyer's miserable existence. Whatever he might have intended for Clara and me, his plans had fallen apart. Was there any meaning to be found?

Oh, but that door. It was a hidden door, a *secret* door, and though I was no longer a child, I had not grown so great that I could not feel the allure of being Alice. I returned to the frozen kitchen, rustling through the empty drawers and cupboards until

I found half of a candle. Then I grabbed a heavy block of wood that might once have been part of an umbrella stand and dragged it over to prop the secret door open; as much as I wanted to explore that dark square in the wall, I had no mind to be trapped inside.

Last, I went into the dining room and took up a piece of a broken chair, heavy enough to serve as a club. Weapons might be little use against whatever ghosts still lived in this house, yet the wood felt good in my hand. As I passed the mirror once more, I thought that I looked rather like a Valkyrie in the old tales, ready to take on all comers.

There was a box of matches in my visiting bag. I had always carried them, though I didn't know precisely why; the only thing I ever used them for was to light Conrad's foul cigars. Staring at the box in my hand, it occurred to me again, much more strongly now, that I had undersold myself, traded away the extraordinary life I might have had for an indenture as Conrad's appendage. Seventeen was old for marriage in our world, possibly the last year before a girl began to be whispered about, marked as a spinster. Yet it seemed that I had been almost impossibly young. I thought of my child's dreams of seeing the Continent, seeing London, crossing oceans like the pirates in my books. Seventeen was far too young to give up such dreams, and yet we all did. Conrad still had no idea that I owned Drosselmeyer's house, and now, standing before the mirror, I was very glad of that fact, suddenly feeling that it wasn't his business, that he had no right to know anything about me. This was my house, not his, not anyone else's, and the idea made me brave, galvanized me into action. Lighting the candle, I ducked through the miniature doorway and crawled into the dark.

————————

I DON'T KNOW WHAT I HAD EXPECTED; SOME VAST UNDER-
ground labyrinth, perhaps. But when I reached the bottom of the
short staircase that lay just inside the door, I found myself in a
single room.

This room would have seemed sordid under any circumstances, but in the thin gleam of my candle, it struck me as pitiful
as well. Against one wall lay a filthy pallet, its cheap straw stuffing
leaking from multiple seams. A plate lay beside it, covered with a
gristly piece of meat so old and dry that even the flies and mag-
gots had long since departed. On the floor was a pile of scattered
papers, covered in the ghostly outlines of drawings. From the wall
above the pallet, two chains dangled to the floor, each ending in
a manacle. On the wall were several splashes of blood.

My one candle seemed suddenly insufficient; the flame flickered, as though in a draft. I forced myself to bend down and retrieve the pile of papers, but they too were a disappointment, for
all the drawings were of toys. Here was a ballerina, here a nutcracker, here a tiny gingerbread man. They were as detailed as
mechanical drawings, and yet I did not see any clockwork, only
strange markings I could not decipher, dimensions and angles that
I recognized from no geometry class. A slow wave of darkness
passed over my vision, and in it I heard screams, infinite screams,
joined together in the wailing wind.

Looking up at the manacles, the diagonal splash of blood on
the wall, I felt that I had seen just such a splash of blood somewhere, and not that long back. This room, this terrible room,
seemed to tell its own story. Drosselmeyer had kept the scarred
boy here, forced him to build, and when the boy failed, he bled

for it. But why? And if the boy was so powerful, why did he only build toys?

Now a breath of wind touched my shoulder, redolent of the sour scent of old ginger. In that moment I was certain I was not alone, that another stood just behind my left shoulder, and if I turned around I would see her, a tall shadow with eyes of deepest black, her teeth gleaming needles, come to see this place where her son had been kept, forced by the old devil with the eye patch to work his magic, do his bidding.

My candle guttered, then went out.

In that instant all my fine resolves fell apart. Dropping the chair leg, I broke into a run, stumbling up the filthy stairway, losing my candle in the process. I didn't care; I could see the door now, that tiny child-sized rectangle of light at the top. And yet I seemed to be slowing, as though something were holding me back, icy fingers clasped round my ankles, trying to drag me back to that dismal room.

"Let me go," I whispered. "I didn't steal him."

A moment later the hands on my legs seemed to loosen, and I scrambled up the last few stairs and threw myself through the miniature door. My skirts tore as I fell into the entrance hall and rolled into a blessed patch of sunlight. This house was haunted, everyone said so, and how right they were. I slammed the small door, watching with dull wonder as its outlines once again disappeared into the cracking stone of the wall. The sunlight that fell through the glass of the front door was warm, inviting me to go back outside, return to the Liebermanns' bright, gaudily nouveau residence, leave this house and sell it, or, if it could not be sold, then perhaps burn it to the ground.

But there was the mirror to consider. That dark shadow remained over my reflection's shoulder, and I didn't want to leave the glass here, where another unwary prospective buyer or estate agent might see something they should not. Of course the property agents had said the mirror could not be removed, but this was my house now; when I reached up and grasped the mirror's sides, it lifted easily—if clumsily—from its hooks, allowing me to set it against the wall.

I fixed my hat, wiped the tears from my face, and brushed the dust and cobwebs from my ripped skirts. Locking the door behind me, I descended to my carriage, waiting at the bottom of the steps. Despite my appearance, the footman did not ask questions, only handed me into the carriage. Home, I told Ivan, but on the way I stopped at the property agents' office to return the key and tell them that they could keep Drosselmeyer's house on the market for at least another six months. The firm's managing partner offered, as he had before, to find a decorator, refurbish the exterior of the house in hopes of increasing the sale price. But I told him that the house would continue to be offered as was, save for the looking glass in the front hall, which I instructed the agents to remove to the Liebermanns' mansion at my own expense.

CHAPTER
34

O N SUNDAY MORNING, AS USUAL, I ATTENDED CHURCH
with Conrad's family. Father Benedict's sermons were just
as dull as they had been when I was a child, but this was yet
another pitfall of the life I had traded for. People noticed Clara,
marked where she went and what she did. She could not stay
home from church every Sunday, as Natasha had once done, and
no one would believe any tales about private religious instruction.
So every Sunday morning I put on my veil, bent my head in the
pew as piously as any grandmother, and made a valiant effort not
to snore.

This Sunday, however, I remained awake, watching Father
Benedict closely as he fumbled his way through the sermon, dropping his spectacles several times. He was no performer, Father
Benedict, but that was all to the good. He was an academic, and
an academic was what I needed.

After the sermon, I told Conrad that I wanted to make confession. He raised his eyebrows at this—Clara had never made confession before—but his mother nodded approvingly; she often

opined that I suffered from the sin of pride. I had instructed Ivan to bring my carriage to church, and so I sent Conrad and his parents on, telling them I would return home later. As they left, I spotted my own parents on the far side of the church: my father impatient to be gone, my mother trying to wrangle Fritz, who seemed intent on molesting one of the half-naked statues that lined the vestry. I had not thought of Fritz in some time, but the sight of him disturbed me, gave me an uncomfortable feeling of imbalance in the universe. I deserved my griefs; I had committed murder, or at least meant to, and so I deserved whatever might come. But Fritz had harmed no one, and his punishment now seemed far too heavy for the simple sin of grabbing a toy and throwing it against the wall. The nutcracker had been Orlov's; had Fritz's madness been his doing as well? If so, perhaps it could be undone, but that would require a conversation with the toymaker, and no one seemed to know where he might be found.

Now Father Benedict retreated and began to take confession. Noble after noble filed forward as I waited patiently in the pew, sorting through the papers I had found in Drosselmeyer's house. No matter how many times I read the letter from the mysterious Grigori, I could not see how it might help me in any practical sense. Whatever Drosselmeyer might have intended on that long-ago day of our christening, his plans surely lay in ruins now, and it sounded as though his friend Grigori had exhausted his sources of information. There was no date on the letter, but clearly it had been written before the turn of the century, and we were now nearing the end of the year 1905. Clara and I would turn twenty-two this Christmas, or at least we would if I hadn't killed her.

But did you?

This was a question I turned over often in my mind. Was Clara dead? She didn't seem to be. I had lived with her shadow for

245

months, the moving air of its passage, the warmth of its touch on cushions and chairs. The Fairy had wanted me to kill Clara; remembering that scene in the forest, I would have wagered anything that she thought I had done so. Yet Clara lived. How could that be?

"Lady?"

Starting from my reverie, I found Father Benedict leaning over me, his dry old hands clasped together, spectacles perched on the end of his nose. It seemed he had not aged a day since my childhood.

"Father," I said, pulling myself to my feet. "If you have leisure, I require some assistance."

"You wish to make confession?"

"No. I have some questions about theology."

The priest raised his eyebrows at this, but nodded. Looking around to make sure the church was in order—it was, peopled now by only a few mourning widows and mothers who clearly meant to spend all day bent in prayer—he beckoned me to follow him through a door at the rear, just to the left of the enormous plaster statue of Christ. We went down a long red-carpeted hallway and then into a surprisingly small room, clearly an office, its walls lined with books that appeared uniformly religious.

"Well, my lady, what can I help you with?" Father Benedict asked, seating himself behind the small wooden desk.

"Do you speak Latin, Father?"

Father Benedict nodded. "Reasonably well, though I admit I am rusty."

I hesitated, for now that it came to the point, I was nervous about giving him the two sheets of paper, which might be innocuous or might confess to a pact with the devil. I needed no trouble with the Church, and Father Benedict reported directly to

Bishop Theofan, who was friends with the King. If one believed the Church's doctrine, the King was appointed by God himself.

"You require some translation?" Father Benedict asked. He leaned forward, a twinkle in his eye. "Yet you are fearful. What is it? Something forbidden? Perhaps some Boccaccio?"

"Nothing like that, Father," I replied, smiling at his unexpected humor, and passed him the sheet of Grigori's notes. "Honestly, I am not even certain what these papers are. I found them in a relative's effects, and can make nothing of them."

"Well, let's see."

Father Benedict pushed his spectacles up and began to read, slowly, moving from word to word as a man would between stones in a river: leap, then pause.

"We tried this . . . division . . . but did not succeed. There was no power to be found in either—mother Mary, what a hand!—either twin. In dividing them, we destroyed the very . . . aspects, which we hoped to increase."

He paused, looking at the paper with bemusement.

"Strange matter."

"Is that all?"

Father Benedict cleared his throat, then bent to the paper again.

"We find that the—*haruspex*, I know that one—the diviner is far stronger than the . . . healing. Indeed, the prophecy is so strong that it begins to drive the diviner half . . . mad. We find no hope of creating a shield. We doubt the . . . utility . . . of the division, unless it might be for the ultimate purpose of . . . reunification."

He cleared his throat again.

"We succeeded once, but only once. The vessel was powerful, but even so it had no power equal to stave off the—"

He broke off, staring down at the sheet for a moment. Then he handed it back to me, his eyes wide behind the spectacles.

"You see that last word, Lady Liebermann?"

Taking the paper, I looked to the bottom and felt a nasty start. The writing was as tangled as ever, but it was hard to mistake the word.

"Demon. I know it in English."

"Well, *daemon*, actually," Father Benedict said. "But yes, the meaning is the same."

He sat back, eying me thoughtfully, his hands clasped on his round belly.

"I must say, I grow interested in the origin of this document. It seems to indicate a fascination with black arts."

"I told you: I found it among a relative's effects."

"Yes, but *which* relative?" the priest asked, leaning forward. "I don't suppose you would be willing to share?"

"We're not in the confessional, Father. What assurance do I have of your secrecy?"

The priest threw his head back, laughing.

"Only this, my child: the curiosity of an old man who would rather discover new things than be the snoop. I will move no higher in my office than this; I am too much scholar, not enough politician. I have no need to tell the secrets of others. I prefer, always, to know."

I considered this, watching the priest thoughtfully. I had never liked Father Benedict in my youth, but I had seen him only in the pulpit. And what could he really do to me anyway, even if he should tell the bishop? Word might get around that I owned Drosselmeyer's house and effects, but that mattered little. What mattered was that Drosselmeyer's money was safe, held in multiple accounts for which I was the only creditor. Conrad and his grasping parents would never find it.

"These papers belonged to Drosselmeyer."

"Ahhhh," Father Benedict replied, beaming. "Your godfather! I should have known."

"Did you know him?"

"No, no. Drosselmeyer was not one for church. The only day I ever saw him here, strangely enough, was the day of your christening, when he invaded your parents' house. God save us, what a nightmare! Your poor mother never recovered."

"No, she didn't."

"But here now, you see! They are speaking of you!" He snatched the sheet from me, rattling it in the air. "Magic, you see! Pagan magic! How wonderful!"

I raised my eyebrows, for Bishop Theofan would hardly think it wonderful. But Father Benedict was beaming again. He beckoned me forward, nearly wiggling in his seat, and pointed at the Latin words.

"Here now, it begins to make more sense. Twins, you see. In the pagan mythologies, twins were always very powerful, for they shared a single soul."

"What kind of power?"

"Oh, all sorts. Healing; twins were always supposed to have healing powers. Knowledge of the future—that must be the *haruspex* they speak of here—and sometimes even foretelling of the weather. Romulus and Remus—they that founded Rome, you know—were raised by wolves, and their descendants were supposed to be able to communicate with animals ever after."

I nodded, though I had barely listened to the end of this.

"Healing, you said. What kind of healing? The sick?"

"Sometimes, but the idea could also be more holistic. Healing of the soul, that kind of thing. A sort of magical protection."

I sat back in the chair.

"Protection."

"Yes."

"Against demons?"

"Against anything, I suppose. In many ancient cultures, twins were considered a sign of extreme good luck, not just for their families but for entire villages. But again, this is all legend and superstition."

But it wasn't. Not to Drosselmeyer, and now I thought I began to glimpse, dimly, what Clara had been to him, what she had been meant to be.

"What if one twin died? What happened to the power?"

"Nothing. Twins were not two souls but one, and the power was likewise indivisible. If one twin died, the surviving twin would become doubly charmed."

I nodded, my face bland, as befitted a simple conversation about folklore. But behind my eyes I saw the shadow of the clown, cartwheeling along the parlor wall. Drosselmeyer had created us, divided us, and then tried to kill me, so that Clara might have it all.

"Would this work with any set of twins?" I asked.

"I couldn't say. My practical knowledge of such things is, of course, limited, though I did read much apocrypha in my youth." Father Benedict looked down at the paper again, his gaze thoughtful. "Of course, you and your sister were not merely any twins; you were born on Christmas Day."

"What does that matter?"

"My child, the pagans worshipped Christmas long before the birth of Christ! They named it the winter solstice and celebrated by dancing around a tree. It was the best of all days to perform magic."

"Healing and divination," I murmured. Yet Clara had gotten all the healing, while I was the diviner, the one who saw. My sight, my knowledge, had brought me nothing but misery. He had divided us entirely, light and dark, and yet again I felt a strange sympathy for Drosselmeyer, a sympathy I could never have felt for him in life. I was not offended by what he had done to us, or even that he had tried to murder me years before. Rather, the mere fact that he had had a plan, some sort of reason and method in his dealings with us, no matter how mad, seemed to render him more human than he had ever been. I had spent so many years thinking him purposelessly spiteful; what might he have said, if we could have spoken together, had private speech?

"Drosselmeyer was a pagan, to be certain," Father Benedict remarked. "I should not be surprised that these were his leanings, but I hope you have no mind to follow in his footsteps, Lady Liebermann."

"Heavens, no, Father," I said, putting on my best Clara smile. "I've merely been emptying his house that the agents might sell it."

I folded up the paper, meaning to tuck it away in my Sunday bag. But my eye fell again upon that word—*daemon*—and I paused.

"Do you believe in demons, Father?"

He raised his eyebrows.

"My church does. Since we are sharing confidences, however, I will tell you that the hierarchy squabbles endlessly over what a demon actually is. No one can seem to agree, even within sects. And it hardly matters anyway."

"Why not?"

"Well, because they are all the same. Fallen angels, old pagan gods, animal spirits . . . it matters not which mythology you hunt through, you will find the same thing: creatures who despise mankind. They await our downfall, speed it along when they can. They seek vengeance upon us."

"For what?"

"For being shut out of the light."

I blinked, thinking of the Fairy's land, the dark moon that rose and fell, with no possibility of sunrise. Father Benedict took off his glasses and began to polish them on his white robe, though his sharp eyes never left me.

"I must say, you have made me very curious, Clara. You were always a charming child, but never one of particularly inquisitive mind. It was your sister, poor creature, who was the scholar in your family. Pity she left the Church so young; she would have made a fine nun."

"I'm sure she would have."

"They never found any trace of her, did they?"

"No." *But they did not look very hard either.*

"Was there anything else you wanted to discuss?"

"No. Thank you, Father. You have been most helpful."

"Have I?" His gaze upon me was thoughtful, almost wistful. "It's so rare that I have a chance to discuss academic matters with a parishioner. Far more interesting than the usual lustful thoughts."

I smiled, for I saw him suddenly, clear as a pane of well-polished glass. I saw that he regretted becoming a priest, regretted leaving the seminary and the study of history to minister to our hopelessly damned neighborhood. Was anyone ever content with the choices they made in youth? Perhaps not, or perhaps it had nothing to do with age. Perhaps we were all fools until life taught us better, showed us what had been before our eyes all along.

"Bless you, Father," I said, feeling real pity for him, and perhaps for myself. "Have a good Christmas."

ARRIVING HOME, I WAS RELIEVED WHEN KROLL TOLD ME THAT Conrad had gone out shooting with several members of his club. I went upstairs to our suite, then moved to stand in front of Drosselmeyer's enormous mirror, which had been placed on the broad wall to the right of my bed. Staring up at the edges of the mirror, I thought again what a powerful wizard Drosselmeyer must have been, to steal over the very borders of the Sugar Plum Fairy's nightmare country and abscond with the only thing she might care about. Perhaps Drosselmeyer had taken Orlov as mere insurance, a guarantee that the Fairy would not simply send someone to burn his house down. But Drosselmeyer did not want to be confined to the house; he needed better protection than that, and so he had created Clara. In my mind's eye, I saw him roaming our neighborhood at night, surrounded always by his pack of pretty boys. How many of them had been twins?

The surface of the looking glass was as clear as ever, free of even the hint of a smudge. The maids might have polished it every morning, but I didn't think so, for I had heard from Eva, my lady's maid, that more than one chambermaid refused to touch the mirror, that they tried not to cross in front of it when they dusted. Since I had brought it into my rooms, they would not even change my bedding, except in groups. When I had asked Kroll about these rumors, he'd said, almost apologetically, "They fear the thing, madam. They are silly girls. They fear what they might see in the glass."

Now I stared at my reflection, at Natasha, at the shadow that waited over my shoulder. It was darker now than it had been the

253

week before . . . or perhaps that was only my own imagination. Was the Fairy watching me? Why should she need to, now that Clara was here? But then Clara was gone now, off on some mysterious errand of her own. Drosselmeyer had meant her for a talisman, but I didn't know what she might be now, when Drosselmeyer's plans had gone awry and so much had changed.

"Come," I told the mirror, and waited. But there was nothing, and after a long moment I realized that I had not expected anything, not really. Our bargain was done; whatever gratitude the Sugar Plum Fairy might have felt to me for giving her Drosselmeyer was gone, and I was only another tool expended. Her kind sought vengeance, the priest had said; they hated us all, and if she would not pity Clara, there seemed no reason she should pity me. So I lay awake most of that night, staring into my dying fire, considering everything I knew about the Kingdom of Sweets, everything I had seen there. I was sure that Clara would appear at some point, but she did not, and I wondered why. Magic ebbed and flowed, she had said, and while I could not guess what she meant, it was comforting to know that Clara did not have free rein in this matter, that she was at least bound by some rules. Ebb and flow . . . I fell asleep pondering those words, and in the morning I felt refreshed, almost reborn, because clearly my *mind* had not slept; it had continued working and working, and now I found myself with the beginnings of a plan.

CHAPTER

35

THE NEXT AFTERNOON I TOOK THE CARRIAGE TO MY PARents' house. The butler who answered the door—a new man—informed me with well-bred regret that my parents were out, but that was fine; I didn't want to see either of them. While I had visited often in the year after my marriage, I had not been back more than a handful of times since, reasoning that it was no longer my job to negotiate Father's desperate social climbing or Mother's circle of green-bottle friends. Viewed objectively, my parents were an unpleasant pair, as unpleasant in their own way as Conrad's family, and I was just as happy that I would not have to drink a cup of bitter tea and make small talk. I pushed past the butler—he started to protest, then thought better of it—and headed straight for the kitchen.

Clara had been with me on the doorstep, but here, in our old house, she seemed to have business of her own, for she drifted up the staircase, vanishing into insubstantiality near the top. Perhaps she meant to visit her old room, to play with her dolls, the bright pink dollhouse that so resembled a castle. Perhaps she merely wished to remember the light.

ANASTASIA HAD COME UP IN THE WORLD. SHE NOW BOASTED A staff of three: two boys and a girl, all of whom likely worked for pennies but were young enough to be happy to have them. The kitchen counters had been resurfaced with fine marble, and the old, chipped pots and pans that I had known so well had long since vanished, replaced by a gleaming set of iron cookware so extensive that it took up two walls of the kitchen. The west wall now opened out into a beautiful conservatory filled with hothouse flowers, the effect only a bit spoiled by the fact that none of them were actually growing, that all of them were in vases.

Anastasia herself looked more prosperous as well. She wore a deep purple dress of expensive wool, and her hair was clipped back with bejeweled pins that gleamed ruby in the light. She greeted me laconically, then asked what I wanted, her tone implying that whatever it was, it certainly rated less important than the luncheon she was beginning to prepare.

I had spent most of the morning's breakfast considering how to frame this request. The old Natasha could have asked the question easily, and probably gotten an answer too. But Clara had never been one of Anastasia's favorites, and even in my frequent visits in the first year of my marriage, I had sensed her impatience with me. Her clear annoyance at the amount of kitchen preparation needed to entertain a future duke and duchess had been one of the reasons I stopped my visits. I considered telling her I was Natasha—telling her everything—but in the end I decided against that course. Anastasia had always claimed that Drosselmeyer was an emissary of Shaitan, and while as a child I had been content simply to have an ally in that sentiment, now I thought that she must have actually known something, might even have been able to sense the darker magic that lay behind Drosselmeyer's parlor theatrics and unnatural grace. If she heard about the Kingdom of Sweets, she would only fear me. No, best for her to know me only as Clara, foolish Clara, with her head full of ribbons and romance. There might still be a way.

"I need some help, Anastasia," I said, smiling Clara's charming smile. "I know we've never been close, but I must ask for this favor."

"What favor?" she asked truculently.

"I need to know where to find the inventor. Orlov."

"What makes you think I know?" Anastasia demanded, but inside my chest, my heart seemed to spark. She did know. All of those long years when she was my only friend in this house, when I had come to understand her as well as anyone . . . she did know, and she didn't care much about the information either, had no reason to withhold it.

"Because you always know everything," I answered in a flattering tone, and this flattery, at least, was true. The servants always knew. Anastasia certainly did, for now she straightened up proudly, a piratical gleam in her eye.

"I will tell you, girl, for a price."

"Name it."

"I have a niece, fifteen years old. She needs a job."

"Here?"

"Yes. She is a good girl, my niece, but she is not content with the country life, she wants to be a city woman for a while. My sister has given her blessing, but the girl needs employment. Good employment, or she will end up on her back down by the docks."

"Why can your niece not work for you?" I asked. My question

was not accusatory, only curious, and fortunately Anastasia seemed to take it that way, for her tone was neutral when she replied.

"Your parents might be in the lap of luxury since you got married, princess, but they're as tight as ever when it comes to staff. These poor wretches"—she indicated the boy and girl peeling onions at the small block table—"make less than the chimney sweeps, but they still live at home. My niece cannot make her own way on such wages."

I nodded, and inside I felt a sharp stab of regret. Anastasia had been my wailing wall for years, about Clara, about Conrad, about Drosselmeyer, but I had never even thought to ask whether she had family of her own. Too late, I wondered how I could have been so selfish. So young.

"I will find her a job."

Anastasia nodded, though her expression remained skeptical. She had no reason to trust any of us, certainly not Clara, and with the memory of our former closeness in my mind, I found myself saying, "Your niece will not be mistreated in any way. No one will offer her insult. She will earn the same as the other girls. I will see to it myself."

Anastasia's eyes narrowed, and I realized that I had been betrayed into carelessness, that I had allowed my old self to come forward and say something that Clara would never have said. Anastasia was backing away from me now, raising her hands, forking them in front of her, making the sign of the evil eye.

"Phantom," she whispered. "Leave my sight."

"Tasia, please—"

But she had begun to mutter a prayer now, and when I stepped forward she darted back behind the carving table. Her two assistants had stopped peeling onions and now watched the drama with bewildered interest.

"Tasia, I need to know."

"Leave my sight, I said!" she shouted, and I knew that soon the new butler and his footmen would be in here. They might not throw me out of the house, but then again, they might. The servants had always feared Anastasia far more than they feared any of us.

"If you answer my question," I said calmly, "I will leave, and never enter your kitchen again. My word."

Anastasia stared at me for a long, fearful moment, and then some of her old iron seemed to seep back in. She straightened proudly, though her fingers remained forked, warding me off.

"The toymaker lives in a warehouse in the industrial district. I don't know the street, but you will be able to find it. They say he uses machinery in there that runs all day and night, and he has strung the whole place with lights . . . not candles, but the new light, the light that comes from wire."

"Thank you," I said, and then, because the game was up and no further harm could be done, and even more because this woman, of all of them, had always been good to me in her own way, even from infancy, even when the rest of the house had dismissed me entirely, I said, "I remember you kindly, Tasia. I will not trouble you again . . . or your niece either."

Anastasia did not reply, but I did sense a kind of softening in her face, and to this day I still hope that she knew, that in the end she understood that it was me, Natasha, no ghost, and that I truly meant her no harm. But that might be only wishful thinking, for she remained behind the table, her fingers raised in the sign of the evil eye, watching my every movement as I left the kitchen.

CHAPTER

36

RETURNING TO THE ENTRANCE HALL, I TOOK MY COAT AND gloves from the maid, meaning to put them on and leave immediately—I'd had quite enough of the old homestead, and if I could manage to leave Clara behind for a few hours, so much the better—but I was stopped by a strange giggle at the top of the stairs. I looked up and spotted Fritz, peering at me through the rails.

"Fritz!" I called. "Are you well?"

He rose to peek at me over the banister. He was only eighteen, but his face looked strangely old, particularly around the eyes.

"I saw," he whispered, clutching the rails as a cloistered nun might clutch at the bars of her cell.

"Saw what, Fritz?" I asked, climbing the first two risers with some caution. I didn't like the way he was looking at me, his face a mixture of wariness and guile. I was surprised that my parents had left him alone, for his proclivities toward arson and general destruction of property were now common knowledge in the neighborhood. Conrad's parents wouldn't have him to visit, even if Fritz had wanted to come.

Reaching the fourth riser, I seated myself. Conrad's mother would have told me that I was wrinkling my dress; in my head, I told the old bitch to go spit, tucking my velvet skirts beneath me. The stairway was actually quite a comfortable spot; I could see why Fritz had chosen it. There was a roaring fire in the entryway fireplace, and my parents had installed a massive tree in the hall as well. The smell of fir, that sharp smell that would never mean anything but Christmas to me, permeated the house.

"Is no one watching you, Fritz?" I asked.

"We are."

Charles and Deirdre stood in the upper hallway, arm in arm. Charles wore his old black velvet suit, but Deirdre had finally abandoned her mannish attire; now she wore a bright yellow silk dress. That color, which would have excited no notice in May, was strangely incongruous in December. I could almost see Deirdre delighting her mother with her sudden willingness to wear a dress, then springing that dreadful concoction on her.

"Mother and Father left you two in charge?"

Charles shrugged. "We're of age now. We're responsible."

I meant to return a cutting reply, but I left it unsaid, for I had suddenly seen something in the two of them, something I had missed. They had always looked like twins, though there was a year's difference between them. I had considered it as the similarity of their faces, their red hair. But now I saw them more clearly than I ever had: identical sets of dark eyes, full of malice. I wondered that I had never seen it before.

"You two," I murmured, shaking my head as I pulled myself to my feet. "You're just like him."

"Who's that, Clara?"

Fritz was tugging at my skirts. He beckoned me close, and after a moment's hesitation, I leaned down to hear him whisper.

"I saw. I saw the dark."

What dark? I began to ask, then stopped, for Fritz had the gleeful look of a child sharing a secret. He was simply mad then, just as the neighborhood said. I hated to think it of him, my little brother, whom I had once taught to write his first straggling letters.

"Did you see it?" he asked.

"Yes, Fritz, I saw it."

"Did you see the pit?"

He grasped my hand, and I drew back in sudden horror, for his words had pulled a veil from my memory, drawing it back as sharply as a curtain. I saw the dark city, but much clearer now, crypt-like buildings and lampposts of bone. I saw a wide smear of blood on white marble steps.

"What is it, Fritz?" I asked him. "Do you know what it is?"

But he had gone back into himself, counting on his fingers as he had when he was five.

"He never stops speaking nonsense," Charles said above me, and I straightened, placing a hand on Fritz's head, as I would do when he was young.

"I'm sorry, Fritz. I wish I knew how to help you."

"Don't be sorry," Deirdre remarked. "We should all be so lucky, to sit around all day setting things on fire and be rewarded with fine clothes and a soft bed. He should have been in the madhouse long ago, but your mother refused."

"So would any mother, I think," I replied, hanging my bag on my arm. "Though perhaps not yours. Reptiles don't inspire parental devotion."

They glanced at each other, then at me with a sudden predatory interest.

"You've sharpened your tongue, Clara," Deirdre said softly. "You're not the good girl you once were. Perhaps the rumors are true."

I stopped short at the foot of the stairs.

"What rumors?"

"Ah, she knows nothing!" Charles remarked to Deirdre, smiling. "She must be innocent!"

I knew I should simply leave; the two of them were nothing but trouble. But Charles and Deirdre did not invent items to make mischief on, not when there were so many real human faults available. Whatever they were talking about, others must be talking about it too.

"What have you heard?" I asked. "Come, tell me some gossip."

Charles shrugged. "Only that you have certain . . . sympathies."

"For whom?"

"For the servants," Deirdre chimed in. "Everyone has heard of it. What we were curious about was whether it was one particular servant—as in the old days, you know—or all of them at once."

"Ah," I breathed, sitting back on my heels. This would be Conrad's mother again, or perhaps even Conrad himself. Easier for Conrad to believe I'd descended to the lower quarters out of whim than to seek his own culpability in my locked bedroom door, just as it was easier for them all to believe I was a harlot than to examine their own treatment of the servants in a contrasting light. In that moment I hated the lot of them: Conrad, his parents, my parents, the King, the vast nobility of the city who rested on their luck and called it wealth. I wished I *had* bedded one of the servants, as Clara undoubtedly would have without thought, just so I could go home and tell Conrad to his face.

"Arne is still here, you know," Deirdre remarked, almost reading my mind, gesturing toward the parlor. "Are you sure you don't want to give him a quick tumble, just for old times? Is the downstairs really as good as we've heard?"

"You'll have to find that out for yourself," I replied, smiling tightly as I pinned my veil to my hat. "Or you could, if you weren't too busy fucking each other."

That, at least, shocked the two of them into silence. Blowing Fritz a kiss, I left my cousins standing there with rounded mouths and wide eyes, and that was the best of a bad business.

CHAPTER

37

ORLOV'S WAREHOUSE STOOD OUT AMONG THE STACKED
stone boxes of the industrial district like a taper in the
darkness, its tiny windows lit with unnatural radiance. For a man
who valued his seclusion, he was not much concerned about an-
nouncing his presence to the neighborhood. But then, secrecy was
only a matter of money . . . or perhaps fear. I had purchased such
silence myself.

"Do you want me to come with you, my lady?" Ivan asked.
We could hear the roar of fire inside, and repeated blows echoing
within the walls, as though a hundred men were in there, swing-
ing cudgels in unison. But Ivan's worries were more prosaic: the
crowds we had seen roaming the warehouse district. In the past
few days, there had been clashes between the King's soldiers and
the workers again, with several people injured. The King might
think he had won the day, but the sullen looks on the gathered
workers' faces presaged more trouble.

"I'll be fine," I replied, patting Ivan's shoulder. "You needn't wait, though. Take the carriage out of here, and come back in half an hour."

Ivan tipped his hat, climbing back into the driver's box. Charles's words of the day before must have stayed with me, for I noticed suddenly that Ivan was handsome, tall and well-built. It was not an erotic thought but a liberating one; for so many years the word *handsome* had meant only Conrad. Now it occurred to me that the world was full of men, and some of them might be thoughtful as well as handsome, might even be kind.

I expected to have a difficult time getting in; after all, a man so invested in his own privacy would hardly leave the front door open. And there was indeed a group of men at the entrance, led by a burly man with a knife displayed prominently at his belt. But he took one look at me and jerked one of the doors open, pointing me inside.

"Go on in."

I moved inside, bemused by my easy entry. As I crossed the threshold, I was astonished to find that the sounds of machinery were suddenly muted, dampened down to a distant thudding.

"Up the stairs!" the doorman called after me, and I looked around until I glimpsed a set of rickety stairs on the right side of the warehouse. "Second floor!"

Much of the bravado I had brought with me on the journey was sapped by that climb. Each step I took was punctuated by a squeal of tortured wood and the sickening feeling of give beneath my feet. The stairs *wanted* to snap, I thought uneasily, and for no reason my mind called up the image of the shortbread trees in the Kingdom of Sweets, their tops writhing and splitting in the moonlight like the petals of some ruined flower. Who knew what trees really thought, long after we had taken them for pleasure and use, twisting them into shapes never intended? Who knew what memories even the dead wood might hold?

At the top of the second flight of stairs I paused a moment, holding on to the railing with vast relief, trying not to think about the inevitable climb down. Then I forgot the staircase as I saw what I had walked into.

The warehouse was enormous, easily covering half the footage of the building. But rather than being full of boxes or equipment, as I had expected, that vast sprawl was covered with people. Families. They spread across the floor for hundreds of yards, crushed into the space. Some were trying to cook, holding pans over small fires they had conjured in steel bowls. Others were huddled together, singing, trying to get children to sleep. The smell was horrendous, but I did not cover my nose with a kerchief, as Conrad's mother liked to do when she was forced to behold the poor. Rather, I did my best to swallow my confounded expectations and started across the room toward the far side, where a tall, thin, dark-haired man sat at a desk, bent studiously over his work. The families looked me over as I passed, their gazes betraying neither hostility nor goodwill, only exhaustion.

When I came within ten feet of the desk Orlov looked up, his expression already betraying irritation that anyone would dare interrupt his work. Though I had been certain I was right, still I was relieved to see the face I remembered, the mouth twisted by scars.

"Who are you?" Orlov demanded. "Do you want to make a donation?"

"I would, if I had brought gold. I didn't know what I would find here."

His brow furrowed for a moment, then cleared.

"I know you. You're the little Stahlbaum girl. The one who broke my nutcracker all those years ago. Light."

"Light," I repeated, and felt my mouth lift in a smile, perhaps the bitterest of my life. "So Drosselmeyer purposed."

"Drosselmeyer is missing."

"Drosselmeyer is dead."

His face seemed to tighten beneath the scars.

"What do you know of it?"

"I know that your mother is full of gifts."

He shot from the desk in a single lithe motion, clamped a long-fingered hand round my arm, and jerked me toward a single door in the far wall. We passed into another room, whose contours I could not see in the dark. Orlov flicked a switch on a box beside the door, and everything was suddenly illuminated. I had never seen electric light before, and though my father often said it would not be long before it lit every house in the city, I hoped he was wrong. The light was harsh and unforgiving, very different from that of day or even candlelight, and it blinded me, kept me from seeing my surroundings until it was too late.

The room was filled with toys: hundreds of them, assembled in lines like soldiers, tiny men and lions and standing dogs and gingerbread men and mice and knights. There was even, in one corner, a row of foot-high clowns, their harlequin faces very familiar. Thousands of beady glass eyes stared at me in the bright light.

"What do you want?" Orlov demanded, closing the door. "Who are you?"

"Natasha Stahlbaum."

"Natasha Stahlbaum is dead."

I removed my gloves. "You once gave me a dire warning, Mikhail, and I should have heeded it. But I did not."

He stared at me for a long moment, his gaze searching, and beneath the surface, the scars and the bitterness, I could suddenly see the part of him that was his mother. His dark eyes were keen and cold, so perceptive that they seemed to be turning me inside out.

"Don't call me Mikhail," he finally replied. "That was Drosselmeyer's name, and I have shed it forever. I am Orlov, and now I belong to no one."

I nodded, shrugging to show how little I thought of the distinction of names, how easily I had discarded mine.

"I heard of your disappearance," Orlov said, leaning against the wall. The electric light limned his scars in grotesque relief; he looked like a doll that had been mended and re-mended until the stuffing was gone. "They said you threw yourself in the river, and I believed it, because I could see the jealousy eating you alive. But that's not what happened at all. You found my nutcracker."

"Yes."

"You wear your sister's face."

"Yes."

"And where is your sister?"

I looked at him for a long moment, not dropping my eyes even when accusation crept into his.

"I see." He turned away, shaking his head. "Jealousy . . . I did warn you."

"You did."

"And now I know what happened to Drosselmeyer."

"You mourn him?"

"Quite the opposite. But I was curious. . . . He had been so careful, for so long . . ." He shook his head. "Well, she has him at last, and I am free of him. But what has she sent you for? To wheedle me one last time? You can tell her I won't go back."

"Your mother didn't send me. I'm here for myself."

I told him about Clara, the familiar who now dogged my steps everywhere I went. I told him what she had said about ebb and flow, but could not tell whether Orlov did not understand her words or merely chose not to share his understanding. I even told him about my long night in the Kingdom of Sweets, feeling as though I had the proper audience now, as though the multitude of small toys around us might listen and nod along. And then I told him what I wanted.

"Why on earth—"

"I can pay you; I'm a wealthy woman now."

"I'm sure you are. Your sister's fiancé was a good catch."

I ignored the jab. "Can you do it? Or was it Drosselmeyer with the skill, after all?"

He smiled, a smile that did not reach his eyes in the slightest.

"You see these?" He touched the scars on his face.

I nodded.

"Whenever he needed magic—real magic now, not sleight of hand—he would use me . . . or, more precisely, use my blood. He was liberal with his knife, your godfather."

I winced, thinking of the tiny room, the bloodstains on the wall.

"When he came to me and said he wanted me to make a nut-cracker, I thought he would simply cut me again. But he didn't. I don't know if he was losing his own power, or simply in a hurry, but he told me to make it, even let me use his tools. He had a won-derful workshop, Drosselmeyer, and that week of work was the first happiness I had ever known in his house. He never knew what I was doing; he thought I made the nutcracker to protect Clara, just as the clown was meant to finish you. He was so pleased with the results that he offered to pay me, but I told him no, that I wanted to attend the party instead."

"Why?"

"Because I wanted to see you two. Dark and light."

"You knew of us?"

"All of Drosselmeyer's boys knew. He thought you would save him from my mother . . . or at least, that your sister would."

"So he divided us."

He shook his head. "You misunderstand. Your sister as talisman, that came later. Drosselmeyer had been trying his luck with twins for years and gotten nowhere. But there is enormous power in the simple severance of twins . . . power enough to open doorways better left closed. Drosselmeyer was only a fair magician, but a first-rate thief."

"What did he steal?"

"Me."

I looked at him for a long moment. "So you blame us."

"I did once, enough that I wanted to have a look at the two of you. But in truth, when I did, I could feel only pity. Drosselmeyer had done neither of you any favors."

"True enough."

"Still, I don't regret making the nutcracker, for it was my only way to get clear of the old man. He could have held me there forever—"

Orlov was silent for a moment. I thought of telling him that I had been to Drosselmeyer's house, seen the room, but in the end I said nothing.

"Well," he said at last, focusing on me again. "I am finally shut of the old man, as I wished to be, and now I am shut of my mother too. So why would I ever reopen that old door?"

"You don't wish to go back?"

"I can't go back."

"Why not?"

"Because I have grown used to this world, to its light and warmth. My mother's world has nothing but vengeance. I will not go back, not even for her. This is my home."

I nodded, though I was certain that I would never be the one to deliver that particular message to the Fairy.

"In all your days with Drosselmeyer, did you ever meet a man named Grigori?"

Orlov blinked.

"How did you know about him? Drosselmeyer was very careful."

"I saw some correspondence. I—" But I stopped, for a movement had drawn my eye: one of the gingerbread men had darted forward from his fellows, his friendly red smile somehow gloating. Two of the clowns were peeking at me, their glittering eyes visible over the edge of one of the tables. I understood now how Drosselmeyer's boys must have died, cut to ribbons as they huddled alone inside their locked flats and attic rooms. A cold hand seemed to touch my spine.

"You shouldn't have come here," Orlov told me. One of the nutcrackers marched forward, almost to my feet, pulling a saber as I backed away toward the wall.

"Why did you kill them?" I asked, temporizing. I had begun backing away, but the first row of toys scuttled forward, matching my steps. They were closing on me now, drawing together as I retreated into the far corner. One of the lions opened its mouth, almost in a yawn, and I saw that its teeth were large and white and sharp. "Drosselmeyer's boys. Why did they need to die?"

He looked at me for a long moment, then turned his attention to the toys at my feet. They halted, but not for long. One of the clowns, I saw, had removed its hat, begun to swing it back and forth. Its red eyes never left mine.

"When Drosselmeyer disappeared, I was quicker than the rest," Orlov said slowly. "I took the gold and cash from beneath his floorboards. But his pretty boys knew of that stash, for they had helped him steal it. Once they found me, they tried to blackmail me. I was in no mood."

I nodded, for this made fine sense. But I knew it was a lie. That terrible room; the cold; the manacles; the blood on the wall. Drosselmeyer's boys had come, yes, and demanded the gold. But that was not why they had died screaming in their solitary rooms, cut to pieces by invisible killers. I pitied Orlov, and it must have shown in my eyes, for his face resumed its earlier cold lines.

"I am sorry for this," he said. "Truly I am. But you know too much about me. And I cannot risk her finding me, not now."

A sudden movement made me look down. Two gnomes stood beside my feet, their tiny axes raised, as though ready to go to work.

"I have no dealings with your mother. Not since Drosselmeyer disappeared."

"You think not?" Orlov asked, smiling darkly. "Look closely at yourself, Natasha. You are no longer what you were."

I jumped a bit at that, thinking of the shadow that peeked over my shoulder whenever I looked in Drosselmeyer's mirror. I felt an awful doom in Orlov's words, a reflection of my own uncontemplated certainties.

"Go ahead," Orlov said.

One of the nutcrackers leapt forward, raising its saber. I grimaced, preparing to feel the sword pierce my satin shoe. The constables would find me somewhere else in a few days, perhaps on the waterfront, perhaps in a locked room, Clara's pretty dancer's body torn to pieces.

But the nutcracker paused at the last second, holding its blade above its shoulder. It looked up at me for a long moment, then turned to Orlov and shook its head. The inventor's expression was shocked, but after a moment the shock melted away into something else I couldn't quite define: craftiness, or perhaps simple wariness. He stepped backward to the other side of the room, placing the army of toys between us. At my feet, the nutcracker had begun to march back and forth, brandishing his saber like a sentry.

"Your sister is no ghost," Orlov said. "She lives."

"How do you know?"

"Something Drosselmeyer said once," he replied, sinking onto the tiny stool that stood beside the table. "I know little of the magic of twins, but Drosselmeyer made quite a study of it . . . a deeper study, I would guess, than anyone alive. More than once, he said that twins were protected by their own magic. Once they were divided, it went away, but until such division was complete, it was a very difficult business to kill a twin."

I considered this, still puzzled. The Fairy had thought Clara dead; I was sure of that, if nothing else. I had hated Clara that night, hated her enough to squeeze the life from her throat. How could we not have been truly divided?

"How do I know if we're divided now?" I asked Orlov.

He smiled, his eyes bright with malice. In that moment, he looked just like his mother.

"Try to kill her again. See if it works."

"If you take sport in this business, you're no better than she is."

"But I am, you know," he said. "My mother thinks only of vengeance. I have a higher calling."

He clapped his hands and stood, becoming suddenly business-like once more.

"I can do what you ask, but it will take a few days. You have the item?"

I handed him the wrapped parcel from my bag, watching him with some suspicion. But he did not approach me again. The rows of toys, too, seemed to have relaxed. The gingerbread men had retreated to the safety of their table, and two of the clowns had begun some sort of jumping game. I could not help marveling at these wonders, though I had feared them only moments before.

"Why do you make toys?" I asked him. "With all your gifts, why not something else?"

"My creations are not toys," Orlov replied. "They only look that way. You of all people should know."

"But you sell them as toys. You—"

I halted suddenly, thinking of the frenzy that had gripped the city in the past weeks, the wild hunt for genuine Orlovs, with every wealthy family determined to have one as a prize. They were not toys, but no one else knew that. The nobility had bought out every shop in the city, taking these tiny murderers into their homes. They were wrapped in boxes now, but after Christmas morning they would be everywhere: in parlors and drawing rooms, on mantels and tables, in bedrooms where children slept.

"What have you done?" I demanded.

"Nothing," Orlov replied, "and I will not. Not unless all else fails. Not unless they refuse to listen to reason."

"Reason?"

He stared at me for a long moment, and I felt those black eyes turning me inside out. Then he began to laugh.

"What?"

"Oh, I see you, Natasha, as plainly as you seem to see me. Lady Liebermann, proud wife of that highborn idiot you could not stop doting on, even all those years ago. But you are not happy, are you? You see more than most nobles. You know how precarious your world is, how poorly balanced."

He reached out with both hands, flexing the scarred fingers.

"You know that terrible things happen when a man is ignored and mistreated for too long."

"And what of that?" I asked.

"For weeks my people have been searching for the identity of the woman, Mother Christmas, who was so generous to the children of the poor. But by happy accident, I think I have found her."

"And again I ask: what of it?"

"We can always use a sympathetic noble."

This time, it was my turn to laugh.

"I spent my life being used by Drosselmeyer. Now you think I will be a puppet for you?"

"Not for me. For them."

He gestured out the window. Moving to join him there, I saw that a crowd was marching through the street below: men and women, even children, their faces grimed from soot, or bloodied from butchering. They were heading for the center of the city, bearing signs before them.

"You sympathize," Orlov said quietly, switching off the electric light. "Enough to risk the wrath of the King. Soon or late, you know, he will call out the full army. He will slaughter them all, unless he is stopped."

I stared at the dark parade, which seemed to go on forever beneath the window. One father held his sleeping child in his arms. And I felt a curious prickling of my spine as another memory fell into place, another piece of the dream I had forgotten, the only piece that really mattered. *Did you see the pit?* Fritz had asked, and I had, that terrible and pitiful tangle of bodies that seemed without end. Orlov was not wrong. There would be slaughter, if it could not be prevented.

"You care about them," I said. "The poor. Why?"

"Perhaps only because I understand them. I spent years working as they do, in a tiny dark room, barely rewarded for my efforts, the boot of the owner on my throat. I have committed myself to their cause."

"You're the ringleader. The one the King is looking for."

Orlov's face tightened.

"I am only one of several. Will you help us?"

"I can help no one until I deal with Clara. Surely you see that. Will you help *me*?"

"What is your address?" he asked, producing a tiny journal from his pocket and switching the light back on. As he opened the book, I saw that the pages were covered with drawings and figures, notes that only a madman could read. I was not sure whether I wanted him to have my address, but it seemed pointless to withhold it when it was common knowledge among the shopkeepers of the city. I gave him my address, and he licked the nib of his pen, then wrote it down on a page that was already filled, with nothing to distinguish it from any of the others.

"You will have the piece back before Christmas Eve."

"Thank you," I said, though the words came only with difficulty. I realized that I was becoming inured to even the idea of gratitude, as though all things I received had been placed before me for my pleasure, as though nothing were given anymore, only compelled. Taking the pins from my veil, I began to secure it to my hat, watching the clowns, who were now playing leapfrog. Their shrill giggles rang around the big, hollow room.

"You need not fear them," Orlov said, mistaking my interest. "I have told them to stand down."

"Why?"

"I have no need to kill you . . . and, if I am truthful, no power to do so. Drosselmeyer's schemes have worked thus far, at least, though he is not here to see it. You and your sister stand at each other's throats, but you both remain."

I nodded, ignoring the judgment in his words, finding it faulty. What lay between Clara and me was hardly admirable, but we stood in a room full of miniature assassins. Orlov might claim that he and his mother were done, but he had more of the old country in him than he thought.

"What about my brother?" I asked.

"I heard about him as well."

"Surely he doesn't deserve such a punishment."

"It wasn't my doing."

"Can you fix it?"

"No. It's between him and my mother, and I will not get involved. All of you should be careful. I know what your sister was meant to be, but I'm not sure what Drosselmeyer has created in you. My mother may not even know. But I would guess she will perceive you as a threat. You and your sister both."

"Yes," I murmured, thinking of Clara, who had been allowed to come back, with her black-stained mouth, hands hooked into claws.

"I did warn you," Orlov said. "You should have left my creations alone. You should do so now, though you will not."

"Why?"

"Because even if you manage to survive, you are still the thing Drosselmeyer made, still dark. There are uses for creatures like you . . . terrible uses, and my mother will find them. She always does."

He pulled out a pocket watch, opened and glanced at it, stuck it back into his pocket.

"Now I must ask you to leave, Mrs. Liebermann. I am expecting other callers. I will send your parcel by courier as soon as it's ready."

I hesitated with my hand on the doorknob, sensing that he had told me the truth, a terrible truth that had nothing to do with me but everything to do with what I had seen in Drosselmeyer's mirror. But it was too late. Done was done, and there could be no wisdom in regret, not at this late date. Before I could reconsider, I seized the doorknob and turned it, nearly wrenching it off, and as I came back into the warehouse, I saw something terrible, perhaps the most terrible thing I had yet seen.

The families still covered the floor, but now they were watching the door through which we stepped. I saw that their eyes were all the same, black and piercing and cold, fixed on the scarred inventor behind me, absorbing him hungrily. She was there, she was there right in front of him, and he couldn't see it. But I always saw, and in the gaze of their endless hunger I lost the sedate retreat I was attempting and found myself running through their ranks, trying not to look at them. I fled down the rickety staircase, almost sprinting, and if one of the risers had snapped beneath me, plunging me through to the floor below, I would almost have counted it a blessing, a great gift of things that could no longer be seen.

OUTSIDE, I WAS ABOUT TO CLIMB INTO THE CARRIAGE WHEN I caught sight of a shadow behind a stack of nearby boxes, eyes gleaming in the thin moonlight. At another time I might have been frightened, but now I was only heartsore, sick of secrets and games and tricks. I marched over to the stack of boxes, heedless of the squeals of my quarry, and grabbed hold of something that turned out to be Clara, hollow-eyed Clara in her rags. She was angry at being caught; her mouth held the petulant Clara-pout that I remembered so well. Her cheeks were sticky with sugar, as though she had been caught eating too much gingerbread.

"What are you doing here?" I demanded, shaking her. Orlov was right; she was no ghost. Her flesh was solid beneath my hands, solid and warm. Belatedly, it occurred to me that I had meant to ask Orlov more about the mysterious Grigori, but forgotten.

"I—I followed you."

"No, you didn't." I stared at her for a moment, then turned to stare up at the warehouse.

"You were here," I said, marveling. "Here . . . for her."

Clara tried to duck away, but I wrapped a hand in her dark hair and held her there, gripping tightly as she mewled and begged. Ivan and the footmen began to approach, but I waved them away. Clara's appearance, which had once horrified me in the middle of the night, would not have raised an eyebrow in the upstairs room of Orlov's warehouse, and I didn't want any of them to mistake what was going on here.

"Let go, you bitch!" Clara hissed.

"She sent you to spy on him?"

"Let go!"

"Answer my question, and I will."

"Yes, she sent me to spy! She wants him home, expected him to come after Drosselmeyer. When he didn't, she was—"

Clara fell silent. She had stopped pulling now, but I released her all the same, unnerved by what she hadn't said. If the Sugar Plum Fairy had really expected her son to come home, she would have been disappointed, and she didn't strike me as one to take disappointment well. Clara turned away, leaning against a nearby stack of empty boxes, and I reflected that if it was odd for me to see my face on Clara, it must be doubly odd for her to look back at me . . . Clara who had spent so many hours before the mirror, who would have known her own face as though it were an old friend.

"What did she do to you?"

"What do you care?" Clara snarled. "I'm free now, no thanks to you, and I won't be going back."

"Then what do you want from me?"

"I told you: I want what you stole. I'll have it too."

"Clara—"

But she had already torn from me, her shadow slipping behind the boxes. When I rounded them, she was gone, and I could hear nothing save the roar of the massive crowd of workers several blocks away.

I wandered back out toward the carriage, feeling as though I could have slapped Clara, who had not changed a bit. The Sugar Plum Fairy had told her to come here, find Orlov, and of course Clara had not asked why, had not wanted to know more than she needed to.

"Where to, my lady?" Ivan asked, as the footmen helped me into the carriage.

"Home, please."

As he clicked to the horses, I leaned from my window to have a last look at the massive warehouse with its blaze of light. The scene was ridiculous; Orlov could not have advertised his presence more clearly if he had taken out a posting in one of the city's circulars. Yet his location was still secret; wealthy parents sought in vain to secure a private audience with the toymaker, while I had been forced to pry the information from Anastasia. If Orlov was so well hidden in plain sight, someone powerful must be protecting him, someone with the heft to sway all those trudging, sullen denizens of the warehouse district. Who would have that sort of broad power?

As if in answer, another carriage drew up before Orlov's warehouse. But this was no expensive conveyance like mine, only a plain rattletrap such as country people used in the rain. I rapped sharply on the wooden bar above my head, felt Ivan pull the horses to a halt.

Several men descended from the carriage. They gave the appearance of a group of friends, all laughing and joking together, save for one of them, a small man who stared up at the well-lit building, his face clearly visible even from my distant vantage. He was bald, with an egg-shaped head. A long mustache drooped and straggled around his humorless mouth, ending in a pointed beard. He was clearly the man in charge, for at his muttered command, the rest of the group sobered and followed him to the door, where they seemed to have no more problem getting inside than I had.

"What is it, my lady?" Ivan asked, leaning down to the window.

I did not reply. Something rang strangely inside me, like a bell. I felt that I should have recognized the little man, as though I had seen him somewhere before, in a newspaper or a daguerreotype. Healing and divination, Father Benedict had said, and if Drosselmeyer had divided us and given Clara the healing, then what was left for me but to see the future? I thought again of the dark city I had seen in my dream, the acres of corpses covering the lawn, and could not escape my certainty that the little man was important somehow. But I could not grasp it. After several moments, I rapped on the roof again, and felt the horses go.

CHAPTER

38

ORLOV WAS AS GOOD AS HIS WORD. HIS PARCEL ARRIVED ON the twenty-second of December, and I did not unwrap it, only set it on my vanity table. Conrad asked me what it was, and when I told him it was a Christmas present for him, he was just fool enough to believe me.

On Christmas Eve we dressed in our opposing bedrooms for my family's party. I prepared with some care, taking extra pains with my hair, my powder, my jewels, though I didn't know why I bothered. The party would proceed as it always had, vulgar and perhaps spectacular in its vulgarity, but I would not be there.

Before we left, I moved to stand before Drosselmeyer's mirror one last time. I had avoided the glass for the last week, troubled by Orlov's words, the changes he seemed to think inevitable. But now I was leaving for a long while, perhaps going to my own death. Clara would not leave me alone; I knew it now. Her sense of grievance had only sharpened during her time in the Kingdom of Sweets, and I knew what that felt like. Whether she was human or ghost, this problem would only be solved when one of us was dead, and so I wanted to see my own face one last time.

I looked, and recoiled.

My eyes were black hollows in the mirror. Shadows rose behind both of my shoulders, bookending me, locking me in. As I turned away, I heard a soft rustle, a sound I knew well: the unfurling of wings. So she had finally come; she was here with me now. Only when I turned back to the mirror, heart hammering against my ribs, did I understand: the rustling shadows behind me were not her wings but mine, vast ebon nightmares sprouting from my back.

"Are you ready, love?" Conrad called, and I clapped a hand to my mouth, stifling a scream.

WHEN WE ARRIVED AT THE PARTY, I GREETED MY PARENTS DU-tifully, kissing my father on the cheek. I could not judge the two of them as I once had, not when my own marriage lay in a similar ruin. Here in my family's old house, six long years later, I could see the contrast of past and present perfectly, and it revealed my younger self as an utter fool. Not knowing Conrad, I had loved him; knowing him well, I had come to loathe him. The Fairy had given me good advice that haunted night in the Kingdom of Sweets, but I had not listened, and I had no one to blame but myself.

My mother kept a protective hand on Fritz's shoulder, turning a defiant glare on anyone who wished to ignore him in passing, any newly arrived party guest who tried to turn away. I saw no tears in her eyes, and when I looked for the telltale lump of the bottle in the pocket of her dress, I did not see that either. Was it possible that she had given it up?

When our turn came, I gripped Fritz's hand as I kissed him,

feeling only sorrow for him, for the nightmares he must have seen in that single moment before the nutcracker crashed to the ground. But Fritz endured my touch for only a moment before he began to howl. Tearing free of my hand, ducking Mother's comforting arms, he fled upstairs, and I heard the slam of a door.

"Oh, for God's sake," Father said. "Don't let it worry you, apple. He's mad, that's all."

"He's not mad," Mother said, her face suffused with anger. "He's only disturbed."

Father rolled his eyes at us, but I did not smile, for that dreadful vision in the mirror was too fresh in my mind. Even Orlov could not say what Drosselmeyer had done to me, where the path of darkness might go unchecked. What were we now, Clara and I? Merely freaks?

When we had greeted everyone, Conrad began to guide me into the parlor, but I excused myself, saying that I needed a moment, that he should go on through and get me a drink. A rush of people had just come in the doors, Kleists and Breyers and Kalenovs all arriving at once, like a heap of muffled snowmen, and in the confusion caused by their arrival I ducked away from Conrad, meaning to go straight upstairs. But it was not to be; Clara could no more remain invisible at these soirees than Natasha had been able to lead a reel. As I put my hand on the banister, I heard a loud, jovial voice call my name.

"Clara! Clara! Over here!"

Turning around, I saw Bishop Theofan in the doorway to the parlor, waving me over. He was standing beside a tall, gaunt man with dark hair, a man I had never seen before.

"I have been introducing my new friend here around the city," Bishop Theofan said, beaming, as I moved reluctantly in that direction. From the smell of him, the bishop had consumed a fair bit of rum, and he certainly seemed jollier than usual. "He has expressed a particular wish to be known to you!"

I looked at the newcomer, sizing him up. He wore the robes of a priest, but his hair was much longer than was the fashion in the priesthood. His beard, too, was unfashionable, sprouting wildly from his face in grizzled curls, like an untamed hedge. Yet his eyes unnerved me. Bright blue they were, sharp as a bird's. As he gazed at me for a long moment, I had the uncomfortable sensation that he was staring right through me.

"He is a grim sort, our Grigori," the bishop said, chuckling. "But do not be fooled by his outward appearance, Lady Liebermann. His advice has been of great value to the King and Queen."

"Is that so?" I asked lightly. Inwardly, though, I quailed. Had I ever found Drosselmeyer's eyes piercing? These were much, much worse.

"My condolences on the loss of your sister," the gaunt priest said, raising the cross around his neck and kissing it. "She resides in the bosom of Christ now."

"Indeed she does," I said quickly. "If you will excuse me—"

He grabbed my arm . . . not roughly, but with enough force that I stilled.

"At your leisure, Lady Liebermann, I would like to speak with you in private."

"About what matter?"

"About my old friend Drosselmeyer. Your godfather."

"Drosselmeyer has disappeared."

He smiled, though the smile did not touch his eyes. "Yes, that is what the constables say. Yet I will be making my own inquiries."

"Come, Grigori, come!" the bishop interjected, his drunken voice now a trifle worried. "The dark sister is long dead, and

Drosselmeyer, bless him, is in the hereafter. Is this any matter for a party?"

Grigori released my arm. Yet I felt marked, all the same. Those extraordinary blue eyes seemed to bore into me, and I had the sudden uneasy feeling that he, like the Sugar Plum Fairy, would always be able to find me, no matter where I went.

"At your leisure, Lady Liebermann," Grigori said quietly, and then allowed Bishop Theofan to pull him away into the crowd. I remained frozen for a moment, then turned and went upstairs, neither quickly nor slowly, with Orlov's parcel tucked neatly beneath the white stole that wrapped my arms.

My old bedroom was unchanged, still lit by the silver moonlight that filtered through the filmy hangings when the curtains were open. But the chamber had a musty smell that not even airing could overcome, the unmistakable smell of an unused space. Neighborhood gossip said that my parents allowed no one to sleep in here, not even guests. Yet I closed the door behind me, for I didn't want anyone to spot me in here, least of all Grigori, who, I felt certain, knew much more about me than he should. If he was truly here to investigate his good friend's death, he might try to get into Drosselmeyer's house; I made a mental note to tell the property agents, then realized that it barely mattered now. Clara was the problem tonight. Grigori could wait for the morning.

My old rocking chair still sat in its place near the window, and I dropped my stole on the bed and sat down. Outside, the city's rooftops spread before me, clear in a clear night, with the white line of the ice-covered river snaking between them. Taking Orlov's parcel in careful fingers, I began to unwrap it, slowly, a corner at a time, keeping my hand gripped around the paper so that a single layer of wrapping remained to cover the creation beneath. I rocked as I worked, pleased to find that the chair's comforting squeak was still just as I remembered it. Many trappings of my old life were here. My bookshelves still lined the room, though they were empty now. My white wardrobe stood untouched, still needing a fresh coat of paint, and the frost-lined windows revealed the oil streetlamps of my childhood, throwing the same shadows I remembered on the walls. The four-poster bed still stood stolidly against the wall, and even the mattress appeared unchanged, that same old mattress where Conrad and I had once rolled together in a wild delirium that I had believed to be love. The pain of those days was gone, but so was the joy, and I thought that I would never again feel anything so strongly as those nights, when I would force myself to stay awake, watching Conrad as he slept, wishing I could hold back the dawn. I closed my eyes and saw it, as though in a flash of cold dawn light: my hand, reaching across the icy void for a piece of torn shirt. How could I have been content with so little? Why had I not demanded more?

"Natasha."

I opened my eyes, and Clara was there, standing in front of the window, a tottering horror in her scraps of gown. She had come for me tonight, just as I had hoped, for here we were, once again, on Christmas Eve.

"Clara. Merry Christmas."

She grinned, revealing teeth that had gone crooked and rotten from lack of attention . . . or, perhaps, from eating too many sweets. I continued to rock, resting my fingers on the undone parcel in my lap. Magic ebbed and flowed, Clara had said, and that was undoubtedly true, for I could feel the power that curled and writhed just beneath the wrappings, and what had once chilled me now made me feel galvanized, as though I could pull off the paper and jump the moon.

"Didn't I kill you?" I asked. "How are you still alive?"

"You were too weak for murder."

"Did the Sugar Plum Fairy say that?"

Clara's face twisted involuntarily, with an agony too misplaced to be anything but real.

"She isn't a fairy. She isn't . . ." Clara paused for a moment, her shoulders moving heavily up and down. "She's—"

"What?" I asked, honestly curious to know the Fairy as Clara had known her, to see what she'd seen.

"She's nothing," Clara replied brokenly. "Only dark. The dark at the bottom of everything."

I nodded wisely, for this seemed to me an excellent description of the Fairy, even better than the one provided by Orlov. And I thought again of my reflection in the mirror, of the black wings arching over my back.

"What did you see?" Clara asked, her voice almost pleading, and from this question I saw that she was perhaps no more comfortable with her choices than I was, that though she might feel them inevitable, they did not resolve her guilt.

"The same thing you saw," I finally replied. "Darkness, but as though the darkness was female." And now, for the first time in a long while, I remembered the name the Fairy had given beneath the overhang of twisted trees, the name she claimed to like best. "The Queen of Spades."

"Yes," Clara replied, her head bent thoughtfully in the posture of a scholar, though her silhouette spoke only of madness. "Strange, that we both saw her the same way."

"Perhaps not. We are twins, after all."

Clara grinned bloodlessly, lurching forward on blackened, frostbitten toes, and I gripped the parcel in my lap, tensing my muscles in preparation.

"We don't have to do this, Clara."

"Oh, you would say so," she snapped, and I saw that she was weeping, black tears on her cheeks. "Do you know how time runs in her country? Five years here, but I have been waiting for an eternity in that room, and you don't know, you can't imagine—"

I had no answer, for no, I couldn't imagine. The woman I saw in the mirror had been screaming, screaming . . . and there were so many doors in that castle. So many doors. Clara reached for me, shambling forward, her hands stiffening into claws, and for a moment I didn't move, couldn't, held transfixed by the picture she had painted. I had meant to kill her; even now, I could not pretend to any other motive on that distant night. But I had not intended the horror she described; not to leave her there. And I felt the first stirrings of anger at the Queen of Spades, that creature who had once seemed so far beyond my anger, or anyone else's. She had lied to me. I had not known, and if I had—if the Queen had told me the entire truth—I would have acted differently. There were things far worse than death, and for the first time I could say it honestly: had I known, I would have acted differently.

But I could not change the past like this, not with Clara's grasping hands coming for my throat. So I stood, unwrapping the final corner of the parcel. Orlov had not cheated me; I could sense the power of the thing a paper's thickness away. At the last moment Clara glimpsed what I held, and her smile twisted, becoming a rictus of horrified understanding, but it was too late, for I had already leapt forward, dropping the wrappings as I went, and pressed the nutcracker into her outstretched hand.

ACT V

NEMESIS

What are the roots that clutch, what branches grow
Out of this stony rubbish? Son of man,
You cannot say, or guess . . .

—*The Waste Land*
T. S. Eliot

CHAPTER

39

T HE LAND WAS STILL COLD, BUT MY FALL WAS NO LONGER
cushioned by a blanket of snow. When I landed, rocks
clawed at me, tearing my arms, shredding my dress, and I covered
my face, trying to protect my eyes, feeling tiny slivers of rock
tear at my cheeks. After a long, painful slide, I came to rest and
lay still.

"Natasha."

I opened my eyes and found her there, a dark shadow without
meaning or sense. The very geometry of her had altered; skin no
longer flowed into hair, but it seemed rather the other way round,
and the wings that had risen so majestically from her back were
now inverted, feathers dripping like ichor from their tips.

"You have returned, Natasha. Not by accident, but by design.
I am pleased."

"Clara," I muttered, sitting up. "She came back."

"Of course she did, child. You took far more than you lost,
and fair is fair. All scales must balance in the end."

Pulling myself to my feet, I found that we were standing on a plain, perhaps the very snow-covered plain of my memory, all of it illuminated by the moon, the dark moon, the same as it had ever been, so powerfully a part of this land that even the Queen's great magic had been unable to disguise it the last time. The moon's light flowed blackly, revealing the land as dark and stony, its endless surface dotted with broken towers crumbling to dust, its vastness infinite and yet bounded by terrible horizons both vertical and horizontal at the same time, and I knew that if I looked at them long enough, I would surely go mad, which would fit perfectly with the Queen's plans because that was what this land had been designed for: to facilitate the journey into madness, to render the downhill slide so frictionless that it could not be reversed. I could not blame Orlov for wanting no part of this land; against that tortured background, even the Queen's senseless silhouette seemed almost sane.

"You thought I killed Clara," I said quietly. "Why is she still alive?"

"Pity," the Queen replied shortly. "I thought Drosselmeyer had already divided the two of you, so deeply that it could be done. Likely he thought so as well. But you still pitied your sister, and that made you weak. Too weak for murder."

"Where is Clara?"

"You will know where to find her."

"And will you stand aside?" I demanded. "Let us settle it?"

The Queen chuckled, and it was a terrible sound, blacker than a curse at midnight. I tried to see if she was smiling, but even her mouth was wrong now, a terrible razored shape that seemed to have five sides, or none, a yawning void that made the idea of upturned corners not simply unthinkable but impossible.

"Stand aside, child? You have been here twice now, one more time than most humans can boast, but you still understand nothing about this place. Human problems must be settled by human actors, and of course we will stand aside, that is what we do: create the arena for redress, and then let events take their course."

"That's a lie. You enjoy this, I know you do."

The Queen grinned, a snarl of needles that made me shudder.

"True enough. I have my pleasures, and take them where I can. I enjoy watching your kind set upon each other like lions to the kill. The Romans knew this; they named me Nemesis, but I was far more to them than the saint of wronged lovers and the angry undead. As they degenerated, they knew me even better, so well that they made me the patroness of their gladiators. Fighters entering the arena might have saluted the King, but they bowed to *me*."

She stepped forward, holding out her hands, those hands that seemed almost infinite, each unspeakable finger extended, and that was when I noticed, for the first time, the shadow beside her: a miniature creature, hunched over and so shrunken that he barely reached her knees. At first I thought it was another gingerbread man, but then it looked up at me and I saw that it was a manikin, a puppet dressed in blue velvet, its tiny hands clinging to the unplottable expanse of her skirts. I felt a single moment of horror, echo of that long night of dreams, but here he was again, one tiny black eye staring at me, the other hidden behind an eye patch.

"Godfather," I said. But he turned away, burying his face in her skirts.

"We will stand aside, Natasha," the Queen said, "just as we always have. We will stand aside and do what we love best: watch."

She flickered and vanished, taking the shrunken puppet with her, leaving me standing alone on the blistered plain.

295

CHAPTER

40

I BEGAN WALKING. THIS WAS NOT AS EASY A MATTER AS IT should have been, for the geometry of the terrain had altered as well, so that what looked like upward slopes often turned out to be dips, and ravines connected with my feet as raised bumps that tripped me fairly, sending me sprawling to the ground. But I stumbled forward regardless, making slow but steady progress through the grey and rotten snow, driven by an engine more powerful than survival or even hunger, an engine I remembered well from my previous journey across this land: the great and immutable force of what must happen. What was right. Such things were much clearer here; I remembered that as well. Until that long night in the castle, I had not understood what Clara was. What she had taken from me.

She didn't take anything from you, my mind whispered. *You only thought she did.*

But it no longer mattered, the old grievance between us. Now it seemed only a matter of survival. Drosselmeyer had laid us on this path, years before, and I was amazed that we had been able to maintain the illusion of coexistence so long.

After a time I began to gain some semblance of bearings, for the terrain which had been so cleverly disguised last time did not hide the lay of the land. Here was the deep ravine that had sunk between walls of fudge, but now the walls were a shapeless grey mass, seeming to go neither up nor down, yet somehow rising so high into the sky that I could not see the tops of them. I didn't dare go into that ravine, thinking vaguely of rockfall, of collapse, of how it would be to become buried in this dead land without even a whisper of breath, a stone to mark my memory, so I ended up circumventing the entire grey structure. I traveled in a seemingly endless half circle until I reached another landmark I remembered: the bed that had once housed a stream of pink gelatin. There was still a stream there, and it sounded like any stream one might hear babbling along in the countryside on a clear summer's day. But the liquid that gurgled happily through the streambed was black, and I veered away from it, thinking vague thoughts of the river of Lethe, certain that if I even touched that water, much less tasted it, I would lose everything. I would need it all, I saw now, every slight and grievance. I knew where I was going; my feet had known their course long before my mind.

Ahead of me loomed the forest, just as I remembered it: blacker than black, topped by the silhouettes of an infinite number of ruined branches twisting into the dead sky. This was where it had been last time, where it had to be, and the power I had sensed in that clearing was drawing me, pulling me back. Clara would be there; I could almost feel her out there, wandering her own path back to the forest, to the clearing at the end of her life.

I reached the edge of the trees, but they did not frighten me now. I charged inside, each stride imbued with purpose, almost daring anything to cross my path. And now I sensed them, parting before me: the spectators, unseen but there, just as they had been before. They would watch, yes, but they would not interfere, and it was well for them that they would not, for I was ready, feeling myself somehow a match for them, utterly unlike but still dangerous, like a blazing torch thrust into a nest of spiders.

Warm.

The trees parted, revealing the clearing, and I did not hesitate but strode on in, feeling them close behind me: her people, the company of spades, binding us in, making an unbroken circle that ringed the clearing. Clara was already there, standing across from me, her left foot pointing daintily outward. She wore my face, and the sight of that was so unbearable that I launched forward without grace, without ceremony . . . and then I halted, as though startled out of a deep dream.

Lightning flashed, tearing a seam in the darkness above, revealing that the sky in this country was not black, as I had always supposed, but rather a dim, dead brown, shot through with veins of purple, the color of a long-healed bruise. In that brief but endless moment of light I saw them all clearly, a circle of shadowy forms. The Fairy stood to my left, the horrible puppet Drosselmeyer beside her, and in that dreadful company she alone was beautiful, a beauty of such utter darkness and horror that I was transfixed by it, unable to look away. In the moment before the lightning vanished, I saw that she watched not Clara but me, and I was complimented, absurdly pleased . . . but I also saw something else. She controlled all things in this land, she had told me once, controlled them so completely that even the moon did not dare rise without her permission. But when the thunder came

next, rending the silence of the clearing, shuddering the earth beneath my feet, I saw something I would not have believed.

The Queen flinched.

The thunder faded, and in its wake the crowd around us
sighed, that slow sigh I remembered as signifying neither agreement
nor disagreement, only the way things were now, the pass that
had been reached, and at that moment I heard a voice in my ear,
as close as though he stood right behind me . . . no longer scarred,
not here, but still drowned in the bitterness of this place, so bone-
deep that it even showed up in his inventions, toys that betrayed
his history as surely as they betrayed his genius, so that he was
unable to make even a gingerbread man without giving it the
ability to weep.

"Abandon this. Now, while you still can."

I whirled, furious; how weak did he think I was?

But Orlov wasn't there. He never had been. My mind had dug
him up in a last, desperate effort to thwart this thing, as though
anything could keep me from the inevitable event of this combat,
the rightness of it. All of our lives, it had been Clara and me, but
now we stood here and the very earth itself seemed to demand
resolution, that we solve our inequality at last, that someone win.
And it was only now, in this place, in that endless moment between the thunder fading and the lightning's next strike, that I
found myself able to consider *why* I had killed her. Many times in
the course of our youth, I had thought that all of life would be
easier without Clara standing in the way, constantly inviting
unfavorable comparison, overshadowing everything with her
beauty, her light . . . but would I ever have murdered her for that?
No; the truth was that I had killed Clara for the oldest and simplest of motives: because I had wanted what she had. Love might

be real, but it was also utterly precarious, just waiting to turn to hate. I might have called Clara's actions betrayal, but the simple truth was greed. I had felt entitled to revenge, and once I returned to Clara's face, Clara's life, I fell in line for the same reason: because it seemed right, and because I could. Murder did that, I saw now: muddled the mind, reduced perspective to only the one, so that all that mattered was moving forward, driving through. Getting away with it. Now we faced each other again, murder in our eyes, but why? Conrad was forgotten, buried in the long-ago past. What could we possibly gain?

I turned this question over in my mind for what seemed like endless time during that few seconds, staring at my twin, trying to see past my own face, past the formless, vulpine crowd that surrounded us, past the bruised history that had brought us to this point. Vengeance was a seductive idea, so beautiful in its symmetry that it seemed utterly necessary, almost a moral imperative, a path without turnings. But if it was symmetrical, that symmetry was undeniably empty, and with the rotten land stretching in all directions beneath my feet, I could feel the contours of that emptiness, almost taste it with my tongue . . . a ruined taste, like that of ancient dust. The Queen wanted us to fight, *needed* us to fight; it powered her, gave her something she considered her due, and this clearing still felt like the very heart of her land. She had learned to wield vengeance like a scythe—or perhaps a spade— but still the past seemed less important than what we might be now. The changes in the mirror, the wings that sprouted from my back, what were they? And what was Clara, if she was no longer Drosselmeyer's talisman or even my twin?

Another crescendo of thunder broke over our heads, shaking the world. The Queen flinched again, and I suddenly glimpsed the turning: a nearly invisible turning, almost obscured by brush, its signage long ago decayed and washed away. Clara had no use for my face, but I did. I was no longer the girl who had hidden in corners. I had more imagination than she; even with my own face, my own name, I could become anything I wished. The part of my mind that demanded justice, that insisted on retribution at all costs . . . that part had been shaped by Drosselmeyer, like so much else, and I would not have him there.

"I have a request!" I called, not able to see the Queen, but knowing exactly where she stood in the darkness, her wings enfolding her like a shroud.

"Yes?" Her voice was so close that she too might have been standing at my shoulder, but the only figure I could see was Clara, standing twenty feet away on the clearing's blasted earth.

"If we're to do this, I want my own face back, and I want Clara to have hers."

For a long moment there was only silence in the woods, not even the faintest breath of wind.

"Why?" the Queen hissed, and I could tell that my request had disturbed her, confounded her somehow. Perhaps no one had ever asked for such a thing before. Clara looked just as confused, her bewilderment out of place on my features.

"I want to see Clara," I told the Queen. "I want her to be herself, wholly herself. And when I tear the flesh from her face, I want it to be Clara's face."

Again there was silence, but this time I sensed approval in it, could almost hear the pleased murmuring of the invisible crowd that surrounded us on all sides. They had come for blood, and it occurred to me then that if I understood the Queen little, I understood them even less, this nameless, formless crowd of creatures who had somehow come into her possession. The Queen was not chaos; she offered choices, and then demanded that one live with the consequences. Perhaps all of these dark things had refused to do so . . . or perhaps they had done. Perhaps these were the consequences. This latter thought disturbed me so much that I closed my eyes, cutting off the entire line of inquiry. If there was any later, I could consider it then. For now, my face had begun to alter again, pain striking between sinew and bone as the upheaval ran its course, and when the lightning struck again, I saw that Clara's face, too, was in the process of metamorphosis. I was going to take a chance, give her everything she wanted . . . but would she want it anymore? Natasha had been content with so little, but Clara wasn't built that way. There was a final, sliding bit of pain beneath my cheekbones, then everything lay still.

"Done," the Queen pronounced from her place in the circle. "Now we will have justice."

For one long moment, I hesitated. I was only human, after all, and the gamble I was about to undertake demanded a willingness to lose everything. Clara had once cut me to the core in a place that had never healed, and now I saw that it never would heal because I had sealed off that entire soft place in my mind, welded it shut. The happiness that people sought all of their lives, that the poets and novelists talked of, I would never have it.

God help me, I thought. *I do belong here. I'm one of them.*

"Clara."

She turned to me. Lightning flashed again, and there was her face, so long resented that I had never grown accustomed to it, not even when it belonged to me. She had taken my pretty white party dress for her own, and her teeth were once again straight, her blue eyes shining. The sight of her made it infinitely harder to say what I needed to say, but somehow I found it within me, all the same, because it was true. The entire track of my own life had been shaped by our differences, so that if anyone ever asked, *Who are you, Natasha Stahlbaum?* I was forced to reply: *Clara's sister.* But here, at last, was a moment in which I might define myself.

"All wrongs are settled, Clara. I forgive you. Go home."

Clara's silhouette, deep black against the ghostly outline of the forest, seemed to shimmer, rippling slightly. Thunder split the world, but even its eldritch cracking was not enough to drown out the Queen's dreadful scream of rage, and then the entire clearing was alive with the sound of her anger, hissings and snarls. For the first time I was truly afraid, but I was not craven enough to think that my fear changed anything with Clara, that I had the right to use her as a shield, and so, in the moment when I might have changed my mind, might have revoked my forgiveness—and I sensed it could be done, sensed that the Queen would offer me that last option to save myself in return for a good show—I remained silent. The clearing stood still for what seemed an eternity, even the air itself unwilling to move, and when the lightning came again, Clara was gone.

CHAPTER
41

B RING HER TO ME."
The Queen's voice was low and controlled, in command once more, but anger hived and tunneled beneath. I felt myself surrounded, clawed hands taking my shoulders, and at that point I felt a rogue urge to recant, a wish that I had simply fought Clara there in the clearing, killed her for good. But the urge was brief, and there was relief in that brevity; if I was a coward, it was only for a moment. Then their hands were pushing me roughly through the forest, fingers pinching and cruel, not caring if they hurt me, not caring if I bruised.

I could not see the Queen any longer, but as we left the trees, I thought I spotted Dmitri, my old dinner companion, off to one side. There was nothing handsome about him now, his form slumped and hunched like that of a scarecrow, but he climbed over fallen trees with a long-legged grace I recognized, a grace that seemed now not athletic but animal, and when he turned, I saw that his mouth was smeared black, as though it had been painted. Then he turned away, and did not look at me again.

Now the land began to slope upward. I chose not to look at the horde of misshapen black figures around me, focusing instead on the ground, following the slope doggedly, dimly aware that while it appeared to go up, it actually went down, that my feet were being drawn inexorably forward. I did not become accustomed to these contradictions; every few feet my legs would tangle, and were it not for the sudden clench of clawed fingers on my arm, I would have gone down. I thought of Clara waking up, perhaps next to Conrad, in the bright world we knew. She too would look in Drosselmeyer's mirror; what would she see there? I wished I had had time to warn her about Grigori, the blue-eyed man who had come looking for Drosselmeyer. He did not strike me as a man to be content with Clara's fatuous explanations. I should have warned her, but would she even have taken my warning? Grigori's letter to Drosselmeyer had said something about reunification, but I was not fool enough to think that we were reunited, Clara and I. Just because I had forgiven her, that didn't mean she had forgiven me, and her grievance was surely greater than mine. Were we truly divided now? I didn't know.

We topped the high hill, and I looked over the edge.

Below, on the floor of the valley, the castle waited, vast and black and sepulchral, its cornices and parapets crumbling, its once-gay bunting faded and rotten. Even without the advancing decay, I knew it for a terrible place, a place where hope shriveled, where all good intentions were lost. In that instant my courage failed, and I drew back, meaning to turn around. But an iron hand grasped my arm, and a voice spoke in my ear, a voice I recognized.

"I am sorry, sister. You must go."

I looked up past the blackened face and saw that it was the captain, the weary soldier who had once helped me so gallantly into the sleigh. He wore no uniform now; his clothes were a ragged ruin of shapeless black, but he retained the same rigid posture and bearing that had originally identified him. As he looked down at me, his clutch on my arm softened, and with a blink of distant surprise, I realized that his hand did not feel cold.

"You were courteous to us, sister," he murmured, "and we, who had almost forgotten courtesy, have not forgotten yours. I am charged to see you safely into the castle. But that is all I can do."

I nodded, drawing a deep breath, trying to swallow my fear. Some of it did go, for even this moment of brief and empty kindness had heartened me. I wanted to thank him, but when I opened my mouth, fingers prodded me roughly in the back, and I began my stumbling journey down the slope.

THIS TIME, THERE WERE NO FIELDS OF JELLY BEANS, NO PEPPERmint lampposts. The Kingdom of Sweets had become a dry black land that seemed to stretch forever, horizon to horizon. The Queen struck me as a woman who had chosen her own exile, but like all exiles, she had been forced to the dead lands that no one wanted. This place refused to hold its shape, refused to conform to any geometry or physics I had learned as a child. As I neared the castle, that rearing black structure seemed to grow smaller, not larger. Sometimes it seemed far away, sometimes very close. And now I realized that she was walking beside me, not a form but a shadow, that flow of deep darkness I remembered from the ballroom.

"My Natasha. What am I to do with you?"

"Whatever you like, I would imagine."

At the Queen's feet, Drosselmeyer began to laugh, the thin wheeze of a broken accordion. The Queen kicked him so hard that he flew through the air and landed with a solid thud on the ground to my right.

"How do you like my fool?" she asked. "He's not very entertaining, I'll admit, for I've removed his tongue. But he still gives me enormous satisfaction."

I stared at Drosselmeyer, feeling a revolted sort of horror. I had thought myself complicit in murder, and I was ready to live with that, but not suffering without end, suffering that I had helped to inflict. If asked, the Queen would no doubt have said that her land was honest, far more honest than ours. Yet I saw it differently, riddled with half-truths and untold secrets. Her version of honesty was like Conrad's: self-serving, constantly in motion.

"Why do you torment him?" I asked, gesturing toward Drosselmeyer.

"Have you not guessed?"

"Of course I've guessed. But your son is happy enough now. He's found his place in the world."

"His *place*," the Queen spat. "In that warehouse? With the wretched of humanity clinging to his feet?"

"He cares for them."

"Then the more fool he. He will learn."

We had stopped now, in front of the castle. To my surprise, I saw that it was no castle at all, but a shrunken model, roughly the size of a child's dollhouse. There was no beauty in it now; rather, it had the look of a mausoleum, long abandoned and worn by the years. Tattered black flags drooped from the battlements.

"You did not have the courage to finish it," the Queen remarked.

"There was no need. Clara did me no wrong, not even back then. And she has been punished enough."

"And what of the others? Your parents, your husband? I have already dealt with your godfather"—she pointed at Drosselmeyer, chuckling, and as her stabbing finger found him, he twitched and moaned on the ground—"but there are plenty of others to blame."

"Why is it so important that someone be to blame?"

Her jaw tightened. "Scales must balance, Natasha. I do not deal in forgiveness but in accountability."

"I have not harmed you."

"And what of your sister? Your godfather?"

"You facilitated those crimes."

"So I did. No law of the universe prevents me from setting my own banquet. Drosselmeyer took you and your twin sister and tried a piece of black magic so old and abhorrent that even the early barbaric cultures wanted nothing to do with it. And you were not alone; he had tried the same thing with many other sets of children before he happened upon you."

"Why didn't it work?"

"Born at Christmas. It grants a peculiar power, Christmas, whether you believe in the Nazarene or not. You and your sister were charmed, but still, such magic always ends in murder. There is no power without it."

We had reached Drosselmeyer now. The Queen stared down at him for a long moment, but he didn't move. Her eyes flared with anger, and beneath my feet, the ground seemed to tremble. Finally Drosselmeyer, with clear reluctance, climbed back up her black skirts, clutching handfuls of them in both hands. We stood before the dollhouse, and I saw that the others around us had melted away. The black moon had risen in the sky again, and we were alone.

"I liked you so much, child, when we first met." The Queen sighed. "As well as I am able to like any of your kind."

"Not much, from what I hear. Does deviling my kind give you peace? Does it win your son's affections back?"

She stared at me for a long moment, and then I suddenly found myself standing in a long corridor, lined with doors. At the far end of the corridor was a window; I took several steps toward it, then jumped back as a giant eye appeared there, black and cold, staring in at me.

"My son will come back," she said, and suddenly I felt myself moving with sickening speed, set down in another corridor, one I recognized. Here was the mirror, and there the clock. But instead of eighteen, its hands were now set at twelve.

"Twelve years," the Queen said. "Twelve years of your kind, that is all, little more than a blink of my eye. Then he will give up his foolish crusade and come home."

"What happens in twelve years?"

The Queen smiled.

"I cannot read the future, child, not as your frauds and mediums claim. I cannot see clear events. I read only the tides, the great movements. You live in an empire of vast inequality, and the trouble has already started. Small skirmishes and uprisings, sparks of flint. But eventually these sparks will grow into a bonfire. My son wishes to help these wretched people, wishes to rebel against his parentage as all children do. But he does not know what I know."

"What do you know?"

"That there is no revolution for man, not really. I have observed your kind since the dawning. They mean well. They wish to slay monsters. But murder begets murder, and so your heroes invariably become monsters themselves. My son does not understand this yet, but he will. He will waste his talents helping to craft an empire of such cruelty that it will make your present

kingdom look like Eden itself, but when he has learned this crucial lesson about humanity, he *will* come home."

There came, again, that sickening feeling of great velocity, and
now I stood at a higher window, looking out at the black land. The
Queen stood there, a formless shadow on the far side of the moat.
Her silhouette seemed to stretch as tall as the clouds, and now, at
last, I understood: the Queen had her own dollhouse. She meant
to leave me here, trapped, the way she had left Clara. The way she
had left all the others in the rooms. I turned my attention to the
puppet Drosselmeyer, who had returned and was now clinging to
her skirts again.

"Godfather!"

He looked up, his eye patch so shrunken and tucked that it
looked as though it were winking itself.

"I found the letter from Grigori! He said something about reunification!"

"Twins," the Queen sneered, giving Drosselmeyer another
sharp kick. "Always twins. It didn't save you in the end, did it,
my little puppet? As for your friend Grigori, he has belonged to
me for centuries."

But Drosselmeyer was staring up at me, his one eye wide.

"I have forgiven Clara," I called down. "What happens if Clara
forgives *me*?"

"He can't answer," the Queen replied. "And even if he could,
your sister will never forgive you. I saw to that."

"You think so poorly of us."

"And why not, child? Your humanity is so easily taken."

Drosselmeyer had begun to gesture wildly, pointing upward,
toward me. He tried to speak, but could only make strange, gar-
bled sounds.

"Watch yourself, little fool," the Queen hissed. "Or I may decide to remove something else."

Drosselmeyer quieted instantly, his one eye wide with fear. But as I watched, he pointed upward again, silently, toward the waist of the Queen's skirts. Squinting, I saw something there, dangling from the Queen's belt. A hint of silver.

"Enjoy your stay, Natasha!" the Queen called. "I may come back to play with you, but I wouldn't count on it. I do have other concerns, after all."

And she withdrew, her dark form fading into nothing, leaving me alone in the castle with the darkness, the silence . . . and those doors. All those doors.

CHAPTER
42

I KNEW THIS PLACE. I HAD BEEN HERE BEFORE. BUT THINGS were different now. The door slammed closed behind me and I found myself surrounded by my own demons: Drosselmeyer as he had looked in his youth; my mother, now a dreadful caricature of herself, her eyes bleeding red, her skin beginning to slough away like fine paper; and last, and worst of all, Fritz, his eyes wide and his fist jammed in his mouth as he screamed and screamed and screamed.

I spent long hours wondering what Clara had seen in here, for I would have thought her incapable of guilt. The thought that it might have been me, that I might have been the one to devil her here while stealing her life outside was intolerable; no sooner had I thought of it than Clara was there, her filthy hair covering her dark face.

If this had been indefinite, I might not have survived it. It did no good to say to myself that I held no guilt for Fritz, for my mother's addiction. Simply being forced to live with these things was punishment enough. But on the eighth day—I marked them on the wall by scraping through the dirt with my fingernail, just for something to do—there was a low tapping at the door. Bending to peer through the keyhole, I saw a tiny shriveled eye: Drosselmeyer.

"Godfather," I said. But I knew he couldn't answer me. Behind me, my mother had begun to weep again. She never stopped, and the sound alone was enough to drive anyone mad. Meanwhile, Clara kept trying to braid my hair, her fingers sticking in the strands, as though they were covered with melted sugar.

Drosselmeyer hopped backward from the keyhole, moving to stand in the corridor, where I could see him. Reaching beneath his shrunken blue cape, he produced a piece of lead and began to draw on the floor. His clumsy, halting movements were painful to watch and I felt unwilling pity, remembering again the sorcerer he had been. First he drew a large, dark eye, then, beside it, a rectangle.

"Can't you write?" I asked, but the little puppet shook his head, returned to his pictures. I realized then that I had never seen any writing in this land, and that seemed the most terrible thing about the Kingdom of Sweets, an entire land locked away from words, from stories, from history.

Drosselmeyer tapped the lead on the ground, clearly impatient, dragging my attention back to the eye, the rectangle. He tapped the eye, pointed at me.

"Me?"

He nodded, then tapped the rectangle. I looked at it for a long moment, not understanding, and Drosselmeyer drew a crude stick figure inside it: a girl with long curling hair.

"Clara?"

Drosselmeyer clapped his hands. He divided the rectangle into four quarters, drawing a different picture on each: a flag, a corsage, a heraldic crest. But I only needed the first two to take his meaning, for of course I knew my medieval knights, their odd notions of chivalry.

"Clara's a shield."

He clapped his hands again, hopping a bit in his excitement.

"What does it matter?" I asked. "She didn't protect you. Or me, I suppose."

Drosselmeyer shrugged, went back to the eye. He circled it, pointed at me, then made a strange gesture: *follow me*, as though I could walk straight through the doorway and join him in the corridor.

"It isn't possible," I said patiently.

Drosselmeyer shook his head frantically. He tapped the eye with his lead again, even harder. I tried the doorknob but found it locked, as ever.

Bending to the keyhole, I saw that Drosselmeyer had begun drawing again. His new picture was a key.

"I don't have a key."

Drosselmeyer jumped up and down, this time in clear frustration. He beckoned me again, drawing away from the keyhole, and I suddenly realized that I could see much farther than before, not only the corridor outside, but the ends of it, the staircases, the places where the hallways twisted and turned out of sight.

"DROSSELMEYER!"

The word came from everywhere, above us, all around us. The puppet dropped the lead with a whimper of terror and ran up the corridor on his tiny legs, like a teacher frightened away from school.

But I had already taken the lesson.

THAT WAS THE DAY I REALIZED I WAS NOT LOCKED INTO MY tiny room. My sight bought my freedom; wherever it went, I could follow. It took me beyond my room and even my small corridor; eventually, it would take me all through the castle and I would realize that many things had changed.

I could hear them, for one thing. No matter where I went in the castle, I could hear them, muttering and whispering and weeping, begging forgiveness from fathers and mothers, brothers and children, those whom they had wronged. Sometimes they would scream. Sometimes they would not stop. Eventually the doors vanished and I could see them all: in one room, a man, drunk and crying, wielding what seemed to be an invisible ax; in another, a woman wailing in anguish, clawing her cheeks as she stared at a strange plaster fresco; two old men sitting down at chess.

Without the doors, I found that I could go anywhere, and every day I made a circuit of the castle, top to bottom. This was less a matter of exercise than of keeping busy, of having some sort of goal. There was insanity in this place, and I knew very well that the Queen had placed me here in the hopes of watching me go slowly mad. Clara, I thought, would have been doomed by her great need for other people, and perhaps she had gone mad here; she certainly looked it. But I had spent my life alone, and so I was determined to thwart the Queen's purpose. Every day I made a tour of the castle, almost an inspection, always by the same route, seeking anything that was even remotely different, from a crack in the flooring to a draft under the gate. Soon I came to know the castle as well as I had known our house, attic to cellar, and that was how I eventually discovered that it was slowly sinking, a millimeter at a time, its floors and ceiling beginning to buckle. The damage had undoubtedly begun long ago, and I often wondered whether its outsct might have coincided with that last Christmas Eve, the night Clara and I stood in the clearing, when this land was denied the vengeance that was its due. I wasn't sure the

Queen had noticed, but after innumerable days spent observing the creeping change, I was certain of it: one day the castle would crumble, sink down into the moat.

THE QUEEN DID NOT COME TO VISIT. EVERY ONCE IN A WHILE I would hear the squeal of hinges, the thump of a lock, and understand that the dollhouse had a new resident. But I never saw them come or go. The screaming woman had mercifully gone one day, faded into whatever quiet might await such creatures, and the room behind the mirror was empty. That was a relief, for every day in my circuit I passed the mirror, and could not help looking in it, to see what I might see.

At first I expected the glass surface to show me what I had seen in Drosselmeyer's mirror at the end, but when I finally summoned the courage to view my own reflection, it was only the same old Natasha, smiling in the rags of her green velvet dress. The shadow that had stood over me, that broad shadow of upstretched wings, was gone. Somehow, by letting Clara go, I had expiated it forever. And so I could not regret it, not even on the loneliest days in that castle, when it seemed that I would go mad indeed, when I would have cheerfully lopped off a limb in return for a book, even one of the trash-filled novels Clara used to read.

THEN THERE CAME A DAY WHEN I REACHED THE MIRROR AND saw that a broad, jagged crack obscured the surface of the glass. I had never touched the mirror before, but now I could not help tracing a finger down the fault. Then I jumped back, gasping. A line of blue liquid had appeared, water as clear and blue as aquamarine, bleeding from the edges of the crack. Soon the entire mirror before me was a bright and sparkling blue, its surface as smooth as that of a pond on a mild day.

I leaned forward to touch the water, then remembered my resolve and decided to continue my inspection. Something this new and interesting might upset the comfort of my routine, take away its power. And so I did not linger before the mirror, not then or in the many days that followed. Each day I passed it, staring into the clear blue water, trying to read a pattern, to understand how the shifting interplay of blue upon blue might create meaning. I learned, too, that there were things to be seen in the blue water, if one looked beneath the surface. One night I stared through the mirror and saw my mother finally cured of her affliction, her cheeks bright with color as she accompanied Fritz on a picnic. Fritz, too, seemed healthier, though perhaps that was only my imagination, for he was happily chasing butterflies. Another time I saw Orlov, bent over his workbench in the dead of night, his spiked hair and scarred face now giving him the aspect of a madman as he worked on a set of murderous nested dolls. I saw Anastasia, retired into a decent flat down by the docks, living with a girl of twenty or so who might have been her niece. They did everything together, the two of them, and Anastasia, who had never been able to have children, would smile when her niece was not looking, a smile none of us had seen.

After that night I broke my own rule, spending more time in front of the mirror each day while the castle groaned and creaked and decayed over my head. Staring at the water, I learned that there were infinite shades of blue, so many that they began to seem their own spectrum. I didn't know whether the visions I saw were real, or only what I wished to be true. It didn't seem to matter. It was enough to stand before the blue pool and see them there night after night. The old Natasha had been too mired in her own sorrows to wish anyone well, but when I stared into the gleaming blue water I felt that there was hope for everyone, even the lost. One night I saw Clara, saw her smiling face close to Conrad's, and if there was pain in that vision, it was the pain of the long-healed limb, the reflexive tug of a girlhood long since vanished. I saw Clara in the pool many times, and as I watched her, I came to understand more and more. She was not happy, my sister. She had finally achieved the life she expected, the life she felt she had earned, but it was not what she had imagined. Clara wanted too much, always. She wanted dolls and extra syrup. She wanted the nutcracker prince, who had squired her about so worshipfully in his sleigh, giving all and demanding nothing. Instead, she had the life of a duchess, which was hardly the leisurely matter of fashion and indolence that Clara had imagined, and she had Conrad, who was inconstant, visiting the whores every week, just as my father had always done. Clara had not encountered such problems before, did not know how to meet them, and so I began to see that what Drosselmeyer called dark was actually a source of great strength. I expected so little, and so I had felt joy where Clara could only desire, not daring to wish for more or better, only stretching out my hand on a freezing cold morning to save a single piece of Conrad's shirt. We had both seen Conrad as the answer to all problems; I was a different sort of fool than Clara, and yet it was a gift, to want so little and appreciate it when it came. Clara could not do so, and thus she was miserable.

That was the day I knew that I could stay in this castle forever, if need be, biding my time. I kept a close eye on the clock, forcing myself to be patient even as its hand moved invisibly, counting away the years: one, then three, then six. I found myself pitying Drosselmeyer, not only the little puppet but our godfather, he of the swirling cape and top hat, the handfuls of gold coins. It had all been an act; he had spent his life hunted, and I pitied him for it, not caring what he had done, not even caring what original sin had brought him to this place, for I understood now that there was no one in the wide world who did not want something they couldn't or shouldn't have. Humanity aspired, yes, but it also coveted, and so the great force that allowed the Americans to raise their buildings to the clouds had likewise brought me to the clearing where I wrapped my hands around my twin's throat and squeezed. None of us were above this place; some of us were simply lucky that we never fell into her hands. She would be back one day or another, for she could no more resist her dollhouse than I had once been able to resist ours, though the furnishings were not to my taste and Clara would never let me play any part but the maid. She would be back, yes, and one day, when the castle had become a collection of steady creaks and groans and the lone hand of the clock stood at four years remaining, she came.

CHAPTER

43

NATASHA."

I spun around, startled out of the mirror's blue dream. My family had purchased a dog, a miniature breed of ridiculous stature, long and squat. He had been intended as a gift for Fritz, "to settle him down," as my father said. And yet Fritz's new pet had drawn the three of them together in some strange way, united them as a family again. They all loved the dog, even Father, who would allow the little creature to leap onto his lap at table and feed it tiny pieces of chicken when he thought no one was looking. My parents and Fritz would take the dog for long walks, down the riverfront and into the park, and there Father would give Fritz money to ride the new carousel, smiling and waving at Fritz each time he came around. There was hope for all of them, I thought, and that was when her voice hissed in my ear.

"There is something in your mind, Natasha. Something I cannot quite grasp. A secret. What is it?"

I turned and found that she was standing beside me in the corridor, no longer monstrous but shrunken to size. Drosselmeyer was with her, standing at her knee, his unblinking eye fixed on me. The child in me acknowledged, not without some envy, that the Queen owned the greatest of all dollhouses, the one every child dreamed of: the dollhouse you could climb inside to play, become a doll yourself.

"You spend long hours here, Natasha," the Queen said softly. "Watching a cracked mirror. What do you see?"

I stared at her, keeping my face still. Yet my mind was racing. Was it possible that she didn't know about the blue pool? How could she not know?

"Nothing," I said. "Only dark."

Something boomed above us, a sound like thunder. Drosselmeyer whimpered, burying his face in her skirts.

"What is that?" I asked. In the mirror the blue water twisted, making another of those shapes that was almost a face . . . Clara's face, I thought, there and then gone.

But the Queen did not answer, only stared upward with an uneasy expression. Somewhere in the distance I heard another low rumble, and then, perhaps fifty feet down the corridor, a massive block of stone crashed from the ceiling, burying itself in one of the flagstones.

"What have you done?" the Queen hissed, her black eyes like twin coals.

I didn't answer, couldn't. Shouldn't she understand it better than I?

Now the corridor itself had begun to groan. Turning, I saw that a massive crack was making its way through the stone, upheaving the flooring. I threw myself toward the wall, grabbing the mirror's frame for balance. I missed it, and as I fell to the floor, something small and silver landed in my lap.

The Queen bent to grab for it, but I was quicker, and she backed away as I straightened, gripping a silver key in one hand. The puppet Drosselmeyer had dropped from the Queen's skirts, and now he stood chortling, laughing up at her, his eye gleaming in triumph. The Queen fetched him another flying kick, this one so hard that he flew down the length of the corridor, but he continued to giggle, even after he hit the wall with a loud snap of breaking bone.

"Give me the key," she said.

"I won't."

The Queen shrieked, bringing her hands against the dark stone of the wall. Her fists left divots, crumbling the stone in ravines and chasms. Another tremor shook the castle, upheaving the floor so strongly that it sent me stumbling and forced the Queen to her knees. The whole place was falling to pieces, it seemed. But the mirror remained as before, its surface placid and blue. The single door stood there, reflected across the hallway, and in a sudden flash of memory I recalled the tiny door in Drosselmeyer's house, the door that could only be opened through the mirror.

She is so simple, I thought again. *Dark and terrible, yes, but master of only a few simple, imitable tricks.*

Key in hand, I reached into the blue pool. The water was as cool and kind as I had always imagined it to be, and it was an easy thing to slide the key into the keyhole. The Queen reached for me, screaming, but I had already turned the tumblers and shoved the door wide. Blue light poured through the doorway, washing the corridor, and I heard them, everywhere in the castle I heard them screaming. But these were not screams of pain.

The Queen grabbed my shoulder. I saw that there would be no discussion now, no bargaining. Her pretty face was gone; now she was the thing I had seen in the forest, clawed hands and wings outswept. Her mouth was a horror of infinite needles. Her eyes were fixed on me.

"You think you have wounded me?" she demanded. "Release them all; I will get more. There will always be more. Your kind never changes."

"Nat?"

The voice was faint, but so real in its tone, hesitant and uncertain, that I did not mistake it for a phantom. I looked into the mirror, and Clara was there, just beneath the surface. The blue water was suddenly blazing, glaring, a torch of blue fire, and before it the Queen recoiled, throwing a hand over her eyes with a scream as she fell to the floor.

"Nat, please."

Clara's voice was closer now. The blue water had broken the surface, extending outward from the glass, reaching for me. I looked down and saw my entire self, covered in that blue light.

The shield, I thought. *Not for Drosselmeyer, but for me.*

"Nat!" Clara cried, her hand reaching for mine through the water. In that moment, I knew that I had forgiven her in truth, for it was an easy business to reach out, take her hand, and let her pull me forward into the mirror. For a long moment I stood there, caught somewhere between reflection and reality as the water closed around me. Dimly I could still hear the Queen screaming, raging at me, telling me that she would have me in the end. But her voice grew fainter with each passing second. Darkness loomed ahead; I flinched from it, but Clara was still pulling me along. Then I was in a dim room, stepping onto a solid surface.

Something exploded behind me, a sound of breaking glass; I opened my eyes and saw that I was in my dressing room, my old dressing room in Conrad's family house, and behind me stood Clara, holding one of the iron shovels from the fireplace, the shattered remains of Drosselmeyer's mirror on the floor at her feet.

CHAPTER

44

DESPITE ALL THAT HAD COME BEFORE, THAT MOMENT WAS the strangest of my life. I looked at my sister, and she looked at me. I barely recognized her, panting as she was with effort, her teeth bared and eyes gleaming. She looked at me, grasping the shovel, and for a moment I thought she meant to hit me as well. Then she dropped it, wiping her dirty hands on her dress. From the doorway came a steady sound I knew: Conrad, snoring in the aftermath of a bottle of brandy.

"I got him drunk," Clara told me. "It's not difficult."

"No, it's not," I replied, at a loss for what to say. Looking around the dressing room, I saw with wonder that everything was exactly as I remembered it: wardrobes, vanity, even the lacquered jewelry box that Conrad had given me for our third wedding anniversary.

"You didn't change anything."

"There was no need," Clara replied. "Your taste is good. I never knew that about you."

No, of course she hadn't. I had spent my youth in the dark

colors and unobtrusive fabrics that a girl was supposed to wear when she meant to blend into the walls. Pretty clothing was part of the light, and I suddenly wondered whether it went both ways, whether beneath Clara's dollhouses and penny novels there was a mind at work, atrophied from disuse yet still shrewd enough to make plans, to understand the workings of Drosselmeyer's glass, to reach through and pull me out.

"Orlov showed me how," she said, following my gaze to the empty silver eye of the mirror's frame. "We made a bargain."

I winced, but she put her hands out.

"Not one of those bargains. An ordinary bargain, favor for favor."

"What do you do for him?"

"Nothing terrible." Clara looked up at me, her eyes gleaming in the dim light of the candle. For a strange moment I felt that we had somehow exchanged ourselves again, not faces this time but selves, so that I was the innocent and she the one with knowledge. I sensed that she was not displeased with the switch. I opened my mouth to thank her, then closed it, unable to bring the word out. Instead I picked a shard of glass from my palm, trying to find the courage to ask Clara the question, the one that mattered.

"You're filthy," Clara told me. "You'll need a bath, and some clothes."

"All right." But I paused, placing a hand on the silver border of the mirror. I had forgotten how solid it was, how cold.

"I have to run," I said. "Run far, where she can't find me. I can't stay here." For I saw now that Clara had not forgiven me. She had rescued me, yes, given me her shield, and that was something. But the shield, it appeared, was a temporary thing, and forgiveness was a more difficult matter. Perhaps she couldn't forgive me, not yet. Perhaps in her place, I would not have either.

Clara shrugged. "If she means to have you, she will find you wherever you go. Me as well, I suppose. We made bargains, and she'll have us in the end."

"There was another too," I said. "A man named Grigori, with terrible eyes."

"Oh, you needn't worry about him," Clara said, sweeping up the glass with the broom from the fireplace. "He has overstayed his welcome at the palace, Conrad says, and they mean to remove him."

"Who?"

"Conrad's political club."

Despite everything, I was disappointed. "He's still a member of that dreadful club?"

"Come along," Clara said briskly. But as I turned from the mirror, I saw that her expression did not match her tone, that her eyes were dark with sorrow, and something worse: pity.

CLARA HELPED ME BATHE, WASHING MY HAIR AND MY BACK, scrubbing away all the filth I could not see. This, too, she did in a businesslike manner, but I sensed a degree of artifice in it. I saw Clara sharply now, and in her dutiful movements I understood that she meant to prove something here, not to me but to herself. After the bath she helped me to pin my hair, and opened the wardrobe to display a green woolen dress, the waist several inches too wide for Clara's lithe frame. The fabric looked new.

"Whose clothes are these?" I asked.

"Yours," she replied shortly, tossing me a corset. "I had them made."

I blinked. The idea that she had planned this—that she had put as much effort into rescuing me as I had into replacing her—was nearly impossible to credit from Clara, who had never looked further than next morning's breakfast. Perhaps Clara had become a different person as well. I regretted that we had so little time, but I sensed that Clara did not regret it . . . was, in fact, anxious for me to be gone. When I was dressed, complete with cloak and boots, she handed me a small leather valise, which felt as though it were full of iron.

"What's this?"

"Money," she replied. "Your money, from the sale of Drosselmeyer's house."

"How did you find out about that?"

"The property agents. I admit it took me some time to understand what they were talking about, but once I did, it seemed to me that the money should be yours. I have no need of it, and Drosselmeyer surely owed you some recompense."

I winced, thinking of the little manikin flying down the corridor, his broken body still lying in the dollhouse. I no longer knew what was owed to whom, but still I took the valise, grunting a bit at its weight.

"How long have I been gone?"

"Eight years."

I nodded. It had never occurred to me that the clock in the Kingdom of Sweets might be wrong, but I needed to know. From the bedroom door came another loud snore, and the rustling sound of Conrad shifting in bed.

"Do you want to see him?" Clara asked. Her tone was light, airy, but I saw in her eyes that this question had cost her more than all the rest, the dress and the bath, even whatever bargain she had made with Orlov. I did not answer, only stared at her for a long moment, astounded.

"You love him."

"I don't know whether I do or not," Clara admitted. "It's not like I remember love being. There wasn't so much pain."

I nodded, understanding. Men were such fools for beauty, and no one woman's beauty would change that, though she be Helen of Troy herself. I wondered whether Conrad had been unfaithful to me as well, and then dismissed the question. It didn't matter.

"Do you want to see him?" Clara repeated, and now I saw that she envied me as well, envied my freedom. I had moved past Conrad, and so she felt compelled to offer me the sight of him, just as a medieval martyr would have worn a hair shirt. I pitied Clara now, pitied her while she envied me, and there was a development I could never have anticipated, not in my wildest imaginings in the Kingdom of Sweets.

"No," I answered. And because Clara had summoned the courage to ask me her own terrible question, not once but twice, I finally found the courage to ask mine.

"Why did you bring me back?"

"Because fair is fair, Nat. I know what it is to be trapped there. You could have left me there a second time. I don't love you. I think I might hate you. But fair is fair."

I stared at Clara, wanting to ask her questions, perhaps wanting to embrace her, but it was too late now, for she was handing me a pair of white gloves. Her eyes gleamed with a jealousy I could scarcely credit from my twin, who had always had the world at her feet. Drosselmeyer had created her to protect himself, and so she should have danced through the world all her life, clear and bright and untouched, just as I should have been relegated to corners and alcoves, the dark sister, knowing a future I was unable to change. But magic was only magic, as Anastasia had always said. Thinking of Anastasia reminded me of Fritz, of that odd day on the stairs, and I grasped Clara's elbow.

"There's one more thing, Clara. I saw something . . . I thought it was a dream, but now I don't think so. I saw a great slaughter. I don't know where it comes from, or what it means, but the Fairy said that Orlov would be involved. She said it would come at the stroke of the clock—the great clock, you know—"

"I know the clock," Clara replied, her voice so cold that I released her, feeling ashamed. Of course. She would know the clock.

"But you are worrying about nothing," she said. "The King relented some years ago, loosened his grip. We have a Parliament now, a constitution. The unrest has settled."

I considered this for a long moment, but it did not make me feel better. The power of that old vision was too strong.

"Be careful, Clara. If your dealings with Orlov aren't done, be careful."

"Why should I be careful, Nat? I know what Drosselmeyer did; we had long talks in the black land, he and I. I am a talisman, just as he intended, but I am not without my own will. I shield whom I please, and most of the time, that means myself. Orlov is no danger to me; if anything, it's the reverse. I don't have to fear his little toys, and that makes him very nervous. Believe me, I'll be fine."

I stared at her for a long moment, struck both by how much she had changed, and by how little. Nothing was worthy of worry to Clara; even Orlov and his army of tiny murderers were not enough to invite concern. I had warned her, but what did warnings matter if the listener was deaf to caution? For a moment my old resentment resurfaced, but there was no sharpness to it, no killing edge, for I knew that Clara's recklessness had not purchased her happiness in the end.

"Here," she said, handing me a hat, an unfamiliar straw affair covered with ridiculous puffs of ribbon. Yet I knew it must be the fashion. Clara always knew the fashion.

"If you're a talisman," I asked Clara, "then what am I?"

"An afterthought," Clara replied, not unkindly. "He cracked us right down the middle to make me what I am, but he never cared what might become of you. Truthfully, I don't think he cared about either of us, save as pawns. The Fairy once told me that he was too reckless to be a good magician, and I suppose she was right; his own magic doomed him in the end."

She grabbed the hat and stuffed it onto my head.

"I'm sorry, Clara," I said, for I sensed it might be my last chance. "I'm so sorry for all of it."

For a moment I thought she would kiss my cheek, but she did not, only turned away.

"We are even, sister," she said. "Now leave my house."

CHAPTER

45

I T WAS EASY ENOUGH TO STEAL DOWN TO THE FRONT DOOR, for they were all still asleep. Only one maid saw me, but she barely raised an eyebrow at the veiled woman descending the stairs. I thought this odd at the time, but later I would come to realize that Clara had clearly been paying the servants for their silence as well, and that I could hardly have been the oddest visitor to that house.

At the foot of the stairs, I heard a rumble of masculine laughter from the long corridor that led to the servants' pantry. It wasn't Conrad, or his father, and certainly it wasn't Kroll. I tiptoed down to the doorway and opened it a crack.

There they all were, a circle of men clustered around the small servants' table. Orlov was there, and several other men, all of them dressed in the rough wool of the working classes. At the head of the table sat the other man I had once seen outside Orlov's warehouse, the small, bald man with his strangely fussy beard and mustache. I did not recognize him then, though I would later, years later, when his face was splashed across the newspapers, when it was too late and the harm had been done. But at the time I thought only how fitting it was that these working men should gather in the Liebermanns' house underneath Conrad's and his parents' sleeping heads, planning their revolution where the King would least suspect. I thought that if this was the price Clara had paid Orlov, then perhaps it was not such a bad bargain after all. I closed the door without a sound, then went on down the hallway and let myself out the servants' entrance, into the night.

CURTAIN

                "What shall we do tomorrow?

What shall we ever do?"

                    The hot water at ten.

And if it rains, a closed car at four.

And we shall play a game of chess,

Pressing lidless eyes and waiting for a knock upon the door.

                      —*The Waste Land*

                      T. S. Eliot

CHAPTER

46

AFTER ALL THIS TIME, I DIDN'T THINK ANYONE IN OUR neighborhood would recognize Natasha Stahlbaum—they had not noted her even when she was alive—but I was taking no chances. In that next week, I avoided all places and people I had known, venturing into the far corners of the city to purchase the things I needed: several new dresses; undergarments; cosmetics; a proper traveling case. It was a revelation to be back out in the wide world, the open air of the city, and as the shadow of the Queen's dollhouse faded, I found myself buying pretty clothes in bright colors. I no longer looked like Clara, but still, I felt I had earned those colors, gleaming silks and velvets, as though I wore them in defiance of the black land. The fashions had changed while I was away; so had the prices, for there were rumbles of a coming war in Europe, the inevitable result of ongoing squabbles over land. Fortunately, Clara had not cheated me; when I opened the valise I found several stacks of bills, many thousands of marks' worth, more than enough to begin a new life.

With a feeling of wild recklessness that I finally identified as freedom, I booked passage on a ship bound for Southampton. I had always wanted to see England, and if I was no longer the child who sat in her rocker staring at pictures of castles and dragons, then I was at least a woman with everything ahead and nothing behind. It was a long voyage, via the Gulf of Finland and the Baltic and North Seas, but I beat the onset of the war by several months, and once I arrived in Southampton I traveled straight onward, boarding a steam train for the city of dreams, the most modern in the Old World.

London was a revelation. I spent two happy years combing its age, the long history written in its cobbles and castles, the winding streets that followed no clear plan and never came out where one would expect. In the summers I journeyed the countryside, practicing and then perfecting my English, and one year I even visited the charming seaside town of Whitby, wanting to see the reality of a novel, the abbey where Stoker's great work had been born.

But eventually, as I perhaps should have expected, life in England began to darken. I sensed figures following in my steps, hostility in faces that I had never seen before. I glimpsed shadows where there should have been none. I had known that my future would be hunted, and so it was, by an enemy I could never quite see. She was there, lurking in the alleyways, in the dark shade of awnings, crouching behind the shelves when I visited a bookshop, seated across from me at a table set for one. I never saw her, but I knew when she was there, hiding behind this face or that. When the German bombs began to fall, targeting civilians for the first time, I saw her face behind the explosions, the bodies in the streets, and having seen her there, I suddenly saw much more, as though a dark veil had been lifted from my sight. I saw London's filth, the way the Thames became nearly choked with shit in summertime, the coal soot that covered every surface in the city, even seeping its way beneath the windowpanes to end up on top of my eggs at breakfast. I saw the workhouses, where children no higher than my waist were driven and beaten in equal measure. I saw that London was a city of extraordinary history but equal brutality, a wild carnival that was just as bad, in its own way, as the Kingdom of Sweets, and after that I could not stay, for beneath the city's pretty trappings, I knew it for what it was. I always knew, and so with some regret I said farewell to England and booked passage again, this time on the great voyage, the journey to end them all: the long steamship ride from Old World to New.

I boarded the ship with an odd conviction that the Queen would not be able to follow. The Old World was her province, her place, the superstitious soil in which she found her most fertile ground. The Americans were heartier, vital and efficient, displaying an energy that the Old World disdained, and I felt—rather than reasoned—that America would not be to the Queen's liking, that she would find little purchase there. Our voyage was a tense one, overshadowed by the danger of German U-boats in the Atlantic and the still-recent horror of the sunken *Lusitania*, but we arrived in New York Harbor without incident, and as the liner glided past the Statue of Liberty, I found myself struck dumb, as so many had been before me, by the sight of that extraordinary figure, and even more by the wonder of the New York skyline, the buildings that stretched almost to the clouds.

I took rooms on Seventy-Third Street, overlooking Central Park. Before leaving Europe, I had taken the trouble to consult the ever-helpful Mr. Armitage, and on his advice I invested the remainder of my money with a thriving Manhattan firm, a firm that would eventually become one of the greatest financial power-houses in the world. Every year they returned to me a sum that was modest but nevertheless adequate to maintain the simple life I had crafted for myself; I had a housekeeper who came twice a week to clean, but no maid or cook. I found a great satisfaction in the simplicity of my life—that I made my own meals and chose my own clothing, that I was free to do with the day as I saw fit, reading and walking, visiting bookshops, or sometimes just sitting in the park, enjoying the spring sunshine, which seemed so welcome after the long, dark wet of New York's winters, milder but somehow grimmer even than those of Mother Russia, set as they were among that vast modernity of buildings and streets that seemed to render even the notion of inclement weather anachronistic.

No shadows pursued me through New York. The city was a world that came as advertised, beautiful and clean and occasionally cruel, yet even New York's cruelties were comforting to me, for they were not the Queen's, grounded as they were in indifference rather than intent. As the years passed, I had friends and even a few lovers, but no intimates, and I felt embarrassment for my younger self, the girl who had once risked breaking her neck for a scrap of cloth, for the love that she had thought she could not live without. At such times I often imagined Clara in her own world, so close and yet immeasurably distant, sitting in front of her vanity table, using the set of silver combs and brushes that I had chosen in the early days of my marriage. I wondered whether Conrad had reformed his ways, whether Clara was happy with the life she had settled for, and on those rare occasions when I considered the matter of my sister, my beautiful twin sister, I found myself hoping that she was content. I was able to do that much, and that was how I knew that I had truly put the past away.

IN MY SECOND YEAR IN NEW YORK, THE NEWSPAPERS BEGAN rumbling with noise of revolution, a great unrest in Mother Russia. The King had finally pushed the workers too far, withheld too much and granted too little, and now the volcano had begun to erupt. The King had indeed created a Parliament, just as Clara had told me, but he also had a pernicious habit of dissolving the Parliament whenever it did not align with his own wishes. When the war broke out, he had made the disastrous decision to take command of his own troops on the western front, leaving his throne in the hands of the Queen and her corrupt advisor, Grigori Rasputin, and though several nobles had finally put an end to Rasputin as an agent of dark forces, the damage had been done, the Crown irreparably tarnished. Workers and peasants flooded the streets of the capital; the army went with them, and at the end the King and his family were placed under arrest.

At first I followed these developments with mild interest, but no more. Russia seemed to me part of another life, and at any rate the great wave of violence the Fairy had predicted had not appeared. Only when the weeklies began to carry pictures did I come to recognize the man with the bald head and the little mustache, the academic Orlov had held in such high esteem, as the ruler of the new movement, and in November, when that little bald head and the brain beneath it masterminded the Great Revolution that toppled the old government once and for all, I felt little surprise.

But in the next year I began to pay closer attention, for other stories had begun pouring in, stories of arrest, execution, torture of unbelievable brutality. Someone had tried to kill the little man with the mustache, had almost succeeded, and now he was determined to purge the landowners of Russia, the royalty, the nobility, even the clergy, anyone whose wealth marked them as enemies of the state.

For two months I read the newspapers feverishly, seeking news of Clara, of Fritz, of my parents, of any of the neighbors I had known. But there was little information in the papers, and none at all to be had from Russia itself. The Red Terror, they called that time, and it tore through the old kingdom and left few names, only corpses. I had warned Clara, but I felt that I had warned her of the wrong danger, assuming that the violence would come from the King. I had not understood the darkening of the world that had taken place in my absence, nor the terrible vengeance the oppressed might take. For four years the slaughter continued, ebbing and flowing, and at the end of it all I had given up hope. The Fairy had been right, of course she had been right, for she understood vengeance even if she was blind about everything else. I wondered often whether Orlov had come home, as she predicted, whether he had embraced his revolution or withdrawn as it devolved into terror, whether the Fairy had understood him as well as she understood us.

Then, in my seventh year in New York, I passed the window of a luxury shop and saw a set of nested dolls, such as one might see in any market stall on the Prospekt. But these dolls had been exquisitely carved, with bodies of silver and heads of bronze. As I watched, the shopgirl tapped the largest doll on the head, and a moment later they were all leaping toward each other, jumping like drops of water on a skillet, each doll hopping inside the next to nest.

That was the first Orlov I saw in New York, but it was not the last. These toys were mechanical marvels and much prized in the city, being notoriously difficult to obtain, for they had to be smuggled from Russia, where the Great Revolution had put an end to all such frivolities, and the popular tale told how the toymaker, Orlov, had been marked for death by Lenin himself after he betrayed the Revolution during the Terror, how a wealthy benefactress had smuggled him away to safety, absconding with him at the same time as she escaped the pitchforks with her own family. This bloody provenance gave the toymaker's creations a fashionable air of danger and subtle vice, so that to have a genuine Orlov became a matter of much pride among the wealthy of New York, almost on a par with having an original Renoir, or a perfectly preserved musket from the Revolutionary War. The Americans were mad for Orlov's creations, but whenever I glimpsed one of them I felt no nostalgia, only a pocket of cold, as though I had stepped into a draft. Orlov had survived, and I could only hope that it was Clara who had saved him, that she might have helped our family as well. Clara was clever, much cleverer than the world had given her credit for, yet she could not have helped them all, those people I had known in my childhood, foolish yet kind. The sight of Orlov's toys brought them back to me, those drunken faces at our Christmas Eve parties, making me wonder how they had died, what had been done to them first, whether their bodies had been dumped into a vast pit before the King's palace or merely burned.

At such moments, I did not see how there was much hope for us. Only the Fairy, I thought, understood these things. Perhaps Orlov did as well, but it was not a comfortable feeling, to see his toys in shops and know that they were gradually peopling the great apartments on Park Avenue. Orlov had turned on the Revolution, so they said, but that did not mean it could not happen again. Such moments were brief, however, and it was never long before I was able to move on, out of the cold patch, back into the light.

CHAPTER

47

ONE DAY IN MY FORTY-EIGHTH YEAR, I WAS WALKING down Madison Avenue. I had always loved to walk this stretch in the spring, but lately it had become more difficult, for I was now encumbered with a cane. Late the year before, I had developed a stabbing pain in one of my feet, a pain that would not subside. When I finally summoned the courage to go to the doctor—I hated doctors, always had, and I waited much longer than was advisable, so that my foot got worse and worse—he informed me that I suffered from gout.

This news hit me harder than it should have, for I knew gout only as a disease of the elderly. I was not afflicted with the need to gaze into the looking glass; my features were as plain as they ever had been, and somewhere around the age of thirty I had finally accepted my own reflection for what it was. But the meeting with the doctor revealed to me that, though I had relinquished pretensions of beauty, I had also placed a great deal of value on my own sense of youth, and despite the doctor's protestations that anyone could be afflicted with gout, that the ailment struck indiscriminate of age, that was a terrible day in my memory, for it was the first day that I knew I was old. The cane reinforced my age, making it inarguable, and I hated the tapping sound it made as I went up and down the sturdy sidewalks of New York.

But now, in the month of April, the sun was shining, the tulips out in full flower, and I could not resist a walk. I had always liked tulips; they were such simple flowers, almost comical, but they somehow produced the brightest of colors, and while in my youth I demanded depth in all things, as I aged I had learned to enjoy simplicity, to understand that beauty could sometimes be its own reward. I was admiring the great spray of tulips, blue and red and yellow, that bobbed outside Canavan's Bookshop at the intersection of Madison and Sixty-Eighth Street when my cane struck something solid on the pavement, shattering it with a brittle crack.

Looking down, I saw that I had broken a glass ornament, a reindeer. A remnant of the winter just ended, likely; it had probably fallen from a Christmas tree when a troupe of servants hauled the dried-out carcass from one of the great houses that stood on either side of the avenue. The texture of the piece, a glassy, crystalline translucency that might almost have been mistaken for spun sugar, tugged at my memory, making me reluctant to touch it. But I did anyway, for the reindeer's legs had cracked, creating wicked shards that might easily cut an unwary child. I picked up the pieces, wrapped them in one of my handkerchiefs, placed the parcel in my handbag, and went on. But I did not get more than a few blocks before it happened again.

This time it was a tiny gingerbread man that I stabbed with my cane, dismembering him, so that four limbs and two halves of a pastry body lay on the pavement before me. I could not tell whether the gingerbread man was a porcelain ornament or a real bit of biscuit, but it did not matter, for when I bent down to examine the remains, I saw that its upper half was still breathing, the tiny chest rising and falling, keeping a nearly perfect time with the reverberation of my own lungs. The gingerbread man began to wheeze, struggling for air, and at the same moment I realized that I too was struggling, that my lungs had begun to labor, that a stabbing pain had invaded the right side of my chest.

Rising to my feet, staggering, I found myself in front of a patisserie, the windows full of cakes and muffins, pastries and pies, even a jellied mass that I gradually recognized as a trifle. But the sweets took my attention for only a moment before I saw what loomed behind me in the glass: a monstrous black shadow, all tangled hair and ragged dress and cold eyes and arching wings, and at the sight I clutched my chest, where it felt as though a small animal were now scrabbling inside, tearing through tissue with teeth and claws. She had found me, and in the end it had not mattered which city I chose or where I made my home. I still belonged to her, for my hands felt cold now, as cold as the ice that skimmed the river in late December, and when I turned from the window I saw not the comfortably astringent stretch of Madison Avenue but a vast darkness, below me not the cracking sidewalks I had come to love but rather an expanse of bare, scrubbed wood, unbroken and infinite. Only then did I understand that I was on a stage . . . not a stage as I had come to know it at the theater, the damnable ballet, but the great stage, the world's stage, and now I saw my audience, there in the center of the seventh row, the best seat in the house: the Queen of Spades, her black eyes gleaming with pleasure, her mouth creased in a smile of needles. My foot gave beneath me; I stumbled and fell, and now, at the end, I understood at last that there was nothing beneath this world, nothing beyond the curtain. There was no ultimate salvation, only the illusion of the stage, the eyes of the audience, the Queen of Spades, and the depth of the fall, and when I looked up, I saw not New York but the ruins of a castle, its jags of black stone outlined against the battered land, the deep grey sky.

CHAPTER

48

SHE WAS NEAR DEATH. I KNEW IT AS SOON AS I SAW HER, when I stepped through the destroyed doorway of the castle and found her shriveled form in the courtyard, her arms like sticks and her black mouth sunken, the corners tucked in pain. But I had known it even before that, when I saw the utterly ruined land outside. The destructive process that had begun the night I forgave Clara in the clearing had now reached its final end. The Kingdom's many shades of black had now faded to an amorphous grey. There was no black stream anymore, no sign of water. It was a kingdom of dust.

"Natasha."

Her voice was faint, thin as paper in my ears. But only a fool would have missed the command there.

"Where are your people?" I asked.

"Gone. All of them are gone, and how did you do that? All I had built, broken in so short a span of time that it would not cover even a human life. How did you do it?"

I thought of explaining it to her, but did not. She had seen me as weak, that night in the clearing, and I didn't think she would be capable of understanding what had happened, how a single act of mercy could outweigh all of our terrible deeds.

"Perhaps Clara did it," I said. "Light."

"And yet, you are the more powerful," the Queen rasped. "Always saw me coming, didn't you? I have been waiting a long time for you to come back."

She held something out. At first I thought it was a stick but then I saw that it was her spade. The metallic head sparkled with blood, blood that vanished just as suddenly at a different angle, so that it was only an ordinary spade, its head red with rust.

"Whose blood is that?" I asked.

"All of them, child." She gasped, her breath beginning to falter now. "Pharaohs, Romans, Vikings . . . If you dug deep enough, you'd find Cain himself in there. This is the record of my dealings, and I give it to you."

She handed me the spade. I grasped the handle, feeling the hidden power in it, as though electricity lived beneath the polished wood.

"I have no heir," she told me. "The last time I saw my son, he said that you would do the job well. He liked you, just as I did, and Drosselmeyer's gifts serve you nicely. I think that very little will be hidden from you."

"What else did he say?" I asked. "Orlov. Will he ever come back?"

She turned her face away from me and didn't speak. In that moment I finally found pity even for her, this creature who had once been able to freeze my blood with a single glance. I had never had children, but I understood what a terrible thing it must be to

349

lose one, and especially to that humanity which she held in such little regard. Yet I could not help being happy for Orlov, that he had escaped this place.

"I don't want that," I said, dropping the spade to the ground.

"You could live forever."

"I don't want that either."

The Queen's breath caught, like a thread on a nail, and hung there. She closed her eyes, and I sat motionless for a long moment, waiting for the next breath to come. It did not. Her skeletal body went limp. Yet the spade still lay beside her, bleeding at me in quiet invitation.

So much power, I thought, and felt again the pull of it, the great draw. But there was nothing there, only the closed eye of vengeance, a pit of corpses. So I turned and went out the gate.

OUTSIDE, THE KINGDOM SAT STILL AND DEAD UNDER A GREY sky. Even black could fade, a fact I had not known. The land was empty, not so much as a vulture circling in the charcoal sky. The moon was down as well, though I could not tell whether it even rose or fell anymore. The Queen had not been wholly boasting when she said she governed the moon, commanded all things here. Only a few of us had slipped through her fingers, and I could well believe that when she fell, the moon would fall with her.

I sat down on the edge of a piece of broken stonework and surveyed the land. Whatever terrible process had begun inside my chest was still working, but far more slowly here, and certainly less agonizing. I thought I might have as many as several days before the end came. Thunder rumbled, and the sky seemed riven by streaks of pale white against the darkness. Light and dark . . . but even Drosselmeyer was dead now, gone wherever the

Queen's people went when they were of no more use. I wondered what would happen to this place. Without the Queen, would vengeance itself simply fold its wings and walk away? No, for Orlov had said that the Kingdom was powered by us. Still, as I sat there on the broken stone, I liked to think that it had not all been for nothing, that perhaps we would all learn to be better, put down our spades.

Near the end, I felt someone sit down next to me: Clara. She was dying, just as I was; we were old and it did not surprise me that we should die so close to each other, just as we had come into the world. Yet we sat comfortably, me with my arm around her shoulders, singing her a Christmas song, just as I had when we were young and hiding in the cupboard. I sang until I could sing no more, until at last the pain in my chest overtook me, and then it was Clara's turn to hold me close, as though I were one of the dolls she had always loved. Bright blue water seemed to surround us, absolving us, and if I felt any sorrow, it was only for the years we had wasted in hating each other, the great things we might have done, the adventures we could have had. We might have been anything and gone anywhere, for in that moment it seemed that we were both dancers, both pirates, both duchesses and knights. Clara had forgiven me and I had forgiven her, and so at last we were together, both of us at the end just as we were at the beginning, free of the Queen's terrible country, as though we had never been divided, as though we had passed through all of it, this wild theatrical of life, and somehow come out whole on the other side. Silence fell around us, soft and welcoming as a velvet curtain, and then all was still.

ACKNOWLEDGMENTS

As I get older, writing is a lot harder than it used to be. The stories don't come as quickly or effortlessly as they used to, and writing a novel has now become an often grueling exercise in endurance. This is an eventuality that I didn't foresee, and neither did my publishers. So this is where I thank Maya Ziv and John Parsley at Penguin Random House, and Simon Taylor at Transworld, for their extraordinary patience and understanding, and for giving me the time I needed to sort it all out.

Thanks, as always, to Dorian Karchmar, the best literary agent any writer could ask for. Thank you also to Pat Polite, Alex Kane, Gabriella Caballero, Isabelle Appleton, and Sophia Ihlefeld at William Morris Endeavor (now and then), for their hard work and help during a difficult period for everyone. Thanks to Alice Dalrymple at Penguin for her editing advice. Thank you, too, to Miranda Ottewell, who is quite simply a world-class copy editor.

Thanks to the seriously underfunded and undervalued workers of the NHS, for keeping so many of us healthy during the pandemic. Many of us still know how hard you work, and what a great thing socialized medicine is. We haven't forgotten.

Thank you to the teachers, who do the most important job there is.

This book would never have been finished without the kindness and help of my father, Curt Johansen, who did me a great favor by instilling in me a lifelong love of classical music. He also took me to see *The Nutcracker* more than a few times over the years. Thanks, Dad.

Shane and George, you both put up with a lot from me when I'm under deadline (and when I'm not). I love you all the way to the end of the universe and back.

To all my dear readers: it's a grim timeline we're living through. I hope you found a bit of escape here, as I did. Thanks for reading.

ABOUT THE AUTHOR

Erika Johansen grew up in the San Francisco Bay Area. She went to Swarthmore College in Pennsylvania, attended the Iowa Writers' Workshop, and eventually became an attorney, but she never stopped writing. She lives in England.